SOUL WEAVER

SOUL WEAVER

QUEEN OF CONQUEST
BOOK ONE

Fudge Esquire

Podium

Podium

SOUL
WEAVER

Prologue

The world was never kind to me. But that was okay. I never expected it to be.

I hadn't thought it was kind when I was taken from the arms of my mother and forced to live the predestined life of royalty.

I hadn't thought it was kind when I was forced to kill the other princess candidates to survive.

I hadn't thought it was kind when neighboring kingdoms went to war over my ascension to the throne.

But I had hoped, perhaps foolishly, that the world would be fair. If I tried my hardest and fought to survive, I thought that, in the end, everything would work out. But I was wrong. Life wasn't kind, and it certainly wasn't fair. No matter how hard I struggled, killed, and climbed the ladders of power, the world simply refused to let me live in peace.

Now, betrayed and abandoned by everyone, I walked before the crowd. The entire city held its breath, enthralled in silence, as I stepped toward the noose. Not a single soul dared to speak up in my defense. I wasn't surprised. No one had defended me since the Duke's men framed me for treason.

The reason for my execution mattered little to the sheep dressed as men and women staring up at me. They, like everyone else in this Godsforsaken empire, only wanted blood. The thrill of seeing a ruler—a queen—heading for a cruel death. Oh, what a tale they could pass on to their children's children for generations to come.

I kept my chin high. They might have sealed my Diamond Core, and they might yet kill me. But they would not break me. No one ever would. My bare feet thumped against the wooden planks as the executioner motioned me forward. With spears at my back, I halted behind the noose. The loosened boards beneath me creaked, eager to let the executioner pull the lever and condemn me to my agonizing end.

"Queen Lilith of Aedronir," a scrawny man beside me bellowed at the crowd, "by order of Emperor Draxis of Aexion, you are hereby sentenced to death by noose for"—he paused dramatically—"the crimes of mass murder of imperial citizens, treason against the Crown, and incitement of war!" The crowd roared in response, fists punching the air in waves of false righteousness.

It was all lies. Lies crafted by the Duke and the Emperor to seize my kingdom. Lies designed to take what was mine. To *steal* it.

"You may speak your final words, Queen of Rot," the scrawny man decreed, clutching the parchment with the imperial mandate before his slight frame. The guard slipped the noose around my neck, tightened it, and then removed my gag. "May your last words be of repentance."

I spat toward the citizens of what had been my kingdom, and then toward the imperials looking down on me from my own balcony. "Each and every one of you will burn, consumed by the fires of your traitorous hearts," I cursed, each word laced with hate and venom. If I'd learned more close combat skills and physical enhancement techniques, I might have broken the chains binding me and killed them all where they stood. I cursed myself for relying so blindly on long-distance skills. "May Ashwash curse your homes and families with death and despair." The executioner's hand was already on the lever. My heart hammered so loudly in my ears that I had to shout to hear my own voice. "I will return! I will return to burn this empire—this world—to ashes, where it bel—"

The executioner pulled the lever. The loose planks dropped, and the warded rope tightened around my neck. I heard a snap, felt a burst of searing pain, and then everything went dark.

But as the last fragments of my life slipped away, something happened that shouldn't have been possible.

My Heart Core imploded.

The explosion of a Diamond-level Core was rare, capable of destroying the entire capital. But mine didn't explode. No, it imploded, collapsing inward. Somehow, the last remnants of my life—everything that made me who I was—were pulled into that implosion.

For what could have been days, months, or even years, I drifted in Nothingness. I had no control, no thoughts, only a sensation of floating. The void's pull began to tear at what was left of me. And, as theory said, all that remained in Nothingness would eventually fade.

But then I sensed the faintest thrum. A tiny beat, like a flickering flame, calling out to me, pleading with me to follow it. With all that remained of my existence, I followed the call—the call of the little voice. Of that dying soul.

I'm going to die, the small soul whimpered. *Please, don't let them kill me.*

CHAPTER ONE

Reincarnation

Pain was the first sensation to greet me, paired with the distinct pressure of a boot against my face. Even through the blindfold, I recognized the feeling of thick hide smashing against my skull. My father had also been quite fond of cleaning his boots with my face.

The world returned in fragments, disjointed and hazy, each piece sliding into place with a disorienting lack of order. A dull pressure ignited behind my eyes, pulsing faintly in sync with—was it a heartbeat? Or footsteps? The sensation felt distant, like an echo buried deep within me. My limbs felt strangely both heavy and light, unresponsive, as though wrapped in layers of thick cloth.

A groan escaped me, oddly loud, as I fought to understand the unfamiliar sensations in my joints and muscles, every motion alien in this new body.

Whether the sluggishness came from the pain or my soul adjusting to its new vessel, I couldn't tell. What I'd done wasn't a polished method of magic, nor even a well-theorized one. For all I knew, I could have ended up in the body of a talking cat.

Thankfully, when I managed to twitch my fingers, I felt the distinct presence of opposable thumbs. Thank the Gods. There were bindings around my wrists and ankles, but the knots were sloppy. Slipping my hands free took only a few seconds. I yanked the blindfold off, only to be assaulted by a barrage of colors and light.

The shapes around me blurred and shifted as I squinted, trying to make sense of it all. Colors were brighter than I'd ever seen; the edges of shapes seemed sharpened, pressing painfully against my senses. I couldn't tell if this was due to the new body's sight or if my perception was still settling, as though I was viewing everything through rippling water.

Another boot collided with my face, and a small, feminine voice escaped my lips in a grunt. Female, then. That was good. My body spun toward the floor, and I instinctively reached out, though the motion felt off-balance. My muscles were sluggish and weak, the arm much shorter than anything I recall ever having. My hand didn't land where it should have, though I doubted it made much of a difference as my muscles instantly gave out without being able to resist the momentum of my fall.

"Pathetic," a young, but rough, human voice sneered from the other end of the foot assailing me. "I can't believe Father let a rat like you into our family."

I blinked, processing his words. Rat?

I looked down at my small fingers, thin arms, short legs, and tiny feet. Definitely not a rat. Unless there were, what, rat people in this land? I'd need to figure that out later when I accessed some sort of mirror.

My thoughts drifted in scattered fragments, struggling to coalesce. I was here, thinking, but not fully. I bared my teeth, squeezing my eyes shut, trying to force my mind to align with this body and its unfamiliar rhythm. It felt like waking in the middle of a dream only to realize I was still dreaming.

My mind still wrestled with where the dream ended, and the reality began.

Another foot came at me, and I managed to raise a hand, albeit sluggishly, to deflect it. Pain tore through my muscles, sore from recent abuse, as the boy's boot forced past my arm, slamming again into my face.

Warm liquid pooled in my mouth, and I spat out blood. I looked up at my attacker as my vision finally began to settle. Young, somewhat broad-shouldered, ugly, and likely stronger than me in this new, weakened state. He loomed above, his body caught in late puberty's awkward promise of manhood, exuding a casual arrogance that set my teeth on edge.

The boy's rich bloodline showed in his refined features, though his crooked nose and petulant scowl twisted his face into a rodent-like sneer.

His attire, finely tailored and embroidered, spoke of privilege. However, even the obvious wealth that dressed him failed to soften the cruel air that surrounded him, a haughty aura that betrayed the entitlement he no doubt had grown to expect.

On the other hand, based on how that foot had just sailed through my guard, I guessed I inhabited a young girl's body, a child's. Not ideal, but certainly better than a talking cat. Or a baby.

As the petulant manchild aimed another kick at my face, I rolled to the side without the usual grace I'd grown accustomed to in my old body. I hit the floor with a painful thud. His boot sailed over me, slamming into the wall with a sound that could have been my skull breaking. He winced, having put all his power into a kick that struck only a stone wall.

Untrained, then, I thought. *A merchant's son? Or a low noble?*

The boy began to rant about rats, giving me a moment's reprieve to assess my surroundings. Expensive furnishings, silk carpets, delicate ornaments, paintings, chandeliers, and high ceilings surrounded us. I was in a lavish hallway painted in deep shades of blue, purple, and red.

The hallway seemed to stretch endlessly, its length obscured by the dancing shadows that flickered in the lights of torches mounted along the stone walls like guardian soldiers. The air was heavy with the scent of burning wood mingled with a faint aroma of aged tapestries. Other than the torches, the walls displayed paintings of men and women in heavy garb. No crowns were shown in the paintings.

The stone floor beneath my hands was smooth and cold to the touch, likely worn by the decades of footsteps that had echoed off the stones with every stride. Massive pillars rose to the ceiling on either side, carved with intricate patterns of dragons, knights, and other mythical beasts I didn't recognize, their eyes seeming to follow my every move.

Between the pillars, richly woven tapestries hung, depicting scenes of what looked like epic battles or quests with guards of armor astride large black horses. The colors were not bright, but faded, as if having withstood the test of time.

Under the torches and the paintings were suits of armor standing sentinel, their polished surfaces casting the torchlight across the stone walls in a ghostly manner. Swords, spears, and shields adorned the space between, their edges dulled with obvious age but hinting at the strength the tools of steel once possessed.

Definitely wealthy—likely noble or as close to that as existed in this foreign land.

I knew killing the boy was not a good idea. It would do nothing to help my situation, so I desperately struggled to restrain the rising sense of anger boiling within me. It urged me to disregard any civility and put the boy in his place—dead and at my feet. Regardless, I couldn't let him continue beating me and the only way to stop his assault was by putting him down. If this new kingdom was anything like Aedronir and the kid was a noble, no one would stop him even if they *were* around.

He lunged, and I twisted so his kick glanced off my shoulder. With my elbow raised, I drove it forward into his groin as hard as I could. It might not have been so effective had he any semblance of guard raised against me. He very clearly had not expected me to fight back.

His mistake.

His eyes grew wide as he dropped to his knees, pain written on his scrunched, ugly features. It was not a royal act, but at the moment, I wasn't a queen. Queens had guards. I had an elbow.

Without missing a beat I slammed my shoulder into his chin, rocking his head back and knocking his already quivering body over. And then I was on him and my thumb found his eye socket, pushing deep into it while he screamed in both pain and abject terror. It was a lesson I'd make sure he never forgot.

Once I was deep enough, I angled my thumb upward to scoop it out.

Despite his lack of skill, the boy's strength was considerable compared to my new body. In his wild flailing, one of his arms whipped into the side of my head, throwing me off and making the world spin. But he didn't move to attack again; he just lay there, sobbing on the floor and cupping his injured eye. Tears streaked down his face, transparent on one cheek, a deep scarlet red on the other. I knew I'd probably blinded him in that eye unless healing attribute heart energy was cast on it. Assuming healing energy existed in this land.

Once my vision cleared, I stood up, a bit shakily but steady enough to not need anything to help with my balance. I stretched my arms and rotated my neck. No pain. No broken bones. Good. Badly bruised and beaten but it didn't seem like I was suffering from any head trauma or any broken bones. Still, I would need a mirror to better judge this body's physical nature. I could already tell it was malnourished from the gnawing hunger in my stomach. I also needed time to check on the state of my Core and see if its level had followed my Soul Transference. I doubted that it had, but it would make things a lot easier.

"Child," I rasped, my voice unsteady as I gave his side a small kick. "Who are you?" I paused, then added, "And who am I?"

"Wh-what?" He cried, still whimpering. "H-how d-dare—"

I kicked him again before he could finish and just sighed. Kids were always so stupid. "Who. Are. You."

He just looked at me blankly. I moved to kick him again. "I . . . I'm Brian Silverwater." He seemed to regain some of his confidence as he said "Silverwater." "Third son of Lord Silverwater, Baron of Silverwater."

I looked down at him in disgust. Third sons were often pricks or just useless. He seemed a mix of both.

"Why did you attack me?"

He set his jaw, lips curling into his perpetual sneer. "Because you're an insect," he spat, blood dribbling down his chin. "My father says your mother was a traitorous whore who—"

I didn't let him finish. I grabbed a nearby vase in both hands and swung it like a club to the side of his head. He screamed and fell backward. The glass shattered over him, deep cuts marking up his face. The rage I'd restrained seeped through my control, cold and cruel.

Images of a woman flashed in my mind's eyes.

Feet dangling. Blood. Her dark, sunken eyes staring lifelessly back at me. Her bony limbs shattered like those of a broken puppet.

I snapped back to reality, anger still thrumming through me. "What did you just say about my mother?" I hissed, cupping his mouth in my hand. "Say it again." I pointed the cracked edge of the vase at his throat. "Come on, say it again."

Shouting erupted behind me. I ignored it, leaning closer to him. They could wait. They had waited this long. What was another minute? I pressed the glass deeper into his throat. "Come on, Brian. *Young Lord Silverwater.* Say it again. Repeat that filth you spewed about the Queen's mother?"

His eyes, or eye, widened in shock and confusion. The other one stayed shut. I was not sure if it could even open.

I did not have a chance to continue. Large hands curled around my arms and shoulders, ripping me from Brian. I struggled momentarily but stopped when the hands only tightened. A group of armored knights surrounded us, horror on their faces.

"Holy mother of Aedonia," muttered a knight with curt blond hair and soft eyes. His hands moved to make some sort of star shape before ending at his heart. "Lilliana, what did you do?" The knight asked gently and glanced over at the largest of his warrior brethren who bore one of the most massive frames I'd ever seen. Each of his movements was precise and controlled, suggesting a high level of martial prowess. His broad shoulders easily carried the weight of his armor, a suit of gleaming steel adorned with intricate engraving and emblems similar to those I'd seen on the men and women in the paintings. A dark blue bird with a beak longer than its body, arching backward to match the angle of the crescent moon at its back.

The darkness seemed drawn to the large knight, his hair as black as the night sky cascading in untamed waves around his sharp features. His eyes, deep pools of obsidian, gleamed with an intensity that warned me of a darker nature than I would have thought a trained knight would harbor.

His countenance was that of a stern commander. Not an inch of emotion was betrayed in his flat, almost bored expression.

This one could have entertained me back in my early years as Queen. He wouldn't have won, obviously, but he would have been an enjoyable challenge. As of the moment, however, the massive knight could squash me with very little effort.

The large knight looked down at me and then at the bloodied noble's son, and let out a deep breath.

"Captain?" The soft, blond-haired knight asked.

"Report the incident to the lord," the large knight, the Knight Captain, ordered. When he spoke, his voice resonated with a commanding authority that brooked no dissent. The words were measured and deliberate. The soft-looking knight was clearly subordinate. "Beatrice, you take the young lord to the healers. Shael, you and I will speak with . . . the Lady Lilliana." I noticed even the Captain hesitated when adding "lady" before what I assumed was the name of this body. "Daniel, you report to the Baron." The blond knight saluted the Captain and took off with a raven-haired knight the Captain had referred to as Beatrice.

The adrenaline was quickly draining and, with it, most of my immediate rage. It dawned on me that I might have gone a bit overboard with the whole smashing his face with a vase. In hindsight, the boy had not been talking about *my* mother. He had been insulting this body's mother, who, for all I knew, *was* a whore.

Still, it wouldn't do to have people thinking they could walk over me. The Captain didn't look angry—annoyed, perhaps, but not angry.

I nodded and followed the Captain as he turned to lead me away, down the never-ending hallway of flickering torchlight and eerie stone walls. Shael followed from behind, so I walked between the two knights.

After a while, we finally approached a plain door that the Captain swung open with familiarity. We had walked down a flight of stairs, so I figured we were likely on the first floor of the mansion-like castle of the barony. Through the door was probably the Knight Captain's office, I figured. I entered the room and I was impressed by the smoothly polished wood and the faint scent of ink. The room was relatively small, yet I could see it had been efficiently organized. A sturdy oak desk stood proudly at the center, its surface cluttered with a mess of scrolls, quills, and inkwells. There was also a large leather-bound tome resting open on the desk, but when I craned my neck to have a better look, the Knight Captain slammed the tome shut. Behind the desk was a worn leather chair that creaked when the Captain sat on it.

Along the walls, shelves were lined with volumes of leather-bound books while various weapons were displayed on adjacent racks. Each seemed to have been meticulously organized, and I would have bet any of them could be used in real battle.

A large map dominated the wall directly in front of where I'd entered with small, colored pins dotting different regions. I wanted to take a closer look, but the Captain coughed, and my attention snapped back to him.

"Sit," he ordered. "Explain." His voice was gruff as he pulled a cup from a drawer in his desk and filled it with water. At least I thought it was water.

I just looked at him and frowned. From what I had been able to collect of this body's life, Lilliana was a lady. I was a lady. No doubt the result of an affair, but a lady nonetheless. And, more importantly, *I* was a queen.

Even if that title meant nothing to the plebeians of this land, I would not be treated as some inconsequential scum. But I knew that men like the knight in front of me could not be forced to give respect. That did not mean I had to accept it.

I sat in silence, glaring. He remained still as well. Together we stayed there like statues for what felt like half an hour before Shael, who'd been squirming uncomfortably since the first few minutes of our stare-off, broke the silence. "Um, Lady Lilliana. Could you explain to us what happened? Baron Silverwater is going to be quite upset." The gentle tone of Dame Shael's voice suggested that this body was possibly even younger than I'd first imagined.

"I'm not sure," I said finally, my voice not coming out nearly as strong or as loud as I'd hoped. Ashwash be blessed, this body had yet to even begin puberty. "I don't remember anything before that boy's boot in my face."

At that, the Captain quirked an eyebrow and Shael covered her mouth. "You don't remember anything?"

I shook my head. "No." I needed information, and pretending to have some sort of memory loss seemed the easiest route. Assuming the knights would help me. The Dame seemed somewhat empathetic. "I remember basic things, like time and what words mean, but I have no memories of anything before about fifteen minutes ago."

"Hmm," the Captain murmured, tapping the chin under his burly beard. I noticed his voice carried an accent quite distinct from that of the others I'd heard speak. It was heavier and dropped the *H* from his words. "This is 'ard to believe. You do speak differently . . ." He trailed off. I knew there would be a disconnect between how I spoke and how Lilliana would have spoken. I was raised to be a queen and an energy user. Lilliana was raised to be ignored. The question was whether they had heard her talk enough to be suspicious of the change. My bet was no one in the castle had heard Lilliana speak more than a few sentences.

"I do not know who I am. Who you are. Or where we are." I gestured around us. "But I understand that I have noble blood in my veins. I have been told that I am Lady Lilliana of Silverwater. I am not sure what exactly that entails, though by the number of times that boy stomped on me, I do not imagine it to be of any great importance."

The two knights looked at each other and the Captain shrugged. "I suppose we will find out, with time," he said without looking at me. "Shael, fetch the 'ealer when 'e finishes with the young lord and then report to the Baron. I will stay with the *young lady*." He emphasized the title.

Ah. There it was. Some respect.

I smiled.

CHAPTER TWO

A Weakened Queen

The Captain leaned forward in his chair, scrutinizing my, no doubt, wild appearance. He didn't speak until the female knight, Shael, left the room.

"Why are you lying, Lady Lilliana?" he asked, his previously gruff voice now taking on a gentle tone.

"I am not lying," I insisted, crossing my legs and resting my hands atop them.

He raised a curious eyebrow, gesturing at my posture with a casual wave. "Explain how that makes sense, given your current behavior. You seem nothing like an amnesiac and more in control than ever."

I returned his wave with narrowed eyes. "Perhaps it's the lack of memory that gives me confidence."

"Perhaps," he said, stroking his beard thoughtfully. "Or perhaps you're simply showing your true colors." I glared, imagining how easily I could have bent him to my will in my previous body. The heart energy the Captain radiated felt no stronger than that of a warrior with a Silver Core and perhaps a heart ring or two. Yet, oddly, the majority of energy radiating from him felt . . . different. It came from much lower than his heart, pulsing from just above his navel.

I frowned, trying to read his expression while probing him with what little energy I had. He easily rebuffed my attempt, now mirroring my frown, but not before I sensed a pulse from that second source of power near his navel.

What is that? I wondered, my curiosity and the beginning of panic coursing through me. I'd never felt a power source originating from anywhere but a heart's energy Core. *Something's not right.*

"What did you just try to do?" The Captain growled, standing abruptly, his face a mixture of confusion and irritation.

"I . . . I'm not certain," I replied, the lie as natural as breathing. "I wondered if you meant to harm me, and something in my heart reacted." I cocked my head, watching his reaction.

How does he not know about energy sensing? It's a basic use of heart energy.

Something was very wrong. My heart began to quicken as the reality of my situation began to dawn on me and I felt my fingers cling to the edge of the chair's armrest. The Captain must have sensed my panic, because he sat back down, his anger replaced with something resembling concern.

"Where am I?" I asked, trying to keep down my rising sense of panic.

The Captain eyed me again before shaking his head and finally releasing a heavy sigh as if not quite believing me, but too exhausted to argue against the wants of a young lady. "You are in House Silverwater territory, within the Lysorian Kingdom."

Lysoria? I had never heard of such a place, and I was confident I knew every kingdom or empire in Ordite. Most of which I'd warred against, at one time or another. There was no way I wouldn't have heard of this Lysoria if it truly existed. Either this Captain was lying, or something unexpected had occurred during the Soul Transference.

I asked the most obvious question I could think of. "How fares Aedronir?"

The Captain tilted his head, puzzled. "Aedronir?" He paused, pursing his lips. "Do you mean Aedonia?"

Who in all the hells is Aedonia? I wanted to scream but choked down the instinctual reaction, relying on my royal training to restrain the panic bubbling in my gut.

"What continent are we on?" I asked, biting my lip, anxiety peaking.

"Pularea, of course." He sighed. "Lady Lilliana, I grow tired of these charades—"

Whatever he was thinking of saying next was cut off by the entrance of a woman I assumed was a doctor, judging by the clean white robe she wore and the large gray bag that smelled strongly of medicinal herbs. The doctor's face was warm, despite the wrinkles of age that she seemed to wear like a badge, each of her steps confident and solid.

She approached me with the quick, efficient steps of someone accustomed to military discipline. Despite the neutral way the doctor schooled her facial expression, however, I could tell there was annoyance there. Disbelief. Perhaps, even a bit of scorn.

Just whose body am I in?

"Captain," the woman said, giving the Knight Captain a quick nod of respect before setting her bag on the floor next to me and kneeling so we were at eye level. Then she turned to look at me. "I hear you are having trouble recalling memories, Lilliana?" Shael entered quietly behind the doctor, but I paid her no mind, glaring at the mere doctor who dared address me without a title.

"Are you a noble, doctor?" I said, lips curling into a scowl.

"Excuse me?"

"Do not make me repeat myself, servant." I glanced over to Shael, disdainful. "This is who you bring? Was there no doctor available with even a modicum of respect for noble bloodlines?"

The doctor looked ready to argue, but Shael stepped in, pulling her aside. The two leaned their heads close together and, although they whispered low enough I couldn't make out any distinct words, it was clear they were arguing. After nearly a minute, the doctor backed up with a loud exhale and waved her hands in resignation.

"Fine, Dame Shael. I understand." She knelt once again before my crossed legs, her expression carefully neutral. "I apologize, Lady Lilliana. Please, describe your symptoms."

I nearly laughed at my impulse to kill her for such disrespect. *What would I even kill her with? These scrawny arms? This nonexistent Heart Core?* No, I'd have to bide my time. If this Lilliana was indeed low nobility, her bloodline would serve me only so far if I killed everyone that bothered me.

"I remember only the most recent events . . . with Brian." I gestured to the bruises on my arm and what felt like a blackening eye.

"May I?" she asked, reaching for my head before I could answer. I gritted my teeth, painfully aware I was no longer Queen of Aedronir. I didn't even know who I was, but certainly not a queen.

The doctor's hands were cold and clinical as they gingerly pressed different spots along my face and skull, making their way to the tender skin around my neck. After a moment, she turned to the Captain with a non-committal shrug.

"It could very well be some form of brain trauma. It wouldn't be the first time concussive force causes memory loss. The bruising and tenderness suggest concussive or blunt trauma was applied to her with quite some force." The doctor didn't seem to care that force came from Lilliana's brother. "There isn't much I can do, but generally symptoms such as these fade over time. I suppose I could brew some medicine for the pain."

"Her memories will return?" Shael's hopeful tone surprised me. Why would she care if Lilliana's memories returned? I imagined most of the Silverwater staff would have preferred if Lilliana vanished quietly in the night.

"I think it's very likely." She still shot me a particularly doubtful expression, but I couldn't tell if she was lying and doubted my memories would come back or if she doubted they were gone at all.

"Thank you, Doctor," the Captain said, dismissing her. She nodded and left without a backward glance.

Some doctor.

"All right, Lady Lilliana," the Captain grunted, leaning back into his plush chair. Shael stood next to the closed office door, her posture at ease if still attentive to her surroundings. "Let's say I believe you. It is my duty, of course, to help the young lords and ladies of House Silverwater find their way. What can I help you with? I do not have much time, but I will impart whatever knowledge I can."

I doubted he'd be fully forthcoming, but I had no other options. He did seem to have a soft spot for the girl whose body I now occupied, for whatever reason, so perhaps he would answer honestly.

I swallowed the building saliva of anxiety and asked my question. "What is the name of our world?"

The Captain's eyes widened slightly as he glanced at Shael. She didn't react to my words or his look, remaining stoic. The Captain shrugged and responded. "Graedon."

My hands gripped the chair armrest tight at his words, dirty fingernails caked with blood and dirt dug into the plush material. *This was not Ordite. Not my world.* Although Soul Transference had been entirely theoretical, I'd never read that it could move a soul to a different world.

A queen does not panic. My father's words rang in my ears, surging through me like a bolt of lightning. My muscles instantly relaxed, fingers loosening their grip upon the armrest, and the turmoil roiling in my stomach all but vanished. *Calm. Calm. Take what you know and turn it to your benefit.*

"Tell me about my family," I said. I'd confirmed my broader situation; now I needed immediate details.

The Captain peered over his desk, his expression still stoic and unreadable. "You must truly have lost your memories to be asking such a mundane question of me. As you likely have already figured out, you are Lady Lilliana Silverwater. Your father is the Baron and patriarch of House Silverwater, Cedric Silverwater. Your mother is Mathilda Silverwater, daughter of House Goldenheart, who rule over the Goldenheart Duchy. Your siblings are Brian, Aedrius, Morgana, and Raphael. You are the youngest. Bri—"

"How old am I?"

The Captain smiled wryly at the interruption. "You are eleven. Your brother, Brian, is fourteen. Morgana and Aedrius both reach the age of majority this year." He must have seen my confused expression since he clarified. "Seventeen is the age of majority. Raphael is the oldest and current successor of the barony." I waited for the Captain to say Raphael's age. When he didn't, and I found I didn't really care, I moved on.

"If we all share the same mother, what causes this . . . treatment?" I asked bluntly, not quite sure how else to phrase the beating.

The Captain hesitated and Shael bowed her head respectfully before opening the door and stepping out. It closed with an audible click. "Baroness Mathilda is, technically, not your mother but your stepmother." That made sense. So rather than being my siblings, they were my half-siblings. "I would not be telling you this if everyone did not already know." He hesitated again and, though he tried to disguise it, I could see there was struggle in his eyes. And disgust. "Your mother was a maid whom the Baron became quite infatuated with. You are the result of that infatuation. Your mother attempted to usurp the Baroness, leading to her banishment from the estate and House Silverwater territory."

"She's alive?"

By the look on the Captain's face, it was clear the answer was a resounding no. Still, he only shrugged. "It is possible."

Sounds like a nice way of saying he raped a maid and then kicked her out, I thought, remembering the many examples of such behavior from nobles even in my own kingdom.

I only had a single, pestering question left for the Captain. If I was going to rise in power in this new world, I would need to be able to rely on my previous knowledge. "What realm is your Heart Core?"

"My Heart Core level," he repeated, lifting an eyebrow. "Why would you want to know that?" When I didn't answer, the Captain relented. "Heart Cores are rather rare. Mere knight captains do not have access to the house's cultivation guides."

"How many heart rings, then?" I pressed, desperate for some answers that would depict this world's general power level.

"Twenty-one rings."

I gawked at the ridiculously high number of heart rings around an un-Cored heart. It should have taken him only three rings per Core realm. To maintain twenty-one heart rings around one's unprotected heart was essentially suicide. If the Captain were to use his heart rings to wield a level of heart energy above the Bronze realm, the pressure would strangle his heart leading to a swift and unavoidable death.

"Do you have any attributes that you know of?" It was a bit of a reach, as energy users wouldn't realize what affinities their Core had until they began reaching for the Bronze realm, but I figured it was worth a shot.

The Captain looked at me like I'd grown a second head and asked him if he'd like one too. "What are attributes?"

Something was seriously wrong with this world.

Fundamentally, raw heart energy without any attribute affixed to it was a neutral energy that all hearts produced as a natural part of being alive. The amount of raw energy a heart could hold, however, was severely limited in mortals and could only be expanded by the process of cultivating the Heart Core; the repeated circulation of that neutral energy and spreading it throughout the body. After an Awakened energy user gathered enough heart energy, they could condense it into heart rings and, later, into a Core.

How was it possible for the Captain to have twenty-one rings and have never heard of Core attributes? It not only meant he had never even attempted to try forming a Core, but that he didn't know he could.

What backward information is being taught in this world?

Someone knocked on the office room door just as I opened my mouth to ask what house cultivation guides were, and a slim, extremely tall man bowed through the doorway. He wore a particularly clean and straight black suit, with a stiff white dress shirt underneath that came together with a red bowtie. "Sir, the Baron has called for your immediate presence."

The Captain nodded and stood, motioning toward Shael. "Dame, show Lady Lilliana to her chambers. Find me afterward at the Baron's office."

The Dame saluted, placing an open palm against her chest. "Yessir." She beckoned me toward her. "Lady Lilliana, please follow me."

I woke the next morning, my head still reeling from the previous night's conversation with the Knight Captain. I was truly in a different world. Far from being able to obtain my vengeance, I didn't even know if my enemies were still alive. For all the information I had regarding Soul Transference, it could have taken centuries for me to reach this new world.

I swung my legs off the bed and looked around for the bell that had adorned my bedchambers for the past thirty years. I felt instantly ridiculous for doing so. Of course, it wouldn't be here. There wasn't anything of use in Lilliana's desolate boudoir.

The room was located in a remote corner of the Baron's stone mansion, far removed from the luxurious and opulent quarters inhabited by Lilliana's . . . more favored siblings. The location itself spoke volumes of her place in the family—out of sight and out of mind.

Neglect hung around the room like some evil curse. It was sparsely furnished with little evidence of Lilliana's noble bloodline. The stone walls were bare, devoid of the ornate tapestries and lavish luxuries that decorated the rest of the Baron's home.

There was a single, narrow window allowing some light to filter into the room. It cast long shadows that had stretched and warped the previous night as the sun set below the horizon. To call it eerie would be an understatement. And the furnishings in the room itself were modest at best and downright awful at worst. The bed still stood but was missing a wood peg at the bottom left edge where there was a large splinter in the wood. What I figured had once been bed linens lay torn in the far corner, and I hadn't bothered to pick them up. I'd much rather sleep without bedding than those rags.

There was a worn writing table near the window. Though it was small, scarred, and very tattered, it was stable enough that I'd found myself spending more time there than on the bed the previous night after I'd returned. I'd found a small piece of parchment crushed into a ball stuck between the desk and the wall. I hadn't been able to find an inkwell or quill, so I'd simply tucked the crumpled parchment into one of the desk's drawers for another time.

I dressed in basic trousers and a shirt. That was all Lilliana's closet had, so the choice was made for me.

Before sleeping, I had located a mirror in one of the empty neighboring rooms and had taken a look at the state of my new body. It was beyond disappointing and quite frankly, horrifying that an entire noble family would allow one of their heirs to fall into such . . . an awful state. There was no muscle or fat anywhere on the body. Lilliana had been on the brink of death.

Everything else was fairly standard, even in my world. Brown hair, brown eyes, small and round face. Though it didn't really matter. Soul Transference would, theoretically, slowly morph this body to match my true appearance which would unlock upon reaching a Silver-realm Core. However, it would take some time to reach as Lilliana's Core had not yet Awakened. She was only eleven and being un-Awakened at that age wasn't abnormal.

Still, based on what the Knight Captain said about not having a Heart Core and their rarity, it seemed like the level of Heart Cores in this new world couldn't be any lower.

I needed to raise my strength back to what it had been on Ordite and, after forcing this world to kneel at my feet, increase the level of heart energy proficiency in the world. It would become my personal army. I would also need the help of energy scholars much smarter than I was to figure out the science of full-body Transference or long-distance teleportation. Some had considered me a genius in war and bloodshed. That hadn't extended to the sciences of heart energy.

I slipped on a pair of heavy and tattered brown boots and made my way to the mansion's training yard. The Captain had given me some rough directions to it, and it wasn't difficult to figure out. Other than the occasional maid or butler scurrying past me, the only noise came from the soldiers training, so I simply followed the familiar sounds.

Although I still couldn't fully wrap my head around the fact I'd succeeded in transferring my soul across worlds, I didn't feel sad about leaving Ordite. There was nothing left for me there except for vengeance. And that would come one day. But everyone I knew or had ever cared about was long dead. Some by my own hands. Some by others. One by her own.

I entered the training grounds and was greeted by a wave of unobstructed sunlight. It was a sprawling expanse of carefully manicured graveled and grassed fields. The air was filled with the sound of clashing swords and the rhythmic thud of training dummies, a familiar symphony of martial training that echoed across the grounds. For a moment, a small, tiny moment, I forgot where I was. What had happened to me? The mansion was connected to the training area, separated only by a wide stone wall. The hallway I'd found myself walking opened into the outside, with no door in sight. An odd structure, but there were doors leading to other hallways, so I figured it wasn't too unreasonable.

At the center of the training grounds loomed what looked like some type of lookout tower. It was clad with red and purple flags depicting the same blue, long-beaked bird and moon symbols populating the mansion. The training ground was split into various training areas, each apparently tailored to a specific aspect of combat. I ignored those and started walking along the outer rim.

I shook my head, clearing it of thoughts, and took off at a steady jog. I ignored the shouts and calls around me. It took all I had to focus on breathing and keeping this body moving. In. Out. In. Out. It wasn't long before my legs started to give out. My lungs were already screaming. I didn't stop. In. Out. In. Out.

I cursed the weakness of my new body and its inability to create energy within my heart. The only way I could properly gather power within myself was by creating a Heart Core for Lilliana, but her body would crumble under the pressure of awakening. Especially with the purity I would aim for. Until that point, I was limited to physical exercise to create energy within my heart. When enough was there, I could condense them into heart rings. Eventually, that would coalesce into a Core, and I could begin circulating existing energy to create more.

But that was a long way off.

This new world seemed to focus on building heart rings without any concept of forming a Core. No wonder this world was so behind. The Awakened here didn't seem to understand how to embed the heart rings into their hearts to create a Core. If the Captain proved to be someone I could rally to my side, perhaps I'd save him from his imminent death.

Eventually, I collapsed. My brown hair was completely plastered to my forehead and my clothes were soaked in sweat. I lay there, breathing heavily, and closed my eyes. My un-Awakened heart beat a little stronger than it had yesterday.

Good.

I started to purify what little energy my exercise had forced my heart to produce. Before the Soul Transference, I'd mastered two forms of heart energy attributes—lunar and necromancy. The latter was an energy attribute type I'd kept completely buried, hidden away even from those closest to me. If I made it back to Ordite, I would unleash the full, unbridled extent of my fury and mastery of the forbidden energy attribute on all that had betrayed me.

I looked within the pathways of my body, spotting two small streams of energy: one a dull white and one a brilliant Silver. The dull white I knew to be neutral energy, raw and without an energy attribute. The gleaming Silver energy, however, was the valuable remnants of my lunar attributed energy. Small and feeble, but I knew it would one day roar like a raging river again.

I grit my teeth at the thought, digging my fingers into the soft dirt, removing a clump of dirt, and twisting my body so I leaned against the base of a tall wooden post, my chest heaving with the effort of each breath.

While creating a Core did improve the speed of manifesting raw and attributed energies, the further an Awakened traveled on the path of cultivation, the more energy would be required to achieve the next level. In my previous life, I had reached the peak of a Diamond Core practitioner, which was practically unheard of in Ordite and had required a tremendous number of resources and time to form even a single heart ring. I had likely spent more time on a single diamond heart ring than I had when progressing from mortal to platinum Core.

This life's climb to power would be similar, except for the chance that Lilliana had a natural affinity for an energy attribute that I did not have in my previous life.

The thought of obtaining a new energy attribute completely unknown flooded me with adrenaline and I couldn't stop the small smile that curled my lips. First, I'd shed the mortality of this body by awakening my Core and achieving the cultivation level of a Bronze realm Core. Then Silver, Gold, Platinum, Diamond, and whatever legendary realms of power lay beyond that.

When some strength returned to my legs, I climbed to my feet toward the soldiers. I wasn't sure they would allow me to join their routine since I was technically eleven years old now. It wasn't like I would be able to keep up. But at least it would give me some physical goals to work toward. In this life, I would make sure to cover all of my past weaknesses. If I had been as strong in close combat as I'd been in long-distance heart energy, the Empire would not have captured me so easily.

This time I would make sure to leave no openings. The betrayers of Ordite would watch as I burned down their world and I would enjoy the despair in their eyes. The thought made me smile. Just a little.

"My lady?" Shael asked, looking at me with concern. Her entire body was caked in sweat and dirt from the training field.

"I want to join."

"You what?" The rest of the knights stopped their sparring to look at the disturbance, bouncing between me and Shael.

"I want to train with the soldiers."

"I don't think that'd be a good idea," she said, hesitant. Some of the soldiers started to laugh and she shot them a glare that shut them up.

Regardless of what the Dame believed, I needed to push myself as far as physically as possible. And I needed some experience using this body in combat. Or as close to it as I could get it. "It's not your place to decide that," I stated simply. "And I doubt the Baron would mind very much, even if I happened to die from exhaustion." That was true enough. None of the soldiers denied it, nor did Shael, but they at least had the dignity to look awkward about their silence. "Anyway, if I fall behind you can just leave me. I'll figure it out."

The Dame regarded me for a long moment and then slowly nodded. "Are you familiar with swordplay, lady?"

"Yes."

Shael looked at me again, disbelief evident. "If I decide your swordplay is not enough to give my soldiers some practice, I will remove you to the wooden dummies." She pointed to a small row of upright wooden logs. "Understood?"

I wasn't pleased with the tone, but considering my current position, I said nothing and walked over to take hold of a wooden practice sword. I swung it lazily a few times to judge its balance and weight. I found it surprisingly heavy.

"Strong wood," I muttered, drawing a raised eyebrow from Shael. The Dame didn't say anything and motioned toward a soldier to approach. The soldier was younger, maybe sixteen or so? Older than the boy, Brian, from earlier. There was some scruff on this young soldier's chin.

"This is Lucid, my squire," she said. "You'll start with him since you're both learning."

Lucid grinned, flashing white teeth in my direction. His brown eyes looked down on me with more pity than disgust, which I found interesting. "Go easy on me, my lady," he said, obviously thinking this was some sort of rich child's momentary desire.

I was never the best at swordsmanship, but my generals had insisted I train at it every day. I hoped to last a few minutes before my arms gave out. Unfortunately, my arms proved to be even weaker than my legs. Less than sixty seconds had passed, and I was already having difficulty keeping the wooden practice sword at the ready.

Lucid's strikes shouldn't have been heavy. They really shouldn't have been. His form was off, his strikes too wide, his footwork was all over the place, and he didn't use his hips properly. In the end, it didn't matter. I was just so incredibly weak. The kid could have slapped me with a pillow, and I would have been blown off my feet.

Okay, maybe it wasn't that bad.

He lunged at me; the point of his wood blade directed toward my heart. I ducked, only using the edge of my blade to redirect Lucid's. It soared a foot to the left of my head. I used the duck to twist around his sword, so I stood outside the reach of his extended arm. Lucid moved to readjust but my wood blade was too close. It thwacked weakly against the side of his head.

He looked at me, perplexed, then broke out in a loud laugh. The other soldiers stopped to see what was happening. Some gawked at my blade still touching the side of Lucid's head. I wasn't sure why. The kid was constantly full of openings. If I couldn't dodge a few wild hits, I wouldn't have been much of a queen.

A clap from Shael sent the soldiers back into practice and their attention returned to their training. "Impressive, Lady Lilliana. I have to say, for someone with no memories and weak muscles, you have rather refined footwork." I just shrugged. I highly doubted Lilliana's memories contained any footwork training anyway. "Keep going. See if you can do that again. Lucid, if you get tagged by her sword again, I'll have you running until your heart rings scream. Got it?"

Lucid snapped to attention. "Yes ma'am!" He turned back to me, sword at the ready. This time his playful little smirk was gone, replaced by a determined expression.

CHAPTER THREE

Marriage Doll

I sat in a corner of the training field, my muscles pounding and sore from the relentless beating of a wooden sword hitting me over and over again. My breaths came in large heaves, each inhale a battle against my bruised ribs and aching joints. My legs trembled, exhausted from the constant moving and efforts of remembering perfect footwork.

The sun was falling toward the horizon now, indicating it was sometime after midday. Shael had left some water next to me when the soldiers departed, and I was truly thankful to her for that, despite the water being warm and the brown tint suggesting it was unfiltered. However, that was what the soldiers had been drinking, so I couldn't fault her for it. I'd asked to join, and she'd treated me like a soldier—as much as she felt comfortable doing, in any case.

When I'd taken my place in the corner, she had tried to approach me, but I waved her off. The group left sometime soon after that. Since then, I'd been purifying any new energies and absorbing them into my heart to shape energy rings in preparation for my awakening. It was slow going, as an un-Awakened body had truly poor absorption rates. For every handful of energy my heart created, I would absorb and purify but a speck of it.

Either because of my focus on absorbing energy or my exhaustion, I hadn't noticed the flicker of shadows as someone approached me from behind until I heard the soft cough of an older man. My head jerked up around the sound, surprised to find I was no longer alone. I had no idea how long he'd been standing there, wordlessly. The servant wasn't tall. He was slightly hunched, his face covered in wrinkles as he stared at me and scratched the edges of a rough beard with gnarled fingers.

"Yes?" I asked, not having enough energy to make my voice any louder than a breath.

"The Baron has commanded your presence."

"Good for him," I retorted a little louder, but not much. My side ached with the effort of even just breathing. "I'm not presentable at the moment, so the Baron will have to wait."

The white-haired man stared at me, open-mouthed. All this staring was beginning to aggravate me.

"Enough gawking like an ogling child," I continued, waving him away and subconsciously falling back into the manner of speaking I'd used before the Transference. "Tell the maids I will be taking a bath. Get it ready for me." When he didn't move, I grunted, still not daring to get up lest I fall. "Now." I reached into my heart energy and released a little, no larger than the size of a needle, to prick the man's skin. He went white as a ghost before giving me a slight bow and disappearing back into the mansion.

I would have laughed at his reaction if my side hadn't been in so much pain. How weak was that man to flee so pathetically after the prick of unrefined heart energy?

It took me some time, but I made it back to my small bedchambers. To my astonishment, a bath had been prepared. The water was lukewarm at best. Given the family and household's dislike of Lilliana, I considered myself lucky it wasn't ice water.

After I bathed and dressed in clean clothing identical in every way but color to my last pairing, I headed in the direction the Captain had indicated was the Baron's office. It proved rather difficult to find at first, though once I saw the giant oak door with dragons and warriors carved along its frame, I knew right away that was his office.

Did Lilliana ever call him "Father"? I wondered. Either way, he would have to deal with me calling him Baron. Though he might have been Lilliana's father, he was not mine. The day I called the lord of a small barony in some backward world my father would be the same day I forgave the Empire.

So, never. He would have to make do with being called Baron.

I didn't bother knocking on the Baron's office doors. They swung open with well-oiled ease to reveal an unnecessarily lavish room. And it was filled to the brim with bottles of alcohol. The smell was repulsive. Was this the office of a Baron, not some slum alley drug lord?

The room was large, at least four times the size of my bedchambers. The ceilings were vaulted, supported by intricately carved pillars of marble. Tapestries of fine silk depicted scenes similar to those on the hallway walls but more vibrant and detailed.

At the center of the room was a desk made of some heavy wood, though I couldn't place what kind. Behind the desk, a high-backed chair of velvet and gold creaked as the Baron swiveled on it to face me. He was a balding man with a comically large mustache and an average build. Sunlight spilled in from outside through the massive windows behind him. When he spoke, the mustache twitched. I didn't laugh. The queen inside me, the training I'd gone through, told me this man should die. He was an unworthy noble, an embodiment of corruption and greed. A coward of wealth. Someone controllable.

The rest of the room was decorated similarly to the Knight Captain's office, though without a large map or parchment. Where the Captain's room had parchment, the Baron's had a bottle of alcohol, cigars, or spilled remnants of one. That, and the giant portrait of the Baron hung directly in front of the entrance, left of where the Baron sat.

"Good afternoon, Baron," I said, opting to speak like myself rather than feign Lilliana. It was a good idea to continue acting as Lilliana, but I just couldn't bring myself to address the Baron like some pitiful daughter. Perhaps it was foolish of me, but I would speak to him with the dignity of a royal. Or, at least, I would try to. "I do appreciate your patience. When I received your summons, I was hardly in a state befitting a meeting of this nature. Now that I am here, shall we proceed?"

Like everyone else in this Ashwash-cursed place, he gawked clearly not expecting me to sound, well, royal. He pulled a cigar from a drawer in his desk and lit it, breathing deeply before moving it away and releasing the smoke in my direction. I didn't so much as flinch.

"So," he said, ignoring my demanding entrance. "Captain Holloway told me you're claiming to have no memories?" That didn't sound like an actual question, so I stayed quiet. His mustache twitched again. "You do seem quite . . . different. Is it true you exercised all day with the soldiers?"

"Yes."

He stared at me and made a sound that was halfway between a groan and a sigh. "Yes, *Baron.*" I returned his stare, debating whether or not to comply.

"Yes, Baron," I finally corrected, resisting the urge to grit my teeth.

He grinned.

"Good. Good! I was worried you were going to wither away in shame, useless to the end." He shifted some papers, squinting at the writings before scribbling what I guessed to be words of some foreign language. I recognized bits and pieces of this kingdom's writing and could speak their language, so it had to be a foreign script since it looked like scribbles. "Good. Good. If you add some weight to that face, I bet Earl Paul would take you when you're of age in a few years." His face scrunched like a confused pig. "How old are you again?"

"Eleven."

The Baron nodded and muttered "Good" under his breath a few more times.

"Baron, why have I been summoned?"

"Hmm? Oh. Oh yes." He put the papers down, not pushing them aside, though he did take his eyes off them to look at me. "I was wondering what I should do with you. I can't keep a wild dog in my home after it bit my son, now, can I?"

Did he just call me a dog? That river of rage inside me that had cooled with the time in the Nothingness stirred and began to boil back to the surface. I pushed it down as images of myself sticking a knife into his eye came to mind. A son and father should match, shouldn't they?

No, not yet.

"So your plan is to . . ."

"Why, marry you to Earl Paul, of course, you stupid little thing." The Baron barked a laugh. I could hear the guards by the door chuckling. Filth. All of them. "Didn't you hear what I said?"

No, Lilith, I warned myself. *Keep yourself steady.*

"That would be a waste." I sat across from him, shoving my rage back into the box.

The Baron waved a hand, clearly done with me. "Make sure she eats more," he shouted at the soldiers. "And keep her training. You'll be the perfect replacement to give Earl Paul."

"Replacement?" I asked, not moving.

"Leave, girl. I don't want to scar you if you are to take your sister's place as the Earl's bride, but you're testing my patience. I don't think he'd mind his next bride a little roughed up."

"I'm eleven."

The Baron shrugged. "Less than two years before you can be married. If you behave, I'll make sure none of your . . . siblings beat you anymore." He laughed again, loudly. "Good! You were like the dead but look at you now."

"The marriage age"—I almost said "in this world" but managed to bite it back—"is thirteen?"

"By the Gods girl, you really did lose your memory." He grunted, beckoning the guards to come and drag me away. "Someone get her a teacher. The Earl will be expecting a lady, not this"—he threw his hands up in my direction—"thing."

Well, that was rude.

I stood on my own and walked out without another word. That had not gone as planned. I had thought to try leveraging the honor I could bring to the family by training as a female energy user. By the end of that "meeting," I would have rather gouged my eyes out than do anything in the family name.

In any case, the Baron had just given me about a year and a half to prepare. By then, I wouldn't be so weak.

I went back to my room, shut the door, and climbed into bed to resume the process of purifying my heart energy. I crossed my legs and placed a palm over each knee. I closed my eyes and focused.

I needed to shape the energy into rings and absorb them as fast as I could without destabilizing my Core's foundation. The longer it took me to do that, the longer I'd remain weak.

CHAPTER FOUR

The Eldest Daughter

The weeks passed in a blur while I focused on building the energy rings around my heart. I needed power, and the process kept me distracted from the ocean of my rage just under the surface. True to his word, the Baron had apparently ordered for me to be left alone. No other encounters with any of the Silverwaters occurred, and for that, I was thankful. Even if it came at the cost of being eventually sold off.

Although I had only just managed to form the first ring, that had been enough to trigger my new body into undergoing some needed physical changes. The changes were minor and nothing like the Reformation that would happen upon achieving a Silver-level Core, but it made using Lilliana's body a lot smoother.

I grew a handful of inches upon achieving the first ring and coupled with the soldier's daily exercise routine, thin muscles now rippled beneath my unblemished skin. The scars of my true body would return, I knew. The scars of an Awakened were not just physical manifestations—they were reflections of the Awakened's journey and a testament to the wounds of their very soul.

Lilliana's brown eyes had also shifted to a reddish brown, the first sign of their eventual total shift to my original bloodred coloring, the symbol of Aedronir royalty.

The maid Baron Silverwater had assigned to me, Dectra, cleared her throat from the doorway. Her lips were always twisted into the expression of someone sucking on something sour. I couldn't tell if that was her natural look or just a face she made when looking at me.

"It is time for your etiquette lessons . . . my lady."

Since the first day the maid had been assigned to me, I'd disliked her. Even without the permanent sour expression staining her face, the woman simply reminded me of my grandmother. My actual grandmother. Gray, beady eyes showing disdain for everything I did. Coarse white hair, messy and untamed, yet braided with a delicate touch. The dichotomy did nothing to aid the hair's ugliness or grease yet spoke much to the person's inherent bias toward hypocrisy.

I raised my eyebrow from where I sat at my cracked and dilapidated desk, reaching over with a quill point to tap a short white paper next to the stack of educational material the Baron had been providing me.

"It is the fourth day today. Next is history, not etiquette."

"The history teacher is not available at the moment, so Madam Elara has stepped in to replace the course time."

"That is unacceptable," I said, clenching the quill in an undignified fist and then burying the point into the white paper. "My education must be properly balanced. Etiquette can wait. If the history teacher is not available, fetch another one. Or must I be the one to fetch?"

The maid was silent for a long moment, and though her eyes had narrowed, I could still see anger and hatred in them. I didn't know why this maid was filled with such anger, but I truly did not care so long as she performed her duties. At the very least, Dectra had so far been quite able in that regard. Sometimes a dog wasn't bad, it simply needed to be tamed and shown where its place was.

"Yes, Lilliana," Dectra said through gritted teeth.

I turned a sharp gaze on her and stood in a single swift motion, the heavy steel blade at my hip jangling against its sheath as I did so.

"If you wish to deign such a disrespectful tone, I will have you serving slop to the hogs in an hour." Not a threat, a fact. While the Baron still did not particularly find any favor with me, he would continue to protect my welfare if only for the benefit of the marriage contract. "In fact, I might have you fed to the hogs."

Dectra paled and gave me a deep bow that brought her nearly horizontal to the floor. The sliver of heart energy burrowing its way into Dectra's mortal heart would be enough to persuade her of my seriousness. It was doubtful Dectra could tell it was heart energy manipulating her senses, but it didn't matter. It was the feeling that mattered.

"I will fetch you a new history tutor, my lady." Without waiting for a response like she should have, Dectra turned and fled out of my bedchambers. I let her go despite the disrespect. One step at a time.

In any case, I wasn't too concerned about etiquette or history courses. While there were certain aspects of etiquette that differed between my current role and previous world, the differences were rather minuscule. What was interesting, however, was the political layout of this world and something called "magic." While there were no textbooks available to me describing the essence of magic in any great detail, my understanding, based on the few lines relating to magic I'd read in *The History of Lysoria*, indicated that magic was similar to heart or Core energy, but that it was created from something called ley lines rather than the heart.

I turned back to the opened geography textbook laid out on my desk and absentmindedly flicked the quill pen around between my index and middle fingers. A single area was circled with ink, and its borders were traced by a mountain range called the Drought Range. The kingdom was a mid to lower-sized territory called Lysoria, where I currently found myself, though technically the Silverwaters were stationed on the outskirts of the kingdom as the Baroness was related to a foreign duke . . . somehow. I hadn't quite figured that part out yet.

The world itself was called Graedon, but the textbooks available to me only detailed a single continent—Pularea. The land was split into six different territories, one of which was Lysoria. I didn't pay much attention to the other five, though I couldn't help but note that only one of the territories was labeled as being an empire, written in enormous font, even on the Lysoria-made map before me.

I thumbed to the next page, which focused on the Lysoria kingdom's territory. The aptly, if unoriginally, named Silverwater town at the Core of the barony was surrounded by three neighboring cities, but none of them struck me as useful. Considering Lysoria's neighboring country to its east, the Kingdom of Cael, traded with Lysoria through a slave-run city on the border of both nations, I was fairly surprised to learn that slavery was actually banned in Lysoria.

Not indentured servitude, but the owning of an individual as property. Yet there were generally no armed conflicts between the two nations despite the opposing ideological perspectives. In my past life, I'd seen many nations enter blood feuds on the basis of slavery.

The relationship between Lysoria and Cael was an interesting one. On the surface, both kingdoms had remained peaceful with each other throughout the centuries. But a deeper reading of the texts indicated a number of intricate political contentions between the two nations. It was as if their governments and people refused to coexist, but also, for some reason, could not wage war against their neighbor.

I grabbed the textbook with the details of Lysoria's territory, specifically the one with a map illustrated on the thin pages and stood to leave the room. I didn't particularly need a tutor in any subject, but it never hurt to have an additional source of information. Regardless, by the time Dectra found a new tutor, I'd be at my next lesson—Religion and Faith, as the Church of Tranquility's Cardinal Lack was so fond of referring to it as.

The information was interesting, as religions often were, but at this moment, those lessons were perhaps my least useful. I summoned my single heart ring in a smoky appearance in my free hand and began to spin my hand around the fledgling ring as I left the room to roam the halls of the Silverwater mansion.

Unfortunately, before I got much farther than the end of the first hallway, I came face-to-face with the Baron's eldest daughter, Morgana, and her entourage of lower nobility ladies-in-waiting and some other high echelon noble ladies. Though I'd never seen her before, I had seen many of her portraits over the past few weeks, and she was easily recognizable by the tight brown curls of her hair and distinct green eyes that had a bad habit of peering down her nose at just about everyone. She couldn't have been older than her late teens or early twenties, judging by her lack of wrinkles. She wasn't all that tall; however, she loomed over me due to Lilliana's body having not yet experienced puberty.

"If it isn't the whore's spawn," Morgana said, flipping open a fan to hide the smirk I could almost hear spread as she spat the insult out. "I hear you went and lost most of your memories? Not that there was much in that crass little head of yours anyway."

I grit my teeth in an attempt to avoid pummeling the woman as images of my mother flickered in my mind's eye. Based on what I'd learned about the Baron's family in the past few weeks, Morgana could likely wipe the floor with my current self. If the gossip I'd overheard from the housemaids and seen in some of the house information books recently updated, the woman was quite gifted with fire energy and magic. At that moment I cursed the Baron inwardly for prohibiting me from accessing any textbooks about magic or energy. Even information as surface level as what exactly magic was and the associated ley lines would have reduced the edge Morgana had over me.

Though, I supposed, it wouldn't do for the marriage doll to learn how to kill her contract owner.

"Good afternoon," I said, my voice coming out as pleasant as I could manage.

"Oh, goodness." One of the many women in Morgana's entourage, likely a lady-in-waiting given the wealth of her overflowing dress, gave a mock gasp. "It even looks like a wild animal." The woman was a good bit older than Morgana, with fresh wrinkles spreading out from her forehead and under her eyes. She was maybe a head taller than Morgana and two more than myself but was exceedingly skinny to the point I was surprised she could walk. Her pale skin was in stark contrast to the thick red makeup on her cheeks and lips that did not pair well with her dark brown eyes.

"How old are you?" I asked. Noble ladies were the same no matter what world, apparently. Fortunately, that should make them fairly easy to manipulate.

"Wh-what?" she asked, matching Morgana by flipping open her own fan.

I pointed to her ungloved hands. "I was just curious why my sister keeps such an old, unmarried maid in her retinue. I have to say, that certainly is quite undignified." The noble lady cried out in insult as the women behind her snickered. Even Morgana had begun to crack a mocking smile until she realized I had not only insulted the other noble but her as well.

She gave me a small warning smile. "Watch where you tread, sister. You may have somehow developed a little bravery recently, but bravery and foolishness are quite closely related. And foolishness never ends well." Her eyes lit up with a glint of something I knew would not be good for me. She suddenly switched to a fond, elder-sister tone I'd heard from other queen candidates as a child. "What is it you're reading, little Lilliana?" I didn't show her. "Oh, she's feeling shy!" The girls giggled, perhaps catching on to Morgana's plan while I was still in the dark. "Why don't you join us at our tea party? We can discuss." She peered around my arm with a false smile that wasn't fooling anyone, much less me after introducing herself by calling me a whorespawn. "Oooh, the history of Lysoria. Yes, that should be fun to discuss over some Pularean tea."

"My apologies, Lady Silverwater," I said, hesitantly switching to a more formal tone to indicate a refusal for one of a higher station. "But I truly must resume my lessons."

Morgana waved away my words with her fan. "Not to worry, darling sister. I hear you have been excelling in all your lessons. One afternoon off will not set you behind at all."

I wanted to protest further, but the noble lady and her entourage swept and hustled me forward, despite my objections. I choked down the snarl and curses that bubbled up at the complete disrespect I was being shown. Lilliana was a bullied eleven-year-old. Morgana was a powerful young adult vying to be the family's head. I could swallow the insults for now to come back stronger later and return it all tenfold.

CHAPTER FIVE

Tea Party

The group of finely dressed ladies-in-waiting, who were noble ladies from lesser or fallen houses, pushed me away from the direction I'd been heading and toward the opposite end of the hallway. After a few minutes of irritating shoves and "accidental" trips, I was led into a large room with enormous windows that allowed brilliant rays of sun to shine through.

"Welcome to my solar," Morgana said, looking momentarily awed at the beauty of her room. The Solar was nestled quite deeply within the east wing of the grand mansion. Curious, though, that it was on the same floor as Lilliana's worn-down chambers. "This is my sanctuary of elegance and refinement. Any actions in this room which do not meet these expectations will not be tolerated." Most of the women around Morgana nodded vigorously at her words, though some seemed to shuffle awkwardly. To me, that seemed like a complete lie. I doubted anything happening in this room today would be elegant or refined.

The room itself was currently bathed in the soft, golden light of the afternoon sun and seemed to have been meticulously prepared for nobility.

The sun's rays filtered through the tall, arched windows adorned with delicate transparent glass; some of which contained small sections of stained glass that created an atmosphere of serene beauty. A gentle spring breeze slipped between the partially opened windows and wafted through the room, filling it with the scent of blooming roses from the gardens of the mansion just below.

The focal point of the room was a large, intricately carved wooden table, draped with a finely embroidered linen cloth. The cloth was decorated with images of wildflowers and vines, its edges delicately fringed with golden threads. On the table, an array of silver platters gleamed, each one carefully arranged with tempting delicacies that I'd never seen before but that smelled better than anything I'd eaten since being tried and hung.

There were small pastries filled with honey and nuts, slices of fresh bread accompanied by rich, creamy butter, and a selection of cheeses that ranged from sharp and tangy to mild and creamy. Bowls of ripe, juicy berries and nuts added vibrant color to the spread. Despite myself, my stomach rumbled, and I cursed as Morgana cast a smirk in my direction and the women snickered again.

Goblets of exquisitely crafted gold glass, each one a work of art with swirls of color embedded within the clear crystal linings, were set at each place, ready to be filled with the finest tea and herbal infusions. Delicate bottles, engraved with scenes of hunting and pastoral life, stood nearby, filled to the brim with a light purple liquid.

Comfortable high-backed chairs, each cushioned with velvet and embroidered pillows, surrounded the table, inviting the ladies to sit and enjoy the afternoon's luxuries. The chairs were positioned to allow easy conversation, and a few low stools provided extra seating for the younger ladies who might join. Next to the most richly decorated and lavish chair lined with lush cushions was a single bar stool. Even before Morgana yanked me toward the stool with her, I knew who it was for.

The walls of the Solar were adorned with tapestries that depicted scenes of courtly love and epic battles, their rich colors and intricate details adding warmth and a sense of history to the room. Between the tapestries, shelves held an array of treasures: intricately carved wooden boxes, delicate glass vases filled with fresh flowers, and a selection of expensive or rare books bound in rich leather and embossed with gold.

A minstrel, dressed in a tunic of green and gold, sat near the window with his lute, softly plucking the strings and filling the room with a gentle melody that contrasted in an almost ominous way with the devious aura of the noblewomen.

As I was pulled to the stool next to Morgana's luxurious chair like some sort of wild pet, I counted the other women taking their seats. Thirteen in total, excluding myself and Morgana, who would make it fifteen. The accompanying maids who lagged behind the lower and upper nobility stood at the outskirts of the Solar.

I, of course, did not sit on the rusted and bent bar stool. My tolerance would only go so far. Instead, I looked at the older lady-in-waiting who'd taken her seat on Morgana's left quizzically, feigning confusion.

"Madam," I said, implying the older age of the woman who'd attempted to insult me earlier in my use of "madam" instead of "lady," and walked around Morgana's seat to put my hand on the older noblewoman's shoulder. "Surely you do not expect a daughter of Baron Silverwater to sit on such a thing, now, do you? That would most certainly be a great disrespect toward the Baron." I summoned a small, thin sliver of heart energy and let it slither over the older noblewoman's skin like ooze.

She gasped and was out of her seat before she looked at Morgana for instructions. Morgana didn't have the opportunity to speak as a different woman laughed. This one with a voice high and much more brash.

"She's got you there, Brie. Just sit on the stool and be quiet." The woman who spoke shamed even Morgana's beauty with her own. Long locks of straight gold hair cascaded like a gentle river over her shoulders and to her mid back, small intentionally made waves embedded into the straight lengths to give a more regal feeling. Bright green eyes sparkled in my direction while her red lips pursed in amusement, a great contrast to her perfectly smooth, fair skin. Even her voice was an elegant mix of levity and command, a style of speaking I recognized instantly as royalty.

The golden-haired woman in question stood at the Solar's entrance, her intricately woven silver gown flowing in a silent trail behind her as she approached the table. All snickering stopped as three of the lesser young noble ladies scattered out of her way, leaving three seats for her to choose from. She chose none, deigning instead to remove a smaller girl from a high-backed blue cushioned chair. The little girl paled to the color of snow and her cheeks flushed a deep red before she, likewise, scrambled out of the way.

"Ah, Princess Isla, I hadn't realized you were planning to make today's gathering, or I would have greeted you at the entrance," Morgana said with barely disguised distaste. Actually, it wasn't really disguised at all.

Princess Isla didn't comment on the disrespect and gave a soft laugh. "That's quite all right, Lady Silverwater. I had nearly forgotten the event was today. Had Lady Haventure not reminded me of it, I may have very well missed it entirely."

Lady Haventure . . . I couldn't place the name, though it danced at the tip of my tongue. I was certain that it referred to the daughter of a duchy. Unfortunately, it didn't seem like Lady Haventure was in attendance and no one confirmed who she was, likely because they all already knew.

"I see," Morgana said and turned her gaze back toward me, clearly intending to switch the conversation back to a more favorable topic.

I didn't give her the chance and sat in the empty seat. "It's a pleasure to meet you, Your Highness," I greeted the Princess, giving her a respectful, if slight, dip of my head. A few of the girls around me inhaled sharply, one even gasped. I looked around at them to see what had caused their reactions. They all glanced away instead of meeting my eyes.

Princess Isla raised an eyebrow, surprise sketched clearly on her face though she covered it quickly. "The pleasure is all mine, young Lady Silverwater. Though, I do believe we have met before . . ."

"If that is true, I apologize for the discourtesy. My head, unfortunately, took quite a beating a few weeks ago. It seems I have yet to recover and there is much missing from my memory."

Princess Isla cast Morgana a puzzled expression, but Morgana only shrugged.

"I do hope you recover, young Lady Silverwater," the Princess said after a moment. "I do say, however, that you have greatly improved your speech since we last met. Do you believe that to be a consequence of your trauma?"

It was my turn to shrug. "I am no medical professional nor am I a healer, Your Highness. I . . . am simply a young child."

"Hmmm . . . I'm not sure 'simply a child' fits you all that accurately. Why don't we—"

The Princess's next words were cut off by the sudden appearance of maids carrying pots of what smelled to be freshly brewed tea.

"Ah, perfect timing, Bella," Morgana said to the foremost maid. "Please provide Her Highness with our best tea. Everyone should get the tea appropriate for their station."

The maid, Bella, nodded and took the first kettle toward the Princess. Other maids scurried into the Solar behind Bella, each with their own kettles. The particularly petite maid then poured steaming tea into the small teacup originally set for Lady Brie in front of me. A slightly bitter scent wafted from my cup mixed with the scent of something sweet and herbal. Normally, a lady would be served tea by the personal maid they'd brought with them to the party. I'd read some history on previous nobilities being killed through their tea ceremonies a few generations back. This was a sort of tradition created in light of those deaths.

Therefore, considering this had been Lady Brie's seat, I was unsurprised when the petite maid left my side and returned almost immediately to Lady Brie's side, who had already been served tea. I figured since I clearly did not have a personal maid for this event, it was perhaps a custom to have someone else's maid serve it. Or not. I wasn't sure.

It was, however, quite interesting that Lady Brie's maidservant had served poisoned tea to where her lady was supposed to be sitting. I recognized the sweet herbal smell mixed with the normal bitterness of tea and it was not something a loyal servant would serve their master. I glanced at the Princess and Morgana, the former looking bemused while the latter seemed almost bored. Or annoyed—it was hard to tell the difference with Morgana.

Neither looked like they were anticipating anything. Lady Brie seemed somewhat on edge, but not enough that I would have thought she was attempting to poison me, especially since the tea should have technically been served to her, not me.

Still, this could be a surprising opportunity to restrain Morgana before any sort of bullying truly began. Since Lady Brie was considered a follower of Morgana, it wouldn't be a stretch for the Baron to assume the poisoning was caused by Morgana's pressure or influence. If I were poisoned and the Baron suspected Morgana of instigating the attack in direct opposition to orders and threatening the financial alliance he'd gain with the Earl, that would give me even more space to build a foundation with the barony and within myself before real trouble began to brew.

Unfortunately, that did assume I survived the poison, and without knowing the dosage or potency, it could prove unnecessarily dangerous. Still, the plan did have its merits.

CHAPTER SIX

A Noble Lady's Blackmail

I circled my finger around the edge of the teacup and leaned back in my seat. Compared to the desk chair in my room, the cushioned high-back chair was quite comfortable. As the other ladies sipped their tea and made compliments to Morgana, excluding Princess Isla who had not touched hers, I continued to trace my finger along the edges of the cup without drinking it.

Noticing my reluctance to drink, Lady Brie apparently decided to comment on it in some sort of mock-insulted tone. "Young Lady Silverwater, is my tea not good enough for you?"

I laughed, though, to my disappointment, it came off high-pitched and young, reminding me once again of my new body's unfortunate age. "On the contrary, Lady Brie. I believe this tea is only suitable for your noble person. I couldn't possibly drink it."

The woman stared at me, confusion, insult, and a hint of pride all written in her expression. She stood with a huff of finality. "While I agree with your assessment of the tea's quality, I am quite insulted that you would use my given name so brashly. I am Lady Ballenci, not Lady Brie." She turned and stormed toward the exit. On her way out, I blasted her with a fist of invisible heart energy that caused her to tumble into a maid carrying a steaming kettle. Lady Ballenci shrieked in obvious pain as boiling liquid spilled over her arms and face, quickly turning the touched skin into areas of sickly-looking red-and-white welts.

Everyone stopped drinking to stare at the screaming woman, but other than the group of maids who'd been at her side, no one helped. When I turned back to the table to see why, Princess Isla was staring at the retreating injured woman with a cold look of indifference. With a surge of heart energy in my hands, I deftly grabbed my cup and switched it with the mostly filled cup of the random lady next to me, whose name I couldn't be bothered to know. She was similar to Morgana with her curly brown hair and build but differed in her brown eyes and a chin that jutted out just enough to keep her from being a conventional beauty. She leaned over to Morgana, whispering something in the Silverwater heir's ear. They both chuckled, clearly on friendly terms. Perhaps even close friends.

I hoped they were.

"Oh dear," Princess Isla quipped, "it seems you've upset Grand Lady Ballenci. How ever will we continue without the precious daughter of a fallen Baron?" Laughs and snickers echoed through the Solar despite Morgana's annoyed expression. Obtaining favor with a royal daughter clearly outweighed two daughters of baronies.

"I should apologize to her," I said, standing more abruptly than I had intended as an idea occurred to me.

Princess Isla waved her hand. "Enjoy your tea, young Lady Silverwater. Lady Ballenci will overcome her . . . irritation sooner or later. Do not fret."

I shook my head. "My apologies, Your Highness, but my conscience will not let this unintentional slight go without explanation to Lady Ballenci." The Princess just sighed and waved her hand again, this time dismissively. I didn't bother looking at Morgana as I followed the burnt woman's trailing maids.

I exited the Solar room and started to fast walk toward Lady Ballenci, speeding past the painting of an old woman with eyes that seemed to follow me down the hall. The stones echoed my footsteps which slowly turned into a jog. The sun was high in the afternoon sky still, and there was more than enough light to soon spot the group of women hurrying away.

I estimated maybe five-ish minutes before the brown-eyed noble lady back in the sunroom whose name I didn't know would drink her tea. "Lady Ballenci!" I shouted and picked up my pace.

One of the maids, the slighter one from earlier, turned my way with wide eyes as she ushered her lady along faster. I stopped bothering with any attempt to appear elegant and took off at a straight sprint until I overtook them and halted directly in front.

I put on a polite and solemn smile. "Lady Ballenci, I wanted to apologize for using your birth name earlier. I hadn't . . ." I trailed off at the sight of the sobbing woman, her arms and face covered in blisters. What would someone who cared say? Nothing came to mind and time was running out, so I just cut to the chase and went straight for my accusation. "One of your followers is a traitor. I believe it is one of your maids."

"Wh-what?" Lady Ballenci rasped, her words coming out in dry gasps. One of her maids with the symbol of a red sun stitched to her garments over her chest reached out toward Lady Ballenci's burns and a warm orange light began to emanate from those outstretched hands. More sweat ran from the woman's brow than Lady Ballenci's, a telling sign for healing magic even from my world.

"Her. I'm pretty sure she used magic to shove you into the maid, intending to burn you." I pointed to the slight maid. Technically, it was possible the girl was not a traitor and the poison had been served on Lady Ballenci's orders, but my instincts were screaming that Lady Ballenci was not someone who would plan such complex assassinations. I knew killers and the older woman did not strike me as one.

"No! That's not true, my lady!" Lady Ballenci glanced at the pleading maid who'd fallen to her knees. "I swear I didn't! What she says are lies. Please, my lady, please do not believe her. She's just a vile girl saying vile things."

I whistled at the instant begging, not caring whether my accusation was on target or not. It was close enough. I raised an eyebrow at Lady Ballenci. Either the maid was a horrible actress or the lady was not quite as fond of her maids as I had originally believed and the girl feared a beating.

"What proof . . . do you have . . . to make such a claim?" Lady Ballenci said, her wheezing words coming out more emphatic as her healer treated the wounds around her neck.

"Your maid panicked when she saw I was in your seat and gave the poisoned tea to the wrong lady," I responded with an accusing look toward the small maid girl. At the puzzled look of the maidservant and her lady, I held up a finger. "Just wait a moment."

Then screaming erupted from the sunroom we'd just exited, right on time. The other maids looked at me and then at the small maid girl with an equal amount of horror.

Lady Ballenci, surprisingly, did not seem panicked. Perhaps it was the burns still marring her face, but her expression seemed more collected than only seconds earlier. Colder. More calculating. Either my understanding of noble ladies had waned over the years or this woman was quite the actress, playing even my senses. The more her body healed, and she regained composure, the more I could see the intelligence behind the disguise. Curious.

That begged the question, though, why had she suddenly decided to reveal her real self?

"Who is screaming?" Lady Ballenci asked in a still somewhat raspy voice, clearly almost healed. I could see veins bulging from her healer's effort to perform a quick healing. It seemed an unfortunate connection between our worlds that healers would live short lives due to the pressure of nobles demanding quick heals. A healer who was constantly pushed to their energy limits, and magical limits too I assumed, would find their life energy quietly drained with it. "Who ended up drinking the poisoned tea? You let her drink it despite knowing it was poisoned? Why?"

"The woman screaming? I have no idea," I lied, shrugging innocently and feigning a worried frown. "How could I, poor, little, and frail as I am, have known about a poisoning?" I continued. "I have always been locked up, after all. Although, perhaps I did hear you scheming revenge on the ladies who laughed at you when I left to apologize . . . Something about poisoning them with your maidservant?" I said, a thick tone of innocence warping my cruel words as I spun a tale that could ruin whatever remained of the Lady's standing in noble society.

Lady Ballenci scowled. "No one will believe you."

"Maybe not." I shrugged. "It hardly matters once the rumor is spread even if you could prove it all a lie." I took a step closer to her and let some of my cold heart energy loose to resume crawling over her skin like ooze. "No one will talk to you. No man will marry you. You will be cast out and your family will be so ashamed of their criminal daughter who, for all intents and purposes, is believed to have murdered another noble girl."

"Even if you don't say anything, if your claim is true, all fingers will point at my maidservant anyway."

"Not true. All fingers will initially be pointed at the poisoned lady's maidservants who served *her* tea. And perhaps you may want to make that evidence a little more convincing. Your choice."

"We'll all tell them you told us this!" one of the other maids hissed. Or maybe she was another lady-in-waiting? It was honestly difficult to tell when they all wore nearly identical clothing separated only by a slight difference in quality given the fact ladies-in-waiting generally operated more like maids, than nobles while working. The maid, or lady-in-waiting, sported raven-black hair and dark eyes that blended well with her ebony skin.

"Shut it," Lady Ballenci snapped at the woman, eyes still on me.

I shrugged again. "I'm eleven, uneducated, and have no support. You'd be putting quite a bit of faith in people thinking I'm more intelligent than a whore's spawn."

She eyed me suspiciously. "You do not speak like a child of only eleven years. You speak more like my aunt." The lady paused, raising her hand to run over her neck as other ladies poured out of the Solar room in screaming messes. I could hear Morgana shouting from inside for a healer. The healer looked at her lady in exhaustion as if begging not to be sent. Lucky for her, Lady Ballenci was not paying the healer any mind, much less Morgana's desperate yells. "Who are you, really? I've met Lilliana before. I cannot believe such a change to occur from memory loss."

I gave her a toothy grin and a half answer. "I'm the new Lilliana."

After a few moments of more ladies screaming and guards rushing into the room, she finally sighed. "I still do not believe you are Lilliana, but if my maid is truly a traitor to my house, maybe that will indeed prove beneficial. But why help me at all?"

"I'm not sure I would call blackmailing you helping," I said with a practiced nonchalance as I made clear her position in our relationship. "It is my understanding that the Ballenci family are quite involved in the information trade. My offer is quite simple. Limit the information traded to Morgana and instead offer it to me. In turn, I will keep this little event to myself. And who knows? Perhaps my mysterious personality change will positively benefit your information trade."

It was a gamble on my part, but at the end of the day, I could just kill her later if circumstances necessitated it. I wasn't entirely sure that the Ballenci family were in the information trade, and I had no real clue just how deep they might be, but there'd been insinuations in *The History of Lysoria* during the section on old Lysorian families that the Ballenci family were the original information brokers. I had no idea whether they still were, but it was worth a shot.

"You are quite vicious, young Lady Lilliana," Lady Ballenci said, straightening her posture and beginning to walk away. "I will provide you with your answer tonight. I must speak with my maid first."

I had no doubt there would not be much speaking involved.

CHAPTER SEVEN

First Interlude of Lady Morgana Silverwater

That had not gone according to plan. Not at all. It had been a complete disaster. It should have been easy. Simple. The maidservant kills the little whorespawn, and the blame gets shoved onto Lady Ballenci, whose servant had served the tea.

That would not only solve the issue of Lady Ballenci's expanding influence over the noble ladies but would also take care of the annoying rat of a girl that Lilliana was. She hadn't felt the need to go about killing the girl, but Morgana couldn't risk allowing Lilliana to marry into an earl's family. With the hatred Lilliana no doubt harbored against the Silverwater barony, her father was an imbecile to risk marrying her into a Countess position. Though Morgana had originally doubted the scarecrow of a girl could so much as hold her own in a conversation much less act on hatred, rumors of the girl's growing confidence had spurred Morgana into planning Lilliana's death as soon as was convenient.

Her plan had been efficient and simple. Perfect.

How had it all gone so horribly awry?

Her friend was dead now, and it was all that little whorespawn's fault. How had she switched the cups? Morgana had barely looked away from the girl the entire time she had been in the Solar, so there was no way she could have switched the teacups. And even if she had, surely Lady Tremmor would have noticed a child switching the teas.

Yet Lady Tremmor had not noticed. She had been completely oblivious, drinking the entire cup before the poison took effect, killing her before a healer could even be notified.

Morgana clenched Lady Tremmor's teacup in her bloodied hands. When Lady Tremmor suddenly vomited blood, shaking violently and foaming at the mouth, Morgana instantly moved to help her friend. Lady Tremmor had never been the most intelligent or powerful of Morgana's allies, but she had been by far the most loyal.

"I'm going to kill her," Morgana mumbled. "By the Gods, I'm going to fucking kill her!" Fire erupted around her, rampaging across the room, and Morgana shattered Lady Tremmor's last cup against the far wall. Fire trailed as she stalked toward her closest maids still silently standing around the edges of the Solar. None of them looked at her or the body of Lady Tremmor, which was still on the floor. Morgana had dismissed the healers who came, barely restraining herself from ordering them to be hanged. They all knew better than to look around, choosing instead to stare at their feet. "I want her dead. Dead as can be. I want her dead at my feet! Dead, dead, fucking dead!"

"There is something odd about her since she nearly killed the Young Lord Silverwater," her second maid, Diedra, said. "Perhaps she's finally lost it and gone crazy?"

"That didn't look crazy to me," Morgana screamed, throwing a plate against the same far wall. "Someone is educating her beyond my father's program, telling her how to speak and act above her place. Her progress is otherwise impossible over a matter of weeks. Who would bother doing something so absurd and useless!?"

"Tell us your commands, my lady," the six women said in unison.

"Find out who is backing her. Go to Lady Ballenci and have her send out some information collectors. She might be upset at having been burned, so appease her however is required."

"What should we do if the Princess interferes?"

Morgana paused, thinking. The Princess had been rather furious at the poisoning, even if the target had not been her or her followers. Perhaps she suspected the target to have been someone else.

"If she interferes, reach out to my grandfather from the Goldenhearts. Mother is still furious at what Lilliana did to Brian, so Aunt Hilda and Grandfather will want to help kill that little whorespawn. Even a princess will not be able to act rashly against a duke and a marchioness." Her flames quieted as her mind formed a plan. "Yes, in fact, I have the perfect way to kill her. The most painful, excruciating way possible." She turned to her sixth maidservant, who usually communicated with Lady Ballenci's information brokers. "Actually, I want you to find out if my grandfather is interested in Misty Veil Sire. I remember he mentioned to me one had taken to hibernating there."

"My lady?" the first maid, Ariel, asked, raising her head slightly, her usual signal that Morgana was sharing too much information. Morgana ignored her oldest maidservant, still raging and infuriated by Lilliana.

"Just do it! Sires are known to love noble and royal blood. That little bitch would make a fantastic lure. And I doubt the Goldenhearts would pass at the chance to weaken my father's growing military influence. I heard he made moves against Grandfather a few months ago that resulted in one of my cousins being killed." Morgana's eyes flared with that dark greed she was thrilled to always let loose.

"What is a sire, my lady?" the sixth maid asked, clearly making significant effort to ignore Morgana's comments regarding her grandfather, a great duke. Normally, Morgana would punish servants for questioning her, but the sixth maid, Nissa, was her go-between with information brokers and Lady Ballenci's family. There was some leeway to ensure Nissa had the necessary level of information.

"Sires," Morgana explained, "are believed to be the original Progenitors of heart energy and their species."

"Is that not a Beast King, my lady?" Nissa asked. The five maids to Nissa's right all shifted nervously, as the young woman was clearly pushing the boundaries of her leeway.

"I cannot give you the details, Nissa. However, it has recently come to light that Beast Kings may not, in fact, be the originals of their species. The matter is currently being investigated." She cast a glance at all her maids, and the fire around her flared in warning. "That is a secret which must be kept in this room, understood? If it is revealed that the information was spread, know that I will know whom it came from."

"Yes, my lady."

Morgana dismissed all but the first maid, who rarely left her side other than when Morgana slept. The older maidservant had been with Morgana since her mother had been pregnant. "She's dead, Ariel. Dead. My friend is dead, and her murderer is gallivanting about my home."

Ariel swept away from the wall and toward her mistress, red hair trailing in the maid's wake. "Your revenge will be ever sweet, my lady." Ariel leaned in and whispered comforting words kept between the two of them only. "My queen."

Before Morgana could smile at the whispered secret wish, her father burst into the Solar, his face the picture of rage. For the millionth time, Morgana was thankful to the Gods for making sure most of her looks came from her mother and not the man her mother had been stuck with.

His noble red-and-purple robes flapped at his back as his heavy belly jiggled underneath. His large and ever-embarrassing mustache twitched with the lord's angry mutterings. The clothes he wore were more silk than cotton or other durable materials, indicating he had likely been disturbed from time spent with one of his new whores. Alcohol permeated the air around him, swept up to an even greater degree of stench due to the unconscious breeze swarming around the angry wind energy user, the Baron.

"You tried to poison her?" he shouted, storming into the room and shoving Ariel to the ground so he could grab Morgana's jaw between meaty fingers. Morgana went to protest the accusation, but the Baron snarled. "Don't play dumb with me, girl. You didn't think I would find out about your little plan? I told you not to touch her. The Earl is paying a hefty sum for a healthy girl. Do you want to be put back on the contract instead?"

"Mother would never have allowed that," Morgana hissed through the pain of his grip.

He laughed and squeezed her face harder. "Don't be so sure about that, daughter. I am the lord of this house, not Mathilda. And she will do nothing to threaten your brother's position as heir. Do you really believe the Goldenhearts care for you so much they would throw away a chance to have their bloodline in charge of a barony with gem mines?"

Morgana just stared at him and said nothing. Though she despised admitting it, her father spoke the truth. Her mother would not risk the Baron's wrath being aimed at Killian, which was why she had not acted against Lilliana despite what she'd done to Brian.

But that did not mean her mother would abandon her to be sold to Earl Paul and have the arrangement disguised as a marriage. The man was disgusting and horrible.

He finally noticed Lady Tremmor's corpse and wrinkled his nose in distaste. "Clean that up," he said, releasing her face. The Baron's air affinity energy had long since suffocated her flames, so she just stood there, naked of her flames. "And clean yourself up. By the Gods, Morgana, maintain your dignity. You are second in line." The guards at the door snapped to immediate attention as he stalked back out of the door. "And this is your final warning. Leave the girl alone. My uses far outweigh your petty anger. Next time, I will have you in the dungeon for a month."

When he'd finally left and the door closed tightly behind him, Morgana collapsed to her knees and cradled where her father had bruised her cheek. She would not cry; she would never cry from the Baron's abuse. But her rage had been tempered, and it burned below the surface, this time cold and measured.

"I'm changing the plan," Morgana said in a low tone to Ariel, who was once again standing off to the side after picking herself up from the Baron's earlier anger. "We're going to get rid of both of them. Fetch me some paper to write a letter to my grandfather and bring me Jeffords. Tell Grandfather I know of a little bitch with noble blood we can use to lure his mythical sire. And instruct Jeffords that I want to start proper matriarch training. Not training to be the wife of a patriarch, but to be the matriarch. It's time I take this situation in my own hands."

CHAPTER EIGHT

Spring Expedition

Lucid sat across from me in the training courtyard, both of us drenched in sweat and breathing hard.

Ever since the Baron's household-wide declaration that I was not to be so much as bruised, none of the knights had wanted to spar with me. Even the mercenaries were shying away, which had been proving frustrating. Without them, I couldn't train my muscle memory properly. Sure, my eleven-year-old body hadn't been providing much of a challenge for them, but it wasn't about them.

Nearly three months of self-training had passed before I'd less so asked and more so told the Baron that I would be getting bruised in sword spars. He had laughed and agreed. I still couldn't tell if his nonchalance was good or bad, but at least it opened the door to my sparring again. Despite the allowance of physical activity, my social activity was still stunted, and I had yet to follow up with Lady Ballenci, though a letter of vague acceptance had been slipped under my door the night following our *discussion*.

Unfortunately, the lack of proper physical training had greatly impeded my ability to form heart rings. Without heightened physical training to push me to my limits, my body still hadn't been able to develop enough to where it could hold the amount of energy necessary to form more heart rings. What little self-training I'd been doing like running until I dropped and, whenever I managed to sneak into the knights' quarters, donning some armor and training weight resistance to increase muscle mass, was providing me with only slight improvements.

It was all very limited.

The past few weeks since the Baron's allowances had been much better for my growth thanks to the sparring, but it was still slower than I'd have preferred. Lilliana's body was weak to the point even the single heart ring was pushing her heart's current limits. I estimated at least another six months before a Core could be formed, and that was if I was able to remain focused the entire time.

"You've gotten a lot better, young lady," Lucid said and took a large swig from his waterskin. "I can finally see some muscles on those bones."

I laughed and gave him a playful shove. "Just wait. I'll have great large muscles and stand a full two meters someday soon."

Lucid snorted. "Yeah, sure. And I'm half giant."

"Don't believe me, do you, Sir Squire?"

"That's huge! You'd need at least one family member that tall to even think that is a possibility! The only person in this household even close to two meters is the Knight Captain." Lucid said Captain with a reverent tone as usual and his eyes seemed to almost glaze over in a moment of admiration.

"I don't understand your obsession with that man," I said, leaning back against a railing separating the sparring sections from the new squires learning horseback riding. "He's strong for a barony but I'm sure there are much stronger out in the world."

Lucid shrugged, taking another sip of water. "Maybe, but he's the strongest person I've ever met. And did you know he's not even a noble? He's a common born, just like me, who got into knighthood through hard work! Even the Baron respects him."

"Isn't he from a duchy?" I asked.

"Yeah, the Goldenhearts," Lucid responded with a nod. "His service to the Baron was part of the Baroness's dowry when the families were married."

He passed me the waterskin and I took it without looking. "Why would the daughter of a duchy marry into a barony?"

The squire gave me another shrug. "How should I know? I'm barely above a servant's station." I didn't respond and instead let a splash of cool water work its way down my parched throat.

"Lucid," I began tentatively, but he cut me off.

"For the hundredth time, Lady Lilliana," Lucid said in an exasperated sigh, using a serious tone only contrasted by his playful use of my given name. He'd explained to me following Morgana's tea party that using "lady" and her given name, rather than the more respectful surname, was only done by someone close to you, though "close to" could be rather subjective. For most situations, I was the young Lady Silverwater, Morgana was Lady Silverwater, and Mathilda was Baroness Silverwater, or in some situations specific to this world I didn't understand yet, she could be called Lady Goldenheart. "No, I can't explain heart energy to you. And I can't explain magic to you."

I grumbled. "Can't or won't?"

"Both. You know the Baron has given very specific orders about that. And yes," he said as I opened my mouth, "he would know. Somehow. I worked hard for this position, and I'm not risking it to satisfy your curiosity."

"It's not curiosity. If I'm to survive against Earl Paul, I must know how to protect myself."

"Earl Paul is a noble. He won't treat you badly. He can't! It's part of a nobleman's dignity."

I just shook my head, but the boy's stubborn naivety was unrelenting. "At least tell me why the Baron doesn't care if I train swordplay."

"The Earl Mar Paul is a master swordsman with an affinity toward physical energy." Lucid gave me a tight smile that I knew to be his attempt at avoiding sympathy. I'd punched him last time he'd shown me pity. "No matter how much you train, he would win. Perhaps he enjoys the challenge of a wife with some skill."

"What is physical energy?"

"Really, my lady?"

"How this barony managed to acquire a squire of your loyalty simply confounds me," I muttered and drank more of the water. I could see Shael stomping around closer to us screaming at the other soldiers and knew our break was near its end.

"I'm not sure that's a true test of my loyalty," he said with a smirk. "Perhaps one day I'll truly be put to the test and show the Baron I would make the greatest knight he's ever seen." Lucid used his finger to draw some stick figures in the dirt. "My dad was a knight, you know? He served under the old Baron, Baron Silverwater's father. Died in a rare border skirmish with the Kingdom of Cael when I was really young."

"Then he died with great honor while protecting those he loved," I said, giving the young boy a slap on his shoulder and smiling. He returned my smile, if morosely before shaking his head as if to clear the thoughts.

"Yeah, I suppose he did."

"Hey!" Shael shouted as she approached us. "Who said either of you could rest? Does this look like an inn? By the Gods, the both of you better get your asses off the ground or I'll have you running until you're dead!"

Despite my experience as a queen and my overall age being at least a decade or two more than Shael's, some part of me had adjusted to being Lilliana. Lucid and I both leaped to our feet without missing a beat, though Lucid nearly lost hold of his sparring sword.

"Lucid, did you almost drop your sword?" She hissed. He didn't get to answer. "Run. Now!" He flashed me an apologetic expression as we set to take off around the training field, but Shael stopped me. "Not you, Lillia— er, Lady Lilliana. You stay."

I halted in my tracks and watched for a second as Lucid took off into the distance at a sprint. When he'd nearly reached the end of our current side of the Arena and followed the border to the right, I turned to the knight.

"Yes, Dame Shael?"

"I'm not supposed to be telling you this, so listen closely. I'm only going to say this once." Shael hesitated before continuing until her jaw clenched in resolution, seeming to have come to a decision. "At the beginning of next spring, the knighthood will be heading out to a forest on our eastern borders to take care of a projected monster overload. Based on your progress, you should be up to it by then."

"Next spring," I muttered, tapping a finger against my chin. It was currently the eighth month of this world's twelve-month cycle, so the knight outing would occur in about half a year.

Shael nodded. "You'll be almost thirteen by then and that's about when most squires will be beginning real training as well, so I believe it to be quite fitting."

I raised my head in confusion. "Thirteen?"

"Did no one tell you? Your birth date was the sixth month. You turned twelve a few weeks after the incident with Lady Silverwater's tea party."

I opened my mouth to say something sarcastic but shut it promptly. Sarcasm had its place. This wasn't it. Though I'd lost track of time some time ago, if what Shael relayed to me was accurate, then I'd been in this new world for a little under half a year. The fact I was just beginning to form the foundations for my second heart ring caused my river of rage to stir in impatience.

"No. No one told me."

"I see. Regardless, I believe this would be a good opportunity for you. Unfortunately, I do not have the authority to admit you into the expedition. You'll have to ask the Captain directly. If he asks who told you, tell him you overheard some knights talking about it. He won't believe you, but he won't press." Shael clicked her tongue, her usual tell that she was done with a conversation. "Finish running with Lucid and then you can go see him if you want to participate. Tomorrow morning is the final day for knights to sign up for the yearly Fourth Month expedition."

The sun had just crossed under the horizon by the time we finished running. At some point, before we'd started gasping for every breath, I'd relayed Shael's sort-of invitation to Lucid to see what he'd thought, but the boy squire hadn't had much to offer. Apparently, it was a yearly expedition into the more mysterious parts around Silverwater territory. It seemed normal from what he told me, but there was something off about the way Shael had talked about it.

I waved farewell to Lucid and made my way toward the Knight Captain's quarters I visited on my first day in this new world. It took me less than half an hour of wandering through the mansion's great halls before I finally managed to track down the Captain's room. First floor, plain door, look for the room with a giant map and a bunch of meticulously hung weapons. I nearly missed the room since the door was open, but luckily the enormous map caught my eye as I walked past.

No guard stood at the door, though I couldn't remember if one had been there the first time I visited either. I didn't bother knocking. If he expected knocks, the door should have been closed.

The room was empty except for the Knight Captain who was busy scribbling something down in the large tome I'd seen previously. Again, the moment he heard me, or anyone really, he instantly slammed the book shut.

"My lady?" He asked as curt as ever, not even gesturing for me to take a seat. I sat anyway.

"I want to participate in next spring's expedition," I responded just as curtly.

"Will you slow us down?" he asked, taking out a slip of paper with tens of handwritten names.

"No."

"Do you understand the risks of such a venture, young Lady Silverwater?" There was something to his tone I couldn't quite place. A warning? Maybe a hint of concern?

"I understand fully, Captain of the knights. I will take care to not succumb to any of those . . . risks."

"Very well. These are the assigned knights and mercenaries who will be accompanying us on the expedition. Unfortunately, I cannot authorize a young noble lady's admittance into an expedition like this, but neither am I obligated to stop you. Do as you wish."

I signed my name without giving it another thought. Good or bad, only time would tell.

CHAPTER NINE

A Giant Fucking Tree

The next eight or so months progressed much the same. I spent the mornings and afternoons training my body, spending as much time in between the two and in the evenings cultivating the minuscule amount of energy I was able to absorb into my heart. Since the Baron had made his decree, the food served to me had also improved, if only slightly. The muck turned to mushy vegetables and borderline spoiled meat, but I made do.

Fortunately, the Baron must have said something to the other Silverwater children after my confrontation with Morgana because not a single one of them showed their faces in front of me the entire time. It was as if the Baron had decreed for a halt of all communication between us. I was hopeful that order would continue for eternity, though I doubted it. I'd also been moved to the mansion's south wing, far away from any of the Silverwaters. What I hadn't foreseen was that moving to the south wing would restrict me from leaving that side of the mansion for any reason other than training.

"Dismiss Madam Elara for today," I commanded without looking at the maid. "The soldiers are going out on an expedition today. I am to join them." The maid, Dectra, scoffed quietly and muttered something under her breath. I turned a sharp gaze on her as I buttoned up the dark red Silverwater Knight outfit I'd commandeered for the trip. It was too big, but I didn't care.

That had, in turn, hindered my plan to interfere with whatever Morgana was scheming and from communicating with Lady Ballenci. The Baron persistently refused to allow me any communication with other noble ladies, including Lady Ballenci, putting an irritating pin in my information-collecting through her family. Still, I'd carried out my side of the agreement and kept my mouth shut. And from what little I'd been able to gather, Morgana had been raging about her failing relationship with Lady Ballenci due to her burning. That was a good sign, for me at least.

While I would eventually need to get a better handle on this nation's political and military landscape with her family's network of informants, such in-depth information was not my current priority. I was in desperate need of more general details regarding the kingdoms and culture.

After digging through the small library, I'd confirmed that this kingdom, the Kingdom of Lysoria, operated similarly to any other nation in terms of hierarchy. Royalty, aristocracy, merchant class, and then everyone else. One archduke, a handful of dukes, a dozen or so earls, and then a smattering of lower aristocracy I didn't care to memorize beyond the necessities and those from Morgana's tea party the previous year.

I glanced down from where I stood before my mirror, which reflected the image of a young girl dressed in fine leather armor. Dectra was on her knees, picking up the remains of the shattered teacup she'd dropped. I let it go.

Dectra mumbled an apology. "Did the Knight Captain ever officially accept your application?"

"He authorized it. Now stop bothering me with these questions and fetch my boots."

Finally. Finally, I get to leave this Ashwash forsaken building.

That was true that he'd authorized it, if only technically. The Knight Captain had never rejected my request to join the expedition though he still had yet to explicitly authorize it. Which I took to imply authorization. Either way, it was none of the servant's business.

I hefted the sheathed steel blade off my bed and clasped its entwined belt around me, so the heaviness bounced gently against my upper thigh. So far, my understanding of the outside world was dangerously limited outside of basic textbooks and theory. Although the Baron had allowed me limited access to the family's library, there weren't many useful books in the collection.

That was disappointing but not entirely unsurprising.

Over the past few months my energy gains had stagnated, causing whatever initial hesitation I'd had to Dame Shael's offer to join the expedition to evaporate. I would speed up my Heart Core formation, live or die.

I could not wait another year. If I could kill a few of the monsters and try to absorb whatever latent energies they leaked while dying, I could advance my pitiful energy reserves by months. Maybe even years. That was, of course, assuming monsters released absorbable heart energy in Graedon.

Still, physically, my body was a lot weaker than I would have liked to be before venturing off to fight monsters. At this point though, it would have to be enough. I couldn't wait any longer. Patience was not one of my virtues.

I ignored Dectra's nagging and complaints, leaving the room behind after slipping my boots on and making my way to the manse's entrance where Lucid, Shael, and the other knights and mercenaries already waited. Some other mercenaries who were lagging behind the main group also trickled in after me. Pavement extended from the doorway to a heavy-looking iron gate that connected to thick stone walls that curved around the mansion. A grown man could climb over the wall but not before he was stuck with a spear or arrow.

The knights and Lucid all sat atop black war horses. The soldiers and mercenaries would walk. Next to Lucid was a small gray horse. It stood out among the black war horses the same way a mouse might stand out among bears. The disparity was almost funny.

I offhandedly wondered if the gaunt animal could even walk the necessary distance on its own. The thought was overshadowed by the excitement I felt as I approached the horse. It had been so long since I'd ridden. I shoved down those memories of my youth as swiftly as they had surfaced. Now was not the time for nostalgia.

Especially not for those memories.

With a confident stride, anticipation coursing through me, I gently laid my hand on its neck and offered the beast a reassuring pat. It neighed at me. My eyebrows raised slightly but I continued to stroke its rough, unkempt mane. Despite its bony appearance, the horse did not strike me as an animal on the edge of death. I immediately changed my evaluation of the horse. I liked its spirit. If it lived through the expedition, I would give it a name fit for a royal steed.

I took a step closer to its side and adjusted my stance to ensure a solid footing. With a deep breath, I grasped the reins, the cool and taut leather chaffing against my palms. Placing my left foot in the stirrup, I pushed down and swung my right leg smoothly over the horse's back, settling into the saddle with practiced ease. The leather creaked slightly under my weight as I adjusted my position and felt the familiar contours of a saddle stabilizing me.

I looked at the Silverwater soldiers, knights, and mercenaries as if they were my entourage. I'm sure none of them liked me enough to be a part of my personal force, but that was irrelevant. I was technically the highest ranked among those in the expedition, so they were considered temporarily absorbed into it even if it went generally unacknowledged. Lately, the extra attention the Baron had been paying to me was causing more of the mansion staff to show me some level of deference. It was an unintended benefit of being the Baron's new moneymaker.

So, although most of them hated me, they tolerated it. If I could, I would change their minds on this expedition. The weak follow the strong. I just had to show them I was the strength they should follow.

"Okay," I shouted, gesturing forward away from the mansion grounds. "Let's depart." With a gentle nudge of my heels, I signaled readiness to the steed, and it took off at a steady trot. After a moment I could hear the jangling of steel armor move as the soldiers began their march.

Lucid, atop a young war horse, nimbly pulled up to my side with his signature goofy grin. "Since when were you so imperious? Let's depart!" he mimicked jokingly, pitching his voice to sound like mine.

I shrugged. "Though many of the family and household may view me as a rat, I should still try to present myself with pride." Not a lie.

Not exactly the truth either.

Lucid nodded thoughtfully. "I wouldn't say we think of you as a rat." He glanced at me and squinted. "More of a stray cat, if I'm being honest."

I laughed. "I suppose that is better than a rat."

"Speak for yourself, Squire," Beatrice said from behind me. I didn't turn around to look at her. She'd made it abundantly clear that she thought of me more as cat shit than a cat. I heard her sniff. "I believe the lady is more similar to a rodent than a feline." I just ignored her. Knights born from nobility with their noses stuck too high in the air were a dime a dozen.

"Do you know where we're heading?" Lucid asked.

I nodded. "The Misty Veils Forest."

"The center of it," he said, grin slipping. "My brother was telling me about a group of knights he knew who ventured too deep into the center of the mist and were never seen again. No one even heard them disappear. The group just vanished from their squad." Lucid shivered. "I bet there's a Beast King in there."

"A Beast King?" That was new.

"A Beast King is the first of its kind," Shael answered.

I let out a gasp. "A Progenitor?"

"I've never heard Beast Kings called that before, but the two may be the same."

If that was true, I needed to put as much distance between myself and this kingdom as I could the moment my Core Awakened. Progenitors were powerful enough to level entire kingdoms on a whim. If the Progenitors of this world were as powerful as those in Ordite, considering the suboptimal heart energy prowess of this world, the Progenitors would be unstoppable.

"Has a . . . Beast King attacked a kingdom before?" I asked, hoping the answer was no.

Shael laughed. "Of course not. No beast can get through the kingdom's wards. Not even a Beast King." I doubted that very much but didn't say anything.

"Regardless, the kingdom knights would stop the Beast King before it reached the main city. Usually, a Beast King can be deterred with a handful of warriors and mages with over thirty heart rings."

I doubted that even more. Maybe if the creature was a princeling it could be deterred. But if a full-out original Progenitor intended to destroy a city and all that was between it and its prey were a handful of un-Awakened Cores, the kingdom had no chance of stopping it.

Perhaps, like the energy level of the world, the Progenitors were also comparatively weakened. I felt like that was a bit overly optimistic and pushed the thought away.

It took a few days to reach the edge of the Misty Veil Forest. It wasn't until we were a few miles from the forest that the Knight Captain ordered everyone to set up a base camp on the final day. The party would venture forward in the morning.

The forest itself was one never-ending canopy of twisted branches and gnarled roots. The closer we approached, the thicker the air smelled of damp earth and decay, and the only sound that ever broke the silence during the nights of our approach was the whispers of rustling leaves and the howl of a lonely wind.

Even at our distance, the trees loomed like ancient sentinels, their twisted limbs reaching out toward us like skeletal fingers wanting to ensnare the wary traveler. Thick green moss clung to their bark, obscuring the trees' true age and lending them an eerie, otherworldly beauty. If it helped, I would have honestly preferred not to go into that obvious death trap. Still, the real combat experience would be invaluable in better understanding my new body's limits and capabilities.

As I had the previous nights, I set up my own small tent near the center of the encampment. I'd attempted to set up on the outskirts, but Shael had protested. Since she was the only knight who seemed not to want me dead, I listened. All around me knights, soldiers, and mercenaries began to set up their tents as well, some faster and slower but all moving with a purpose. A couple of men I guess were mercenaries even broke out into a mock fight using their tent stands as pretend swords and were shouting strings of playful curse words at each other.

One of the men hit the other and everyone watching broke out into an easy chorus of laughter.

That calm complacency was broken like a dry twig, snapping under the weight of a thunderous roar that echoed deep within the forest. The trees around, behind, and in front of us all shook as if the hand of a God had come down to wrangle them. Even as far out as we were, the dirt trembled as animals scrambled desperately in the opposite direction.

The encampment sank into a heavy silence, whatever cheerfulness or calm existed was extinguished by the reality of what we faced. I had no idea what had made that roar but by the way all the soldiers had gone dead silent, and their faces paled to the color of snow, I figured they probably had some clue, and it was not something any of them wanted to fight. I glanced toward the Knight Captain's tent to see if he was going to come out and say something to return the soldiers' spirits. When his tent flap didn't budge even as the seconds flew by, I dropped my eyes to the bowl of . . . sludge in my hands. There was a soft clanking of metal as others also resumed eating or putting together their tents.

I was about to brave a mouthful of the sludge when the forest roared again. I dropped the bowl and jumped to my feet, eyes wide. That roar had been a lot closer. I ran toward Shael's tent and threw open the flap. The Knight Captain probably wouldn't listen to me, but there was a chance Shael would.

"Shael," I shouted, bursting into the room-like tent ready to warn her. There was no one in the tent. I checked Lucid's tent. Empty. When I went over to check the Knight Captain's quarters, it was also empty.

My heart pounded in my ears as I realized something was wrong. Very wrong. I sprinted from the tent toward the nearest group of soldiers but stopped immediately in my tracks as screams of utter agony filled the air from every direction, causing the small hairs along the back of my neck to stick straight up. Many of the soldiers who'd just a second ago been eating, chatting, or putting up their tents had gone still, their mouths wide open as blood poured from their eyes, ears, and nose. Their eyes were empty even if they still breathed, glazed and lifeless. In my daze, I didn't realize a soldier or mercenary, I couldn't tell which, had run up to me and was shaking my shoulders.

"What have you done?" He screamed, his spittle landing on my cheek. "You bi—" He didn't get a chance to finish. His body suddenly locked and straightened, mouth dropping agape as blood began to pour from his orifices like the others. Fortunately, the shock of a man dying right in front of me pulled me out of whatever frozen state I'd been in. One of my hands dropped to the sword sheathed at my waist and I looked around, taking in the chaos.

I need to get out of here, I thought. But where would I go? Back to the Silverwater estate? That felt like a bad idea. I shook my head. *Never mind that, Lilith. Focus on getting the fuck out of here first.*

Screams and shouts reverberated through the camp as some of the soldiers and mercenaries fled loudly while the braver ones scrambled to help their comrades who were in that odd, freely bleeding stasis. One soldier seemed to try pulling his friend down from where he stood stock-still, but all that happened was the man trying to help fell under the same affliction.

"Okay, don't touch them," I muttered, scrambling away from the man who'd been grabbing my shoulders. What the fuck was going on? And where were the knights? No matter how much I looked around, I couldn't find a single one of them. Not even that one bitch who'd clearly wanted me dead. Only mercenaries and soldiers remained.

Are all the soldiers even here? I wondered. I didn't know all the soldiers, though, so it was impossible to be sure.

I heard footsteps behind me and whirled on them, sword flying from its scabbard in preparation for whoever was coming for me. Instead of an enraged soldier or monster, I found myself facing off against a panicked Lucid, his eyes full of wild fear. Before I could register what was happening his eyes rolled back into his head and a high-pitched voice squeaked from beyond Lucid's opened mouth.

"Hello, Lilliana." When I didn't answer, the voice repeated. "Hello? Can she hear me?" the voice seemed to ask, briefly sounding farther away. "Oh, okay. She can." It then became louder. "I was told not to speak to you, Lilliana, but I don't see why it makes a difference. You're going to die soon anyway. I just wanted to tell you—this is what happens when you mess with my brother and kill my . . . when you kill a noble lady like Lady Tremmor. I hope you die painfully, whorespawn."

Despite the chaos that surrounded me and the wild, fearful eyes that stared at the puppeteered Lucid, I found myself hyper-focusing on the voice. I didn't have time to deal with the fleeing survivors or the unlucky majority of soldiers who were being bled dry. If this was a calculated trap, I doubted any of them were going to survive in the end.

For one reason or another, those here were either expendable or deserving of death. At least from the perspective of whoever laid the trap.

The gears of my brain spun as I pieced together the voice's identity. I hadn't killed anyone since arriving, so this massive murder attempt was over the top. Whoever it was must have had some underlying hatred for Lilliana before I arrived in Graedon.

Then is it even about me? Or am I just part of something else? A bonus to a plan already in motion?

The voice, however, did sound familiar. And her words . . . Where had I heard those words before? Then it clicked. Brian had also called Lilliana's mother a whore. And he only had one sister. I supposed it could have been the Baroness, but the voice sounded too young.

"Morgana?" I asked tentatively.

"Wow, that didn't take her long, did it?" the voice said, sounding surprised. "I did think since you lost your memory and were acting differently that you'd been undergoing some advanced education. Or were you hiding your real self until now or something? Never mind. It hardly matters now."

So the expedition had been a trap for me. That would explain why all the knights were gone.

"Why did you kill all the soldiers?" I asked. "Did they annoy you as well? Where are all the knights?"

"The soldiers?" The voice was dismissive. "Sacrifices for the Beast King, of course. You don't think it can be summoned that easily, do you? Gods, you are so ignorant. And the knights are my knights, why would they he—" Morgana's voice cut off again for a moment. "Oh, but I'm having fu—fine.

Fine! I hope you die in pain. Goodbye, Lilliana. This is for Lady Tremmor, Brian, and the dishonor you have forced upon the entire family."

Lucid's mouth shut, and the young squire fell to the ground at the same moment a towering mass of gnarled wood and tangled vines erupted from the forest. The creature's immense form reached a height that seemed to brush against the very sky.

"Holy Ashwash," I swore in disbelief. "I'm going to be killed by a giant fucking tree."

CHAPTER TEN

Queen of Rot

Calling the creature a tree was a massive understatement. It was more of a giant, hulking mass of roots and vines. Green moss covered nearly a third of its frame, giving it an almost sickly appearance. I tried to see if the thing had a face. It didn't. Or perhaps I couldn't discern it. Either way, I turned to run from the rampaging Progenitor.

"By the Gods," Lucid muttered, apparently regaining consciousness after face-planting at some point. "It's Apocryth, the Beast King of Nature. I—I thought that was just a ghost story!" He didn't stand; instead, Lucid sat there, dumbly staring up at the moving forest.

I reached over and yanked him to his feet. "Get up. Run!" The moment he was up, he seemed to collect himself, and we were off. Whatever spell Morgana cast had hopefully worn off. If there were still lingering magics controlling Lucid's body, he'd be a dangerous enemy to have at my back.

At the moment, there wasn't any time to think about that. I pushed this new body to run faster than I ever had before—faster than during soldier training and faster than my morning sprinting exercises. I knew that I couldn't outrun a Progenitor. No one could, especially not some un-Awakened child.

Apocryth roared from behind us and slammed one of his heavy, gnarled vined limbs into the encampment. Dirt exploded up and away like angry bugs, but beneath the tentacle limb, everything was flattened. From tents to soldiers, anything in its path was forcefully merged with the sunken ground.

Cracks burst out from the canyon Apocryth created, jutting out around us. All sorts of smaller critters scuttled from the cracks. I turned to Lucid, gritting my teeth. We both had stopped running after the cracks had formed. There was nowhere for us to run to. The critters chirped all around us, utterly eviscerating anything they came into contact with, like starving children.

"Do you know any fire energy techniques? Or magic?" I asked desperately, glancing up at the setting sun. If we could delay it until the moon rose, I could make use of this.

"I know a bit of fire energy. Some fire magic too," Lucid responded, putting his back to mine. I risked a glance back and saw small whisps of flames begin to circle above his palm. Then they all melded together into a single ball of fire.

"A fireball?" I sputtered, unable to keep the annoyance out of my voice. "Put that out and create a flame wall, Squire."

To his credit, Lucid didn't hesitate to follow my orders. The ball of flames in his hand expanded outward as he spun his body to draw a ring of fire around us. It wouldn't even slow Apocryth down, but it didn't need to. If it stopped the bugs and delayed our death, that was all I needed to escape this.

Lucid grunted, and I could see the spell was rapidly draining his energy.

"This is why you build a Core," I muttered, then turned to slam my palm into Lucid's back. My power rushed out my heart rings and flooded Lucid's fledgling heart with energy. The flame wall flickered once and then crackled upward with energy.

"Thanks," Lucid said. "But I don't think this will hold for long."

"Just focus. It doesn't need to last forever. Just hold it as long as you can."

The forest insects swarmed around us like cascading waves crashing against a crumbling shore. At first, the insects were reckless, droves of them flying into the flaming circle only to be disintegrated within seconds. The smell of burnt bugs quickly filled the air and my lungs. I nearly gagged, stopping myself through sheer will.

After a while, they no longer suicidally rushed headlong into the flames but instead chittered around us, little legs clicking with each movement.

"What are those things?" Lucid shouted as the circle waned under a sudden onslaught of the creatures. I didn't answer. I couldn't. I had no idea what in Ashwash those things were either.

I looked up at the sky, tracing the descent of the sun. It was almost below the horizon. The moon had become clearer. A full moon. I didn't have time to consider how incredibly lucky that was for me. It would still be another couple of minutes before the sun was low enough that I could begin to draw on the moon's lunar energy.

The fire would hold out at this rate. Just a little longer—

My thoughts were cut off by the roar of Apocryth and the many tendrils of thick vines that slammed down to crush the insectile creatures creating hundreds of ten-foot-wide graves, the closest ones throwing up clouds of dirt just a few feet outside the circle.

Quickly, I shot more energy through my pathway and into Lucid's, causing the ring to flare and lash outward, expending all its energy in a large area of effect. In the chaos that erupted and just as the ring's base flickered away, I bolted from the circle with Lucid on my heels. The two of us shot through a gap I spotted in the swarm before the insects could close around us.

Unfortunately, the direction of the gap led us to where Apocryth rampaged. One problem at a time.

The swarm, scattered by Apocryth's attack, fortunately, did not follow us as we bolted. A quick look behind me told me why—the swarm covered the bodies of the dead soldiers. Disgusting, wet chewing noises came from that direction.

Lucid screamed. He was staring up, his eyes wider than I'd ever seen someone's eyes go. Then he looked at me, filled with fear.

Thump. Squish.

Apocryth's tendrils crushed the boy before I could blink. One second Lucid was running next to me, and the next he was just gone, replaced by a bundle of squirming vines and moss. Death was nothing new to me. Death was a familiar friend, accompanying me in all parts of my life.

I still gagged when the tendril lifted and revealed the scrunched, disfigured, and smushed version of Lucid. It was hardly recognizable as a human beyond the distinct iron smell of blood and one of his blue eyes somehow having survived the attack. It stared at me now, devoid of life and yet somehow still filled with despair. I wanted to scream or at least shout his name, but the warm liquid rising from my stomach kept me silent.

Finally, the sun dropped fully below the horizon. I pushed all my remaining energy from my heart rings and flooded it through every inch of my body, exposing the energy to the moonlight. In reality, I knew the energy I'd gathered around myself was not much, minuscule even, but it still roared through me, making me feel stronger than I had since setting foot in Graedon. Then my energy synchronized with the lunar energy radiating from the moon, empowering my energy well beyond my cultivation level, and I felt invincible.

Power not my own seeped into me and replaced my own lesser energies until my heart thumped and blood gushed from my nose and leaked from my eyes. My eardrums exploded as the pressure inside me built.

I continued to draw in even more of the moon's energy, screaming as the pain wreaked havoc throughout my body with chaotic glee. The energy veil I had created around myself tightened, squeezing muscle and bone until they tore and broke. It dawned on me that the energy I absorbed was temporarily forcing my body into an early Reformation. If I could have felt anything beyond the shrieking pain, I would have panicked.

I could feel myself growing taller, muscles expanding in response to the increased energy coursing through me. Some part of my mind tried to warn me that the recoil from forced absorption would be much, much worse. I ignored it. I needed this. Right now. Or I would die a miserable death, just like Lucid.

The instant my vision cleared and the thudding in my ears lessened, I dashed—not away from the forest but toward it. Between the forest and Silverwater were mostly grasslands. My chances of surviving by retreating backward were none. Moving forward into the forest . . . That was only maybe a fraction better, but I figured at least my death wouldn't be immediate.

I hoped the Beast King might be more cautious in the forest. Most Progenitors tended to be guardians of a region more so than wild predators, though some viewed offense as the best defense. That hope was shattered the moment I entered the forest's domain and four bundles of vines whipped out from Apocryth's chest to decimate the top half of at least a hundred trees.

I dodged the sundering by diving behind a heavy stone halfway buried under a massive oak tree. The attack snapped the oak tree in half like it was a twig and not ten feet wide. The Apocryth barked and grunted, savagely continuing to rip tree after tree either in half or straight out of the ground. The creature was like a tornado of vines and wrath.

Then, without warning, everything froze. A blanket of silence fell across the entire forest. A sense of utter and complete fear spread across the still space, threatening to strangle me as I gasped for breath. I couldn't move, couldn't make a sound.

A calm, eerily emotionless voice echoed around me. It was soft, yet I could hear it as if it were speaking an inch from my ear.

"Halt." The word was spoken, and I knew everything *would* stop, even the wind. It had been uttered in a language I recognized only as Ancient, the language of the Progenitors.

Oh fuck. Oh fuck, I thought, still unable to move. The Apocryth was not the Progenitor.

I forced my head to swivel, straining my muscles to turn even an inch. I saw only a slight silver gleam starting at Apocryth's head, and then it was at its feet. A second later the silver light was gone and the creature fell, split in two. The massive tree was felled in a single attack, one faster than my current abilities could track.

"To all those that remain," the deep voice continued as if it hadn't just felled an Apocryth. "Leave now."

The pressure holding me still disappeared, and I spun around to glimpse a horned human with completely black eyes looking directly at me.

Wait a second. I . . . I knew that being. Was that the Demon Progenitor? But that wouldn't be possible. I had delivered the final strike ending its reign of terror in Ordite.

Our eyes locked for a split second, and it smiled at me. Cold and cruel.

"Run, Queen of Rot. Run."

CHAPTER ELEVEN

Burn It All to the Ground

Part of me wanted to stay. To ask the Progenitor how he knew that title. That awful title. That lie. I didn't. Couldn't.

For the first time in many years, I fled. I didn't flee to survive or regroup—no, I was fleeing from pure abject terror. Not a terror of something common like death or fear. It was a primal terror. It had no rhyme or reason. But it clung to my heart, deep and unmoving.

I wanted to scream. To cry out in despair at the abyss the Progenitor's presence was causing in my mind. And I very well would have if the lunar energy protecting me hadn't deflected some of that pressure. I ran from the Misty Veil Forest like a bat out of hell. Tears sprang unbidden in my eyes as the shame and cowardice of what I was doing poured over me, hot as lava.

There was no chance for me to survive if the Progenitor didn't let me go. I knew that. Running wasn't the wrong choice. It wasn't even cowardly in and of itself. But I wasn't running to survive. Terror drove me. I fled, tail between my legs like a common mutt. I tried to stop the tears, but they came anyway, tracing wet tracks down my cheeks before being swept away by the wind. The only other time I had fled like this, I'd been fourteen, and my mother, the Queen, was being murdered by my father.

This was worse. This terror had no real cause. It was simply a human child reacting to something akin to a God. My body responded instinctually, and my mind was simply along for the ride.

Even when I left the ancient trees of the forest long behind, I continued to run. I ran until I couldn't sense even the slightest hint of the Progenitor's pressure. And then I ran more.

When I eventually collapsed, the sun had begun to rise. I was drenched, though I couldn't tell if it was from my sweat or if it had rained at some point. Maybe both. I dropped to my knees, hands splashing in a puddle as I heaved. My legs were shaking so badly I wasn't sure that I'd be able to stand anymore.

For a second, I wanted to just wrap myself into a ball and let it all go. Was all this really worth it?

Poor Lucid.

I let out a long, low growl and grit my teeth against the weakness in my mind. I would not let the terror win. I would not kneel before this new world. It would kneel before me. I reached over and grabbed a rock that fit nicely into the palm of my hand.

And I brought it down on my left pinkie finger. Hard. I let out an involuntary gasp before forcing myself into silence. Accept the pain. Accept it.

I took a deep, steadying breath as that sharp burst of pain broke the blanket of terror that'd been cast on my mind. I ripped off a sliver of my torn sleeve and wrapped it around the broken pinkie and the adjoining ring finger. The broken finger would only be a temporary inconvenience. Once I Awakened my Core, the natural self-healing of an Awakened would kick in.

Then, with a *whoosh*, the lunar energy left me, and everything went instantly dark.

The next thing I could remember hearing was a female voice, loud but surprisingly deep. Or maybe it was a high-pitched male voice? The person's voice was underlined by a woman screaming. Who was screaming like that?

"By the Gods," the voice shouted over the shrieking woman. "It's a child."

"A human child?" another voice asked, this one distinctly male. There was silence during which I assumed the first voice was nodding. For some reason I couldn't figure out how to open my eyes . . . Why couldn't I open my eyes? The girl screamed again. "I didn't even realize a human could reach that pitch." The man laughed. "What you think she's doin' in the middle of the path?"

"Just give her a healing pill," the voice said. "Then load her into the back."

The back? The back of what?

Hands reached down and grabbed me. I could feel the fingers in my hair as others pinched my cheeks. Then something was shoved into my mouth followed by a stream of liquid. Water. It was warm and tasted like metal, but it was water. And by the great God Ashwash, I was thirsty. I hadn't realized just how severely until now. I drank the water with a greed I didn't know I had.

"Okay, that's enough," the voice said. "Any more and she'll just vomit out the pill."

Much too early, the water was taken away. I wanted to protest. My mouth still felt dry. Again, my body refused to listen.

The hands forcing the water into my mouth moved under my neck and knees. A girl screamed, and I felt myself being lifted into the air. After a moment, I hit something hard, and the darkness welcomed me back into its fold.

I groaned, sore muscles welcoming me back to consciousness. I blinked rapidly a few times, trying to clear the grogginess from my vision as I sat up. The first thing I realized was that the world kept moving. Not exactly spinning. More like . . .

The second thing I realized was that the world was not spinning. I sat in some box surrounded by a handful of other battered people.

And then the third thing I realized was I was not surrounded by *people*. The others in the cart were a variety of species. I recognized only a few from my own world. One of them was a half orc. I'd met a couple of them during the time I'd spent at war. The species tended to be warmongers. His hulking size and tusks jutting from his lower jaw made him look perpetually angry. Or maybe he was angry. I didn't know.

The other I recognized as something similar to a female fae spirit. She had the long, pointed ears of a fae but was much taller and slimmer than any fae I had ever seen or even heard of. So perhaps something else entirely? I wasn't sure. The female's slim figure, scant clothing, and pretty face didn't bode well for the situation I found myself in. Neither did the fact she was curled in a ball and seemed to be trying to bury herself into the corner of the wagon. Carriage? As I looked around, I got a bad feeling. The six of us were surrounded by four walls that connected to the floor and ceiling without gaps. The center of the ceiling had a single hole maybe two feet in any direction that gave those beneath it air and light.

"Hello, child. I'm happy to see you're awake," said a creature I did not recognize. I assumed it was male by the sound of its voice, but I couldn't be sure. With how dazed I felt, I didn't feel sure of anything. It—he—was bipedal and humanoid-looking but with an unnaturally lithe build stretching for what I figured was a little over two meters tall. His skin was an iridescent blue that shimmered whenever he moved under the sunlight poking through the moving room's hole. He possessed large, luminous eyes of deep indigo that looked to have some sort of filter over them. When he reached over to remove the wet towel from my forehead, I noticed he also had elongated fingers with delicate web-like membranes between each one. His voice came out with a gurgle like he was talking while submerged in water. "I thought you would surely return to the Water Goddess, ya know." I thought he might have looked happy, but considering I'd never encountered the species before, there was an equal chance he was angry.

"Was it that bad?" I asked and winced when I tried to stand. The box we were in bounced, and I was sent slamming back to the floor.

"Oh yes," the creature answered, its blue head bobbing in a nod. "You were screaming the first night, and then you went silent. I heard they found you almost dead. You were lying face down in the mud, ya know? The horses nearly stomped you dead." It eyed me worriedly. "Why were you alone, child?"

The half orc grunted. "You probably woulda been better off if you 'ad." He looked at me. "You're gonna be the first to die. You know that, right?" I ignored the half orc and the blue creature's latter question. I asked the blue creature what its name was.

"I'm Marisar, one of the honorable Selenian who serves the Almighty Goddess of Water," Marisar said, his long fingers slapping against his chest. "Ya know."

"And you're gonna be the second to die, you blue shitstick," the half orc grunted. "There ain't gonna be any water for you in the Arenas. Better start praying."

"Arenas?" I asked, looking at the now smiling half orc.

"Oh, you probably won't have to worry about that girlie," he said mockingly. "I doubt they'd let something like you inta them Arenas. You'll probably be sold off to a pleasure palace. It's where all the homeless slave girls are sent to. You're worth more there than getting slaughtered by fighters like me." I just stared at him.

"I am the daughter of a Baron," I said. Although I wasn't a fan of using the Baron's influence, it was looking more and more like this was becoming a situation where that couldn't be helped.

The half orc just barked a crude laugh. "Don't matter. He'll never find ya where we're going. Now you're just a worthless slave like the rest of us, Princess."

I groaned and slumped back into the box. "What are the chances I'd get found by a slaver?"

"Decently high around this time of year," Marisar responded, his large eyes looking over me like he wanted to say something else. He sighed and brought his raised hand back to his side. "Only slavers travel between the cities right now. Too many monsters lurking for merchants and normal people to risk it, ya know?"

Okay, one problem at a time.

I could figure this out. And then I could figure out how to get back to the Silverwater barony and take control of it. Then I'd turn my eyes on the kingdom itself. Then the world.

Still . . .

One problem at a time, Lilith, I reminded myself. *Start with the small issue. Figure out where you are, find out what can be used to your advantage, take it, and then burn the rest to the ground.*

CHAPTER TWELVE

A Queen's Dignity

All right, you lot, get out," said a familiar voice. It took a moment, but I realized it belonged to the person who had forced the water down my throat.

A heavy thud of metal resounded as a line of light split the far wall in two, eventually opening up to expose me and the others to the early morning sun. Not a wall. Doors.

The man wasn't a man after all. He was short and sported shimmering green scales all along his body. Yellow eyes fell on us as the doors opened, and I immediately became more wary of the man. I couldn't be sure, but if the lizard-like creature was what I thought he was, he could burn us to ashes in seconds.

Those slaves who could move on their own gingerly stepped out into the sunlight, while the others, too feeble to jump down from the box, were roughly pulled to the ground by the male slaver. I hopped down by myself. If my slave tattoo hadn't been stained onto my forearm while I was unconscious, it would have been the perfect opportunity to escape.

I wasn't completely certain what the slave tattoos did in this world, but back in Ordite, a slave attempting to escape would trigger its tattoo to inject powerful poisons into the System. Not enough to kill the slave, but enough to temporarily put them into a coma, making retrieval easier.

Until now, faced with the threat of that poison and with the embedded skull wrapped in chains tattooed on my arm, I had never truly understood the cruelty of slavery. I don't think I'd even tried to consider it. Slavery was simply a result of war and disputes between kingdoms. If you won, you gained free labor. If you lost, you became it. Like everything else in war, it was a gamble you took by putting your life on the line.

Or that's how it had always been portrayed to me. Did I ever take a moment to think about the slaves not created from war? I hadn't done that either.

Luckily, the energy usage in the world, other than the Progenitor, proved itself incredibly weak. The energy from a properly formed Core would shatter the tattoo's binding like a knife through warm butter. I just had to get there.

The box I exited was an odd contraption. It was almost like a carriage, but not exactly. Like a carriage, it was horse-drawn and had wheels. That was where the similarities ended. The entire body of it was a large, singular wooden box with hundreds of wards carved on every inch. Other than the door on the far side of it and the hole on top, there weren't any openings. Just a space of about ten feet by ten feet. As I looked around, I counted at least twelve other similar contraptions arriving.

The area we'd been deboarded into was completely barren. No trees or grass in sight. No animals either. Other than the box-like wagons and the slaves, there was only sand. Piles, no, hills of sand.

"Okay, listen up," the lizard creature barked, his voice cutting through the tense silence as the line of captives stood side by side. "Let's get one thing straight. Most of you have probably figured out by now that you're screwed. Those slave tattoos you've got? They bind you to whoever I choose to sell your sorry hides to." His eyes swept over the group, lingering just long enough to make everyone squirm. "Some of you are here because you're criminals, some because you're poor, and others . . ." His gaze landed squarely on me. "Well, some of you are just really fucking unlucky. Tough shit. No, I don't care about your sob stories. No, begging me won't work. If you cause me problems, I'll kill you. Or better yet, I'll sell you to the nastiest bastard I can find. I don't like doing that—they don't pay well—but I'm a petty motherfucker, and I enjoy making examples. So don't test me." He motioned to the figure beside him—a woman-like creature I recognized as the voice giving him orders when they'd found me. "My associate here is going to have a little chat with each of you. We'll decide where to sell you, and if you lie, you die. If you cry, you die. I don't care about any of you, so don't give me a reason to waste my breath ending you."

With a nod from him, the female humanoid stepped forward, towering over the first in line. The first thing I noticed about her was her size. She was massive, taller even than Marisar by a good margin, and every movement she made felt more like a stomp than a step. Her species wasn't immediately clear, but she bore a striking resemblance to a watered-down giant—a diluted bloodline, perhaps.

Her broad shoulders matched her stocky build, giving her an imposing presence. A hard-set jaw and muddy brown eyes, like frozen dirt, made her look as unyielding as stone. Dark brown hair spilled down her frame, swaying slightly as it brushed against her waist.

"Name," she demanded, her voice low and guttural as she towered over the half orc, who was large in his own right. Much larger than me, in any case.

"Gronch," the half orc replied, scratching his nose. By the way he wiggled it and sniffed, it looked like he wanted to pick something in it but was resisting the urge.

"Tell me, Gronch . . ." She didn't so much say the name as she spat it. "Are you good for anything other than bloodshed?"

"Nah."

She moved down the line, going one by one. Sometimes she conversed with the slave, and other times she simply asked a few questions. On rare occasions, she would ask a single confirming question before moving on, as she had done with Gronch.

There were a lot more human slaves. In fact, the odd races I'd been faced with in the box were rare. Other than the ones I'd been trapped with, I saw only maybe four or five of their kind. Weird.

I was in the middle of the line, stuck next to a fat dwarf who kept muttering words I didn't understand, but figured to be curse words by his tone, and an older human woman to my right who kept casting annoyingly furtive glances in my direction. The look in her eyes was . . . strange. Like she was looking straight through me. The fact her eyes were completely white didn't help the eerie feeling.

When the giant woman finally reached me, I knew what my options were. There were four main places we were being "interviewed" about: the pleasure palace, the Arenas, the mines, and the front lines. The pleasure palace was easily the most desired place among the slaves, which I understood. Of the four, it sounded like it would be the safest. Perhaps even good for those who didn't have an issue with what they'd be giving away.

She barely looked at me for a second before scribbling something in the little red book she'd been carrying around. "Hmmm . . . I think the palace will do for you. Don't think you'd fetch much coin anywhere else." She started toward the dwarf.

"No," I responded, not letting her move on. "You will send me to the Arena."

"I don't think so. Now, be quiet before I—"

"I will fight," I interrupted. Whatever threat she had been about to say died on her lips. "I can fight in the Arena or I can fight in the pleasure palace. Either way, I'm going to fight." The words might have sounded silly coming from any other young girl, but even to my ears, it did not sound ridiculous. I was royalty in my blood and my soul. Others had always felt that back in Ordite even if I wasn't announced. I knew now wouldn't be any different.

"If you insist." The giantess jotted something else down. I had a feeling it was not a comment about the nobility of my stance. "We'll see how you do. If you survive your first fight, I'll consider making it permanent. Be prepared. The slavers spent some good coin on that healing pill they saved you with. The only fights letting them break even will be definite death for you."

"We'll see" was all I said. The woman next to me was also being sent to the Arenas. There was no sense to that decision, and I was fairly certain the woman was blind, despite how often I caught her staring at me.

The dwarf was sent to the mines and the fae-looking girl from earlier was being sent to the palace. She screamed and begged for anywhere but there. She whimpered something about elves being tortured and killed in the palace. Her tattoo mark knocked her out almost instantly. Her cries ended with a sad choking noise.

Those headed to the palace were placed back into the boxes and carried off first. The next to go were the miners. Then the front lines. The Arena fighters were last. We didn't set off until the last of the new slave soldiers disappeared over the horizon. There were around a hundred of us left. We all stood there, unsure what to do until the giantess clapped her hands.

"Let's go, fighters. I'll introduce you to your new homes."

She walked in the same direction as the slave soldiers, and we followed. For the first few minutes, the giantess simply led us further into the desert. Maybe she was leading us into the desert to die.

Then, with a pop, I was somehow at the entrance of a city gate. The gray stone walls of the city glowered down at me as I gawked in surprise. Just like the boxes, these walls had strange warding etched into their surfaces.

Circulating around the city boundaries appeared to be an endless ocean of sand. I realized at that moment we had stepped through some sort of energy barrier. I hadn't felt the pull of being teleported, but this giant city in front of me had not been there a second ago. Standing guard at a single, giant entrance gate were a group of armed men each strapped with a decorated Sheathe embedded with a red hawk.

"Ah, welcome back, Chella," one of the men clad in full suit armor said, giving a nod to the giantess. "And, Dralos, you too." The last one was said with disdain. The male slaver shot some insult at the guard with equal vehemence. "Good load?"

"Aye," Chella answered. "Lots of spirit among these new *meats*. Got some I bet folks will be real excited to see die." She stuck a thumb at me. "This one even volunteered. Some real guts she's got."

"Meh," the armored guard mocked. "We'll see whether she can keep those guts inside her." The two of them laughed while Dralos snickered, despite his animosity toward the guard.

"Any of 'em gonna be thrown inta the evenin' fights?" the guard asked after his laughter died down.

Chella shrugged. "I doubt it. Unless the Boss already booked fights for some of them, I'd bet the spots are all taken." The guard grunted and let Chella through. I followed close behind, trying to catch a glimpse of the inner city.

Unfortunately, the barracks for Arena fights were less than a full minute's walk from the city gate. I barely had time to see anything other than a few buildings that looked like inns or taverns. The outline of the Arena loomed over everything else in the city except for the actual city walls, so I'd seen that fairly easily. There had been some distant noise of commerce, so I figured there was maybe a bazaar, but I had no way of knowing if that was true. All too soon the group of us were herded into a barren stone building and down a long flight of stairs. The walls of the stone building and all the way down the stairs, there was nothing. Not even a single torch. Little balls of white light dimly illuminated the stairway, but that was it. I figured the light was manipulated by wards somewhere in the building since I didn't spot Chella or Dralos supplying any of the heart energy running them.

We climbed down the stairs for what felt like hours. It took at least ten times as long as it had taken us to get from where we'd offloaded the wagon to the city gates before we finally reached the bottom. According to Chella, there was a tunnel connecting the barracks to the Arena so we wouldn't have to climb back up, but that would only be accessible to us when accompanied by a slaver or Arena official.

The bottom was also quite empty aside from some cubicles of space we were told were called personal areas. Each fighter was given a personal area containing a bed, a small sewer hole, and a single shelf. I sat on the bed, still utterly exhausted. Everyone's beds were placed against the stone wall, cupped on either side by bland and dirty gray curtains. With us at the bottom were more of the dim white balls of energy. Or maybe it was from that "magic" I'd heard about. I thought they seemed dimmer down here than they were on the stairs, which seemed wrong. Why would the lights be dimmer where there was less light? I was assigned one near the middle, which I assumed was supposed to match up with my spot in the slave line earlier. We had likely been numbered at some point. I sat down on the bed and almost laughed.

It was sturdier than the bed in Lilliana's bed chambers.

A fat man with an incredibly bulbous head suddenly came bumbling down the stairwell, wheezing hard like the very air was playing tag with him. Sounding panicked, he shouted, "Madam Chella, the Boss needs at least three meat sacrifices for tonight's Arena bouts. Princess Aurora just now notified us of her appearance during this evening's Sun-Setting Festival."

"What's the Sun-Setting Festival?" I asked Marisar, moving to push aside the curtain of his personal area on my left so I could get a view of him. He was also sitting on a bed, glancing up at me when he heard the shambling of his thin privacy being shoved to the side.

CHAPTER THIRTEEN

Sacrifices

Marisar looked at me in a way I thought might be his species' way of conveying confusion. "You don't know the story of the Sun God?"

"I'm not from around here."

"Where are you from?" Gronch asked from the area to my right, dispelling my idea that the sections were assigned based on some numbering System. The half orc looked at the Selenian with disbelief. "You realize that she ain't even told anyone her name, right? Not even the slavers know."

"My name," I hissed, "is none of your business, half orc." I spat the last part out in sheer annoyance. Orcs and I had rarely gotten along. They never respected anyone. Half the time not even themselves. The vehemence of my current twelve-year-old posh voice, unfortunately, couldn't quite convey the level of intimidation I would have liked. I honestly probably looked more like an angry mouse to Gronch than a pissed-off Diamond-Cored queen. At least the half orc was visibly shocked. Not scared, but I'd take what I could get.

Before Gronch could collect himself and, by the increasing redness in his face, explode with indignation, Marisar started speaking.

"The Sun-Setting Festival is a story of the great love between the Sun God, Asoras, and the Moon Goddess, Lunaria.

"The Sun God was known for his passion and strength. He ruled the day and brought forth daylight with the heat of his brilliance. Within his fiery heart, there burned a longing—an uncontrollable yearning to touch the unending darkness of the night, to cast his burning gaze on the moon's soft glow."

Marisar told the story as if reading it from a book, which I suspected he was, in a way. I wondered how many times he'd read the story. And to whom.

"One night, the Sun God didn't go to sleep. He stayed and he waited. He waited for the moon to rise. And there she was with the rising moon. The Moon Goddess, ethereal and serene with a luminescent beauty, also desired love. She harbored a silent ache, you see. She loved the Sun God and dreamed about the day they would meet.

"And on that day, they did meet. For a fleeting moment, the heavens held their breath, captivated by the forbidden love of sun and moon.

"But alas, their union was not meant to last. As dawn approached, the Sun God knew he must return to his domain, lest the world be plunged into eternal darkness. With a heavy heart, he bid farewell to his beloved, promising to cherish the memory of their brief encounter for all eternity.

"And so, the Sun God returned to his place in the sky while the Moon Goddess lingered in the fading night. Though they were destined to forever remain apart, their love would endure, a timeless tale whispered among the stars. Ever since then, the people of the Caelos kingdom have always celebrated their love during the Sun-Setting Festival."

I just looked at him, irritated, though I couldn't tell if it was with myself or Marisar. I had not asked him for the entire mythology, only to explain what the festival was. And he still had not done that. I was about to ask him to explain the festival when he continued.

"The festival itself is held yearly for two weeks. Everyone participates, and the kingdom opens its borders to other reigns in the region." He gurgled, and his voice went up a pitch. I still couldn't get used to that sound. There was no water, so why did it sound like he was drowning? "Every year, the Arena puts on shows depicting historical events where slaves like us—I've heard the slaves are referred to as 'meats'—are used to play the side that lost. The villains. I have never been in the capital, which is where we are now, but the Arena festival shows are well known."

I swallowed down the building sense of foreboding. "When did the festival start?"

Marisar shrugged. "I'm not sure. It felt as if I was in that box for so long."

None of that sounded good.

"NO!" a man screamed, and my head snapped away from Marisar, toward the commotion. "This is not what you said!" He looked accusatorily at Chella. "You said I'd be fighting, like a gladiator."

Chella shrugged. "You will be. If you're good enough, you might even win."

"The Gods curse you, slaver. And your family. I hope you all bur—" The man's slave tattoo flashed, and he folded to the ground as if all the bones in his body had been removed. Two other men stood next to the fallen body, their eyes downcast and lifeless. Defeated. All three of the men looked sickly, too skinny to put up much of a defense. Or attack. I guessed that was the reason why they were picked for the festival.

"Sacrifices," Marisar whispered, his voice low enough that I could just barely hear him.

The small man with the bulbous head started shouting at Chella. "Madam Chella." His face was turning almost as blue as Marisar's. "Please explain to me how I am to bring this man to the Arena now. I certainly cannot carry him."

Chella just shrugged, turning to the rest of us.

"The rest of you get into your beds. There are wards around each of your beds to protect against other slaves. You are all warned, do not attempt to cross into another's bed. It will not end well for you," the giantess said, ignoring the shouting man until his face turned a shade of purple. She sighed and bent, grabbing the unconscious slave by the ankle. "Let's go." She dragged him to a crack in the wall and tapped it twice. A door opened inward and into the barracks; the rooms beyond were illuminated by torches many times stronger than the spheres of light attribute energy floating around us. She, the bulbous-headed man, Dralos, and the three slaves vanished down the pathway. There was a *click*, and the door closed. Thirty seconds later the balls of light winked out of existence, and we were plunged into darkness.

I didn't sleep that night. Based on what Marisar had told me, I knew I'd be called up before the end of the festival. That's what Chella had been warning me about when I chose to fight.

An hour before the lights turned back on, I finally finished my second heart ring.

"Rise and shine, meatheads," Dralos cackled as the balls hovering overhead flashed on and a dim white light flooded the damp underground area. I opened my eyes, still sitting on my bed with legs crossed, stabilizing my new heart ring. The center of the underground was still empty, the personal areas creating the outer rim. However, where there had been nothing by the stairs that we had entered through, thick steel bars now blocked our path, along with two crates, the insides of which I could only speculate. "I've brought you some presents. Over 'ere." He slapped the first crate. "We got y'all some food. If you can call it that. And over there"—he motioned to the other crate a few feet away—"some training weapons. If ya ain't called up as one of them sacrifices, we expect ya to win. If ya win enough coins for us, maybe we do you a li'l favor. Spice up those disgusting personal areas." His yellow eyes betrayed the niceties in his words for the lie they were. I didn't know what would happen if I brought in a lot of coins, but I knew it wasn't the favorable situation the lizard slaver was trying to hold over our heads. Though, by the looks on the faces of the others, like Gronch, not everyone caught the glint in the lizard's cruel gaze.

"What in the Gods' anuses?" a different, new voice shouted, this one female. I hadn't realized there'd been another female slave sent to the Arenas. I stood from the bed and peered around the ring of personal areas for the voice, as did many others. After a while, I saw her. Her, and the corpse that still twitched next to her bed.

Dralos tutted. "There're always one or two of them folks that don't listen to the rules. I don't much care what y'all do down here, but we ain't allowing ya to kill each other. That's like stealin' from us. And we dun like when people try to steal from us." He opened the first crate, dumping it on the grimy floor. A few dozen small balls tumbled out from it. Their exteriors were translucent, showing thick brown goop clomping and sloshing around inside. "Everyone gets a single ball. One. If ya try to steal it, well, you can join your friend in the shits."

No one moved at first, though one person eventually took a tentative step forward. I couldn't tell who or what it was due to the limited light, but after seeing nothing happen to the first person, the entire underground of slaves instantly cascaded upon the food balls like starving dogs. Even Marisar ran forward to grab one of the spherical containers of the debatably edible slosh.

I didn't move. There would be one waiting for me at the end anyway. I could tell that Dralos wasn't done. I doubted the lizard would have come all the way to the underground if that was all he meant to tell us. There were subordinates for that. He was here because he was taking pleasure in it and that meant the worst was yet to come.

When the number of people scrambling for food lessened, he continued.

"As many of you heard yesterday, the Festival of the Setting Sun is happening right now. Three of your compatriots fought last night. Unfortunately for them, none of them won. Fortunately for me, I already knew they wouldn't and made some good coins!" He let out a loud, cruel haw of a laugh. "Today, we will be picking another ten of you. But, this time, with some variety." His last words were said to the crowd of slaves. His eyes, however, never left me.

My suspicion regarding Dralos's species was instantly confirmed. The way those yellow eyes expressed hatred for me, the way he talked and walked, those eerie green scales. The way he seemed to want me dead the moment I reached the second heart ring.

Dralos was likely Dragonborne, one of the only races in existence I knew to instinctively despise Lunaris. Which meant the more I increased my lunar prowess, the more he'd come to despise me. I needed to figure out a way to kill him and fast if I wanted any chance of making it out of here alive, assuming I survived being selected as a sacrifice.

He called out the names of seven people, then walked around, grabbing the other two by the arms and shoving them toward the door the other slaves had left through the other day. Finally, last and certainly least in his eyes, he stopped in front of me.

"You're last," he said. "Let's go."

CHAPTER FOURTEEN

The Blood of Orpheus

The eleven of us left through the same stone door that Chella had used to take the slaves the previous night. As the previous sacrifices were led through, I could have sworn there were stairs leading into even deeper darkness.

However, when I walked into the shadows, I was met with a standard hall-way lit by torchlight—not the balls of white energy floating in the dungeon area. The stone walls were covered with some sort of pinkish slime that dripped down its length like goo. Fortunately, there was no slime on the floor, which incidentally was clean of any blemishes. While everything else was stone, the flooring was made of a yellow-white marble-like material. It was so slick that I nearly slipped when Dralos suddenly stopped. Being at the back of the line, I had enough time to slow my momentum. Three of the others did not and collided with each other. The Dragonborne gave them an annoyed expression.

But then Chella came into view from further down the dark path, and all irritation left Dralos's face, replaced by anticipation. His yellow eyes lit up, and the scales along his body seemed to chitter, which was weird, even for a Dragonborne.

"Is it ready?" he asked, his voice trembling with obvious excitement. Chella, who usually wore a stoic expression, appeared almost somber, even sad. She hadn't seemed the slightest bit upset at having sacrificed the three slaves the night before, so the fact that she looked like that now sent a wave of goosebumps through me.

"It is," she responded, slamming the flat of her hand against an area of the wall devoid of slime, revealing the rectangular outline of a door. Before the new door had opened more than an inch, the walls of the tunnel began to shake from the overwhelming pressure of an inhuman roar deep into the new path.

"Come on, slaves," Dralos said, gleefully shoving all of us into the pathway. "We're trying something new for the festival this year. Come meet Orpheus." His smile was as wide as it was malicious.

At the far end of the hallway from which the roar reverberated, I could see a dim red glow. The red light pulsed, accompanied only seconds later by the deafening scream of Orpheus. It wasn't until we reached the end of the hallway that I saw what exactly Orpheus and the red pulses were.

The hallway opened up to reveal a dilapidated chamber thick with the scent of mildew and decay. This room was made of marble like the outside floor, but here, even the walls were marble. Most were stained red with a seemingly endless amount of blood and gore. There were no other cells or prisoners aside from a single, solitary figure. Dense, heavy black manacles wrapped tightly around his wrists and continued up into the ceiling, so his arms were perpetually raised. Golden chains curled around each leg like snakes, so tight I could see dark purple bruises like spots on a cow. The golden chains did not connect to the ground; each end hung loosely at the sides.

The solitary figure was not a man; that much was clear from the three large horns protruding from the top of his head and smaller spikes tracing down his spine. If he had been able to stand at his full height, I guessed he would have easily matched Chella. Eyes black as coal stared at the twelve of us, though his mouth stayed open in an ear-deafening scream. His face was a mask of exhaustion and despair, eyes hollow and empty as he stared at us. Black hair hung loose and unkempt around his face, plastered with sweat, dirt, and blood. The way he looked at us, at me, gave me the impression that any hope of escape he may have had was long since extinguished. His gray, almost translucent, skin flashed red again.

I watched in absolute horror as a gaunt man with more wrinkles lining his features than anyone I had ever seen removed a foot-long syringe from the horned man's leg. Blue fluid filled the syringe's barrel. The man moved over to a large gray desk where a small crystal tube sat and slipped the syringe needle into it, before emptying out the blue contents into it. The room was silent except for the steady pouring of the fluid and the labored breathing of the captive.

After he finished his task, the gaunt man deigned to cast a glance our way and grinned when his soulless black eyes fell on Dralos. If I hadn't known better, I would have thought the man was a scholar by his lank form and glasses. The white coat that drooped down to his knees, however, indicated to me that this was likely a researcher of sorts.

"Ah, Dralos. I appreciate your speed in preparing some new test subjects," the researcher clasped his hands together, examining each of the slaves in turn. "Oh yes. Oh, how wonderful." When he got to me his eyes lit up. "A child? How absolutely magnificent Dralos. You have brought me such a diverse group. We shall reap such great information from this test. How perfect." He walked over to a counter where he picked up a smaller syringe filled with blue fluid. "Who would like the honor of being the first of you ten to be imbued with the Blood of Orpheus?"

What in the name of Ashwash . . .

"Her. Start with her, Darmond," Dralos said, giving me another shove. The tattoo tightened, and my entire body went rigid before I could argue.

Gods be damned, I cursed. Given enough time, I knew I could break through the slave bonds with the power of my newly formed second heart ring, but the damn slavers weren't giving me any time at all.

Darmond reached out, grabbing my arm and yanking me forward so I faced the horned man. Orpheus. "Look into his eyes," the old researcher commanded, grabbing my chin so he could point my face toward Orpheus. Despite my resistance, the slave tattoo forced my eyes to meet those of the captive.

And then Darmond plunged the needle deep into my arm. I wanted to scream, but the tattoo held me still and silent. I couldn't even watch as the blue blood was drained into my bloodstream.

There wasn't any pain. In fact, nothing happened. Darmond simply examined my eyes for a moment, nodded, and handed me back over to Dralos, who looked a bit disappointed that I hadn't spontaneously combusted.

The process was repeated with the other slaves, and one by one they all lined back up next to me. After all of us had been injected with the Blood of Orpheus, the researcher jotted down some notes in a leather-bound brown book that lay a few inches from the test tube filled with the fluid. "It should kick in once they enter the Arena grounds," Darmond explained directly to Dralos and Chella, not bothering to even pretend the explanation was for us. "The blood will remain dormant until then. I'm not sure whether the blood will return to being dormant afterward, or whether the effects will linger since the previous subjects were all killed in the Arenas. If any of them live, return them here for further examinations."

"Will do," Dralos said. Chella stayed silent. She hadn't looked up from her feet since we'd entered the room.

As we exited the way we'd entered, heading back toward the hall of slime, I ventured a question toward Chella when Dralos made his way to the front of the morbid parade.

"What did that man inject into us?" I asked. She didn't answer, so I pressed. "What exactly is the Blood of Orpheus?" Chella winced as if that very title made her uncomfortable. "If I'm going to die, I at least deserve to know what was put inside of me," I argued, still making sure to keep my voice low enough that Dralos wouldn't hear. While I'd gathered that Chella outranked him, I didn't think she'd answer if Dralos was actively listening.

After a moment, she looked up at me, and her brown eyes were full of pity. "It's not so bad," she muttered. "It might make you much stronger than you'd ever believed you could be." It was my turn to remain silent. There was more to it than that. "Orpheus is . . ." She started to say and then trailed off.

"He is *what*?" I pushed, needing to hear it. My life was about to be thrown into utter turmoil, and the more unknowns involved, the more likely a blade would find its way into my chest.

Chella gulped. "He is the sire of a Beast King."

My mouth dropped open as I let out an involuntary gasp. The only beings I could fathom siring a Beast King would be a Progenitor. How had anyone in this world captured a Progenitor? I thought back to the time in the dungeon room and then my meeting with the Progenitor in the Misty Veil Forest, where the pressure had been magnitudes more deadly.

But then an image of the golden chains snaked around Orpheus came unbidden to my mind. I hadn't been paying attention to the chains because of what had been happening. I tried to recall whether there had been any wards carved into them.

I couldn't remember.

"I was injected with the blood of a Progenitor?" I whispered, barely audible even in the brisk silence of the tunnel. That wasn't something I'd even thought was possible. Progenitors were individual species. The common belief was that two Progenitors couldn't reproduce with each other, and that's why there had never been any cross-species. "That's insane" was all I could say.

Chella nodded and then after a few seconds added, "It's blasphemy against the heavens. The Blood of Orpheus can open the mortal mind to the way of the Gods. It is not a realm mortals should be interfering in."

I was about to ask what that meant when Dralos shouted from the front. "Welcome to the Arena! Get out of there and die, ya worthless scum." Chella shot me another pitying look and then increased her pace to walk ahead of me toward the steel doors that swung open to open air. Like a procession, all ten of us walked out into a screaming crowd. When I looked around for Chella, she was gone. Dralos had vanished as well.

All around me, the cheering of an audience was deafening, drowning my thoughts in a myriad of noises. I had figured from its title of "Arena," but I still had not expected the sheer size of the colossal amphitheater—a perfect specimen of ancient architecture and engineering.

The Arena was encircled by towering stone walls, each with distinct markings of different animals carved along their lengths. Their weathered surfaces bore thousands of scars indicating the countless battles that had occurred within. Archways and columns stood heavy along the Colosseum's perimeter, adding to the obvious wealth and grandeur that had built the amphitheater.

Within the Arena, the dirt floor covered the entire interior adorned with sparse weapons and obstacles like a broken-down wagon or a large boulder. Patches of the black dirt were stained crimson with the blood of past warriors.

Tiered seating spread outward along the periphery, rising steadily in concentric rings to fill the entire outer rim. Despite the colossal size, not a single spot seemed to be empty. Hundreds of rows of stone and wood benches filled the concentric rings to accommodate the crowd, excitedly waiting for the next participants to enter the Arena below them.

I looked up at the audience, attempting to shade my eyes from the blistering sun overhead when a monotonous voice rang coldly in my ears.

[Welcome to the Arena. Please state your name so it can be recorded in the System.]

I spun instantly, hands out to protect myself against whatever had talked over my shoulder. Nothing was there. There was no one except for the other slaves, who were all shouting at each other for some reason. I still couldn't hear them.

**[State your name so you may proceed to choosing your preferred
class for the upcoming Arena challenge.]**

There was no way I was going to engage the disembodied voice, much less tell it my name. One of the slaves to my right pulsed with a red light akin to Orpheus's own pulse.

In the blink of an eye, the withered slave man with sad blue eyes disappeared, replaced with a much taller, stronger man decked out in shining silver and gold armor. Even the man looked shocked as he stared down at his new armor.

The Blood of Orpheus can open the mortal mind to the way of the Gods, Chella had said. Is this what she meant?

"Lilliana."

A blinding blue light exploded across my vision. When it dulled and coalesced into a semi-translucent blue wall in front of me, I was able to see words written on it that echoed the voice in my ears. The blue screen flashed, showing six different options. Swordsman, mage, archer, spearman, tank, rogue. Before I could do anything, the opalescent blue screen disappeared and then reappeared a second later, this time a foreboding pitch-black. The words laid out before me were written in a deep blood red.

[Error: Core System interfering.]
**[Choose whether you would like to mix the Core System
with the Blood of Orpheus.]**
[Ability to choose overridden. Combining System . . .]
**[Systems combined. Blood of Orpheus benefits will continue.
Status window only applicable within Arena territories. No access
allowed outside the jurisdiction of Orpheus, Progenitor of the
Sun God.]**
[Defeat your enemies to gain energy toward your Core.]

CHAPTER FIFTEEN

Reenacting the Massacre of Filth

There wasn't any time to spend trying to understand the blue walls of text hovering in front of me. A hoarse male voice boomed across the Arena, energy crackling with each word as some external energy increased the words to a deafening volume, echoing them across the vast space. It was too far for me to tell whether it was heart energy, or something else. I figured it was likely a good amount of people in the city were skilled with magic since no one yet had managed to build a Core for their heart energy.

"Laaaaaaadies and gentlemeeeen," the voice screamed, and the audience roared in response, "Welcome to the 103rd annual Sun-Setting Arena battles! My name is Jarold Evergreen, and I will be your play-by-play caster tonight. This year we have a special treat for all our blooooooooodthirsty fans." Jarold, the caster, punctuated each word with so much excitement and frenzy I was surprised he could still talk after the first syllable. His throat must have been incredibly raw. "Princess Aurora of our gorgeous and powerful Cael Kingdom is here to witness our famous reenactments of the kingdom's bloodiest wars and our fiercest noble warriors." He paused, and amazingly the crowd went silent in response. The air was tense with anticipation like a predator prowling in the night. "For our first fight, we will see the great battle between Cael Kingdom and the Rednatch Tribe." The caster's voice spat "Rednatch Tribe" with clear disgust, and the sound of boos filled the air. "Many of us were not born yet during the Great War between our people and the elves of Rednatch, but we all have heard the stories of how those barbarians would break into our cities, break into our homes. And then . . ." A silence fell over the crowd once more, and even I couldn't help but feel entranced by the story. The caster did his job well. "And then they would kill our children, our parents, our brothers, and sisters. Then, they would eat them, those vile, vile barbarians." More booing. "But then a hero stood at the forefront of our armies and fought them off. He pushed them back into their forest and burned it all to ashes!" Before the man had even finished his final word, the crowd had jumped to its feet screaming.

"GI-DE-ON. GI-DE-ON. GI-DE-ON," the mob of people chanted, stomping their feet and clapping their hands repeatedly. The Colosseum vibrated with the force of that pure, rage-filled excitement. Despite my situation, despite the horror of that story, despite knowing if I fought and killed, I'd be serving the needs of slavers, the sheer, burning exhilaration overflowing from the stands was making me eager. By the sound of that story, I was going to be fighting a death match with warriors—probably slaves with more experience, ones the audience favored.

Defeat your enemies to gain energy toward your Core, that voice had told me. It sounded like a lie. Probably *was* a lie. Even if it was real, I should despise it. Whatever it was, it had spawned from the blood of a Progenitor, who was an enemy of all living beings. I doubted such a thing could be anything but a promise of lies.

Still, I couldn't deny that what coursed through me at that moment was anticipation. I wanted to see if it worked and if the promise was true. If it was, I had somehow stumbled on the opportunity to build my remaining heart ring weeks in advance. Maybe even combine them into a Core, though there was no way I'd trust some unknown entity with the creation of my base Core. Considering my present circumstances, I'd have to take a temporary risk on this System thing. Good or bad, I'd deal with the consequences after. Sometimes risks needed to be taken for victory to be obtained.

Besides, it had been injected into me already. I wasn't in a place to do anything about it yet. Might as well use it for all it's worth in the meantime.

I suddenly felt myself grinning. A familiar feeling of peace and thrill for battle flooded through me like an uncontrollable tsunami. These fools were in for a surprise if they thought their Cael Kingdom would be victorious in the reenactment. My grin widened as my Arena enemies filed out from the other side, clad in scant armor. Parts of their bodies were covered in rusted steel, but the majority of the coverage was done by thin leather.

There were twenty of them in total, ranging from twenty years from youngest to oldest, give or take a few. I guessed the youngest was in his twenties. None of them struck me as particularly well trained. They walked too lazily and held their myriad of weapons either too tightly or too loosely, and the smiles on their faces were full of relief from being on the winning side. Some of them might die, but most of them would probably live, and they likely knew it.

Unfortunately, I was going to make sure none of them walked out of the Arena. Not if my own life depended on their deaths. The worry I'd felt about my situation drained away with the crash of the tsunami, and I could feel nothing but the frantic buzz in the air as the audience roared with the approval of the newcomers.

"GI-DE-ON! GI-DE-ON!"

I realized then that the audience had not stopped chanting the name Gideon since the end of the Caster's introduction. One of the enemy fighters raised his eyes as the crowd cheered and was running in wide circles, though taking care not to approach us. Unlike the others, he was covered in a completely golden suit of armor. His golden visor bounced and clanked as he ran. The crowd ate it up.

I thought he looked like an utter fool. That was probably why the crowd loved it.

"FIGHTERS," Jarold shouted over the screaming crowd, "GET READY!" That was when the door at the far side near the opposing soldiers opened again, and a chariot was rolled out, pulled along with two war horses, black as night. Eight more of the beasts followed. And then, at the very back, something that made my jaw drop. Again.

A long snake-like creature slithered into view out from behind the horses. The creatures gave it a wide berth, as did the soldier slaves. The creature was covered in dull gray scales that slinked along its twelve-foot length and ended where the torso split. Two heads tittered from the scaled body, each without a single eye. The entirety of the "heads" was a giant mouth filled with sharp red teeth that seemed attached to some type of spinning jaw. In between the horrendous maws was a single, black eye encircled in a bright white lining. It stared directly at me, and a whirring sound erupted from the two mouths.

"Holy Ashwash," I swore, taking a step back as some of my earlier bravado slipped away. "A desert tunneler?" An image of myself running away from the Demon Progenitor sprang to mind. I gritted my teeth and forced myself to take two steps forward.

Not again. Never again.

"We have the Soldiers of Cael Kingdom," Jarold introduced, and a golden light flashed down on the other slaves with a thunderous boom. The crowd roared, the magnitude of it dwarfing Jarold. After a moment, when the audience's applauding had died down, he switched to us, and an ominous red light flashed over our heads in silence. "And the nasty, dirty elves of Rednatch."

His words were met with a scattering of boos, but it was clear the audience was ready for the bloodshed to begin. Most of them were watching the desert tunneler spitting red fluid everywhere. The liquid splashed around it, sinking into whatever it hit with an acidic squelch.

"In the year of the Sun God, YSG 263, the Great War began. Five years later, the Hero King, Gideon of Cael, stepped in and fought back against the elven scourge." The man playing Gideon climbed onto the chariot and was given a long spear with a point that gleamed with a dangerous, enchanted aura.

Great.

"It wasn't until YSG 270 that the final battle occurred. The Massacre of Filth, where our soldiers tracked down the vile elven savages and destroyed them all, one by one in vengeance for our families, our friends, our children." A pause, letting the audience warm to the rage Jarold was building with his words. "Warriors," the caster shouted, the golden light illuminating the slaves playing Cael soldiers flashing even brighter, "bring salvation to our lands! Fight for glory! Fight for honor! Fight for your kingdom and your lives!"

The earth once again shook beneath me as every person in the stadium jumped to their feet, and the opposing soldiers surged forward on their horses, the golden soldier on his chariot.

Some of those around me still stood in shock, poking the thin air in front of them. I momentarily wondered if they were seeing the same blue and red boxes that I was. I pushed the thought aside as an arrow whistled over my head by inches.

I took a chance, figuring "class" was referring to what combat specialization someone had.

"I choose Lunari," I commanded the System. The red box vanished for a moment. Then a white one replaced it.

[Granted. Lunari class approved.]
**[NEW! Abilities grante—Error: Class override. System incompat-
ible with individual's foreign Core. Core System will progress.]**

That sounded like the Blood of Orpheus was going to allow me to progress the same way I had in Ordite.

Despite the moon not being in the sky, I was shocked to find lunar
energy flowing into my body from everywhere in the Arena. Not a lot, but
more than should have been in the air during the day. I pulled in all that
I could up to the very last second; until one of the mounted combatants
was only a few feet from me.

The soldier atop the horse was clearly untrained and not in good control
of the war beast. With a flick of my wrist, I released a small burst of light
energy and threw myself to the side, rolling with practiced ease back to my
feet. The horse made a panicked sound, and the man shouted.

I couldn't hear what he said, though I knew it was about his eyes when
his hands rubbed at them frantically. His horse bucked from underneath
and the man was thrown from the horse, slamming heavily into the ground
as his armor clanged in discontent.

I didn't give him time to recover. I pushed off from my position and
leaped at him, a crackling yellow-white light spreading around my right
hand. With a thrust, I buried my empowered hand into the soldier's chest,
piercing the leather armor without an obstacle. When I retracted it, there
was no blood staining my skin. Whatever flesh or gore remained quickly
burned to ashes in the inferno of light energy radiating around my arm.

[You have received a percentage of heart-ring energy.]

I didn't pause to observe what I'd done. I was on my feet dodging blades
and batting them aside with my empowered hand. All but one of the slaves
from my side were, surprisingly, still alive. Bloodied and injured, but alive.
As we fought, I noticed some of them improving at an impossible rate. The
realization that they were experiencing the same phenomenon that I was
came late. I grinned even wider. Oh, what a mistake the slavers had made.

The glint of gold flickered in my peripheral vision, and I instinctually
ducked. A long, deadly golden point speared overhead, skewering the man
I'd just been fighting. Hooves stomped by, and then wheels followed. The
crowd broke out into cheers of "GI-DE-ON." I looked up, laying my eyes on

the golden warrior. That spear strike had been too accurate for an untrained slave. I noticed the golden flecks in the man's eyes as his gaze met mine, and he smiled back at me, teeth polished with a clean white.

That was when the desert tunneler lashed out, its whirling noise temporarily interrupted by the sound of tearing flesh and the dying screams of slaves. Apparently, the tunneler was not particular about who it ate.

The energy empowerment around my hand winked away, and I grabbed a shining steel blade that had fallen a foot from me. The man playing Gideon didn't move. He stood there on his chariot; an arrogant smirk permanently plastered on his face as he looked at me. At the twelve-year-old girl, he was trying to kill.

Filth.

An enormous beast burst from our end, a massive hammer clenched in each hand. It stood at least ten feet taller than Gideon on the chariot and possessed a muscled humanoid body covered in thick, fur-covered skin, the matted silver fur spotted with stains of crimson blood. The creature's head resembled that of a goat more than a man, with a flat face and amber eyes made small by the large, curved horns spiraling outward and then sloping slightly downward at the end. It lowered its head with a scream and charged the chariot.

"Oh no, folks," Jarold said, "it looks like the vile elves had a trick up their sleeves. Does anyone remember how Gideon dealt with the Beast King protecting the elves?"

As one, the crowd chanted, "Kill. Kill! KILL! *KILL!*"

CHAPTER SIXTEEN

A Queen's Stand

It was as if the entire Arena froze in time. Enormous ice spikes rose, instantly covering the entire desert landscape in sharp, ragged edges. At least five people were killed on the spot as the ice spears tore vertically through them until each of them had small points at the top of their heads like little hats.

A moment earlier as the goat monster had charged at Gideon, I'd seen the man raise his hands. Seventeen heart rings . . . or maybe magic rings based on the oddity in the foundation of the man's heart energy, whirling around him in demonstration of his power. Other than the Silverwater Knight Captain, the man acting as "the" Gideon had the strongest foundation I'd seen since arriving in this new world. But there was something very off about his foundation. The energy was different—I couldn't sense it coming from his heart. Instead, the majority of Gideon's power seemed to originate around his stomach, fortifying my belief that he was using "magic."

Blue-white light had danced around his outstretched palms while he'd drawn power from the hovering rings. The ground had rumbled, and the temperature had plummeted.

I lived thanks to my honed instinct screaming at me to dodge. I had rolled to the side just before a great white spear of ice launched itself from the ground where I'd stood.

Gideon was laughing, that arrogant smirk still clinging to him like a bad rash.

"The Frozen King has descended!" Jarold announced, the audience responding with screams of "GI-DE-ON."

I figured this was clearly some sort of reenactment of what the announcer was referring to as a Massacre of Filth. Something about elves, whatever that was. I had no idea why they were trying to force me into a reenactment. Were candidates supposed to play along? Was playing along part of the test itself? Was I supposed to know about the battle—to know what I was supposed to do?

I glanced around, taking in the *magical* destruction. I still wasn't sure what exactly magic was, but my instincts were screaming that what Gideon had done was magic. Three of the five men killed were from the ten I'd entered with, but the other two were from his own team. The steel armor they adorned clinked against the ice while their bodies collapsed onto it limp and lifeless.

"The Hero King kills his own people?" I shouted, spinning the steel blade I'd looted until its flat side landed softly on my right shoulder. I didn't really know who the Hero King was, but I tried playing along with whatever weird reenactment bullshit was going on. My words rang loud and clear thanks to the energy I imbued into them. It wasn't a difficult bit of heart energy manipulation, though it did require a refined touch. The poor slaves around me with under five heart rings and poor foundations likely didn't even know it was possible.

Gideon's smirk twitched but didn't slip. The audience, however, had completely stilled. I couldn't tell if it was out of shock or anticipation of what I'd do next. It didn't really matter. I was absolutely sick of this world tossing me around left and right. If I died, so be it.

But I was done being kicked around. No more.

"I didn't realize the great Hero King Gideon was a coward not fit to lick Ashwash's balls," I taunted, adopting the tone and way of speech I'd heard from the knights who'd served me. "Pathetic."

Not even Jarold spoke as the entire amphitheater held its collective breath, waiting to hear what the man playing Gideon would do.

I reached into my heart rings and drew on their vitality, lunar power flooding my energy pathways with a rush that nearly caused me to gasp. Instead, I held up my hand and flicked the would-be killer spear at my side. It didn't just break. It shattered.

"Now what, O Great King? Do you plan to kill a twelve-year-old girl?" I again taunted the still-silent man. I could see him gritting his teeth, clearly not having come prepared for being taunted by a child. Strictly speaking, he was much more powerful than my current self—well, at least where raw energy was concerned. Raw power, however, was not the only factor in war.

"Child, you dare question the honor of the Frozen King?" He finally and lamely bellowed. The crowd gave a cheer, but it was hollow, a husk of what it had been. Most of them just looked on, wide-eyed. He paused and spoke quietly, as if to someone unseen. "Who is this kid? You never told me the child had magic; this was supposed to be a slaughter reenactment. She was supposed to be the weakling elf offspring, not—not . . . not whatever she is!" I didn't give him time to receive an answer.

"I question the honor of the pig before me, slaughtering his allies. Are you the Frozen King, or some fool pretending to be something greater than himself?"

He snarled and raised his hands, blue magic swirling around them with a deadly flourish. Before his magic was completed, I condensed lunar energy into a single point above my finger.

And then I flicked it at him like I'd done with the ice spear. The white dot collided with the swirling blue energy, and both blinked out of existence. No sound, no explosion. Just gone.

I laughed, but it was without mirth. The laugh was cold and cruel, unfitting and unnatural for a twelve-year-old girl. I knew that. I didn't care. This was not a Progenitor. This was a man from a small, backwater world who didn't even know about Cores or cancellation techniques. All I had to do was send a dot of condensed heart energy toward him before his internal energy was released and poof, it dissipated. While everyone was enraptured with the drama, I made my way toward one of the opposing slaves who squirmed, a steel shard sticking from one of his eyes. The other slaves stared at me, open-mouthed and without understanding.

All except an ebony man, no older than his mid-twenties, with black eyes that sparked with rebellion. His face was plastered with sweat and his body was covered with scars, blood, and gore. But I liked that expression. Our eyes met for a fraction of a second. A single fraction but I saw understanding dawn in them as I approached the downed man. He whispered something to the man next to him, who looked much older and weathered. This one with pale skin and hair a dull red like a dying fire.

Both of them gingerly stepped backward, away from my spectacle and toward some of the injured slaves. As I drove my foot into the man with the steel shard in his head, they also acted, each killing an injured slave. I didn't know if the killed men were our opposition or not, but it didn't matter.

[You have gained heart-ring energy.]
[Two others have chosen to transfer their obtained heart-ring energy to you. Absorbing . . .]
[You have absorbed sufficient energy to create a third heart ring.]
[Attempting to form heart ring . . .]
[Error: Formation failed. Fighter's name unknown. Unable to register with the System. Provide Fighter Identification.]

"I already said 'Lilliana,'" I growled.

[Fighter Identification not accepted. "Lilliana" restricted to individual's name. It is not acceptable for Fighter Identification.]

"Fine," I whispered between clenched teeth. "Lilith."

[Accepted. Creating temporary title based on Fighter's past experiences, achievements, and sense of self. "Queen of Rot" established.]
[Class override. Classes Necromancer and Lunari combined. Current class: Soul Weaver.]

Gideon, clearly oblivious to the System, didn't react to the deaths of three more of his allies. That put the slave soldiers down from twenty to around thirteen now, some having been killed before the ice shards. On the other hand, only four in total from my original slave group had fallen, leaving me with five allies.

Luckily, the System seemed to be working for the other five. I could sense properly structured heart rings among them, though not all. The five of them no longer slumped or looked ragged. Their breath came in heavy bursts, but their shoulders were back and the look in their eyes was no longer hopeless.

I clamped down on all three as the third ring formed around my heart. They appeared around me, swirling in a uniform circle much as Gideon's had done. The man in the golden chariot bellowed a mocking laugh at my three circles, his seventeen rings still dancing around him. What Gideon didn't know, what no one here seemed to know, was that without a Core, high-Bronze-energy techniques would be a heart-ring user's max. Any more and the power would begin to tax their heart. The Knight Captain with his twenty-one heart rings had built a solid foundation despite not having a Core himself, so he could likely reach the strength of a high Silver-level Core before his heart gave out. If he'd had a Core, he could have fought me at my prime for some time.

Gideon, however, did not have a proper Core nor did he have the solid foundation of the Knight Captain. His heart rings were more foundationally solid than others I'd seen in this world, but not by enough to matter in this fight.

The audience began to jeer with Gideon. Right up until the moment my heart rings collided with each other, spinning radically off their normal trajectory. I technically didn't have to show this. Broadcasting heart rings was something anyone with a heart ring could do if they wanted to, but it wasn't necessary.

I wanted Gideon to see. I wanted all of them to see. To know that this— this was the beginning of their end.

My heart rings became intertwined, spinning across each other's axis. I put as much focus as I could without risking losing sight of my surroundings into the Core's formation. I had done this before. It wasn't easy, but once someone learned the methodology, it became a straightforward task. If slightly arduous.

I could feel the entire stadium enraptured at the scene before them. Even Gideon, who I figured would have tried to attack me, was staring dumbly at the spinning heart rings. After a moment there was a deafening crack as the heart rings exploded into particles. Then, quickly, as if being pulled toward an invisible magnet at the very center of their rotations, the particles turned inward. All together and all at once.

What remained where the heart rings had circled was a single Bronze sphere thrumming with refined, pure energy. With a silent command, the spherical Core vanished and took its place within my heart as the foundational Core.

The spectacle took no more than thirty seconds, and I doubted anyone watching knew what had happened. Soon they would come to understand.

I cracked my neck to the right and then the left, my grin having never faded. The sheer amount of pure lunar and necromantic energy coursing through my veins was electric. Though I didn't know how my body was so easily handling necromantic energy with a Bronze-level Core, I figured it must have something to do with the System assigning me the class of Soul Weaver. Unfortunately, that was not a class I was familiar with.

Vaguely I remembered the System giving me the title of Queen of Rot. I decided to ignore that for the moment. It seemed someone, or something, knew who I was. Who I *really* was. And I would find that out eventually.

I looked down at the body of the slave soldier my foot had killed and was surprised to find a small, reddish-white ball of energy hovering above his heart.

"W-what was that?" Gideon asked, his voice also heightened by energy now. I wasn't sure why he hadn't attacked me yet, even after the spectacle had ended. I suspected it might have to do with the fact I looked like a pre-pubescent child. He'd seen me kill, but no doubt didn't really believe I'd be a threat to his seventeen rings.

Jarold, the caster, echoed the question. "Folks . . . I don't think I've ever seen anything like this before. That little girl had three heart rings and . . . did she destroy them? And was that a Core? By the Gods, I believe it was. Mother of the Gods . . ." There was some static as the caster's voice grew distant, as if he was speaking with someone.

I ignored them, staring at the ball of energy. Eventually, I shrugged and reached down to grab it. When my hand should have touched the energy, I instead passed right through it. The ball, with a whoosh, slammed back down into the body.

A single, thin string, one nearly invisible, remained attached to my palm and led to the corpse.

A corpse that rose from the ground. Headless.

And then with a *pop*, his head returned to his shoulders. He looked around, questioningly.

At first, I thought that might have simply been how this world handled necromantic energy manipulation.

No. It isn't necromancy, I realized, reaching out my senses to examine the man. The *living* man.

"Holy hells," Gideon said as a panicked clamor in the audience broke the silence. "What is that?"

The soldier was alive. Not undead. *Alive.*

CHAPTER SEVENTEEN

Nobility and Divinity

What I had just done was impossible. Not simply difficult or requiring high levels of energy refinement—it was impossible. No one could bring the dead back to life. It went against the laws of reality. The dead were gone.

At least that's how it was supposed to be.

When his eyes met mine, all the fear and confusion previously sketched across his newly fashioned head vanished. Where there had been fear, there was now worship. Instead of confusion, determination. He bowed at my feet, and I vaguely noticed the tunneler clamping both its jaws around the goat creature's shoulders.

"My queen," the resurrected man said, his voice suddenly raspy and ancient. "Tell me your desires."

I didn't respond, still reeling from how I'd apparently broken the fabric of reality and somehow changed the man's fate.

"What are you?" I whispered, low enough that he shouldn't have been able to hear.

He heard. "I am whatever you want me to be."

[Welcome to the Orpheus System, Awakener. You have achieved the minimal requirements for entry into the Main System.]

This was a new voice. A deep, almost melodic male voice, not the monotonous one from before.

"This is blasphemy against the Gods!" Gideon shouted, his accusations repeated in screams from the audience.

Intermixed with the accusations of heresy and trickery, I could hear vastly different . . . accusations that I wasn't sure I liked much more than being a blasphemer.

"It's the Saintess."

"The Saintess is here."

"The Goddess of Life has sent to us a messenger."

Different voices collided with each other as I watched the audience high above me begin to turn toward each other. Loud voices and angry faces at first. Then, slowly, patches of arguing onlookers broke out into brawls.

I nearly broke out in a genuine laugh of disbelief. How religious were the folk in this city for them to believe I could have ever been the Saintess of anything? True, I didn't view myself as a villain, but I certainly was no shining beacon of divine will.

I was not a saintess nor a villain; I was merely a survivor, ruler of my own path.

If only they could see the Queen of Rot title oh so graciously forced upon me by the System.

The goat creature staggered when it finally broke through the rock slabs. It was too late. The tunneler, expecting the slabs to break, pounced the moment the creature was off-balance. Blood sprayed like a geyser as both mouths bit down on both sides of the goat's head, causing the thing's skull to collapse inward. I wanted to vomit.

I raised my sword in Gideon's direction, the sight of him a stark difference from the gloating noble a moment earlier. He now looked as confused as the man kneeling at my knees had upon awakening. Gideon's brows were scrunched in thought, and I could see his eyes constantly flickering from me to the area where I knew the rich and noble were. The section was at the Arena's peak and jutted out overhead, the sun above us all blocked by a golden embellished overhang.

He raised his sword in a tentative manner, his lips forming words too far away for me to hear. I doubted he was speaking to me anyway.

Taking advantage of his distracted focus, I wrapped both my hands and sword in the new black and white swirling Soul Weaver energy and launched myself over the fifty feet or so separating us. Much like the goat creature, he'd been caught off guard.

Gideon raised his ice-covered arms up in defense just a fraction late, and my empowered hands slammed into his chest. That should have greatly injured him if not straight killed him.

Instead, I found myself having phased through the man. Not a scratch on him. Gideon turned around, his eyes nearly bugged out of his head. We just stared at each other for a moment. And then, without a sound, he collapsed to the ground. His life energy fled the vessel like it was being evaporated.

The energy fled toward me. Toward the reddish-white ball sitting in the palm of my left hand that absorbed every last drop. The more energy sucked into the ball, the more drained Gideon's soulless body became. Little by little, it became nothing more than a sunken husk. I probably could have stopped the absorption. I knew instinctively that I could have.

I didn't.

I once knew some nobles who refused to kill, believing it would turn them into the very evil they fought against. They were all dead, and that belief was bullshit. They died with their honor intact, but they died all the same.

Gideon was an enemy. My enemy. If he hadn't died from my mysterious new abilities, he would still have died from a blade through his heart.

When I finally finished draining Gideon, his heart stopped. At the same moment, a shrill scream pierced through the noise of the stadium. It wasn't so much the woman had screamed louder than everything else. It was the pain in her voice, the desperate disbelief mixing with the pressure of high-tier energy coalescing into something I had only heard described as physical sound.

"No!" the woman cried, her voice clear with tears. "Damien, no!"

[A large amount of energy has been collected. Absorb energy?]
[Yes/No]

I ignored the message, not sure what to do with it and pushed it to the back of mind to worry about later.

The gates on either side of the Arena that each team of slaves had entered parted with an uncaring slam. At least a hundred soldiers from both directions flooded into the Arena. Some with swords at the ready, some with crossbows, all looking . . . hesitant.

It wasn't fear, exactly. At least, it wasn't a fear of me. Fear of their Gods? I couldn't tell.

I stayed calm despite the thudding of my heart and the ache from my Core that thirsted for the thrill of battle. I quirked an eyebrow at the approaching soldiers as nonchalantly as I could. By the looks on their worried faces, I might even have pulled it off.

"Is this how you greet Your Saintess?" I asked, holding what was probably a physical manifestation of Gideon's soul in my hand. "Should I ask the Goddess to strike down all her nonbelievers?"

That stopped them cold, and I tutted.

"You should show more deference to a messenger of your go—"

"Enough with this nonsense," screamed that same shrill voice from earlier. I turned to face its owner. It was a tall, scrawny woman with a sunken face and an overly large nose. Her blue eyes and cheeks were stained wet with tears. It looked disturbing in contrast to the woman's prim golden-purple dress that hung an inch above her similarly colored shoes.

Next to her, looking not particularly perturbed, was an older man with the same colors, though he wore a large crown on his head. I noticed at that point a thin circlet was on the woman's. The man had the silver remains of a once youthful head of hair and a beard of silver with golden flecks.

In between the two was a young woman, maybe sixteen or seventeen, with golden hair to her waist. Light blue eyes stared out at the Arena dispassionately. Almost bored. Only the man had any semblance of combat training, though I could tell both women had been rigorously schooled in the etiquette of royalty. It was in the way they walked. In the way their bodies moved with their legs, yet their heads remained almost still. In the way their eyes seemed to try to look beyond the facade of Lilliana.

Ah. What had the man told Chella the previous night? That princess . . . Aurelia? Aurora? Something like that. She would be attending the festival?

The situation had quickly escalated further than I would have preferred. I'd hoped to gain enough attention to attract the Arena runners and make a deal with them. An Arena, despite its inherent flaws, wouldn't have been the worst place to train myself before returning to the Silverwater barony.

Though this situation wasn't too awful. I could always bring back Gideon—no, Damien. Probably.

As the trio drew nearer, I sketched a bow to the King first, and then the two women who were likely princesses. The taller woman didn't strike me as a queen, but just in case, I bowed to her second after the King but before the younger girl to avoid any potential disrespect.

My bows were slight, no more than a respectful dip of my head while keeping my back at a very slight incline. Generally, such a bow was used when greeting an equal. In this world, I had virtually no status. I should have given a proper curtsy, bowing my head deeply at the end. I scoffed at the idea. They were lucky I even dropped my gaze.

"Your Majesty," I spoke after straightening, ignoring the hysterical woman. Again, I broke the rules of etiquette by initiating a conversation with a higher noble. I didn't care. And I doubt the King did either considering he was staring at me with growing interest, and I was still basically cocooned in gore from the earlier melee. "Are you enjoying the show?"

Like when I taunted Gideon, the audience was as silent as the dead. Listening at the edge of their seats.

Sheep, I thought. These worlds are full of sheep just waiting to leech off the misery of others.

One of the guards who'd entered from the opposite entrance of the royal family took a step forward, his golden suit of armor jostling from the movement. Instantly, the resurrected man who'd been like a statue at my feet sprang up, a sword in his hand. He placed himself between me and the rest of the army, body as steady and determined as one who'd trained their entire life for that singular purpose. The guard halted and looked at his king, who shook his head no.

"I can't say that I am," the ruler stated flatly. His voice came out weathered and aged yet held a strength I remembered from when I would hear my father talk. My real father. "You've killed my son-in-law."

The way the King said "son-in-law" gave me the impression the man was less annoyed by the death of the man than having to call him *son-in-law*.

"Do you want me to bring him back?" I asked, tossing the manifested reddish-white soul into the air a few times.

The King shook his head with a glance toward the still-nameless resurrected man. "Not if he turns into whatever that is." He paused and then looked at me. "Who are you? What are you?"

"I am Lilliana Silverwater, second daughter of Baron Silverwater, and fifth in line to the Silverwater barony," I declared to all who could hear. With my energy-enhanced volume, that was everyone. "I was wrongfully detained in this Arena and I demand satisfaction." I nudged Gideon—Damien—whatever his name was with my foot. "Though I've received some measure of satisfaction already."

Based on *The History of Lysoria*, it was commonplace for nobles who had been wronged by another noble to request satisfaction, some type of restitution for their injuries. If the King acknowledged me as a daughter of the Silverwater house in Lysoria, my chances of living went up significantly. Or, at the very least, I wouldn't be executed for killing a member of the royal family.

"You're . . . a noble lady?" The younger woman said, cradling the other sobbing woman in her arms. She looked dubiously at my gore-covered figure and I shrugged.

"Is it so hard to believe one would fight for their life, even a noble's daughter?" I responded. "Would you not have fought?"

"Of course, I would have!" The girl shot back. "But yo—"

The King put a hand on his daughter's shoulder. "The daughter of a Baron and the Saintess for the Goddess Dhalia; those are both very heavy claims, warrior. To claim both nobility and divinity have been lost to a slaver's market is quite . . . perplexing." He motioned to me and the group of guards to my rear. "Let them take you back into the dungeons. I will see if your words are true. If you have lied to me, you will be hanged for attempting to lie to the Crown of Cael. Do you understand?"

"Yes. Yes, I do, Your Majesty."

CHAPTER EIGHTEEN

Advent of the Soul Weaver

I was not taken back to the dungeons with all the other surviving slaves. While we were being shepherded back toward the cells, a handful of guards grabbed me and split us off from the main group, dragging me down the path where I'd been injected with the blue Blood of Orpheus, the Progenitor. The chamber was the same as it had been—barren but with a single desk cluttered with all sorts of experimental tools and liquids, and the Progenitor chained up against the far wall. This time, however, there was one difference: a wooden chair had been placed a dozen or so feet from both Orpheus and the desk. That's where I was forced to sit. The two guards proceeded to tie my hands behind my back with warded chains. I instantly felt all the new power I'd accumulated drain away. Then they bound my feet.

"Is all this truly necessary?" I said, casting a glance at the guard locking the golden chains around my ankles. "I still have the slave bond on me—what do you think I could even do with that brand on me?"

He grunted. "Ain't my job to think about that. Stay still."

"Oh, it should be your business though," I warned, putting the saintess facade back up. "I don't believe your Goddess will be too pleased about this."

The guard, again, gave a noncommittal grunt and shrugged. "Them Gods have better things to do than worry about what I do."

"Maybe," I hissed. "But I don't. Be warned, Soldier—my Goddess may be a Paragon of forgiveness. I am not." Truth be told, I had no idea whether or not that was true. I didn't know anything about this Goddess I was supposedly the saint of other than the fact she was the Goddess of Life. The guard's face paled, and beads of sweat formed at the edge of his forehead, but he finished tying me despite his obvious discomfort with my presence.

I didn't have time to continue my threats and warnings before Darmond entered the room, gaunt as ever. The researcher's inhuman dark blue eyes stared at me with the grimmest smile I'd seen him wear. Last time he was full of academic joy. That joy seemed to have become a maniacal resolution.

Without saying a word, he strode up to me and I could smell day-old sweat and the slightest hint of cooked meat wafting from his direction. Had it really been so long since I'd had a real meal that I could now smell it on another? He took a small scalpel from his pocket and sliced the side of my forearm with a short, quick cut. Reddish-blue fluid seeped out. I expected the academic to yip in excitement, but he just nodded.

"Outstanding. It looks like the two bloods have mixed perfectly," he murmured, making a similar cut on my other arm and then right above my right hip. "Simply outstanding. It's a perfect mix. Truly, you are a marvelous child." He took a small vial from his desk and used my cuts to fill it with blood. "If only we had more time, I could study you more. Find out why you. Why does your blood match so well." He sighed, putting down the vials and wiping the scalpel clean. "Unfortunately, it looks like the King will be taking you from here soon." Out of nowhere, his eyes darkened, and he slammed his fist down on the table. I tried not to wince in surprise and was success-ful. Orpheus didn't budge either, though I noticed at some point he had opened his eyes and was now staring openly at me. "He doesn't understand! None of them understand what you can give to us. To all of us." The gaunt researcher stepped directly in front of me, his nose mere inches from my own. "Child, I believe somewhere inside of you is the key to immortality. And it goes beyond that—to give immortality to everyone. This king, this country"—he shook his head, the wild look in his eyes raising goose bumps along my neck—"they don't understand. How could they? This is the realm of the Gods. The heavens!"

It was at that point Orpheus chose to release a hoarse chuckle. The sound was deep and ancient, reverberating through my bones as it echoed around the chamber. "Fools," the voice rasped with hollow pity. "My blood . . . is not the blood of Gods. No . . . You have brought . . . forth . . . your end." Orpheus's eyes had never left me. Those black coals which had been hopeless before, dead, even, had rekindled with a sort of . . . pride? "It is . . . the advent of the Soul Weaver." His voice became increasingly clear and more pronounced even as his Progenitor pressure began to seep even through the golden chains. Finally, those black eyes of his that seemed to look right through me looked away, up at the ceiling as if he were praying. "The Guardians will chase you to the end, O Queen of Rot. Your fate . . . is ever your own to weave."

Then he was silent, his head bobbing back to his chest with a soft thud. For a moment no one moved—well, I couldn't even if I wanted to, but Darmond didn't move. Then he jumped and scrambled forward to Orpheus, rapidly performing a series of tests I wouldn't begin to understand. The researcher let out a final, relieved breath. Still alive then.

There was a bang on the door and then a third soldier whispered into the ear of the soldier that'd tied my legs.

"You have five minutes left, Darmond," the guard stated. The researcher spent those remaining minutes running various diagnostics on me, different from what he'd done to Orpheus, injecting me with more blue fluid and removing more of my blood. I didn't know why, but I couldn't wait to get away from the madman who spouted increasingly nonsensical mutterings until the very last second. The guards had to physically drag me away from the researcher who was shouting and screaming at the guards that he wasn't done.

The guard I'd spoken to had slung me over his shoulder and I bounced as he moved to slam the door shut with a final, resounding thwap. The sudden silence away from the screaming researcher was jarring but in a nice way.

"Well, that was something," the new, third guard said and the other two laughed. I attempted a short laugh too, since it had been quite bizarre and the guards seemed friendly enough, but the constant jostling and sharp pain of metal armor being jabbed into me like I was some sack of potatoes made laughing impossible. It was all I could do not to grunt every time the armored shoulder sank into the soft flesh of my stomach. Which now had a bunch of small cuts thanks to the mad researcher.

"Can you just let me down?" I was finally able to say. "I have the slave tattoo and nowhere to run. Just let me walk. In the name of the Gods, put me down."

The three looked at each other and when the third one shrugged, I felt large hands reach up and bring me down back to my feet. "You will have to walk with the chains on your hands, but we will take off the ones around your feet. Don't try to run. I don't want to harm a child."

"Run?" I just barely restrained myself from spitting the word. "Where would I run? Back to the Arena? Back to wherever in the Gods' names that madman is? No. No, thank you. Just let me walk back to my bed." The second guard unlocked the chains around my ankles, and I shrugged off the hand that steadied me when I was immediately unbalanced from the sudden removal of weight. "I can walk fine. Leave me be." I could tell the guards were confused by my tone. It was likely their first time being ordered around by a child, much less a slave child. On the other hand, I might be a saint and a noble, and it didn't look like they had any orders that I couldn't walk on my own in the tunnels. They eventually relented and as the walk continued, paid less and less attention to me, engaging each other in various topics like women and the King. Which was fine by me.

The next morning, I was sitting cross-legged on the tattered mattress called my bed, trying to eat the bowl of slop when the bulbous-headed man came marching into the dungeons surrounded by a handful of guards, none of whom I recognized.

He cleared his throat and held up a scroll of parchment stamped closed with the claw of a dragon. "Ahem. All bow before the word of His Majesty, King Isadore the Seventh, Lord and Ruler of the Kingdom of Cael, Savior of the High Humans, Destroyer of Elves, and Master of the South." The bulbous man paused, apparently waiting for us all to bow or kneel in deference to the words of the King. None of us bothered. I doubted any of the slaves were actual citizens of Cael.

I filled my mouth with the slop and forced back my gag reflex as I chewed the goop and unknown lumps and swallowed. Disgusting. The King's messenger, I assumed he was, staring at Chella and Dralos as if telling them to use the slave mark to force us into kowtowing. Neither of them had gone down on the floor either. After a long moment, the bulbous man took a deep breath and, furiously, undid the seal to open the scroll, and began to read. "By decree of His Majesty, King Isadore, Slave Number 33122 is hereby recognized as Lady Lilliana Silverwater, daughter of Baron Silverwater. Baron Silverwater has been apprised of the situation and is headed here now and should arrive within seven days. The issue of whether Lady Silverwater is the Saintess of Goddess Dhalia remains to be decided. However, as Lady Lilliana has already declared herself to be so, the King has decided, with recommendations from the Church of Life, to continue the Arena battles with Lady Lilliana as her saintess trials. She, along with any slave she chooses, will face three trials. Each a combat in the name of the Cael Kingdom. Should the Goddess's light truly shine upon Lady Lilliana, she shall be victorious. That is all." He rolled the scroll up and tucked it away. On his way out, his eyes caught mine, and his nose wrinkled.

Guess I knew what he thought of the King's decision to find me of nobility. I sighed and forced down another mouthful of the slop.

"Wow," Marisar said, pushing aside the curtain separating our personal areas. "You really are nobility."

"Much good that did 'er," Gronch said from the other side. "She still 'as to fight."

CHAPTER NINETEEN

Just One Hit

Despite Gronch's arrogance and wholly unpleasant demeanor, I quickly understood within seconds of our spar how he'd won his earlier death fight without so much as a scar. He was, by far, the strongest of the slaves in the dungeon's Arena in terms of raw skill with weapons.

In response to my killing the King's son-in-law, the slavers had imposed stronger restrictions on us, preventing the use of our heart rings outside the Arena floors. While we could still gather energy and create new rings, the new ring would be instantly sealed upon formation. Instead, they provided us with new steel blades, with a warning not to kill each other.

Unfortunately, despite training for decades in my previous life, in this life, my body was not physically fit for combat. While forming a Core had aided in developing Lilliana's body into a weapon to some extent, it was nowhere near capable of fighting off a rampaging half orc without any physical empowerment.

Soon after the bulbous-headed messenger had departed, Chella handed me a smaller, unsealed roll of parchment that outlined the trials with absolutely no detail. It read:

Lady Silverwater, by order of the Church of Light and the King, your trials shall be as follows, each separated by three days: the first shall be a test of faith, the second of strength, and the third of destiny. May the Gods and Goddesses be ever leading you upon the correct path.

Signed,

King Isadore

I stuffed the useless letter into the pocket of my worn pants, not bothering to keep from crumpling it. Since then, it had been around two days. I'd chosen to spend the first day sparring with the other slaves using whatever weapons were available, displaying varying levels of mastery. I preferred the sword if it had proper balance, though I had next to no training for wielding the hammer. That's where Gronch came in.

The majority of the second day had been spent getting tossed around the dungeon like a sack of trash by Gronch, who was clearly a well-trained hammer user. If Gronch was to be believed, he was not just well trained—he was a captain of the Diamond orc militia that had been warring with the Kingdom of Cael for years at the northern border. I had no idea if that was true, but Marisar didn't say anything, so I figured it probably was accurate.

At least the part about the militia existing.

Gronch swung diagonally with his war hammer, the flat of the hammer's head colliding erratically with my steel blade. I mistakenly leaned into the battle of strength, and my sword flew from my hands, spinning away under some slave's bed. I cursed. The body of a child was simply so different from my own, and I had yet to gain enough experience with the body's limitations. For better or for worse, my new body was also continually growing in strength, and due to that constant change, I was significantly misjudging the new parameters.

I jogged over to where my sword had been flung, while Gronch stood in the same spot, looking a combination of bored and pleased with himself. I knelt and yanked the sword out. The blade slid out with a shrill noise as it scraped against the stone floor. My breath somewhat calmed, and I stalked back toward Gronch, staggering my feet to enter into a proper fighting stance. "Again."

Gronch yawned. I lunged at him, steel blade aimed directly at his throat. The large half orc swatted my strike away almost lazily with the butt of his hammer, then rotated the weapon to crack against the side of my skull. I could always see the blows coming but could never react to them. I couldn't figure out why. Gronch wasn't faster than me; I'd established that early on. Yet, his blows came hard and straight, without wasted movements, and I always received the end of it. Or my blade did.

This time, my face did, and I flew back a handful of feet, rolling smoothly to my feet in an attempt to disregard the thumping pain that now screamed from where he'd hit me. To say I was surprised wouldn't do the shock I felt justice. I was never the greatest close combat fighter, since I had trained from an early age as a Lunari mage. That didn't mean I hadn't trained for decades in close combat. Even with the disadvantage of size and strength, this was proving ridiculous.

"How are you doing that," I attempted to ask politely. It came out as a snarl. Gronch didn't seem offended, though. Rather, he beamed with pride that pulled his lips into a smile so wide it showed the base of the tusks jutting upward from his lower jaw. It looked particularly menacing like he was baring fangs at me.

He didn't answer. "Come," he said, beckoning me forward with his hammer. "Land a hit on me, and I will teach you. Raise your sword again, mage child. I am having great fun!"

Now I snarled for real, unrestrained. The orc seemed to love it, savoring the bloodlust radiating off me in waves. With what felt like inhuman discipline, I kept myself from charging the orc warrior. That hadn't worked the first time or the fifth time, and I had a feeling it would continue to not work.

I spun the sword around my hand by its hilt and slowly crouched so that my weight leaned over my feet. One of my trainers from my Kingdom of Aedronir had been a Therianthrope. A beastman of the Tiger Nation. I knew only the slim basics of his kind as I'd never spent much time with the Tiger Nation nor any of the beastmen nations. The majority of what I knew was that usually they were abnormally strong and brutal. Fortunately, I'd witnessed his fighting style a few times, enough that I understood the basics.

Instead of charging, I kept a dozen or so feet of distance between us and began to prowl in a circle around the orc. He raised an eyebrow at me, moving lazily to keep his torso facing in my direction. We circled a few more times, and I could see he was getting annoyed. When he finally took a step toward me, my entire being surged forward with enough speed to turn me into a blur of motion. His eyes followed my movements for a split second and then became unable to keep up with the sheer speed with which I was moving.

His hammer raised as I stuck my left foot in the ground right in front of him and pivoted right to circle to his back, where I swung my sword diagonally up from my left knee. It should have struck him, just like all my other attacks.

It didn't.

Luckily, the tiger fighting style I'd switched to emphasized nimbleness and adaptability. When Gronch's hammer swung toward me at an angle that should have been impossible with a speed that had no business keeping up with my own, I ducked under the horizontal hammer, which then slammed through the air above me while I redirected my upward slash to cross against the back of Gronch's legs.

The river of rage contained inside of me absolutely roared at the incoming bloodshed. Swiftly as it'd come up, I shoved it down and halted my swing. I'd halted a bit late, so a thin bright red line blared from the back of Gronch's legs, tiny crimson drops sliding down to disappear beneath his bare feet.

Gronch snorted and gave out the friendliest laugh I'd ever heard come from an orc or even a half orc.

"Aye, ya got me there. That was risky of you," he said, ostensibly unbothered by the cut on his leg. If he'd even noticed. "That was *some* split-second drop. If ya mistimed it by even a second, my hammer woulda cracked your face."

I just shrugged, panting. "Life is risks."

"Ain't that the truth," he bellowed, walking over to clap me roughly on the back. "Ya know what, girlie? I changed mah mind about you. I kinda like ya now. You got some real spirit. Like an orc!"

I . . . I wasn't sure that was a compliment, even if Gronch had meant it as one. A full human that was like an orc? Wasn't that basically calling me some type of wild beast? Though I suppose I had used a fighting style based on the movements of a tiger beast so maybe that assessment wasn't far off.

Marisar clapped from where he sat on the floor, his large blue fingers slapping against each other with a wet sucking noise.

"I will never get used to this Selenian," Gronch grumbled, heaving his large hammer against his right shoulder. "In my nation, the Selenian are powerful water warriors. Many of my brethren have died by being pulled into the depths of their waters." He motioned toward Marisar as we approached, not bothering to lower his volume. "But of course, this Selenian refuses to even hold a weapon."

"I am a pacifist," Marisar responded, his calm demeanor not matching the drowning gurgle sound he made while talking. "We do not fight, even when we would die." Gronch scoffed, and I stayed silent. It wasn't my place to pass judgment on Marisar's beliefs. If he wanted to die in the dungeons, that would be his choice. I'd met many pacifists as Queen of Aedronir, and only the lucky ones had lived more than two decades. Even the most fortunate always died before four decades. Except for Droth, one of my advisers. He'd been the only pacifist I'd known to reach six decades of life.

The three of us sat side by side against the dungeon's stone wall in silence. I had never been someone who took in friends. I'd found the idea quite bizarre. A queen did not have friends. She couldn't. No weaknesses.

Yet here I was, sitting between two creatures without worrying one of them would kill me. Were these friends? Or were they allies? A sort-of "the enemy of my enemy is my friend" situation? I couldn't tell, and I didn't want to think about the answer.

"What's the first trial for tomorrow?" Marisar asked, his wet voice soft and somewhat awkward like he'd been pondering the same questions I had a moment earlier.

"A test of faith," I said. "That is all the King's message warned me of. A test of faith sounds . . . not particularly difficult."

Marisar shook his head in disagreement. "No, I do not believe that is correct, Lady Lilliana." Most of the slaves had taken to calling me that since the King's decree. "Faith is always the toughest of challenges. You will not know what is right or wrong, up or down. You will have to rely solely on your faith in the Goddess Dhalia, most likely." The Selenian looked at me with a worried expression, the blue skin around his eyes quivering slightly. "Do you truly have faith that Goddess Dhalia will protect you throughout these trials?"

"No," I answered honestly. "Gods and Goddesses do not help even their most devout believers." Never once had I ever seen any divine being lend aid to a survivor. If they existed, they did not care. "The King's note never mentioned it was a trial of faith in the Goddess of Life. Only a trial of faith." I looked at both Marisar and Gronch. "I, at least, have faith in myself."

Gronch, once more sinking into his usual arrogant and unpleasant demeanor as the fighting adrenaline left him, snorted. "Yer gonna die tomorrow, I just know it."

"Well, why don't you teach me that speed skill you kept bashing my head in with? Who knows, maybe it'll stop me from having my skull caved in tomorrow."

Gronch just grunted.

"You know I'm going to pick both of you for the trial, right?" I said, already standing up. "Shouldn't you help me survive to help yourself survive? Plus, you did promise."

He muttered something but followed me to his feet. Marisar stood as well. He stared at both of us and frowned as if making his mind up about something. "I will teach the two of you something as well. Tomorrow, we all survive."

Us and whatever other slaves I picked. The decree had not stated what number of slaves I could bring, so I planned to bring every slave in this dungeon to the trial. If they all gained access to Orpheus's power, that would only benefit me in my eventual escape.

"Wait a second." I turned and jogged toward the two warriors who had shared their energy gains with me during the massacre reenactment. Julius and Romeo, Marisar had told me. I wanted them in whatever training we were about to do. The two seemed trustworthy enough. If they weren't, well, I would handle that if it came to it.

I needed to start rebuilding my forces somewhere.

CHAPTER TWENTY

You Must Survive, My Queen

As it turned out, both Romeo and Julius were formidable fighters in their own right, even without the System's boost. To my utter and complete surprise, Julius went toe-to-toe with Gronch. It wasn't until Gronch pulled out his slow-but-fast movement that he finally scored a hit on the human fighter. Julius had an interesting appearance. His skin was extremely pale and dotted with many freckles that nearly buried his actual skin tone. He had orange hair of a brightness matched only by the lightness of his blue eyes. The man stood perhaps a head shorter than Gronch but was still tall for a human.

While Julius was well trained and light-skinned, Romeo was the exact opposite. Though Romeo had the same lithe musculature as Julius and was of similar height, the younger fighter's skin was as dark as midnight. His eyes were somehow even darker as if an abyss lurked within him. He wore his thick black hair short and without any signs of an unruly beard, unlike his older comrade who was quite fond of his growing orange beard. The two made an odd pairing.

Marisar had also tried to teach us some healing, though that hadn't really stuck with any of us. Healing magic, I discovered, was different from heart energy with a healing attribute in this world of Graedon. The tattoos did not block it since they drew on natural energy to increase the speed of one's recovery. It was interesting, but I'd never had any luck with magic or energy that involved creating or fixing. I promised Marisar if we lived that I would practice it every now and then. He had looked disappointed I hadn't shown more interest. I'm sure I hadn't looked particularly pleased that his big reveal was healing magic. I had to admit though that I was a bit curious about the difference this world held between magic and energy, and how that interacted with the slave tattoos.

As we watched Gronch take the upper hand against Julius in what was supposed to be a demonstration of the slow-but-fast movement, I tossed a glance over at Romeo. "How did you two meet?"

Romeo shrugged, not taking his eyes off the fighters. "We just happened to meet and got along."

That sounded like a lie. "Just happened to meet?" I pressed. "And you just decided to have some random slave you just met guard your back in an Arena?"

The young fighter shrugged again, still not looking at me. After a few seconds, I mirrored his shrug and let the issue go. No use forcing him to tell me something he didn't want to, especially when the chances of him dying during one of the trials were high. At that point, the boy's background wouldn't matter. That didn't stop my brain from trying to analyze the relationship between the two. Eventually, I settled on the ebony fighter being some sort of foreign highborn, maybe a fallen noble, and Julius was likely some sort of guard. A knight, perhaps. Of course, there was no way to be certain, but the way Julius seemed weirdly protective of Romeo and the way Romeo always acted with dignity about him suggested my guess was at the very least, close enough to the truth.

There was a thud and Julius collapsed, momentarily stunned as the hilt of Gronch's hammer slammed into his temple. I winced, remembering what that felt like.

"Lady Lilliana," Marisar said from my right, the three of us sitting against the dungeon's wall with myself in the center. "This may be inappropriate to ask, but if we are going to fight for you, I would like some answers to my questions. How did a noble like yourself, especially one of the Lysorian Kingdom, get captured by slavers? Were you kidnapped?"

"Who cares," Gronch grumbled with a self-satisfied smirk on his face as Romeo sprang to his feet and dashed over to Julius who still sat on the ground, massaging the side of his head. "Our princess of slaves can explain herself if we all survive. First, she needs to learn the slow-but-fast movement."

"I care," Marisar insisted, keeping his eyes locked on me. "How can any kingdom require such a small child to fight, especially one of noble birth?" He shook his head and small droplets of water flung from his face. "It simply does not make sense."

I placed my hand on Marisar's shoulder and climbed to my feet. "I may be of noble birth, but it was not Baroness Silverwater who gave birth to me. Though," I let a smile play across my lips for a moment, "I doubt the Baroness expected me to end up here."

She probably thought I'd died in the belly of the Beast King. I kept that part to myself. Both Marisar and Gronch were proving to be useful allies, but that didn't mean I wanted them to know I'd encountered a Beast King and a Progenitor. That might lead to questions I wasn't ready to answer.

Turning to Gronch, I rolled my shoulders and staggered my feet into my regular fighting stance. "Okay, let me try this again."

'You must only appear to move slowly,' Gronch had explained to us earlier, for the tenth time, after we'd all failed to grasp even the most basic form of the slow-but-fast movement. 'All beings leave a small path of heart energy when they move. You must spot the remnant energy, and you must allow your movement to be pulled by it. Do not fight the flow, ride it.'

The problem was none of us knew what in the four hells he was talking about. Not a single trainer I had ever worked with mentioned anything about remnant energies that shadowed physical movements. We all continued to try throughout the day, even as the white balls of energy began to flicker, the signal that it was time to return to the personal areas.

I growled when the balls of light flickered again, and I still hadn't done the movement even once. "This does not make any sense," I raged while repeating the forms Gronch had shown us. "There isn't any remnant energy—the tattoos sealed it all!"

Gronch shook his head from his personal area. "Remnant energy ain't sealed, girl. It can't be. It ain't part of us but of the world."

"That doesn't make any sense either!" My frustration was clearly building. I should have spent the past two days training my heart energy and newly formed Core. I was a mage, wielder of the world's energies. What was I doing trying to learn close combat techniques within a day?

The lights blinked, longer this time. I had around ten minutes left. Fuck.

A lanky man approached me from the dimmed distance, his torn clothes and deadpan gray eyes sent the familiar goosebumps up the back of my neck. When I'd first resurrected him, the slave had looked fine. Healthy, even. Normal.

As the days progressed, however, he'd gotten progressively worse. His skin had gone gray, withered, and wrinkled. The fight and determination in his eyes had slowly faded into a blank stare. Whenever he spoke, we were greeted by an inhuman rasp that was like grating steel.

It was incredibly disturbing. Raising the undead never did that. The undead always rose as living skeletons of whatever the creature had once been. Occasionally, if the undead were powerful enough, they would retain some of their former physical features.

Never had I managed to raise anything with individuality and sentience. Then, to watch it slowly dissipate from the . . . man . . . was particularly horrible. The thought of simply killing it had occurred to me. In the end, I let it keep living, or whatever state it was in. I needed to learn more about my new abilities, even if it was at the cost of this man's suffering beyond death.

"Let me help, my queen. You must survive the trials tomorrow," came the gravelly voice of the resurrected, coming to kneel at my feet, his eyes cast down to the floor. "You must open your mind to the energies around you, not strangle it."

I wanted to shout at it that its words didn't make a lick of sense either. I didn't get the chance. The resurrected being rose to its feet in a single swift motion and then placed his thumb on my forehead, his thin, elongated fingers curling suddenly around my head.

An unfamiliar power washed over me. It wasn't an uncomfortable energy. Rather, it felt right. Like it was a power that belonged to me but wasn't my own.

"Accept my energy, my queen," the resurrected said, his body becoming increasingly gaunt as power flooded me. "You must survive, my queen. This should open your senses using my knowledge." The dying being looked up at the ceiling and whispered something into the nether, then it simply folded like it had no bones to hold it up as the final strand of his energy swam into my Core.

"What in the Gods' names?" Marisar gurgled. I heard his wet, shoeless feet slapping against the stone ground approaching me. I didn't look, my eyes wide as a rainbow of colors silhouetted the form of the fallen man from before he had fallen. Then the colors slowly fell, mimicking the resurrected's fall.

"Holy hells," I cursed in amazement, finally turning to Marisar who was similarly followed by a delayed silhouette of colors. "Is this remnant energies?" Marisar sank to a squat next to the fallen resurrected. I didn't bother. The moment the final bit of energy had finished sinking into my Core, something had snapped inside of me, and I'd known the man I'd resurrected had returned to the beyond. When I looked at him now, the reddish-white soul flame I'd seen hovering over him and Gideon earlier was nowhere to be seen. Snuffed out of existence.

I didn't know how I knew that. I just knew.

The white balls of light overhead blinked once again. This time, they did not flicker back on.

"What do we do with the body?" Marisar whispered. Even though I knew he was only a few feet to my right, I couldn't see him and the disembodied sound of someone talking from out in the Nothingness was disconcerting.

"We have to leave it," I said, trying to remember which direction my personal area had been in. "There's not much we can do about it anyway but to leave it."

"Did you . . . kill him?" Marisar asked in an even smaller whisper.

I shook my head. Then, realizing he couldn't see me, I said, "No, I didn't do anything. You heard him—he gave me his energy. I think he gave me all of it until he collapsed."

"I have never seen someone give away all their energy like that. I did not believe that was possible." I could feel the Selenian on the verge of tears. I patted his shoulder. Or was it his head? The lack of light made it hard to tell. "Let's figure out where our beds are before someone tries to kill us." He didn't say anything, but I could tell by the sound of wet skin slapping stone that he was up and moving.

"Over here, ya idiots," Gronch barked, his thick foreign accent coming up even stronger than usual when he attempted to say the word "idiots." "Follow my voice. And if anyone's planning on attacking because you can hear my voice, I will rip your fucking head off your Gods-damned shoulders." Silence. Then Gronch spoke again, and I made my way toward it, followed by Marisar's constant wet slapping.

I knew Marisar was thinking about the loss of life before his eyes. I shook my head, my disagreement covered by the dark. Life was not fair or kind. Some would die, and some would live. In this current place, most of us would die, and if we stopped to lament each death, we would all die.

And now we were one man short for the trials.

CHAPTER TWENTY-ONE

The Red Cardinal and the Mask Without Senses

Laaaaaaadies, gentlemen, and everything in between—I'm looking at you, ya purple slime," Jarold the Caster shouted as a row of purple glob creatures bobbed up and down with what I could only guess to be laughter. "We have a very special treat for everyone today. And we have very special guests as well." He quieted his voice in mock seriousness. "The royal family is here today with one of only three Church of Light Cardinals. They are here to see . . . WHO?"

"The Saintess!" The shout went up around the Arena in an awkward scattering accompanied by some booing and the occasional heathen calls. Personally, I figured I was probably closer to a heathen than a Saintess for the Church of Light. It was the irony that put a small smile on my face as beams of gold light fell upon two overhangs at the opposite ends of the Arena's upper seating area. The show of theatrics was too rich for my taste.

"Today," Jarold continued, "we see whether the young lady of the Silverwater barony, Lady Lilliana Silverwater, is a true Saintess of Light, blessed by the Goddess Dhalia. Whether she has the faith necessary to be a saintess. The first saintess trial in what seems like forever, here! In our city of Sealrite!"

The crowd roared its approval. Jarold's words echoed around the Arena. I still hadn't managed to figure out where he actually was. Thousands, if not tens of thousands of people filled the stadium seats and bellowed their bets and hopes and predictions to anyone within earshot. I'd originally wondered whether Jarold cast from one of the two overhanging seating sections, but one was filled by the royal family and the other by some sort of religious group. Unless Jarold was one of those, which I truly doubted, the caster was hiding somewhere else.

"Before we start, one of our special guests of honor has something to say. Then, he'll kick off the trial and I'll be back!" Jarold said. Then there was a soft click and even the static of his volume enhancement skill died away. No one spoke other than the occasional hushed whisper, as everyone waited for the guest to speak. Or at least identify himself.

I cast a questioning look toward Marisar. He just shrugged.

"Can't we just get on with the fight," Gronch growled, slipping on a pair of gauntlets and smashing his fists together. The gauntlets the half orc had taken from his last death battle in the Arena looked fairly low quality and a few sizes too small for his massive hands. Still, the half orc, by all appearances, quite liked them. The sound of one metal gauntlet smacking into the other one, which was typically drowned by surrounding sounds, now bounced off the silent Arena walls with a resounding *crack*. "Oops."

I groaned, and Marisar shook his head in defeat.

"Good morning," said a woman's voice over the sound enhancement, wherever that was. There was a gentle lilt to her voice that seemed to float elegantly across the Arena's great distance, containing an undertone of subtly fake sweetness. It was a tone common in aristocratic families back in Ordite. While the words would sound nice, each would be carefully chosen, delivered with such a delicate touch that the smooth voice often belied the calculating mind behind it. Without being of nobility, I wasn't sure if the others sensed or even heard the small, almost imperceptible hint of malice dripping from those two simple words, like shadows squirming just out of sight.

The woman continued, her words hypnotic and seductive, drawing the eyes of all the Arena to the sky where her voice seemed to descend from, "I am Mirabelle of the Red Cardinal, serving at the behest of Goddess Dhalia and her servant, Pope Betrant." No one cheered or applauded, though some gawked. I had no idea what was so impressive, but I kept that to myself. "It is upon this day during the 205th year since our great kingdom's birth that I am pleased to announce the nineteenth trial for a Saintess of Dhalia, Goddess of Life and Light. It has been close to five decades since the previous challenge where the saintess candidate Delarose met her untimely fate. She had not been blessed by the Goddess as I and my sisters were. I pray Lady Silverwater has truly been blessed lest her soul feel the brunt of the Goddess's anger."

As the queen of a nation who believed wholeheartedly that the God of War, Ashwash, was the most powerful and righteous God, I was absolutely certain this Goddess of Life would not grant me any blessing. Not that I had ever been granted any type of blessing, nor had I wanted one. Even with the entire nation praying to Ashwash, I never did. Whatever I would have prayed for, I instead fought for.

"Well, jeez," Julius said, the broadsword he'd picked out before entering the Arena stuck into the sand at his feet. He moved a strand of chin-length orange hair out of his eyes, nearly tucking it behind an ear before stopping and simply dropping it. "What a pep talk. Are all religious leaders in Cael like this?" His eyes turned toward me, of course, as the only noble in our group who might have any knowledge of religious leaders.

I didn't respond, frowning in consideration of what I'd learned about religion so far. The orange-haired man laughed, clearly not having expected a response and finding it funny that I'd given it serious thought.

"Focus, Julius," Romeo said, having long since palmed both his daggers and was casting furtive glances to the three Arena doors surrounding our group of five, which had been herded into the middle of the Arena. I had asked for all the slaves to be included. The response I'd gotten from the slaver, the Dragonborne, Dralos, had been equitable to being spit in the face. Actually, he had spit in my face. There hadn't been an opportunity to kill him yet, but for that offense, there would be. Soon. Part of me had hoped with the Lunari aspect of my energy merging into whatever a Soul Weaver was, that the Dragonborne hate Dralos instinctually harbored would have waned at the very least.

But no. The forming of the Core had only exponentially increased the hate and fear.

"The test today will be one of faith," Mirabelle of the Red Cardinal said, a knife through the silence unlike our small voices. "As faith should be, the test is simple. Lady Silverwater has been allowed to recruit as many followers of the faith as her persuasion granted." Gronch snorted at the lie. "The lady will be required to wear a Mask Without Senses for the entirety of this trial. The mask will block her sight and her hearing. Heathen creatures will be released into the Arena for the saintess candidate to slay in the name of the Goddess. If she succeeds, it means the Goddess has given her the gift of grace and mercy. If she does not succeed, she will be returned to the Goddess's embrace and the cycle of life." Without any further fanfare,

Mirabelle announced the start of the trial. "Place the mask upon young Lady Silverwater and release the beasts."

"That's it?" I asked, louder than I had intended. In fact, I hadn't intended to say that out loud at all. The Arena, static without sound as it listened to Mirabelle's announcement, stirred at my accidental words.

"What do you mean 'that's it?'" Romeo asked, a questioning look sketched in his raven eyes. "You must fight blind and deaf against beasts of Heathens. You will die in seconds, even with our help."

I snorted at the lack of, ironically, faith. "You have a surprising lack of faith, young warrior," I said, beginning to stretch my legs as an Arena official wearing a too-long blue cloak with the image of an Arena came stumbling over to me with a gold-red mask in his hands. The mask appeared to be normal, aside from the remnants of strong heart energy I could see flowing from it whenever the guard moved. And whisps of something else that I was beginning to recognize as strands of magic.

"Young . . . young warrior?" Romeo spluttered and I laughed. The boy's surprise was as evident as it was understandable. It was hard to remember that this body was only twelve, almost thirteen. Especially now that my Core was formed, and Lilliana's body was undergoing physical changes every day in preparation for the Reformation it would undergo when I reached a Silver-level Core.

And while I didn't trust this System or the Progenitors, the System was undeniably beneficial in furthering my strength at a quicker speed than otherwise. That being said, nothing was free. Life was not fair, and it was not kind. Quick power would always come with a cost, even if I didn't yet know what that would be.

The Mask Without Senses was placed before my eyes where it sat heavily on the bridge of my nose. A strap wrapped around the back of my head from one side of the mask to the other and, with a word from the Arena official in a language I did not understand, the strap tightened until it was just slightly too tight. A magic- or energy-based lock, I deduced.

The instant the straps finished tightening my heart jumped and the world disappeared. It wasn't so much that I was thrown into a darkness— that happened every night. The world was gone. Color was gone. I wasn't surrounded by black. I was surrounded by nothing. A void.

I could feel myself stumble as sound also winked from existence around me and I was pitched into a soundless, sightless nothingness. Large hands caught me and helped balance my unsteady posture, discombobulated as I was.

The laugh that escaped from my lips, though I couldn't hear it, I knew to be cold and, yet, full of mirth. I had existed and lived in a much greater Nothingness for an endless period of time. They thought a momentary glimpse of such Nothingness would bring hardship to me? Perhaps once, but no longer.

Although I was temporarily without sight, hearing, or balance, as the deafness would also void my vestibular sense, I could still rely on the other senses and, despite what was taught by most lower academies in my Kingdom of Aedronir, I knew from higher learnings that there were actually seven senses rather than five. Most schools of thought left out vestibular and pro-prioception, choosing to combine them with the other five.

I was left with taste, smell, touch, and proprioception. While the former, taste, was clearly useless in this situation, the other three would keep me alive.

The floor rumbled under my feet in one long tremor. The gates were releasing the beasts. The rumbles originated from three different directions, so probably at least three 'heathen' creatures, whatever those were.

A thick scent of blood filled the air like a thick sludge making it hard to breathe. I slowed my breathing and made sure to keep it steady despite the smog in the air.

I didn't move, groping around me. I felt the sand below my feet thump again, this time in a patterned rhythm. Almost like a horse, but not quite. The legs were longer. Body heavier. Either it had more legs than a horse or it was much faster.

The thumping became heavier. While it had started out faint, the sand now jumped with each step. It was getting closer. Then I smelled it, the distinct, putrid smell of an undead.

No, that wasn't exactly it, I realized belatedly. It had an undead smell to it, but there was something more. Three other somethings. A Chimera?

I tightened an unsteady hand around the hilt of my single, worthless blade and readied myself for the charge. The charge never came and the thumping stopped.

Then a large *thud* somewhere next to where I'd tracked the creature. A bunch of smaller pounding was coming from that location. Someone had intercepted the raging beast. Gronch, probably. Or Romeo. I couldn't imag-ine Marisar being able to or Julius bothering to.

I was about to head toward the area to join the fray when something pierced my left shoulder and I could feel something warm and sticky tracing down my arm. As I screamed with pain, I felt a soft fluttering of air by my ear before quickly fading.

"Shit," I swore. Or I *think* that's what I swore. "Something's flying!" Again, not entirely sure that what I wanted to say came out like it should have due to my current deafness. I tried anyway.

I turned to face the direction the feeling of fluttering wind had disappeared in but didn't feel anything more. No vibrations in the air or trembling of the ground. That was only two of the three. Where was the third? Then, in front of my vision, inside the Nothingness, I heard a vile laugh. A cold, merciless sound that reverberated in my ears like nails to a chalkboard.

"Eeeet has beeeen soooo looong seeeeence I have had huuuuman flesh," the telepathic voice whispered in my mind. *"Fiiiinally, another saaaaintess to devooooour."*

What in Ashwash's name is that? I thought to myself. Privately.

Turned out thoughts weren't so private, and the monster chuckled, a grating steel sound sending a shiver through me.

"Yooour peeopple, the huuuumans caaaall mmeee a Miiindscriiibe. I aaaam Vullor. Aaaand you arreee myyyy preeeeeey."

CHAPTER TWENTY-TWO

The Mindscribe

Okay. Okay. I had this. One Chimera, one winged creature, and some sort of telepath called a Mindscribe. The flying creature would be the most difficult to deal with, so I would have to rely on my party to deal with it. Even if the most they did was hold it off, that should work.

The Chimera was going to be slightly easier. It made a lot of noise and smelled like death and sewage making it easy to track regardless of where it moved. The Chimera also needed to be held off by my party. Luckily for me, one of them had already engaged it.

I needed to deal with Mindscribe first. It had somehow invaded my thoughts, giving it the power to speak directly into my mind and bypass the magically induced deafness. Telepaths were not new to me, though even in my old world, the power was rather rare. Luckily, a telepath's strength was determined by the weakness of its prey's mind, and it had chosen me as its target. That would be its first and last mistake.

There was a short and painful stabbing in my head. I could feel myself falling to the ground right before I opened my eyes to an odd space. The space was not bright, nor was it dark, though there was no source of light. No furniture adorned the area and there were no actual walls or doors. Below my feet, an unexpected and unknown path seemed to stretch out infinitely into the far distance. The path was a soft, almost translucent white. Other than the maybe ten-foot-wide expanse that looked like a path, I was surrounded by the Nothingness.

And I could feel myself as if I had been somehow transported away in my physical body. That was, of course, not true. This was my Mindspace.

Telepaths, who had weak combat prowess, relied solely on invading the Mindspace of their prey to achieve victory. Although I had never experienced an invasion into my Mindspace, stories and warnings of Mindspace battles were always prominent in popular songs and stories brandished by bards in taverns and celebrations.

Once the continent war had started in Ordite, telepathic assassinations had become commonplace at unexpected speeds. Yet none had ever tried to kill me in a forced Mindscape.

"*Thiiiis is aaaan iiiiinnntereeesting miiiiiind,*" hissed the Mindscribe, a huge monstrosity taking corporeal form someway down the white road of my mind. "*Whheeeere doessss thiiis paaath leaaad tooooo, I wondeerrr?*"

"I'm sure I will find out one day," I said casually, not a hint of fear in Lilliana's small voice. "But you won't."

The cold, grating metallic sound erupted from the forming creature in a pitch so high I had to restrain myself from slamming my hands to my ears. "*Ohhhh, IIIII don't knoow about thaaaat.*"

As the creature formed, I tried not to cringe back in disgust. It was absolutely hideous. Each of its eight legs was thicker than my body and bristled with a thin layer of coarse brown hair. Its abdomen was a bulbous mass, housing the creature's organs and likely a sac of deadly venom. Its eyes, however, were where its terrifying figure became hideous. Hundreds of eyes dotted the creature's ball-like head looking in every direction. Each eye seemed to blink with a unique tempo, creating a terrifying wave of motion. Facing me were the arachnid's four largest eyes, all focused on me and unblinking. From its mandibles swung strands of something white and gleaming.

"You are not a Mindscribe," I muttered, recognizing the species. The arachnid creature existed, to some extent, on Ordite I realized with not a small amount of surprise. While the ones from my world were more humanoid than the full beast before me, I recognized its horrible visage. Its revulsive eyes. "All I see before me is some type of deformed Cave Crawler."

"*I haaaave gone by maaany names. Huuuumaaaans raaarely livvvve to naaaaaame meeee.*" The moment the creature was fully formed, it lifted one of its heavy legs and slammed it forward. The white path trembled, and I could see it had cracked under the arachnid force.

"You probably shouldn't do that," I said, grinning. "The more you damage the girl's Mindspace, the stronger the presence of my own will be."

The creature didn't stop pounding its legs into the path, one at a time. I was pretty sure the creature, Vullor, could have moved more than a single leg at once. It was taking its time. I just watched as it attempted to destroy the remnants of Lilliana's Mindspace. Based on what I knew, the girl's soul was gone. She had died, leaving the vessel open for my own.

This Mindspace, its emptiness, and its mixture with the Nothingness was likely a result of the soul swap. A remnant.

"I'm not sure you want to experience what happens after the path is destroyed." In fact, I knew it wouldn't. There was a reason no one had ever attempted to invade my Mindspace.

The arachnoid spat something at me, silver liquid glimmered as it erupted from Vullor's mandibles. The stringy liquid latched to my arm, the one still in pain from the winged monster's earlier stab and began to smoke right before a searing pain erupted and pain flashed. Acid.

I put a hand to the wound and tore into the burning skin, using energy to cut off the dying flesh. The pain was sharp but quick as the heated energy cauterized the wound. The putrid smell of burnt flesh wafted over the area. I winced at the removal, still keeping my eyes on the creature. Vullor, on the other hand, chittered at my obvious pain and spit a few more globs in my direction. I raised an energy shield in response and the spray simply slipped off the invisible wall to the ground.

It chittered again, legs still stomping and continuing to send spikes of energy down into the path's foundation. A large crack finally spread from where Vullor's eight legs plunged into the ground and the crack started to move, running through the center of the illusionary landscape which melted away as the cracks grew, revealing it to be not a path but a bridge.

It continued to break away, the arachnid's shrill laugh filling the space once more while its eyes turned to stare at me. To watch me fall into the expected madness and insanity. Each gleamed with pleasure for its incoming kill.

But there was no prey in front of it.

I stared back, fully in control and smiling as we dropped through the bridge into the Nothingness below.

Before either of us had time to comprehend the feeling of falling into Nothingness, everything around us shifted. The Nothingness turned into a raging fire. The infinite path morphed into dirt stained with a deep crimson. A river rushed through the bloodied dirt, its natural clear color long since dyed by endless blood pouring into its stream from the eternal continental war that raged throughout the land. Two suns hung at their apex and rained down heat in dry waves while a single crescent moon held static between them. My suns. My moon.

"What . . . whaaaat is thiisss?" Vullor shouted, its triumphant expression dashed as all its eyes spun around, taking in the Mindscape. *"Hoowww can youuu have two Mindscapes?"* Then one of its eyes landed on me. The creature's entire body froze. Its four eyes centered on me while the others looked away as if refusing to look in my direction.

I knew what the creature was looking at. It saw me. Not Lilliana. Me. My Mindscape would reflect my true self, not Lilliana.

In the arachnid's large eyes I saw the woman, the queen, I had once been in Ordite. I now stood well over six feet tall, every inch of my body covered in thick, hardened muscle and flesh scarred from long periods of war. My eyes were a deep, bright red that stared back at me with a horrible cruelness and ferocity. A single scar etched my face, tracing its way vertically through my right eye. I remembered that scar. Remembered the King who had put it there.

Remembered him gurgling blood at my feet.

And there, centered on my forehead, was the marking of a Lunari. A crescent moon colored with a deep yellow. A black line crossed through the marking, identifying me as a Lunari who had turned her back to the moon.

I grunted as the memories came flooding back to me, shoving them away and turning to the arachnid who still stared at me. I knew it wasn't fully the change in my appearance that kept it frozen.

My Mindscape. My world. If the Cave Crawler could not overpower my mind and take control of the Mindscape, it was *my* prey.

A large gray sword materialized in my hand, its blade sharp enough to cut the air around it. I swung it down and it whistled as air parted to make way for its destructive power.

"Ah, welcome to my Mindscape, Cave Crawler," I snarled. The feeling of once again being in my own body, even if as an illusion, was immeasurably satisfying. I raised my empty left hand and curled it into a fist, my old muscles spreading and then tightening with disuse.

When I spoke, Lilliana's little voice was gone, replaced by my true voice, rich and commanding. There was a regal resonance to it, a timber that demanded respect and attention. Even the wind stilled when I spoke, power radiating off me like an inferno.

I began to stalk the stilled creature who was releasing screams of panic. I could see tendrils of energy pulsing around it while its muscles pulled, straining for release from my Mindscape's authority.

With each step I took, the bloodlust around me curled and reached out as if it had been sleeping since my Transference into Graedon and it was finally getting to release itself.

"*Whaaa . . . Whoooo,*" Vullor screeched, its large mandrils chittering in fear.

"I am Lilith," I roared. The entire Mindscape, its very ground and air, shook and pulsed with the power of my Will. "Ruler of all Lunari. Bane of the Empire." I raised my sword, fueled with a storm of pride and rage. "Queen of Aedronir!" The large blade flashed down and cut the shrieking creature in two with a single wet *schlick*. Even when the two halves split, crashing to the ground, I refused to release the Mindscape. I watched the enormous spider's flesh melt away, eaten by the acidic venom spilling over the body.

The first time I'd ever killed a monster, I'd felt so much guilt. I'd thought life itself, whatever its form, was something beyond my ability to understand or value. That had been beaten out of me within months as the King had forced me and the other queen candidates through the Ma'johong desert.

Our lives were valuable. *My* life was valuable. The life of this monster was an obstacle in my path and its value amounted to how much its death would further the progress I made toward my goals.

My judgment was passed on the creature's worth at that moment, not a single string of emotion pulled by slaying the monster. The Cave Crawler was nothing but an obstacle. Perhaps even one placed on my path by the Gods—if they truly existed.

I turned my eyes to the sky, the sky of my world. I knew it was just the illusion my mind had chosen, but I didn't care.

"I will slay all who stand in my path, and I ***will*** return to what is mine," I screamed, my words echoing into the depths of Ordite's endless sky.

CHAPTER TWENTY-THREE

Reenactment of the Three Fates

The moment I was ejected from the Mindspace, I jerked back into my unfortunate reality of being both blind and deaf. Something hard jutted into my jaw and I tasted metal on my tongue, probably blood.

I fought against the rising sense of discombobulation, locking it away and attempting to rely on my sense of proprioception to rise to my feet. I might not be able to see my body or my surroundings, but I knew where my feet were in relation to my other body parts, and, using that sense of under-standing, I staggered back to a standing position.

I poured large swaths of heart energy into my remaining senses of feeling, smell, and proprioception. The scent of blood clung in every direction, adding to my confusion about what had happened during my fight with the Mindscribe.

But I felt something. A ripple in the calm, a small yet quick wave of wind cascading over me. Then it stopped. Then it started.

When I felt the fluttering wind of the second beast slam against me with increasing pressure, my fingers curled reflexively as if gripping a blade in preparation to wield it. Instead, my hand wrapped around the air. No hilt. I must have dropped it at some point while I'd been unconscious in the Mindspace.

My heart thrummed with anticipation of battle while my mind raced through all the different scenarios and possible angles the second beast could be approaching. It really depended on whether, assuming it had wings, the wings blew air in front of the creature or to the side. Or behind it. Judging from the way the vibrations in the air increased with the waves of wind pressure, it was likely pushing air in front, most likely with a slightly downward angle.

Like a dragon lifting off. I tried not to think about the possibility of the winged monster being a small dragon. Or a wyvern of some sort.

There was a sudden shift in the wind pressure as it completely vanished. My shoulders started to relax when I realized the wind pressure was gone, but the vibrations were increasing. I was being charged.

Without thinking, I threw myself to the side and felt something rough and scaled brush past me with another whoosh of wind. This time the pressure had enough force to propel me off my feet and tumbling in some unknown direction. The ground trembled as whatever the creature was blew past me and into the ground for what I guessed to be a really rough landing.

Then there were a few more light tremors from that direction and the vibrations also ceased.

With a *pop*, the latch behind my head keeping the Mask of No Sense firmly around me was undone, the magical item falling softly like a leaf from the bridge of my nose to rest by my foot. If I thought the silence and darkness of the mask had caused me to be discombobulated, that thought was out the door compared to the sheer disorientation that threatened to swallow me whole once my senses were reintroduced.

I'd never been tortured before, but I assumed it would have been a similar feeling.

I clasped my hands tightly over my ears and shut my eyes as tight as I could, hoping to block out at least a little of the stimulation. It didn't help at all. The roar of the crowd was thunderous, and the sun was blinding to the point tears of pain threatened from the corners of my eyes that I knew would spill if I so much as attempted to open them.

Something heavy patted against my back. I couldn't see what it was, but I recognized the voice. "Damn 'em all to the four hells," Gronch said, and I could picture spittle flying around his sharp tusks as he complained in anger. "Crazy bastards."

"Did . . . did we win?" Romeo asked and I could hear the youth in his voice now, brought to the surface by their obviously hard-won battle.

"Define 'win,'" Gronch muttered. Even despite what felt like complete disorientation to me and the heaviness in Romeo's voice, I would have figured a war orc like Gronch, even a halfling like he was, would have found great joy in the victory. But the half orc's attitude was surprisingly muted.

After a while, though my hands remained firmly against the flat of my ears, my eyes began to readjust to the light. Enough that I could squint at my surroundings. When I managed to find Gronch, he'd moved quite a bit away from me, toward a blue creature collapsed next to the body of a human-size creature with giant, bat-like wings. I couldn't see the details of the beast, but my eyes widened at the sight of the fallen Selenian. The light burned my vision, and I quickly shut them.

When I was able to squint, I once again found Marisar and made my way over to him. As I approached, I saw what had injured him. At the end of a large, sinuous tail was a black barbed stinger jutting through his stomach. All sorts of gore lay splattered around, ripped from where the stinger protruded. Black veins spread from the protrusion, the dark lines wiggling with the constant movement of the venom within.

Gronch's large hand again found my shoulder as his voice came out, gruff and just barely holding back either anger or agony. Maybe both. "The cursed Selenian tackled the Drakoryx when you dodged it," he said loud enough to just barely be heard over the still cheering audience. "Its tail would have pierced you. Like it did him. He moved to intercept like he was possessed or something. I didn't think he had it in him."

I took a squat next to the body of Marisar, examining the Selenian with a deep frown. Death of comrades was not new to me. I might even go so far as to say I was starting to expect it. But no one ever truly became numb to the death of allies. Despite that, I had no tears left to shed. All my tears of sadness had long since been spent.

"How was this beast, what did you call it, a Drakoryx? How was it killed?" I asked, tracing the tail back to the winged beast. My voice was steadier than I'd expected. Steadier than Gronch had expected, given the curious glance he shot my way. I just felt empty. Cold and empty in the face of the inevitable.

The Drakoryx was something of a monstrosity. Its large, dead eyes stared up at me from where it lay. I couldn't help but feel an odd sense of foreboding as I gazed into the unseeing slit pupils that, even in death, radiated a bright amber. Its body was covered in tough, overlapping midnight-blue scales now splattered with its silver blood and Marisar's blue fluids. Its head was sleek and angular, almost feline if it wasn't so easy to tell its reptilian ancestry. Protruding from the back of its skull were a set of elongated, spiraling horns giving off a sense of being a nightmare. Its mouth hung open, razor-sharp teeth outlined the long black tongue that lolled slightly out the side.

Most disturbing, however, were the wings. They spanned nearly twelve feet and were covered in horrible iridescent scales that seemed to sing with blood, death, and other horrors. Attached to each wing's edge were claws that gleamed with the Drakoryx's casual deep blue coloring.

A single dark blue-gray ball hovered above the corpse of the Drakoryx. Next to it was the Chimera, a terrible combination of a griffin's head, a lion's body, and the end of a snake all mashed into a single entity. Large hammer dents concaved its entire left side, pulverizing the beast. Gronch's work was vicious.

"The healer cast some sort of magic," Julius said, pulling up to Marisar's other side with a downcast expression. "It kept him and the Drakoryx in a stasis so we could attack it while it was pinned in place."

Romeo nodded solemnly. "Only reason we won."

The four of us stared down at the still-bleeding body of our comrade, of our healer. Marisar lay there, empty and without even the smallest of lights.

"Wait, that's weird," I muttered, focusing my energy on my vision while I stared hard at the Selenian.

"Do not bring 'im back," Gronch warned, his usual gruff but somewhat good-natured tone completely gone. "He died a warrior's death. Do not taint his worthy death."

"I don't see his soul." No matter how much I focused or where I looked, I couldn't see his soul. And if I couldn't see his soul, then—

"In the very first year of our kingdom, of the old world, Gideon's trusted healer was struck by his adversary and was near death!" Jarold's voice suddenly boomed through the Arena and the audience's cheer froze. "The voice of the Gods called down to the hero Gideon and told him he had only two options to save his healer. If at least one of the options was satisfied, the Gods would save the healer who was on the brink of death. The first option was to prove his loyalty to the Gods by stabbing a sword through his own heart and giving his life for his ally. Or, second, to test his strength and win against the might of the divine." The announcer paused for an obvious dramatic effect. I thought it was rather corny, but the audience seemed to love it. "Which choice will the Gideon of today choose?"

I didn't answer right away, though I knew which I would pick. It was unlikely the slavers who'd planned the show would allow me to pick neither and simply let Marisar die. And if I was being honest with myself, I didn't want to let him die. Each of the warriors had grown on me and they would be extremely helpful in my eventual escape. Should the need to force them to remain in the world of the living occur, I would do what was needed to increase my chances of victory and survival.

Now, however, was not the time.

"I choose to challenge the Gods," I said, not quite answering the question posed but providing one close enough that Jarold did not seem to have an issue with it.

"So be it! Let today's Gideon, our saintess candidate, test her mettle against the Gods!" Jarold screamed as armed soldiers exited from both ends of the Arena, just as they had previously when I'd killed the King's son-in-law, flooding into the combat zone. Each fighter, other than myself, was swiftly surrounded by half a dozen guards and was roughly forced back through the passageway we'd entered from. Within a moment, I was alone, surrounded only by the corpses of the dead beasts and the Selenian. "Today, our Gideon is challenged by the three Fates: Lyrielle, Thaloria, and Eirindel. All are the great enemies of our Goddess of Light and Life, Dhalia. As our champion of the Light and Life, Gideon must defeat all three and take back the soul of her comrade." The announcement was followed by a round of cheering. I was becoming so incredibly sick of that sound.

A large shadow fell over me, and I glanced up at the sky where I saw a great beast flying no more than a few hundred feet above me. It looked almost exactly the same as the Drakoryx we had slain, but larger. Much larger. Sweat swam down my back as I faced the underbelly of what looked to me like some type of dragon or wyvern.

I hoped to the Gods that this world did not have true dragons. At my current level, I would be easily squashed by one.

Fortunately, the monster did not descend. Three smaller shadows leaped from its back and dropped into the Arena with three synchronized thuds. They each landed on a different side of me, so I was stuck in the middle of the trio.

The figure directly in front of me raised her hands and waved at the crowd. She towered over me, clad in shining silver armor that gleamed with an otherworldly light the instant the beast overhead moved, and the sun resumed its heated glare. Her helmet, adorned with small, angelic wings, framed her blue eyes that seemed to dance where her armor gleamed. Shoulder-length blond hair extended out from under the helmet, signaling to me that either the woman was not as trained as she pretended to be or was not taking this seriously. A large golden hammer rested on her shoulder, its head pointed instead of flat, making it look more like a pickaxe than a hammer.

"Playing the First Fate, Lyrielle," Jarold continued, "is Brynhildr, our very own Shieldmaiden of Caelos!" A bright light descended on Brynhildr. "Next, we have Eir, our ferocious and deadly Valkyrie." A second light descended around the woman to my left, who wore black armor over what looked to be a flowing green and white robe. However, where Brynhildr's armor had no decorations, Eir's was covered with different images I didn't have time to bother deciphering. "And last, but not least, we have Skuld, the Seer of Caelos!" A third light illuminated the woman to my right.

The third woman worried me more than the other two. I'd thought she was clad in black armor like Eir, but she wasn't. Rather, the woman was clad in heavy shadows. Even under the authority of the sun overhead, it was as if the woman somehow melded into her own shadow, which I was struggling to comprehend. A book, marked with hundreds of runes, floated around Skuld, its pages flipping randomly as if they were being blown by a nonexistent wind.

CHAPTER TWENTY-FOUR

Never Lose Your Head in Battle

Brynhildr's icy blue eyes fell on me in all my ragged glory. Her eyebrows shot up as her wide grin flipped into an equally large frown. After dealing with the uncaring nature of the Mindscribe and the apathetic audience, the clear empathy plastered on the Shieldmaiden's face caught me off guard.

"What is this?" she asked, her question quieting the audience, which had once more begun to stomp their feet. "She is a child." The Shieldmaiden cast an accusatory glance at the overhanging section where the royal family watched. "This is your saintess candidate whom I am to test? Putting the life of a child in mortal danger goes against the very ethos of my creed." The warrior let her hammer drop to the ground, the heavy metal sinking lazily into the sand.

Eir snorted. "Age has no bearing in our commands from the King and the Cardinal." Unlike Brynhildr, who spoke with a melodic, almost rhythmic accent, Eir's accent came off as rough and brutal.

"You would attempt to kill a child?" Brynhildr accused and glared at the Valkyrie opposite her.

"Do not attempt to manipulate my words, Shieldmaiden," Eir responded, her nose raised just high enough for her to peer down it when she spoke. "Where is your shield anyway? I wouldn't have thought one of your kind would part with that toy of yours."

Brynhildr snarled and bristled at Eir's words, but her reaction was cut off by the soft and ethereal voice that emanated from the cloaked figure of Skuld. "That is not a child." Goosebumps raced up my spine, and I could feel a cold, curious gaze rest on me from somewhere in Skuld's shadowy form.

"What?" the Shieldmaiden asked, furrowing her brows in confusion. Skuld didn't elaborate, but Eir scoffed.

"Who cares what she is? Pick up your hammer, Shieldmaiden, and do your duty to the Crown," Eir said with no small amount of irritation in her voice.

"No," Brynhildr said in a voice that brooked no argument. The warrior stalked over to the gate closest to me that I knew led back to the dungeons. Three guards stood there, each looking increasingly unsure about what they should do the closer the Shieldmaiden got to them. When she eventually reached them, Brynhildr didn't say a word and grabbed a giant shield from the first man. As she stormed back to her original position, she released a stream of curses I was sure would shock even the most weathered of sailors. "I will not attempt to kill a child, even on order from the Crown. I am a Shieldmaiden." She grabbed her hammer and slammed it against the shield. "And I will not allow anyone else to kill a child before my eyes."

"You think you can stop me?" Eir sneered, her green eyes locking with Brynhildr's blue pair. And, for just a moment, a split instant so fast I might have imagined it, I saw a spark of amusement in the eyes of both women.

They're acting, I realized. Just like everything else, the disagreement between the Fates was part of whatever historical act I was apparently starring in.

The river of rage I'd managed to push down reared its ugly head and surged to the surface. I could feel my energy gurgling up, screaming at me to seek release and annihilate those who mocked and jeered.

A deep, familiar voice interrupted the playacting and boomed in my head, unwanted and unannounced.

[Mindscribe killed. Heart energy being provided to Awakener Lilith, Title: Queen of Rot, Class: Soul Weaver.]
[Absorb your stored energy?]
[Yes/No]

Yes, System. Now!

[You have absorbed sufficient energy to create the first heart ring atop your Core. Proceeding with formation of heart ring.]
[Formation complete.]
[One of three heart rings obtained until an upgrade to Silver level is available.]
[Error: Heart Core overriding the Blood of Orpheus. New heart ring unstable.]
[Jurisdiction of Orpheus being contested.]
[Heart-ring formation undone. Heart energy is retained. Heart Core rejecting the Orpheus System's attempt to proceed with automatic formation.]
[Unable to override Heart Core.]

Before I had a moment to contemplate the interactions between my Heart Core and the Orpheus System, an enormous wave of energy slammed into me like I'd been hit by a horse. And yet, I felt no pain. Rather, I was invigorated. While the heart energy I'd received from the fight couldn't do anything about the bloodied rags that I used as clothing, it sealed the wound on my shoulder from the Drakoryx's stinger. As the puncture wound began to heal and new skin slowly crawled over the opening, black fluid poured out and down my chest to be absorbed into my already disgusting clothes. The pain and lethargy I'd been fighting against since the stabbing vanished in an instant.

I blinked, only vaguely understanding what had happened.

"What the fuck was that?" Eir asked, and I realized then that the three women were staring at me, eyes wide. Well, at least Eir and Brynhildr were. Skuld remained cloaked in her shadows, so I had no idea what she was thinking.

"The Gods have warned of this," Skuld hissed from her shroud of darkness. "They have prophesied the Soul Weaver's advent."

"Okay, hold on," Brynhildr said, holding a hand up. The bewildered look on her face, as she turned toward Skuld, didn't look like it was part of the acting. I figured I could be wrong since Orpheus's muttering about the "advent of a Soul Weaver" hadn't exactly been discreet. Still, it was odd to mention if this was supposed to be some type of saintess candidate test. "The advent of the what?"

In a voice so low that, even despite the silence of the audience, I had to strain to hear, the Seer whispered her answer. "The Goddess of Life balks in the face of the Soul Weaver."

"Skuld, what in the Goddess's name are you going on about?" Eir said, rolling her eyes. "How many times do I have to remind you that you are a seer? Not a prophet. You can't know what the Gods think. Are you having another one of your episodes?"

"I'm not having an episode," Skuld snapped, the ethereal voice she'd been projecting instantly broken, revealing the voice of a girl who couldn't have been older than her late teens. "You can't just disregard my visions as episodes, Valkyrie."

"Uhhhhh," Jarold's voice interrupted the bickering as if he was, like me, unsure whether the trio was still acting. I was no scriptwriter, but it seemed they were way off whatever script they'd originally been given. None of them had even referred to me as a saintess or Gideon, which I figured should have been at the Core of the test. "E-even in the darkest of moments when our hero, the great Gideon, was faced with the death of his comrade and tested by the Gods, his strength and determination made him unfathomable," the man rambled. "One of the three Fates, the first of the Fates, Lyrielle, chose to protect Gideon against the unreasonable nature of her sisters. Her sisters were angered by the decision, believing Lyrielle to have betrayed them. But Lyrielle knew that Gideon's destiny would save them, would save us all." Halfway through, Jarold had found his stride again. His voice grew increasingly louder as he spoke. "Whooooo's ready to see Gideon and Lyrielle triumph over their foes to save the healer and the world?!"

The crowd bellowed, and I could feel them stomping their feet as the ground rumbled. Despite Jarold's encouragement to start the fight, the three 'Fates' simply remained where they stood, Eir and Brynhildr casting uncertain glances at each other. I could tell they were debating whether to continue the play in the face of Skuld's real warnings.

Unlike them, however, I had no intention of proceeding with any such playacting. Above each of the three monster corpses left to rot where they lay hovered a blue-gray ball of light. In the chaos of Jarold's announcement and subsequent hesitation, I extended three strings of invisible light outward. I wasn't sure if the strings could be seen, but since no one had mentioned them when I'd brought back the slave soldier, I could only assume.

"I am unsure what it is you speak about," I said. All three figures snapped their attention toward me. Brynhildr's blue eyes found mine in the same way they had searched for Eir's.

"Do you truly have no understanding of my sister's warnings?"

I shrugged, buying time for my tendrils to reach their targets. Hopefully, once they did, I'd be able to revive them instinctively. "I'm not even certain what she is talking about, much less the meanings of her warnings. What is a Soul Weaver?"

While the two women whose faces I could see continued to cast furtive looks at each other, Skuld the Seer began to shriek, and the shadows around her quivered.

Then, like a whip, they unwrapped Skuld from her cocoon of darkness and whipped out toward me with a crack. In my attempt to trick the sisters into letting their guards down, I realized I'd inadvertently lowered my own just enough that Skuld's surprise attack actually did manage to take me by surprise. I only had a moment to cross my forearms in front of me before the dark tendrils lashed into them.

The whips split my skin like hot butter while the force of the blow sent me tumbling backward, kicking up a cloud of sand in my wake. I heard one of the other women shouting in alarm, but I'd hit my head at some point during my fall and couldn't hear properly. I focused on my tendrils of power that reached for the monster corpses and redoubled the energy I was pushing into them.

Perhaps if I had been a Silver Core at that moment, I wouldn't have bothered with resurrecting the creatures and simply fought the Seer's magic with my own abilities. Unfortunately, I was not a Silver Core. I wasn't even close. The other women hadn't released any energy and were apparently good at hiding it from prying eyes, so I had no idea what levels they were at. But Skuld was not bothering to hide it from anyone, her full twenty heart rings on full display.

I used the moment of my tumble to land back on my feet and immediately started running toward the Seer and her tendrils of power. If I could get close enough, maybe I'd be able to steal her soul somehow like I had with Gideon.

Skuld seemed to know that was my plan. Most of her tendrils stayed in proximity to her after the initial attack while only a handful stretched forward to lash out at me. Brynhildr and Eir still hadn't moved from their starting positions.

That was fortunate.

Whack.

One of Skuld's tendrils struck from my blind spot, and my vision swam. Blood ran in warm streaks down the side of my face and blinded me in my right eye until I found my balance and flicked the liquid out of my eye.

Then, like a click in my mind, I felt my three links of energy connect with each of the felled creatures. I glared at Skuld and met her now visibly fear-filled, snow-white eyes. I grinned and screamed as each of the souls sank back into their old bodies and immediately began to drain my energy. The souls pulled energy from my Heart Core with such hungry ferocity that it felt as if my heart was being ripped out of my chest.

My vision flickered between black and red. The energy was sucked out of me like it had never wanted to be mine in the first place. I remembered the slave soldier who'd forced his energy to flow inside me, and I suddenly understood. These resurrected creatures require sustenance in the form of energy.

I had to feed them heart energy.

Time slowed as the souls fed further from my reserves. When they finally stopped pulling from my Core, I was drained and exhausted as if another eternity had passed in the Nothingness. But my head still stuck, and my ears still rang from Skuld's attack. The Shieldmaiden and the Valkyrie still stood watching, uncertain.

An eternity of only seconds, I mused and collapsed to the ground where I sat, heaving.

"The mighty Soul Weaver," Skuld snickered, her voice taking on a raspy undertone completely different from her initial ethereal whisper. I might have asked what was wrong with her if my heart and lungs had allowed for it. "Felled by the shroud of a See-"

The Seer didn't have a chance to finish her sentence as the giant maw of a lion's head closed around her from above. The woman disappeared in a blink and a splash of red blood as the resurrected Chimera chewed down on her. The creature devoured the Seer with such speed that the only remaining sign of her existence in that spot was a single splatter of her blood.

Screams burst from Brynhildr and Eir. Both tore past me and headed for the remains of Skuld, carrying mixed looks of panic and rage.

CHAPTER TWENTY-FIVE

I Will Make An Example Out of You

Brynhildr's hammer sank deep into the Chimera's torso, eliciting a scream of anger from the creature. Its serpent tail lashed out at the Shieldmaiden and swiped her to the side just as Eir swung her large sword at one of the Chimera's hind legs.

Eir was too fast for the Chimera, and her sword bit two entire feet into its thick hind legs. The Valkyrie ripped her blade from the abomination's flesh, spraying Silver-black blood in the wake of her vicious attack.

I watched the action from where I sat, legs splayed out in front of me as my chest heaved desperately for oxygen and my muscles continually cried with exhaustion. The resurrections had completely drained me of my heart energy, and though my Core was working to restore my expended reserves, there was no way it could work fast enough after that level of draining.

Right as Brynhildr would have dealt a finishing blow to the Chimera's skull, a slightly larger than human-size shadow launched itself at the combatants. The shadow, the Drakoryx, slammed its full weight into Brynhildr and sent her flying. Hammer and stinger collided in a fury of blows that I was too low level to visually track.

Eir screamed and scrambled toward her remaining sister to help but was quickly intercepted by the Chimera who widened its lion's maw and bellowed a challenge toward the Valkyrie. It crouched into a prowl, all thirty feet of its lithe frame extending and tensing. An enormous paw raised, just a little, then smashed into the ground as it charged forward.

I was fairly certain in a normal situation the Shieldmaiden and the Valkyrie could have dealt with the two creatures with relative ease. But these were different. These were my creatures, and they would not fear death. I felt it in my very bones. In my soul. The only thing these resurrected creatures feared was *my* demise.

And they would fight until nothing remained of themselves to prevent that from happening.

I couldn't help it. Despite everything, despite my situation and the exhaustion keeping my legs pinned to the ground, I laughed. And this time it was a real laugh. Still cold and ruthless, but real.

The sound distracted the Shieldmaiden for a moment. It was only a split-second mistake and shouldn't have cost her anything in a normal fight.

Unfortunately for her, the Drakoryx was not a normal fighter. Its stinger sprang forward at an unparalleled speed from Brynhildr's blind spot and stabbed into the woman's stomach, piercing through the shield as if it was made of paper.

She gasped, and Eir screamed. The Drakoryx shrieked in victory only to have Brynhildr's hammer, still clenched in her hand, slam into its face and pummel the creature away. In the aftermath of the hammer strike, the winged creature lay still, a rainbow of energy flowing out from it. I tried to reach out and redirect the leaking energy back into the Drakoryx, but the translucent wisps refused. Whenever I tried, it was like trying to grasp smoke.

I tried a different tack. Instead of pushing the energy back where it was leaking, I attempted redirecting it with a small wind of my remaining heart energy. It wasn't much, but I hoped it would be enough to lead the leaking energy into the Chimera vessel.

As if attracted to the pull of the Chimera's resurrected soul, the Drakoryx's released energy was sucked into the Chimera, and the creature let out a roar that was overlaid with a second vibrato. Almost like the Drakoryx's soul remnants had merged with the Chimera.

When I managed to pull my gaze away from the Chimera, which was somehow still releasing its distinct roaring shriek, my eyes met Eir's. The Valkyrie glared at me with open hate, having clearly put the pieces together.

I shrugged and mouthed silently, "Too late."

The Chimera leaped at Eir, and I grunted with the effort of pushing myself to stand. While the Chimera and the Valkyrie exchanged blow after blow, I stumbled my way toward the Shieldmaiden who lay crumpled next to the dead Drakoryx, clutching the stinger still protruding from her stomach.

Tears ran down her face, but they never turned into sobs. Brynhildr struggled to push the stinger out from her stomach. When she saw me approach, she stopped struggling against the stinger and instead grabbed both her weapons, her eyes becoming set with fierce determination.

"You are no saint," she said, accusation and hatred clear in her determined stare. Brynhildr said nothing more as she used her elbows to climb into a sitting position and winced when the stinger was forcefully shifted down. "In the name of the kingdom and the Crown, I wi—"

I didn't let her finish. With a wordless command to the resurrected Mindscribe, Brynhildr's stare glazed over, and her mouth froze where it had been in the middle of a word. I knew the Mindscribe was challenging the Shieldmaiden in her Mindscape, but at this point, all that hardly mattered.

Eir still screamed in the background, and I could hear the panicked fear and desperation in her voice. I didn't care. They had tried to play me. To kill me. All of them had tried. Were still trying. All of them were always playing with me and scheming, ever since I'd arrived.

They enslaved us all.

Then they killed Marisar, a peaceful healer. The first and only truly kind person I'd met in many long years. The river of rage in my mind erupted and surged forward like a tsunami.

It was time to set an example. Clearly, stealing the King's son-in-law's soul had been too clean, too kind, and the death of the slave soldiers too irrelevant.

They wanted a show? Then a show I would give.

I knelt by Brynhildr and closed the woman's hanging mouth. With a gentle hand, I pushed her back to the ground so she lay prone on her back.

I kept her eyes open, even though I knew she couldn't actually see me.

Then I pried her large hammer from her tight grasp. It took me a moment to do so, the woman's fingers clutching to the hilt like she would have clutched to life had her mind been present.

I placed my other hand on the hilt and stood, the hammer's head still firmly on the ground. The Arena had gone silent. Not a single movement as the entire audience held their breath.

The air around me was cold, and my eyes were brutal as I raised my gaze to the overhanging section where I knew the royals resided. And then I turned my gaze to the Church of Life. And finally, I allowed my eyes to roam over the entire audience, letting my stare rest on the slavers in the distance.

"I chose to challenge your Gods," I said, my voice somehow resounding across the Arena with a volume enhancement, despite the fact I hadn't used any such skill. Although I didn't know who was enhancing my words, I didn't particularly care. "And I have judged these Gods, these three Fates, to be lacking."

And I swung the hammer down on Brynhildr's head. Blood sprayed, and I tasted the hot metallic taste in my mouth. I raised the steel weapon and slammed it down again. And again. And again.

The Arena stayed completely silent. No one laughed or jeered anymore. What they were watching was not a historical reenactment or a play. It wasn't even a fight. What they watched was a brutal slaughter.

I wanted them to feel my wrath and to understand my promise.

That this was just the beginning. Not even their Gods could stop me.

When Brynhildr was so fully destroyed that the hammer hit nothing but bloodied and gored sand, I stopped swinging. Still, I didn't allow myself to fall back to the ground. Perspiration soaked freely into my ragged clothing, mixed with dirt and blood, both my own and not my own.

Eir was still locked in combat with the enraged and enhanced Chimera. The Valkyrie, for her part, fought like the four hells incarnate. Her every strike was fueled by raw power and desperation, and though the Chimera fought with equal ferocity, it was clear the beast would eventually lose. It had already sustained deep gashes to both its hind legs, and it was missing half of its serpent's tail. A line of thick fluid trailed the severed tail, and I wondered just how much blood the creature had lost.

The Valkyrie had sustained similar damage with many cuts crisscrossing her torso and legs. At some point during my slaughter of Brynhildr, the Chimera had managed to take one of her arms.

"It wasn't supposed to go like this!" Eir screamed, her sword drooping with the effort of holding it at the ready. "No one was supposed to even get hurt."

"Except for me," I said pointedly, not bothering to disguise the heavy layer of sarcasm.

"You're a slave," she hissed, and the Chimera thundered its disagreement.

I just shrugged. "Am I? Aren't I a Saintess Candidate for the Goddess of Light and Life?"

Eir barked an empty laugh. "Goddess of Life? What life?" Her voice was reaching a manic high, and I could see the sanity beginning to slowly drift from the woman. I'd debated having the Mindscribe paralyze her as well, but in the end, I decided not to. I wanted the audience to witness someone they idolized feeling the pain of the slaves they watched as entertainment. "I'd sooner believe you're a messenger of the Death Goddess than a saintess blessed by the Goddess Dhalia."

I thought about that for a moment and chuckled. "I guess we'll find out. Well, not you." I gestured at the disastrous state of her body.

"How can there be a child such as you?" Eir snarled in disbelief and anger. "How can one be so cruel at an age so young?"

"Cruel?" I spat and motioned toward myself with a wave. "I am not the one attempting to murder a child."

The Valkyrie shook her head. "I simply do not understand. It is impossible that you are the young lady of a noble family."

I gave her a feral grin and, low enough that only she could hear me, I said, "I'm not."

[You have killed 1 Shieldmaiden of Caelos.]
[You have absorbed enough heart energy to form 2 heart rings.]
[Proceeding with formation . . .]
[Error: Orpheus System overruled. Retaining unformed and unrefined heart energy for manual integration.]

I laughed as the new energy poured into me and renewed my strength and spirit to about a quarter of my full capacity. Still, watching Eir's weakened state as she struggled to fight against the Chimera and her wounds, I knew it would be enough.

I raised the hammer, one hand gripped at the bottom of the weapon's long hilt and placed my other closer to the steelhead. Then I heaved it into the air and followed the Chimera into a frenzied charge.

Eir batted away my strikes with the ease of someone much stronger than her foe, but she quickly found herself in a difficult situation when every one of my blows was immediately followed by a variety of attacks from the Chimera. My sole goal was to throw her tempo off, and after a moment, I achieved it. She was too lazy in recovering from moving to block my hammer strike, and as a result, the Chimera swatted her with a giant paw. Long claws raked canyons into Eir's body as the pure force behind the Chimera crumpled the remains of her armor.

There was a sickening crunch as Eir's body crashed into the Arena's far wall. After a moment, it slid from the wall, forming a lifeless heap. Unlike the other two, a reddish-white light hovered above the body. Immediately, I went to grab the soul sphere and push it back into the body to serve at my command, but nothing happened except for a sharp, nauseous pain spiraling through me and my vision suddenly flickering with black dots.

I looked into my Core and groaned. Empty again. I waited for a moment, hoping to get some energy from Eir's demise but, just like with the Seer, nothing came. I groaned, with pain and annoyance, the silence indicating to me the Orpheus System or whatever only rewarded its Awakened for the final blow. I stumbled over the dead Drakoryx and slid down its bloodied side to sit on the wet ground.

"Uhhh," Jarold's voice was harsh against the silence, and even I winced at the suddenness of it. "It . . . it looks like Gideon is victorious in his trials! She moves on to the second stage next week!"

While he spoke, I slipped my weak arms behind my back and wrapped thin fingers around the Drakoryx's broken midnight-blue scales. I was careful to make sure a slight aura protected the open wounds on my hands from Skuld's whip as I yanked a scale loose.

When the guards came to bring me back into the underground dungeon where the slaves were kept, my hands were empty.

As I walked, however, I could feel the sharp edges of the scale rubbing against my leg from the pocket it hid in.

CHAPTER TWENTY-SIX

First Interlude of the Red Cardinal

Prepare the medicine," Mirabelle, the Red Cardinal, commanded, beckoning to her manservant with a flick of her slender hand.

She sat perched high above the Arena in a section that jutted out from the walls and hung over the cheering audience below. The height and size of her overhang cast a large shadow over part of the audience, much like the royal seating on the Arena's opposing side.

The section was open-roofed to the sun cresting its apex and was rimmed with a waist-high stone railing. At this vantage, she was able to easily witness the events at the Arena's center even without magic to magnify her vision. Perhaps thirty feet to her back, at the furthest spot on the section, was the exit, framed with stone slabs carved with depictions of hundreds of years of the Church's history and scenes of past heroes from the kingdom's many wars.

Unlike those of her following who filled the emptiness of the section and wore drab black robes with high white collars and a pair of golden wings adorned right above their hearts, the Red Cardinal herself was covered in a pure and thick red robe and was seated. The robe flowed with her every movement as if a living being. If she were to believe the words of the Pope and the Saint, it likely was alive to some extent. Her red robe and moniker were succinctly matched by her bloodred hair that curled around to her mid-back and the set of bright red eyes that peered out with an otherworldly glow set with diamond-shaped pupils.

Her manservant bowed, his lesser black robes billowing in the wind of their open section before he moved to adjust the parasol blocking the sun's rays from hitting her marble-white skin. He bowed again and moved with purpose out of the section. As she had promised, she would allow the Selenian to be healed. It was a waste, honestly, to expend a precious elixir on a lower life form like a Selenian. But alas, she was a woman of her word and as a Cardinal of the Priestess of Life, she would not go against an oath.

She couldn't. But that didn't mean everything would go the way the slave girl expected.

"Your Eminence," a member of her entourage, Draven, said with the same steady caution all her followers approached her with. He bowed in respect and deference, and likely a bit of fear, as she turned her gaze to meet his bowed figure.

"What is it?" Mirabelle drawled, a natural tone of light and beckoning seduction dancing dangerously in the word. She could see the man visibly swallow his nervousness.

"I . . . I do not believe the life of a mere Selenian is worth the elixir bestowed upon Your Eminence by His Holiness the Pope."

The Cardinal sighed and tapped a polished hand against the wood of her chair upon which she sat. No other chairs filled the near-empty platform save for a perfect gold throne to her left, though none but the Pope or Saint would ever dare to sit upon it. "Yes, you are correct, Bishop. Its life is not worth the expenditure of such a valued elixir."

"Then . . ."

"It is simply fate," she answered and leaned casually against the back of her Blackwood chair. "Perhaps the Fates have arranged it such for a reason." While the elixir was precious and a gift from the Pope, the Cardinal hadn't had any use for it in over a decade and it wasn't the only one available to someone of her position. "What had transpired with the saintess candidate was . . ." She shrugged. "Unforeseen."

The large orb in her left hand flickered to life and the scene of a young girl brutally slaughtering one of the Church of Light's Shieldmaidens started to play within it.

"Unforeseen indeed," Mirabelle muttered. Even she had underestimated the Silverwater girl. She'd forgotten that unlike the previous saintess candidate, the girl did not truly believe in the Church's plan—that much was fairly obvious. There existed in Lilliana no faith that the Church was leading her along the right path; and so she fought like a wild beast. Tooth, nail, and all.

The trial the girl had gone through earlier was supposed to have been, as all first trials were, a planned event. As an Administrator of the System, Mirabelle had upgraded the Selenian to a Soulbound, binding his life to whatever destiny she predetermined within the jurisdiction of Orpheus's power.

He'd played his part in the show, the System forcing him into a near-death state through a minor quest to protect the girl. Unfortunately, the historic reenactment had been ruined when the Seer had gone awry. Still, the entertainment value of the trial had been quite magnificent even if it was not historically accurate as the festival managers had wanted.

It was, however, particularly unfortunate that the elixir was needed to bring back the Selenian. Though, the side effects of the elixir could prove beneficial.

"What are we to do with her?" Draven pressed.

"What can we do at the moment but see if she survives her trials and allow fate to play out?"

"But Your Eminence! That . . ." Draven hesitated as if unsure how to broach the topic considering Lady Lilliana's noble heritage. Finally, he said, "That girl is not a saintess. She cannot become a saintess. Her powers are no miracle. They reach into death, not life."

"Enough, Bishop Argole," the Cardinal snapped. "It is not your place to question the Goddess's will."

The Bishop, Draven, clenched his jaws and his fists went white against the black of his robes. "It is impossible for that girl to be part of the Goddess's will. She killed a Valkyrie and massacred a Shieldmaiden!"

"I am aware that your niece was the slain Valkyrie, Bishop," the Cardinal responded dismissively. "Though Lilliana's actions were . . . unusual, her words were not wrong. We were the ones who insisted on challenging her in that way. The entire point of these trials is to test the Goddess's favor. Can you truly say she was not blessed on this day?" Even with the Seer acting out, the actual trial had played out rather perfectly. Right up until the resurrection of the trial monsters, which had been unexpected. Her mages had done a proper job in protecting the slaves as they fought the monsters to guarantee the fatal injury of only the Selenian, as per the religious historical event of only one injury to the historic party.

However, Lilliana's resurrection ability had, somehow, completely evaded her mage's sense, both those of magic and energy. The method in which the Silverwater girl had done that, Mirabelle had not a clue.

"I believe she was blessed by a demon," Draven spat, and there was a murmuring of agreement from the other followers. "Or possessed by one."

"Hmmm," the Cardinal hummed, and her voice took on an ethereal vibration that silenced the discontent in a second. She extended her charm outward and enveloped the Bishop in an invisible haze until his brown eyes paled with an unseeing glaze. "Bishop?"

"Yes . . . Your Eminence?" Draven said, his voice enunciating each word with an inhuman tempo. Like he was confused, his mind muddled by her charm.

"I believe you need to enter isolation and pray for the Goddess to bestow upon you a clearer understanding."

Draven nodded and left without another word. The Cardinal turned back to the images flickering within the sphere on repeat. It wasn't so much that the Bishop was wrong. Rather, he was actually quite right about the child. She was no saintess and her resurrections were not life miracles but a way to cheat death reminiscent of the Necromancers of Larcos, though with some sort of limited free will. Generally, a Saintess of the Goddess Dhalia would radiate their heart energy as a halo of white light and the resulting feeling was warmth and belonging. The power was both seductive and comforting, wrapping those nearby and the user in a loving embrace.

Even an energy user with half the Cardinal's rings could tell the heart energy coming from the young Lady Lilliana was anything but warmth and certainly didn't create an aura of belonging. It was instead cold and domineering. It didn't grant life back to the target; it commanded continuing servitude and the resulting resurrection was nothing but a tool to that end.

Where Lilliana had learned that power, or really how she had gotten herself captured as a slave, the Cardinal had yet to discover. What information she'd gathered suggested some scheme by Lilliana's sister, though the Cardinal couldn't know for certain until she met with Baron Silverwater, who was watching the events in the King's overhang section. Where she'd learned to wield such foreboding abilities or even what method developed, she'd shown earlier with her heart rings, remained completely unknown. No one knew, not even the slavers.

Despite that, however, the Cardinal felt a great interest in the girl. It would not do to kill such an interesting specimen before discovering whether or not she could be used.

After a moment longer, the Cardinal swept to her feet, and the dozens of followers straightened by her side. "Bring me to our fallen sisters," she said as a visible halo of bright white heart energy began to emanate around her and forty heart rings swirled in a hypnotizing rhythm. "Perhaps the Goddess will once more be generous in her blessings on this day."

CHAPTER TWENTY-SEVEN

Second Interlude of Lady Morgana Silverwater

Morgana had been completely asleep, amid a rather pleasant dream about a certain prince, when she was abruptly awoken by the Silverwater household's head manservant, Jeffords. He had rushed into her room. In an instant of fright, Morgana had leaped to her feet, her fire energy illuminating every candle in her bedchamber and the hallway beyond. She now stood in the middle of her pink and gold bedroom as the lights of her energy flickered with an ominous aura that she quite enjoyed among all the pink. Her leg bumped slightly against the delightful bed with its oak framing and thick comforters now thrown about in a messy clump that made her eye twitch. The usually pleasant scent of lavender incense was sour to her nose, and when she moved, she nearly rammed her toes into the leg of her nightstand.

And there she stood as Jeffords detailed what he knew about Lilliana's survival. Her fights. Her enslavement. And the Baron's rush to her location in Cael. The more he spoke, the angrier Morgana became until her blood was boiling so loudly in her ears, she could barely hear herself think.

"You told me she was dead!" Morgana snarled in an explosion of rage, long brown curls bobbing around her head in messy strands as she whirled on the manservant she had previously ordered to follow the whore's daughter around. The sheer amount of money she'd spent on purchasing monster corpses to lure the Beast King from the forest had been only worth it because she'd believed her revenge had been achieved. Now Morgana was finding out her money had gone to waste and her people had utterly failed in every aspect. "How can she be alive? Are you telling me you not only failed to capture the Apocryth but couldn't even kill one pathetic child?" In her rage, Morgana grabbed the ceramic cup half-filled with scalding tea from her nightstand and threw it at the manservant, who nimbly shuffled out of the way.

That only enraged her further, and she screamed in frustration. None of this was going according to plan. The girl had been alive and kicking all this time. She was supposed to be dead. For the dishonor to Brian. To her. To her family. Though, it had been survival at the cost of being a slave. The thought briefly made her anger cool into a small satisfied smile. Right up until she remembered the girl was now facing the trials to become a *saintess*. How absolutely absurd. The girl was lucky to be a slave that fights—she belonged in the pleasure houses like her whore of a mother. Yet somehow, this whore's daughter kept ruining her plans. Morgana still didn't know how Liliana had swapped her poisoned cup with Lady Tremmor's under Morgana's nose, a constant and persistent annoyance whenever it came to mind. And then Lady Ballenci's weak maid had squealed all her little secrets to the Baron. All of Morgana's little secrets regarding the poison. Following that the Baron had forced all contact between her and the Ballenci girl to be blocked. That hadn't mattered all too much to Morgana as by that point Lady Ballenci had all but cut off communication on her own. For whatever reason. "The child who shamed my little brother, shamed this family, shamed me, killed my friend, and has done nothing but shame herself, is still alive?"

"That is correct, my lady," the manservant said, bowing. Despite the boiling water that splashed on his skin when the ceramic cup shattered against the wall of Morgana's bedchamber, his expression remained stoic. That wasn't surprising considering the old manservant had served her household for a little over a century. His face was nearly covered in wrinkles, though he somehow maintained a full head of white hair. Morgana sometimes suspected it to be some sort of trick from an energy specialist. She had never cared enough to confirm the thought.

"Is she still enslaved as of now?" If the news had made it all the way to Silverwater, Lilliana's identity must have been revealed.

"Yes, my lady. While it was revealed that she is of our house, the Cael King has chosen to hold her in his dungeons. The Baron suspects this to be an intentional showing of disrespect toward the Silverwater house and the Lysoria royal family."

"Has our king responded?" Morgana had no doubt their own royal house would be quite enraged, especially Princess Isla who seemed to have developed a soft spot for the little whorespawn.

"He has not. However, we have recently managed to detain the Beast King's sire using the elixir. We may be able to use the harvest to stay the King's hand in this matter completely."

That caused the Silverwater barony's eldest daughter to pause mid-tirade. "It was finally detained?" He should have led with that. Ever since Morgana had used Lilliana, her father's more loyal knights, and some of the mercenaries the house had recruited as lower soldiers as bait for the Beast King's sire, a large portion of the Silverwater barony's knights had been in battle with the Sire. Her personal forces were on a bogus mission waiting for further orders from her, though it would be a while before the Baron's forces were weak enough for her to do anything overtly aggressive.

The Baron had initially balked at the thought of combating a sire, but with pressure from the Goldenhearts and the Church of Light, he'd caved fairly quickly. Normally, a midsize barony like the Silverwaters would never have been able to defeat a sire. Though that was no secret nor shame on the house, it had ceased to be true when the Church of Life had presented her household with something the Red Cardinal had called the Elixir of Resistance after Lilliana's 'disappearance.' Even a drop blessed the receiver with resistance to a sire's authority.

"Has the harvesting begun yet?" she asked, taking a seat on her lovely comforter as she suddenly calmed.

Apparently used to her quick shifts in temperament, the manservant simply shook his head before answering further. "Not yet. The news of the Sire's capture was brought to me only moments before the news of the girl. The harvesting will begin tomorrow at dawn."

"No, that's unacceptable," Morgana said, not as a command but as a statement. With her father gone for what was likely to be a few weeks, there wouldn't be much time for her to put her plan into action. "We'll start it now." She reached above her head and yanked down firmly on a thick red string that dangled from the ceiling a little left of her bed. In the distance, though faint, she could hear a loud and crisp ding. Moments later, a chorus of footsteps gently clapped their way toward Morgana.

Six maids entered the chambers, Nissa at the back and Ariel at the front like always. "My lady?" the head maid asked. Morgana eyed the older lady with the neutral expression of someone far superior. Which she most certainly was. Her matriarch lessons had been very insistent on making sure all servants knew their place, even those with whom she had a past. "Dress me."

The six maids snapped to work, their worn-down maid outfits ragged compared to the grandiose opulence of the chamber they shuffled into. Shifting her maids into worn-out outfits was another recent change caused by her matriarch lessons. The Baron, despite his support of treating lower-class workers without decency, continued to be at odds with her taking matriarch lessons. Only her eldest brother had any support when it came to leadership lessons.

Morgana climbed barefoot onto the dais at the far end of her room where she was always dressed, her delicate features illuminated by the rays of a waking sun streaming in through great windows.

She spent a moment directing the maids to the outfit she wanted to wear before returning her attention to the manservant. "Once the servants complete their tasks and I am prepared, you will escort me to the dungeon lab. I want a full progress report, and I want to see the Sire."

"My lady," Jeffords began, "I'm not sure that would be wise—"

Morgana cut him off. "I do not care what you believe to be wise, manservant. You have already failed me twice, and I am extraordinarily displeased. Your understanding of what is wise very clearly comes with great limitations." The maid directly behind her grunted as she pulled the corset strings around Morgana's midriff. "Tighter," Morgana hissed when the maid went to loop the strings closed.

"My apologies, Lady Silverwater." The manservant gave Morgana a low bow. It was a much lower bow than what her station rightfully commanded, but most of the servants in the household were aware of the true authority she held. And those who did not yet know soon would.

The six maids bowed similarly low and backed away simultaneously, indicating the completion of their duties. Morgana dismissed them with a casual flick of her wrist and followed Jeffords out of her room and into the mansion's hallway. She paid no mind to the rows of suits of armor and tapestries lining the stone walls as she'd seen them all thousands of times over the years. No, what she really wanted was to see the Sire. Something new. Something powerful.

"Right through here, my lady," Jeffords said with a small bow of his head. He reached over to a large iron door and rapped his knuckles against it three times, each harder than the last.

"Who is eet?" drawled a gruff, almost intoxicated-sounding voice.

"It's Jeffords and Lady Silverwater. Open the door, Dresden."

"Oh fu—yeah, okay, one second, my lady," Dresden muttered, and Morgana could hear the jingle of many keys being bounced around. Then there was a click, and the enormous metallic door creaked open.

A small man stood on the other side, his clothes infinitely more ragged than her bedchamber maids. There was a small table next to him covered in cards and a few empty bottles.

"Take me to it," Morgana ordered. The small man, Dresden, gave a bow so low Morgana thought his nose might touch the floor.

"Yes, yes, of course. Whatever it is the lady desires." Dresden snatched a torch from its position on the wall and beckoned them to follow him down a set of spiral stairs leading deep under the mansion. The air quickly became damp and cold as they descended ever deeper.

When Morgana finally heard the sound of muffled voices and the clanking of metallic chains, the temperature suddenly spiked as if they approached an inferno. Sweat quickly poured down her, drenching her and causing her recently applied makeup to droop. Part of her was tempted to complain about the environment, but there was something powerful in the air that kept her quiet.

As the three of them reached the final level, a blood-curdling scream of pain erupted, and Morgana could feel how even the walls shook. Her eyes widened at the sight of her beautiful prisoner.

Had she not known it was a monster chained and gagged, she might have thought it the most handsome man she'd ever seen. Dark, rich black eyes peered out under long locks of equally black hair with bright diamond-colored pupils that sparkled even in the dimly lit dungeon. The Sire was humanoid and a gorgeous one at that, his every part bunched and tensed with sinewy muscles that seemed to constantly test the restraints holding him to the floor.

The only nonhuman aspect of the Sire was a single horn jutting from the center of his forehead. The horn was the physical manifestation of darkness, she'd been told. Against the dim light of the dungeon, the horn could barely be seen at certain angles until light flickered upon it.

She'd thought the scream might have originated from the Sire, but a single look at the Sire's calm demeanor extinguished that belief.

That, and the fact a white-robed mage twitched at the edge of life on the floor where the Sire was being forcibly knelt, a hole punctured through the man's throat. She hadn't seen any blood on the horn, though, so she took a closer look, careful not to approach too much. No, there was no blood on it. Had he absorbed it?

"Take him away," she ordered, waving at the dying mage. Her nose wrinkled in disgust at the smell and the general scene. "Try to heal him. I want to see the effects of being stabbed by a sire."

"Where is the girl?" a smooth, casual voice asked, and Morgana glanced at the captive creature. The chains around him lit up in a brilliant red, no doubt absorbing the magic and energy attempting to radiate from the Sire.

Morgana shook her finger and clicked her tongue. "Uh-uh, no using your energy here."

"Ah, you speak of the bindings?" The Sire shrugged, unimpressed. "It is not so impressive as you may believe." His voice, while smooth, seemed to strain with the words as if unfamiliar with the language. "Your ancestors, the creators of these bindings, all perished despite them. As will you."

Morgana laughed. "I hadn't thought a monster with your strength and age could indulge in such . . ." She waved her hands around in a mocking gesture. "Naivety." She pulled out a small vial of orange liquid. "I wonder what would happen if you were injected with some of this elixir?"

"Where is the girl?" he asked again, ignoring her threat.

"What girl?"

"The one whose blood called to me."

"Ah, you mean the whore's daughter?" Morgana barked a laugh. "So it's true! Sires of myth cannot withstand the blood allure of children with royal blood in their veins, even when it's as limited as that of a bastard daughter of a baron."

The Sire just smiled and shook his head. "You are correct, descendant of Silverwater. But you are equally wrong. I would warn you against conflict with that particular . . . girl."

"We'll see," Morgana said, grinning down at him. "Inject him with the elixir."

The chains embedded with thousands of unreadable wards flared red once again. The Sire's muscles bulged and then froze, unable to move under the paralyzing energy of the restraints. Under his feet, a large circle of similar wards flared white, and a single mage made his way toward the Sire. A small needle hovered over the mage's hand for only a moment after he walked into the magic circle's perimeter. Then it surged forward and embedded itself directly into the Sire's left eye.

He screamed, and Morgana felt herself smile wider than she had since she'd had the Baron's whore mistress killed all those years ago.

CHAPTER TWENTY-EIGHT

The Orpheus System

Just as promised, Marisar was healed back to full health. In fact, the Selenian casually strolled through the underground dungeon's entrance, escorted by two guards, not half an hour after I was unceremoniously dumped back with the other slaves.

I'd been pacing up until that moment, with Gronch muttering a constant string of unintelligible words. At first, I'd been somewhat worried the others would have a negative reaction to my actions during the fight, but I quickly learned it had not been broadcast to them.

It wasn't until Marisar was in my sight and alive that my need to pace halted. No one ran to congratulate Marisar on living or to let him know he'd been missed. The reality was none of us could spare that type of emotional capacity, and even if we'd wanted to display such a potential weakness for someone openly, it was inapplicable to the current situation as Marisar would have probably been better off dead. Nothing much awaited him as a Selenian slave in a combat Arena. At least it'd been relatively painless.

"I see not even the nine hells wanted you," Gronch snorted, the first of us to break the stillness, and clapped Marisar on the shoulder. I raised an eyebrow at the expression. This world believed in nine hells? Not four? I'd have to look into that and the associated cults. At least on Ordite, the Cult of the Four Hells had been a massive pain in the side of every nation. Their atrocities never had any rhyme or reason, simply violence for the sake of violence.

"I was granted a Pill of Resurrection," Marisar responded, his large eyes wide, and his words slurred as if he was dreaming. Julius whistled, and Romeo frowned. Gronch said nothing and just gave another snort. I couldn't tell if it was out of disdain toward the slavers or mocking Marisar's surprise.

Julius rubbed his growing beard in clear thought. His beard was no longer a solid orange and was now peppered with flashes of white and gray to match his ever-growing wrinkles. "That is quite a precious elixir. Even a king would think twice before using it. I wonder why it was used on Marisar. When I heard the announcement, I just figured a high-ringed healer from the Church would heal him."

"Perhaps it was too late." Having seen Marisar and that he was in relatively good health, I allowed my muscles to relax and collapsed to the ground in exhaustion. "I'm not sure. Even when I left the Arena, there was no sign of your soul exiting your body. So, my understanding is that you should have still been far enough from death for a healer's magic or energy to work."

Marisar nodded along and raised an eyebrow at my description of not having seen his soul. Despite that, he didn't look surprised. "I think I can explain the soul part, you know." His hands moved like he was clicking through something in front of him.

"You were injected with the Blood of Orpheus as well?" Romeo asked, suddenly perking up.

"Mmm," Marisar confirmed, his eyes still flashing with the glint of the Orpheus System's invisible screen. "Ah, here it is. I received a class change when the Drakoryx stabbed me, you know. The System says, 'Class change: Soulbound Healer.'" His long blue fingers swiped down, and he continued. "Effects: Your destiny is set and cannot be changed. All events within Orpheus's jurisdiction that threaten your destiny will be nullified." He glanced up at us, eyes wider than I'd ever seen them. "I'm not . . . I'm not sure I would have died even without being saved."

They all looked at me.

"What?" I asked, meeting their expressions with a quirk of my eyebrow. "I didn't touch his soul. Whatever the Orpheus System did to him had nothing to do with me."

"Lady Lilliana, why do I get the feeling that's not true, ya know?" Marisar said with a small sigh. Gronch and Julius burst out laughing, but Romeo's eyebrow furrowed with thought.

I just scowled at the lot of them.

"Even if I wanted to, only high-tier necromancers can forcefully Soulbound," I said, still frowning. "That's not even a type of heart-ring energy I've awoken to." I was tempted to add that I probably would awaken to it within the year, but I was still unsure about how this world considered necromancers, so I kept that bit to myself.

If it was anything like Ordite, where most necromancers were killed on sight, that information could easily be the death of me. Fortunately, based on what I'd seen of the Soul Weaver abilities, there was quite a bit of overlap between it and necromancy. Passing one off for the other wouldn't be too difficult.

"In any case," I said, changing the subject, "What do the rest of your classes say?"

I wanted to see whether any other interactions with the Orpheus System were similar to mine. Marisar's description of his experience with the System was dramatically different from my own, where I only received the occasional notification.

Only after the rest took turns sharing their interactions with the Orpheus System did I realize just how different and limited my own had been. The four of them described things like experience points, stats, abilities, and explanations for each ability. Apparently, the System also laid out their strengths and weaknesses in numeric numbers. I had none of that.

"I got Berserker," Gronch grunted in his usual rough-natured way of speaking, but I could hear the pride in his voice. "The more I fight, the stronger I become. Even my intelligence seems to be rising from my fights. I didn't even realize that was something that could be improved. Went from 23 to 40." He explained a little about his new abilities to increase his strength by ten times and cover his weapons in energy. Apparently, that had been their saving grace against the Chimera.

"Knight of Questionable Morality," Julius said with a half smile, half grimace. Snickering ensued until we realized he wasn't joking.

"That's an actual class?" I asked, truly perplexed.

Julius shrugged. "Suppose so since it's mine."

"What does it do?" Gronch grabbed some type of orange triangular fruit from his pocket and took a large bite from it.

"It just says I haven't unlocked additional abilities beyond base stats yet."

"What level are you?" Gronch asked.

"Level?" I could see the confused expression on Julius's face as he seemed to flip through his invisible screens.

"Upper right corner." Romeo moved to stand next to the older warrior and pointed to where, if a screen was to appear in front of Julius, the upper right corner would have been.

"Ah, I see it. I am level twenty-seven."

"I think you gotta hit thirty for additional skills. I'm thirty-one." Gronch tapped his invisible screen that only he could see.

We looked at Romeo. "I'm level twenty-five." He frowned. "Must have been given less experience since I wasn't able to do much against the Chimera." His black curls shook as he shifted uncomfortably from where he stood against the wall. "My class is something called a Lesser Wizard of Caelos."

Julius scoffed as if that title for Romeo was the worst fitting title he'd ever heard. "Bullshit."

"Lilliana?" Romeo inquired abruptly, clearly wanting to change the subject, his face still tinted red from shame or embarrassment, it was hard to tell. I suppose he probably wasn't a fan of being called a lesser.

"It says my class is a Lunari," I lied. "Some sort of warrior that gets strengthened by the moon." It was true in that I was a Lunari and Lunari warriors *were* strengthened by the moon. There was a small twinge in my gut as I lied to the people who fought with me in life and death but pushed the feeling aside for the same reason I hadn't told them of my inclination toward necromancy. Regardless of whether they could be trusted or not, sharing unnecessary information led to being blindsided by a third party. Always. That was taught in my lessons during the time I spent as a queen candidate and something I experienced on numerous occasions as the queen.

When asked about my "stats" I just shrugged and said they were no different from everyone else's. In truth, I wasn't sure what they meant by "stats," but I understood insofar as that they were some sort numeric evaluation of their limits.

The four men continued to discuss their stats and basic skills. At some point I'd tuned them out, choosing to eavesdrop on surrounding conversations. Discussion about the Orpheus System wasn't an uncommon discussion topic anymore, though it was still one to be cautious about being overheard. Not all the slaves had been injected, and others hadn't been affected for some reason, but that didn't mean you wanted everyone to know the intricate details of all your abilities and limits.

The one thing all of us did share, however, was the initial warning about the Orpheus System only being available or accessible within Orpheus's territory—the Arenas. Which may or may not be limited to the current Arena we fought in, there was no way of knowing.

"I'm really curious how the Orpheus System can be used outside the Arenas," Romeo said, tugging at the steel collar newly placed around his neck. We'd all had one clasped around our neck after returning from the first trial, including any other slave in our enclave who was a System user. I didn't know about the other slave groups.

The dark blue Drakoryx scale was heavy in my pocket as I gave Romeo a small, knowing smile. "I have a feeling we might find out sooner than we expected." The boy's eyes snapped to mine out of surprise and seemed to be looking for some hint or clue as to what I was thinking but I gave none. Not yet. I was completely drained of energy and so were all of them. We had a week to recover before the next trial and needed to make good use of it.

None pressed me and I climbed back to my feet, noticing for the first time in a while how small they were. Fresh cuts wrapped around my thin, pale legs and they screamed in pain with each step I took as the healing flesh tore ever wider. I ignored the pain, ignored the exhaustion for just a moment longer as I approached the bed I'd chosen my first day here.

It had looked like trash to me back then. Now, it looked like absolute paradise.

I could hear them theorizing about the restrictions that being outside Orpheus's jurisdiction would cause, but I ignored them. At the end of the day, it was my *own* strength that would save or kill me, not some strange power given to me. Like everything else in life, the System was naught but a tool. If it conspired to be more, it would simply need to be better controlled and utilized rather than relied upon.

Thoughts for tomorrow. I sighed and fell into a blissful sleep of Nothingness thanks to my complete exhaustion fending off the nightmares beckoning at the corners of my mind.

CHAPTER TWENTY-NINE

Discretion Is Not My Strong Suit

Nothing happened for the first five days following the initial trial. The five of us took the time to heal and prepare for the upcoming seventh day. Using the heart energy granted to me by the Orpheus System for killing the Mindscribe and the Shieldmaiden, and the smaller amounts for contributing to the deaths of the Seer and the Valkyrie, I was able to refine two new heart rings around my Bronze Core.

It was a surprisingly quick jump to peak Bronze level, but I wasn't complaining. A Silver Core was the true start, and the journey to the higher realm Cores became exponentially more difficult.

Though perhaps not quite so difficult if the Orpheus System continued to allow for the absorption of heart energy by defeating others. Normally, such heart energy had to be accumulated and refined through meditation and cultivation of your Core. Occasionally, one could advance greatly by absorbing the Core of the defeated enemy, but it was more normal for the Core to break on death.

And no one I've seen has had a Core, anyway, I thought.

On the sixth day, however, Dralos and Chella made an appearance to inform us, mainly me, of the second challenge. The moment he laid eyes on me, Dralos sneered, his Draconian pupils dilating with unbridled hatred.

I didn't bother to react. The Dragonborne's hatred wouldn't matter in a few moments anyway.

"All right bugs," Dralos said with a grunt, pulling out a new scroll adorned with the King's dragon claw stamp. "We've received your new test." He slipped a finger under the seal, and it came off with a low pop. Dralos opened his mouth as if to begin reading, then scoffed and seemed to skip a good paragraph of information before starting again. "By decree of His Majesty, King Isadore, Lady Lilliana is judged as innocent regarding her killing of the Shieldmaiden as all events were within the jurisdiction of Goddess Dahlia of the Light. Lady Lilliana's next trial will be a Test of Compassion. Let the Light fall upon her in failure or success." He closed the scroll, looked at us, and laughed. Then he tucked the scroll away and headed toward another group of slaves in the opposite direction.

"Well," Gronch said, slapping me on the back and causing all the air in my lungs to rush out. "It was sorta nice knowin' you guys." Julius chuckled, but Romeo scowled in a way that reminded me of a young noble facing some kind of punishment that was out of his hands. It was a fairly apt expression.

"Don't give up yet, Gronch," the raven-haired fighter said, giving the laughing Julius a hard look. "Maybe we can teach her how to fake it?"

"In a day?" Gronch shook his head.

Compassion. The word took me back decades to when my father had still ruled with his harsh iron fist. *Compassion,* he had told all the queen candidates, *was a tool. And just like any other tool, used correctly it would make the wielder strong. But used incorrectly, and it would turn even a queen into a fool.*

I was no fool.

"Compassion is naught but a tool," I interrupted, my father's words out of my mouth before I could help it. His lessons and his way were ingrained into me. Into all queen candidates. "If necessary, I will wield it as needed. For now, compassion can only do us harm."

"You saved me, Lady Lilliana, ya know?" Marisar said, quietly. "I would call that compassion."

I shook my head. "No, that was not compassion. It was simple necessity and circumstance. Your life and my life were intrinsically linked that day. If I failed to win the elixir, it's likely the cause would have been my death." I looked at all of them with as serious an expression as Lilliana's twelve-year-old face could manage. "I believe, for now at least, we live and die together. So, just trust me. I've dealt with worse than slavery before."

"When?" Gronch said, clearly doubtful. "You ain't even grown yet." I didn't answer. Maybe one day I'd explain the truth to them. Probably not, but it certainly wouldn't be as a gladiator slave in a dungeon.

The awkward moment was broken by a sauntering Dralos who stopped by our little group, an eerie grin having pulled his lips wide. "I've just been told that it's time for everyone to get their first check-up! Our Dr. Darmond is insisting that we start with the young noble girl." His scaly hand whipped out and wrapped around my wrist, pulling me away from the others with an easy tug. At my slightest resistance, the slave mark on my forearm burned with a rage matched only by the glee in Dralos's eyes when he noticed me wince. "Oh, ain't gonna hurt ya, girlie. The doctor is just gonna poke and prod a little."

The others appeared to want to interject, but I shook my head. I sent Marisar a pointed stare, and the Selenian's eyes widened. Right as Dralos began to shove me toward the large doors and into the dark corridors of oozing slime, I saw Marisar's blue fingers gripping the half orc's forearm and returned to me a knowing look.

I would have begun my plan even without Dralos taking me away from the eyes of others, but the isolation was an unexpectedly convenient boon. I began to sink the loose heart energy into the tattoo. The tattoo and the collar.

As Dralos reached into his pocket where I knew handcuffs would be, likely etched with the same skull and chains as the slave tattoo, I asked, "Why do you hate me so much, Dragonborne?"

Dralos froze in front of me, his body still slouched slightly, and his eyes lingering on his hands at the rim of his trousers. Orange, diamond eyes looked up at me slowly, all the glee gone and replaced by barely repressed hate and, maybe, surprise?

"How do you know of the Dragonborne?" The words were quiet leaving his lips but resounded loudly in the empty, slime-filled hallway.

"Are you not Dragonborne?" I pressed, ignoring his question as he'd ignored mine. "Based on your pure level of spite, I wasn't sure what else you could be."

He didn't answer for a long moment. So long, in fact, I thought he'd launch himself at me. Instead, his orange eyes blinked, and then he barked a laugh. "Look at this little girl trying to act so tough with the bit of knowledge she has." Dralos finished fishing into his pocket for the cuffs and tossed them at me. They bounced off me and landed on the floor with a clank. "The Dragonborne do not work in slave dungeons."

"Then what are you?"

He spat at my feet where the cuffs had landed. "None of your business, mutt."

"You should be careful how you speak to your betters," I taunted, nudging the loose cuffs with a look of disdain. "Though I do not plan on allowing you the chance to make that mistake a second time."

Before Dralos could so much as finish raising his hand in threat as the scowl formed on his face, I reached into my own pocket. The slave mark seared, and my entire arm burned as if sprayed with lava. Dralos started to laugh at the brilliant red light that indicated the mark's activation when the mark lifted off my forearm like a parasite rather than a tattoo and then shattered. The slave collar tight around my neck similarly exploded outward. The sounds pierced the air with a shrill metallic shriek, and the illuminating red light winked out from existence.

The dim light of a distant torch casually flickered toward us as I pulled the broken Drakoryx scale from my pocket and buried it deep into the side of Dralos's neck. The sharp edges of the Drakoryx scale slid through Dralos's own with deadly ease. Black lines surged from the wound as venom spread like wildfire through his body. Almost instantly, he began to shake and spasm, his mouth opening into a wordless scream as the venom dyed his orange eyes with the black of Nothingness. Then he dropped to the floor, dead as the ground under us.

A red splotch of burnt and simmering flesh remained where the tattoo had been. I had been fairly certain the magic or energy contained within the tattoo could have been overcome by even a base Bronze-level Core formed correctly, so my peak Bronze level had easily crushed it. The power dampener around my neck and the cuffs at my feet may have made it more difficult if I'd still been at base Bronze. It was hard to tell since both the power dampeners and being under Bronze limits were new to me.

Doesn't matter now, I thought and looked down at the Dragonborne-looking creature, frowning as his reddish-white soul light appeared over the corpse. I'd imagined this very situation multiple times and hadn't been able to come to a proper conclusion.

On the one hand, I could resurrect him and hopefully glean an incredible amount of information from the creature.

On the other hand, I had no idea how someone with at least some level of dragon blood in their veins would react to becoming the servant of a Lunari, whom they so hated. If Dralos came back with enough free will to betray me, then any and all information he provided would have to be presumed poisoned with some number of falsities.

I supposed I could require him to perform acts that would test the loyalty bond, but for all I knew, that could be faked. Still, I didn't know how much time I had before someone spotted the body since it wasn't as if there was anywhere for me to hide it. So if the body could move and act alive . . .

As time ticked by and my indecision started to become a weakness to my plan, I straightened my shoulders and set my jaw. Then I sank a large amount of power into the soul of Dralos and shoved it back into his body.

At first, nothing happened. Right when I was about to leave the corpse as some sort of mistake or misunderstanding of my abilities, he stirred. I summoned a small white ball of light with my lunar energy between myself and the resurrected being who began to sit up.

Under the light, I saw Dralos's eyes were no longer their sharp orange and instead were still dominated by the black of the Drakoryx venom. Dralos came to a halt upon reaching his knees and bent one to kneel before me.

"My queen," he rasped in a voice more similar to the first man I had raised than Dralos's own just moments ago. "I have come to serve you."

A thought occurred to me. "Who . . . who are you?"

He tilted his head. "I am your servant, my queen."

"No, that is your duty and your role. What is your name, resurrected one?"

The Risen Servant stilled like the dead he had once been, in either thought or rebellion, I couldn't tell. Minutes passed, and I knew Darmond would begin to wonder where we were if this took much longer, but something told me the Risen's answer was too important to miss.

"I am Dralos. I have returned to serve my master." He tilted his head, black eyes staring at me. "But I am also not Dralos. Or at least, I am not only Dralos. I was once the Draconian hybrid known as Dralos, long, long ago. Centuries in the timeless Nothingness have long since turned me into something . . . else."

CHAPTER THIRTY

Highly Addictive

Despite myself, his words caught me off guard. "You spent centuries in the Nothingness? But you were dead for only moments."

Dralos simply raised his shoulders in acknowledgment of his lack of knowledge. "That is beyond my understanding."

Many questions fought for priority at that moment. How did he retain his sanity after hundreds of years of isolation? Was it isolation? Was his experience in the Nothingness the same as mine?

But I was running out of time. I needed to move fast if my plan was to work. If anyone raised any alarms or notified anyone higher up the food chain than Chella or Darmond escape would become orders of magnitude more complicated. So I picked the two most relevant questions.

"Who is in charge of this slave Arena?"

"His name is Radford Coldrun, my queen."

"Does he have any position within the Cael Kingdom nobility?"

Dralos shook his head. "I apologize, my queen. I do not recall that answer."

I clicked my tongue and frowned. "How much of your memory is gone?" He started to answer but I waved him down. "Never mind, we don't have time. Lead me to Darmond like you were going to do. Act exactly like the Dralos you were while you were alive. I need Darmond to think he has me so he'll provide the information I need now that I can't raise him since he'll just lose his memories," I grumbled, signaling Dralos to take the lead.

Silent as the dead, Dralos stepped in front of me and began heading down the long corridor of slimes.

"You do remember the way, correct?" I asked, suddenly worried he was leading us in the wrong direction.

"I remember," was all Dralos said and gave no explanation. That was certainly a conversation we would need to have. The memories he retained after the Nothingness were much too relevant for our current situation to be coincidental.

"All right, then lead on, Draconian." I wasn't sure how exactly a Draconian differed from the Dragonborne; another conversation we would need to have later.

It wasn't long before I started to hear the screaming of a man and a woman reverberating along the ooze-filled corridor. When we rounded the corner into the open doorway of Darmond's laboratory room, I saw the reason for all the screams. A man and a woman fought under Orpheus's gaze, ripping into each other with nails and teeth like wild animals.

"That is utterly fascinating!" came Darmond's usual wheezy, irritating voice. "Human nature and its weaknesses never cease to amaze me!"

The instant we'd entered the room, the entire aura around Dralos shifted to match his old persona and his eyes had returned to normal. In fact, he looked and acted as if the prior moments had been all in my imagination. "What are you doing, Doc?" He glanced at the wild fighters with an arrogant smirk. "And why are the mutts fighting outside the Arena?"

"I'll let them answer you," the doctor said gleefully. He turned to Orpheus. "Make the girl answer."

Orpheus shot Darmond an annoyed look, but a moment later the girl looked up above the guy she was fighting, a blue glint flashing in her eyes, indicating she'd received a notification from the Orpheus System. Then I saw the same glint in the man, who stopped fighting immediately. The girl turned to look at Dralos, her expression filled with fear and resolve.

"It is a quest. Fight or lose the System and die." She shivered. "I-I can't lose the System." Her entire body trembled as she spoke, but I could tell it was only partially due to fear. I recognized that look in her eyes and the shaking from a time my people had been infiltrated by a drug cartel. "If I lose the System's power, I'm just normal. I'll be weak again. I can't, I can't be weak again! I've worked so hard for this strength. It's mine and no one will steal it from me!"

"Holy Ashwash, is she addicted to the System?" I whispered, keeping my words low enough to reach only Dralos and covering my mouth by standing behind him.

Dralos chuckled, not showing any visible sign he heard me. "Dumb dogs are crazy for your System, aye Darmond?"

The crazy scientist laughed with the Draconian. "An unexpected boon, I must admit. We'd known the Blood of Orpheus could control the Infected with things called quests and missions, but I had no idea the blood itself was so addictive!" Darmond swept a pipe from his table and showed Dralos a dark purple substance. "You probably don't know, but this is Aexon, an incredibly potent hallucinogen that's been banned in most kingdoms of the western continent. The Sire's blood," he gestured to Orpheus, his smile large and eyes saucers as he bragged openly, "is three times as physically addictive and ten times as mentally addictive if used for long periods of time." He moved to pet the head of the girl who stood as if frozen in time, her gaze unseeing. "These were some of our first trials." Darmond grabbed her hair and shook, all without bothering to look at her. "Unfortunately, its addictive nature is only of such power among some species, like humans. The closer to the ancient generation they are, the less potent it becomes. You would likely be barely affected, Dralos. We can try it out if you'd like!"

Dralos snorted and reached behind him to grab me, shoving me forward. "Stay in your lane, Darmond," he snarled.

The scientist held up his hands in mock surrender, dropping the girl. "Of course, of course. No offense, oh great descendant of the Dragonborne." He turned to Orpheus. "Resume their quest." A blue flash could be seen in both their gazes and the two addicted slaves began tearing into each other without hesitation or remorse.

I wondered if they knew they were addicted or truly believed they were fighting with a resolve to keep the strength they'd earned.

Darmond strode over to me and checked me up and down, a frown forming as he grabbed me and yanked me toward the chair where he'd injected the Blood of Orpheus into me. "You should be showing symptoms of addiction by now. Why aren't I seeing any blue lines? Hmmm." His eyes wandered down the length of me and for once I was thankful the rags I continued to wear had long sleeves, covering the burnt skin where the slave mark had previously been. He pulled out a new syringe, again filled with Orpheus's blood but in a larger quantity. "Perhaps the nobility of your blood is stronger against the effects."

"Why are you doing this?" I cried out, struggling. I forced tears into the corners of my eyes, my nose becoming wet with the effect. "What did we ever do to deserve this? I don't want more of that blood!"

"Don't you like the System?" Darmond asked with an unfriendly smile that showed his dark yellow and brown teeth. "Hasn't it made you stronger than you ever imagined?"

I gulped, sniffling as tears trickled down my cheeks and off my chin. I glanced at the two slaves still fighting, pieces of flesh and gore falling off them and littering the floor. "I don't want to be like that," I whispered, adding a tone of fear to my words.

"Oh, don't worry, deary. I have other plans for you and your section. Although I'm not seeing signs of addiction, you have certainly become less feisty. That's good! A good sign indeed."

"Why is he making them fight each other?" Even as Darmond put the restraints around my wrists, binding me to the chair, I was able to wiggle a finger in Orpheus's direction.

"Hmm? Oh." Darmond laughed. "Oh, don't worry about that. Unless we tell him to hurt you, he's harmless."

"He listens to you?" I asked as innocently as I could, looking at Darmond with the widest eyes I could muster.

The scientist, apparently, couldn't pass up an opportunity to brag. "Of course, he does, like an obedient child."

"Why?" I pressed, hoping the crazed man's ego would push forward. "He's so strong and scary-looking."

Darmond didn't disappoint. "His restraints bind him to Administrators."

"What are Administrators?" I asked, probing for answers with more haste than I should have. Too many Core questions too fast.

The scientist stopped laughing, and I instantly knew he'd realized I was perhaps not as innocent as I would have him believe. His face scrunched in thought, pig-like nose twitching under his beady eyes. "You're asking very particular questions, girlie."

I tried to distract him with more tears, but the look on his face said he wasn't buying it.

I tried a final time to pass as a curious little girl, afraid of death and buying time. "Please, I won't ask any more questions, I promise! Just please, don't put that in me. Stop, no!"

Darmond was no longer smiling, but I saw the corner of his lips twitch at my plea. He lifted the sleeve of my left arm that had no burn and brought the syringe down toward the forearm.

I sighed and created a layer of lunar aura around the limb, causing the syringe of blue liquid to bounce harmlessly off me. "Kill the wild animals, Dralos."

The Draconian was a blur of movement, somehow leagues above what he'd been during his death, as he dispatched the fighters without hesitation. Until I figured out the limits of the System, I couldn't risk letting them live. Not after I'd seen the extent they would go to for the System. Even before they'd been dead, I could hardly recognize them as humans.

Darmond lowered the syringe for a moment, spinning around to watch the Draconian behead both his fighting slaves.

I pulled against the restraints but was surprised to find them holding tight, small gold runes inscribed on the leather bindings sprung to light with a blinding light as I tried to break them with energy. Interesting. I could wield energy while bound, but only if it wasn't used to break them.

"Free me. Then collect these bindings. They may come in handy."

Without a word, Dralos grabbed the back of Darmond's white coat and launched him across the room into the remains of the dead, addicted slaves.

"What in the Gods' names are you doing, you stupid lesser born?" Darmond howled at Dralos as he tried to scramble to his feet and slipped on the gore strewn about around him.

Still silent, Dralos undid my bindings and stepped to the side, waiting for further orders.

"Oh, don't blame him, dear Dr. Darmond," I said, using the scientist's previously mocking tone. "Poor Dralos is only doing what he was told to do."

"I don't know what you did to the Draconian, child," Darmond hissed, drawing out a short dagger with intricate runes written throughout the blade, a single, enormous ruby adorning the base of the hilt. "But you have no concept of what you're doing, of what you're obstructing!"

He stabbed the dagger into the flat front of his hand, skewering it through. Red and blue veins spread from his hand into the dagger's blade and up into the ruby hilt. The gem shattered, revealing a living, beating organ that seemed morbidly similar to a heart.

Dagger still skewering his hand, Darmond pointed at me. "Kneel to an administrator, lesser being."

Instantly, I felt a powerful force from within me surge to the forefront, struggling against my will to compel me into obeying the scientist. The effect was similar to what would have happened if I'd lost in the Mindscape of the Mindscribe. Similar to the Mindscribe, however, Darmond would not find me such an easy foe to fold.

Still, the force from within was strong enough that I was paralyzed in movement, every ounce of my mind and body resisting with maximum effort. I could feel the Blood of Orpheus burning inside, raging against my resistance. There was a need, a desire building in my mind to obey the System's Administrators.

I rejected that building force with every ounce of my Will.

[Quest creation: Obey the Administrators. Obey Administrator 005. This Quest cannot be refused.]
[Quest objective: Stab yourself with a Syringe of Orpheus's blood.]
[Reward: 2x absorption of heart energy!]
[. . .]
[Error: Core System interfering with Administrator 005's Quest.]
[Unknown error.]
[Attempting to assign new quest . . .]

As the blue screens flashed in front of me, I noticed Dralos looking at me almost imploringly. Was he still waiting for an order? My mind raced with possibilities and questions, mainly whether Dralos was still under my authority or whether the System had control as he was resurrected with powers granted to me by the System.

Or were the powers of a Soul Weaver granted to me by the System? Hadn't it simply merged my own previous affinities? Could it claim authority over a power it did not grant when it only merged already established skillsets?

Only one way to find out. In long, drawn-out words, I said, "Drrrraaaaalloooos. Kiillll . . . himmm."

With perhaps even more speed than when he'd dispatched the rabid fighters, Dralos closed the space separating him from Darmond. Large, scaled hands gripped the scientist's neck and heaved him into the air.

[NEW EMERGENCY QUEST: KILL DRALOS THE DRACONIAN. THIS QUEST CANNOT BE REFUSED.]
[Reward: 10x absorption of heart energy.]
[NEW EMERGENCY QUEST: SAVE THE ADMINISTRATOR! THIS QUEST CANNOT BE REFUSED.]

Dralos snapped Darmond's neck with a sickening crunch accompanied only by the man's last gurgling plea.

[Error: Quest terminated.]

The blue flashing screens vanished. The room was deathly silent compared to the screams of the System and man only seconds earlier. That silence was pierced only by the soft chuckling of Orpheus, still chained by his golden restrictions. With a subsequent pop, the surging tidal wave compelling me to act against my Will vanished, and the paralyzing hold on my body was released.

That had been closer than expected. Whatever ability Darmond had used as an apparent administrator to paralyze me had been wholly unexpected. It was simply fortunate Dralos himself had not been affected. If he had been, I was honestly not sure how I'd have survived. I needed to remove the System and all Orpheus's blood from my body as fast as I could.

Orpheus's once gaunt, hopeless face was now a picture of satisfied rage. "The advent of the Soul Weaver cannot be denied," he whispered. Turning his eyes to me, he relayed a request that turned my blood hot with anticipation and, in no small part, worry for what would happen next. I had a feeling I was about to begin a path never before even imagined to be possible. "Absorb my soul and Core, Soul Weaver. And then devour my heart. The Soul Weaver must rise."

CHAPTER THIRTY-ONE

The Gamble

I knelt next to the chained sire, letting my distaste for his request show clearly on my face. "Now, why would I do that, Progenitor?" But, seeing as how he was conveniently chained up and wasn't going anywhere, and considering that I'd been drowning in the agency of others since I'd arrived in this world, I figured I was finally due some answers.

"It is my duty to perish for the creation of a Soul Weaver Progenitor. The System demands it," he answered, his black eyes filled with fanatic excitement, but there was also a distinctly exhausted note in his words. "I am so very tired, Soul Weaver. My existence has been a long one. Too long. I am the last of my kind. The last Angellic."

"An Angellic? I've never heard of them before."

Orpheus nodded with a sullen expression, though the fervent gleam in his eyes hadn't wavered. "My progeny. I am a sire to nothing now, extinguished by the progeny of the Dragon and Demon sires. Allow me to fulfill my destiny, Awakened. I yearn to return to the Nothingness."

"What is this 'Soul Weaver'?" I asked, still frowning. There was something extremely unnerving about the Progenitor chained in front of me. While I'd encountered and even killed a Progenitor before, none had ever spoken to me, much less entertained an entire conversation. Perhaps this Progenitor, the Angellic Progenitor, was truly, simply exhausted from his eternity of life.

"A Soul Weaver," Orpheus said with a grim smile, "is how the System refers to the Progenitor of a race called the Marzana. The Main System chose you for that purpose. That is what it seeks for you to become."

"To what end?" I pressed, feeling that there was some piece of information being omitted. Why was it so important to create these Marzana?

"I do not know. But devour me, oh Queen of Rot. Devour me and it will tell you itself."

I raised an eyebrow in feigned ignorance, though in real surprise, at the nearly begging plea to be eaten. "I am but a baron's daughter. Why do you call me Queen of Rot?"

Orpheus gave a grunt of irritation. "Do not play games with me, Queen of Aedronir. Even without access to the System, you cannot fool me with a Soul Transference, no matter how rare such an occurrence may be."

I leaned in closer so our noses practically touched, his fervent expression a stark contrast to my building impatience. "The System knows who I am then? Who I really am? And so do these sires that have access to the System?"

Orpheus sighed, letting his head droop a bit. His bindings clanked and danced with the motion. His mouth moved to say something but then suddenly snapped shut as a blue glint appeared in the corner of his eye. A screen.

"You do not control the System," I realized, grabbing back his wandering attention.

Orpheus shook his head and sighed. "I may be one of its creators, but even I find myself bound to its authority. Only a few sires can resist its claim." He paused, a thoughtful look crossing his features as he debated his next words. "Beware the Demon Sire, or the Demon Progenitor, as you call him. He is not the same being you previously defeated. He is much more . . . devious."

"Then who are the Administrators?" I asked, ignoring the warning. The Demon Progenitor had already allowed me to escape once. Even if he was a threat, it wasn't an immediate one. In any case, he wasn't my problem unless he got in my way.

Orpheus sneered at the question and spat in the direction of Darmond. "Some fortunate mortals figured out blood directly from my heart provides a higher level of authority within the System than normal. Administrator is what they called themselves and I suppose the System approved of the title. It means nothing to a Progenitor, guardians of the System. Once you join our ranks, you will be able to squash them like an insect."

I snorted. "Unless they bind me like you."

Orpheus just smiled as if it was no big deal. And, perhaps, to him, it really wasn't. I wanted to ask how they'd captured him, but I doubted he'd put up much of a fight judging by how desperately he was asking me for death.

"What is the System? Is it alive?" I asked instead.

Orpheus smiled but said nothing. He simply gazed at me with expectation and anticipation, as if he was reading the very lines of my destiny. Eventually, he said, "I do not know, Soul Weaver. It was once simply an amalgamation of our Authorities. But it has been many millennia that the System has ruled over the Progenitors. It is what it decides to be."

That would explain why the Progenitors were so powerful if their growth had been boosted by the System for millennia. I wondered just how old the Progenitors really were. They couldn't be millennia old, or there was no way I should have been able to kill the Demon Progenitor. If they'd been even close to my rate of growth under the System, they would have exceeded my prime strength long ago.

Yet I *had* killed him. But not from raw strength. No, I had managed to defeat the Progenitor with the help of others in a combined attack on the Progenitor's Mindscape before killing it in the physical realm.

The power of Will. Perhaps . . .

"Why had my world never heard of the System?"

He, again, merely shrugged. "Perhaps your world did not look in the right place. Or perhaps it did and you simply were not aware. I do not know."

"How do I rid myself of this System?"

"You don't."

"I do not want your System," I hissed, feeling my impatience at Orpheus's uncaring attitude boil over. "Nor do I care about your prophecy. Just tell me how to get your Ashwash-cursed System's authority out of me." I could still feel the blue Blood of Orpheus squirming through my veins and it made my skin crawl.

"You can't," Orpheus said, his gaze far away. "It is a part of you now. You belong to the System. You all belong to the System just as many of the other Progenitors now belong to the System." His eyes refocused and the restrained creature gave me another pitying smile.

At that moment I decided to take the gamble I'd been debating.

"For someone who claims to know what I am, you do not seem to have any grasp of just who I am." His confidence seemed to waver for the first time since Dralos had killed Darmond. "My power is my own. I will take what belongs to me. Always." I leaned in even closer and lowered my voice.

"Your System is not the first to challenge my sovereignty, and I doubt it will be the last. But all challenges end in the same way." My hands snapped from where they hung to grasp either side of Orpheus's head. "You are correct about one thing, Progenitor of the Angellic. I *am* the Queen of Rot. I *am* the Queen of Aedronir. And I am *indomitable.*"

I drew heart energy from my Core and directed it out through my hands. The moment it connected with Orpheus's Core, I opened my Mindscape, forcing Orpheus within it. And, hopefully, the System as well. I expected the runes on Orpheus's shackles to burn with its golden light, but nothing happened. He wasn't resisting my invasion into his mind. He didn't even try to summon his own Mindscape for dominance.

Similar to my fight against the Mindscribe, my Mindscape took on the appearance of Ordite. But that was where the similarities ended. Instead of being surrounded by the rays of Ordite's double suns, there was solid darkness illuminated by three dim moons. Each was high in the sky at different times of its phase: one full, one waxing, and the third waning.

I found myself on a large, smooth boulder opposite Orpheus, who had been placed atop a hill of rocks and sand. A single river, perhaps a dozen meters wide, ran between where I stood and Orpheus, the rushing of water silent in the reality of my Mindscape. In fact, there was not a sound in the dead of darkness other than the beat of our breathing. The distance showed a thick curtain of trees and bushes, but there was nothing in our vicinity other than boulders of varying sizes and sand that wafted in spirals with every brush of wind.

"Interesting," Orpheus muttered, looking around. "Why do you summon me to your Mindscape? We are outside the realm of reality here. My authority is free of those restrictions."

I smiled at the same time Orpheus released a wave of his authority, sweeping rocks and sand into a tornado around himself before launching it outward. Although not directed at me, I let out some heart energy to deflect whatever ended up in my direction. My Core jumped and cheered in anticipation, ready to be used to its full capabilities.

"I suppose I'm not entirely free of the restrictions then." He flexed his fingers, clearly disappointed the restrictions were still there, if lessened drastically.

"Summon your System," I said, motioning around me. "It should be able to take a more corporeal form here."

Orpheus stared at me, mouth almost hanging. It was a long moment before he responded. "That is not how it works."

I closed my eyes, grasped my Mindscape with the full effort of my Will, and bore down on the Progenitor. Unlike the Mindscribe, it did little to affect him. He winced ever so slightly.

"You do not need to fight me," he noted, not bothering to put up any defense against my mental ambush. "Like I said, I want you to kill me."

"Summon the System," I repeated, glaring at him. "Now."

Orpheus chuckled. "I am not its master."

"It's inside of you, isn't it? If your heart grants authority over the System, it must be a part of you."

He nodded. "It is also a part of you now."

"System!" I shouted at the fake reality of our surroundings. "Speak to me! Cease hiding behind your pawn." Still nothing. I redirected my words to Orpheus's heart and willed a cut to manifest vertically across my forearm, red-blue blood spilling out. "I have come to make a bet with you. I may not know why you so desire the creation of the Marzana, but I know you need me alive." I willed the cut longer and wider. Though the blood pouring from the widening cut was not true blood, injuries in a Mindscape affect the strength of one's mind and sanity. "How far will you risk staying silent?"

I was about to cut an arm off when a blue screen of the Orpheus System popped up.

[New Quest!]
[The System has acknowledged its interest in your welfare.
Speak.]
[Reward: ???]

"Finally." I snapped a thread of power, and the wound sealed itself, though the life essence lost wasn't recovered. "Orpheus tells me he is your guardian, or at least one of them. I'm sure you have granted him great strength and abilities, much as you have with the others who were injected with his blood. But I have a question for you. Do you trust the strength of his mind?"

Orpheus blinked at me, clearly confused. "Soul Weaver, I have lived for thousands of years. A mortal could not withstand a battle of wills with any Progenitor, much less one as aged as myself."

"That's what the Demon Progenitor said to me," I hissed back, "before I drove him insane and took off his head."

[Alert: Additional Quest information!]
[Quest type: Optional. This Quest is optional.]
[The System is willing to accept the Soul Weaver's bet of mental combat.]
[Goal: Defeat the Progenitor of the Angellic, Orpheus, within the Soul Weaver's Mindscape.]
[Punishment: Failure to defeat the guardian Progenitor will result in the Soul Weaver becoming a Progenitor under the System. The Soul Weaver will be tasked with starting a new bloodline: the Marzana.]
[Reward: ???]

"I want my own System as a reward." My heart raced as I made my demand. "Cut off a piece of yourself and give it to me." It was a huge risk asking for such an existence to harm itself, and an even larger risk to assume I could subdue even a piece of it.

But I had faith in the strength of my mind. That, at least, had never left me.

[Alert: Additional Quest information!]
[Quest type: Optional. This Quest is optional.]
[The System accepts the Soul Weaver's terms.]
[Reward: Upon defeating the System's guardian, a piece of the System will be removed from the Original entity and absorbed into the Soul Weaver.]
[Quest start!]

Orpheus shrugged, his eyes scanning something in front of him I couldn't see, though I knew it to be likely the same messages I was being presented with. "If this is what you desire, then so be it." I couldn't tell if he was speaking to me or the System. Perhaps he was not truly speaking to either of us. The Sire didn't stretch or ready himself. His smooth face had greatly aged in the Mindscape as his mind formed his true self. His face was now a mess of wrinkles, old gray eyes staring longingly into Nothingness. His body shrunk as his hair turned gray. The once great being looked at me and all I saw was a haggard old man.

On the other hand, my body grew once again in height and musculature. The hair on my head lengthened as my eyes deepened to a blood red and hundreds of old scars littered every inch of my skin. The glow of the lunar crescent adorning my forehead morphed into existence, though it was still struck through by a thin black line I didn't fully understand.

The scar that ran through my right eye began to throb like it always had in Ordite—a familiar, yet haunting feeling that was somehow also comforting. A new feeling I hadn't felt in my previous Mindscape combat presented itself now; a deep, angry burning around my throat. Although I couldn't see it, I knew instantly what it was.

The markings of a rope burn. The rope that had hung me to the very last string of my life.

The mark of my everlasting rage.

Waves of authority began to radiate from both of us simultaneously, the powers clashing and slamming into each other with promises of death and pain.

Putting forth all my Will and ramping my Core to full capacity, I surged forward.

CHAPTER THIRTY-TWO

Lilliana

Despite the small hope I'd harbored that my Will would be able to dominate the Mindscape, Orpheus proved me wrong. In fact, he proved my assumptions to be wildly wrong, and he did so at breakneck speed.

Literally.

Orpheus was on me again, his hands as large as my face and gripping either side of my head. Crunch. He twisted his hands, and my neck snapped. Again.

The Progenitor let my incorporeal form drop to the ground before he put a bit of distance between us, looking quite bored. A moment later, I was back on my feet, the illusion of my neck back to the angle it was supposed to be. The Mindscape was an interesting phenomenon. While the inhabitants fought with their will and their minds at stake, the way they fought with their will was represented through the physical actions of their soul bodies.

"Aren't you getting tired of this?" Orpheus asked, a hammer materializing in his previously bare hands. He leaned casually against a giant boulder my skull had previously been shattered against, some dried blood scraping off the stone as his shoulder brushed against it.

I stretched and rotated my neck around so that it cracked a few times. "Not particularly. Rather, I am relieved. The kink in my neck is gone. I give you my thanks for the treatment, Progenitor."

Orpheus sighed. "Your Will is tough, but it is not yet strong enough to match mine."

"We'll see," I said, continuing to stretch out my neck, which was in an incredible amount of pain. "Perhaps you will tire." No words were spoken in response. I blinked, and he was suddenly in front of me, hands reaching out to snap my neck for the fifteenth time.

Predicting the way he'd reach out toward me based on the previous approaches, I threw myself to the side the moment he vanished from my peripheral. I may not have been able to see him move, but there was only one place he'd go for. My throat.

I tucked my chin and entered a roll as my body flew through the air. Before I landed, a dull, blinding pain erupted from my ribs as Orpheus smoothly shifted his attack from a single-handed grab to arching his new warhammer upward into my side.

Without hitting the ground, I was again blown into the air. He allowed me to simply slam into a nearby boulder and didn't bother to approach as I struggled back to my feet.

His frown deepened when I flashed him a grin. I'd dodged him that time. He had missed me. I had predicted his movement, and he knew it.

"It won't matter. I will simply change my approach if you start guessing." The hilt of his hammer bounced against his shoulder like it weighed nothing. Which, I supposed, it didn't really since we were in my Mindscape.

I shrugged. "That may be. However, you will, eventually, run out of variations. And I will learn your preferences. Your habits. And then I will find your weakness." I bent my knees and dropped back down into a fighting stance, hands at the ready and light on my feet. "You may be more powerful than me, but you will never be able to break my mind."

Orpheus groaned in frustration as the glint of a blue screen flickered in his gaze. "Yes, yes. I know." He turned to face me with an annoyed expression. "It was a well-played trick. I cannot defeat you, not truly, because if I break your mind to forcefully end your Mindscape, there will be no mind left to raise into a sire. Still, that does not mean I cannot bring you close to the breaking point. When you're begging for death, maybe then you will see the future the System is presenting you with."

I felt the ire inside me rage at the promise. It should have been a threat. He was threatening to beat me to death. Yet, it didn't feel like a threat. It felt like Orpheus was stating a simple fact. A promise that he would beat me within an inch of breaking. That he would then let me heal and do it all over again. That he would slowly and painfully break my mind since breaking my incorporeal body within the Mindscape was proving impossible. Or, at least, overly arduous. I let out a snort.

All I needed to do was keep my senses open. Learn. Adapt. Grow. This was as much training as it was a death battle, though that was likely not Orpheus's intention.

A proper warrior, her father had told the young queen candidates as they lay on blood-soaked dirt, exhausted and surrounded by a field of corpses of their own making, "They will take everything as a lesson. They will learn even when it seems like they will not live through the experience. The moment you stop learning, stop adapting, is the moment you die."

When Orpheus's warhammer slammed into my chest, I did not scream. When he crushed my skull, I did not wince. Even when Orpheus morphed his hammer into small daggers and slowly cut me piece to piece before allowing me to heal, I did not show him weakness. Each time I healed and each time I stared him down, letting him know the pain he inflicted on me only stirred the fire within me. Pain would not destroy my mind.

It only fueled my infinite rage.

I wasn't sure how long passed in my Mindscape. Weeks? Months? Years? It hardly mattered. Time in a Mindscape was fractions of reality. Either way, the Nothingness had long since devoured my innate worry about time. What difference did time make when one had already spent endless time in the Nothingness?

No, I was single-mindedly focused on one simple goal—predicting Orpheus's next move.

For the longest time, I could not read him beyond two moves. The variations he had mastered were too great and numerous. But as time passed by, I learned which ones he favored. His first move was always a quick approach, swiftly followed by a movement shift ability that allowed him to reposition as needed. Once I'd pinned that down, I tested it. Over and over again, desperately trying to not let him catch on to what I'd learned.

I found that his repositioning was limited to shifting attack patterns. It did not lend itself to defensive maneuvers. Once I was positive my counter would work against his general movements, I set it into play.

It was my first time striking Orpheus. When he moved to reposition into a swing of his axe after I'd dodged the initial blow, I quickly moved inside his reach. Orpheus tried to shift his weight into an upward swing instead of a brutal horizontal cleave, but the handle was locked in place by the hard bone of my shin.

The surprised expression on his face filled me with satisfaction as I, at last, absolutely buried my fist into his skull with the full force of my Will.

His head snapped back and twisted with the familiar crunch of a broken neck.

I stumbled forward into his limp body from the force of my blow and nearly tripped over it. Unlike Orpheus, who had allowed me time to heal each time so that he could keep inflicting pain without completely breaking my mind, I wouldn't allow him time to heal. Pushing my Core beyond its capacity, I circulated every ounce of heart energy through me and released it throughout my Mindscape along with the most powerful burst of Will I could muster.

My authority over the Mindscape manipulated the illusionary mental world, twisting the space and environment around Orpheus into a coffin filled with sharp stakes of my energy and Will. With another push of my authority, the coffin Orpheus's broken body now lay in snapped shut and impaled him with the thousands of little luminescent stakes that shone with my heart energy until the moment the coffin closed, and I couldn't see them.

The Mindscape went silent, but I did not release it. I debated releasing it for a moment but decided not to until the System admitted its defeat. If Orpheus's Will and mind had not been broken, I was worried the return to reality would release his mind from the coffin. Based on the information I'd learned from Orpheus, I was wholly uncertain whether the golden chains binding him were actually stopping the Progenitor from breaking free or whether he was simply choosing to remain chained.

I sank to the ground, sitting on a blood-covered boulder as I waited for the System's message. Wet blood squished underneath me when I sat. As disturbing as that felt, every rock in the vicinity was similarly drenched in gore. At least the Mindscape wasn't portraying brain remnants on this rock.

And I was too tired to manipulate the Mindscape into cleaning itself. Or walking somewhere else.

I leaned back, propping myself up against the hard stone, and stared up at the three moons in the sky. It took me a while longer to catch my breath enough that I could speak coherently. "Hey, System? I believe my victory is now only a matter of waiting. It would be convenient if you would surrender before I am necessitated to waste more time."

The System did not answer. Not even a single ding or beep. I understood what it was likely thinking . . . assuming an entity like the System thought at all. It was likely waiting for a complete result. For a mind to break or surrender.

With Orpheus locked in a coffin that would constantly rip apart his soul body during its recovery, he would be prevented from fully forming again. It would be an eternal loop of dying again and again. A very deserved loop considering the number of times he'd pummeled me. He had asked me to kill him. Multiple times. In a way, I was obliging his request.

I smirked at nothing, intending it to be directed at the System, and allowed myself to sag down the boulder in relief. I knew I shouldn't. Never relax until there is confirmation of death, my father had always warned. But I didn't have the strength. My Will was pulled thin, my mind weary, and my Core drained. If Orpheus burst from the coffin somehow, I wouldn't be able to put up any defense regardless of whether my guard was up or not.

If the Progenitor escaped, I would have to find a different way to defeat him. However, I'd cross that bridge when it started to burn. For the moment, I relaxed and tried to allow my mind to recover from its beating.

I was very lucky, I knew. If Orpheus had truly intended to kill me or break my mind, even in his current weakened state, it would have taken him a fraction of a second. Probably not even that long if I was being completely honest, and he would not have needed to move his soul form. Within the first few deaths, it had become painfully obvious that Orpheus could have simply and easily crushed me with the pressure of his Will alone.

How the Kingdom of Cael had captured Orpheus was beyond my under-standing. The strength of Orpheus's weakened Will still dwarfed mine. Not even the Demon Progenitor I'd defeated had eclipsed my Will to such an extent. In fact, mine had been nearly on par. It seemed like Orpheus had perhaps desired to be captured. To speak with me? To relay the System's message to me? The extent of the Progenitor's designs was unclear. Hopefully, he would die and it wouldn't matter anymore.

While I continued to wait for the System to admit its defeat, I made my way over to the shallow river and started to wash my face. It was a useless act. The moment the Mindscape ended, my soul form would vanish, and my mind would return to its physical body. But that didn't mean I had to suffer dry blood cracking whenever I moved and wet gore from Orpheus's skull sliding down my face and torso. I knelt and reached a hand into the water to scoop some into my face.

The water, even if fake, was cool as it washed over my face. My body relaxed and I could feel some of the blood being washed away. I wished the water could do the same for my utterly depleted Core.

My heart leaped into my chest as a hand burst from the river reaching straight for my face. After the time spent practicing dodging Orpheus's initial move, my reaction was instinctual. I dodged, tucking my chin and body into a roll as I smoothly rotated away from the lake and back on my feet.

I reached into my reserves to pull on energy or Will. Nothing responded and I cursed, unsurprised. Gritting my teeth I glared at the hand that gripped the river's edge and began to haul a body up the river.

While readying myself for another eternity of being pummeled, a head peeked over the river's edge, and it was not Orpheus. It wasn't even close to Orpheus. It was . . . me?

No, her eyes weren't red, and her hair was a darker shade of brown. The girl was also much smaller. Wait, I recognized her. It was me. The 'me' right after I transferred to Graedon. She even wore the torn, brown peasant clothes I'd originally worn when I came to in this new world.

"Lilliana?" I asked, my mouth dropping in pure disbelief. Could it be a trick? My eyes had just started to dart around for Orpheus when the girl spoke. Her voice was soft and seemed almost rusty, as if unused for a long period. Which, in a way, it hadn't.

"We don't have much time," she said quietly, glancing toward where I'd buried Orpheus. "He'll escape soon."

"What? How do you know that? No, hold on. How are you even here?" More questions came to mind, and my mouth was quickly unable to keep up with the piling levels of confusion. Whatever answers I may have gotten were interrupted by a terrible trembling of the entire Mindscape. "Ashwash curse it," I groaned. He was escaping.

"When I say to, I want you to close this realm," Lilliana said, gesturing around herself. "I can't do much for you even though you've done so much to keep me alive. But I can do this. My soul is nearly gone anyway." The girl gave me a thin, gentle smile that was so different from my own that it completely changed her features. Or, maybe, it was my expressions and personality that distorted her body.

"What are you going to do?" I didn't need to ask, not really. There was only one thing she could do in this situation, other than join me in a beating.

"Whatever you've done to strengthen yourself has also strengthened my own soul," she explained. "We are the same person. But we're also different.

I . . . I don't know how I know this, but I know I can defeat him. I've been with you the entire time. I know you have struggled. You've struggled so much to keep us alive." Her small voice trembled, betraying her true feelings despite the resilience I saw in her eyes. "I can do this. We can do this." She walked up to me, and I didn't back away, watching in awe as her small hands gripped my own. I realized I was in my original body, not Lilliana's, so I towered over her. Still, I couldn't take my eyes off the little girl who fought against her fear. In another time she may have grown to be a powerful entity in her own right. "Just promise me one thing." In my exhaustion and general bafflement at everything happening, I simply nodded. "Kill the Baron and Morgana," she hissed, and I felt my heart energy stir at her vehemence. "For me. And for my mother."

Again I nodded.

Lilliana released my hands and ran over to where Orpheus was buried and sat on the shaking ground even as cracks spread like spiderwebs throughout the Mindscape.

"Not yet," she said, closing her eyes and holding her hands together in what I could only believe to be a prayer.

I said nothing. Part of me didn't want to allow Lilliana to do what she was going to do. I was the queen. I protected what was mine and annihilated what threatened mine. And, wasn't she mine? She was a part of who I was now. My rage flared. Lilliana *was* mine. I would not allow Orpheus or the System to take what was mi—

As if sensing my thoughts, Lilliana opened her eyes and smiled. "You have been protecting me since I called out to you. Now, let me return it." She took a deep breath. "May we one day see each other again."

"That was quite surprising," came Orpheus's voice, no longer bored or lazy. Instead, it was filled with malevolence, cold as frozen steel.

He was still deep in the earth of the Mindscape but sounded to be quickly rising. The instant he showed, Lilliana screamed, "NOW, LILITH!"

I snapped off the Mindscape just as a second, smaller Mindscape overlapped with mine and imploded around Lilliana and Orpheus.

The sensation of the transition was jarring, as if my very essence was being pulled through a narrow tunnel. I was back in my physical body, gasping for air and drenched in sweat. My surroundings slowly came into focus. The cold, sterile environment of the chamber in the Kingdom of Cael.

"Lilliana?" a voice called out, tentative and concerned. Dralos.

"I'm here," I managed to say, my voice hoarse. A headache painfully pounded inside my head as something ugly squirmed in my gut at the last, sad smile Lilliana had given to me.

Dralos's voice came low and gruff. Older than I remembered. "Did it work?"

I took a deep breath, feeling the weight of exhaustion settling over me once more. "I am not sure. The System has yet to respond. Orpheus . . . He might still be alive." Both of our heads snapped toward the body of Orpheus, which still hung limp in the cradle of his golden chains.

As if on cue, a faint chime echoed in the chamber, and a holographic display materialized before me. The System's message was brief, but it carried the weight of finality.

[System announcement: Victory confirmed. Orpheus terminated.]
[Reward: You will soon be provided with a piece of the System.
The Main System will not interfere with the split System.]

Relief and something close to sorrow washed over me in equal measure. Lilliana's final act had ensured our victory but at the cost of her life. Even though I had not even known she was alive within me, I now felt something empty in my Core. As if something important was missing. The Baron and Morgana would both die. I would make sure of it.

I climbed to my feet from where I sat, a small amount of heart energy beginning to circulate. I didn't have time to labor over what had happened or what I had unknowingly lost. Or whether it was even lost. I didn't have the information, and I was running out of time for my plan.

Nor did I have time to think about the cracks that had appeared in my Mindscape. I would deal with it later. I needed to continue moving forward.

The throbbing pain in my head intensified, but I buried the pain just like I had buried Orpheus. I was the Queen of Aedronir. People around me died. I killed whatever stood in my way, no matter what they were. People fought and died for me. That's just how it was.

That's . . . how it was. How it should be!

Something came over me and under my breath, I whispered, "We will have our vengeance, Lilliana." Dralos shot me a confused look, but I ignored the Draconian. The fire of vengeance igniting within my Core as I spoke the words.

The battle was not over, but with Lilliana's sacrifice, we had gained a crucial victory, and I needed to cement it. I didn't know whether Orpheus's death, assuming he truly was dead and not merely "defeated" like the Demon Progenitor had been, would cancel the System's hold on the slaves already embedded with the System. If the System was still running in them, I needed to move quickly before the Administrators caught wind of my movements and blocked me from obtaining my slave army.

"I need to understand what I have gained from this victory," I commanded Dralos, stumbling over to the cushioned chair Darmond had used. "Prepare the slaves in our section for me. I want them armed by the time I'm ready. Don't kill Chella just yet. I made a mistake telling you to kill Darmond before we figured out where Radford Coldrun is. I want to . . . speak with him."

"As you wish, my queen." Dralos bowed low and made to depart.

"How long was I gone for?" I asked as Dralos reached the still-opened door to the slime tunnels.

The Draconian's lips pursed in thought for a moment. "My queen, it is my belief you were in combat with the Sire for somewhere around three to four hours."

I nodded and dismissed him. That was much longer than I'd planned for when I'd begun my attack on the Colosseum's slavers. Fortunately, if no one had attempted to find me, then they were likely under the belief that Darmond was still doing his experiments. But that wouldn't last forever. I doubted it would last past the hour considering the Cael King had acknowledged my nobility. Even if I was a prisoner of war and some sort of disrespect was intended toward the Lysorian King by keeping me in the slave dungeons, there would be a limit. I knew from experience nobility despised allowing common-blooded individuals to feel superior to those with noble blood, regardless of how they felt about the other noble. Someone would come looking at some point, even if only out of a misplaced ego trip.

I closed my eyes and turned inward just as a new System message dinged. The expected blue screen and white text never appeared.

What appeared in front of me was a heavy, pitch-black screen adorned only by scribbled texts in blood-like ink.

[System announcement: Congratulations on your victory, Awakened.]

[Reward: You have been awarded your own System based on the color of your soul.]

[Main System warning: Systems were not meant to be controlled. A System being controlled by a Host will fight back. If the System is not kept under absolute control, the Host will face corruption.]

CHAPTER THIRTY-THREE

A System of Desire

[System announcement: Beginning merge of Host with System.]

It was like a bolt of lightning slammed into my already worn body, setting my mind aflame in a deadly thrill of electricity. The System power melded forcefully into me, both intoxicating and immeasurable. I desperately kept in mind the Main System's message regarding corruption and struggled to maintain the walls of my mind as firmly as I could against the intoxication of this new System.

Just as the Main System had warned, the new System began to fight back against my hold almost immediately upon rebounding against my mental defenses. While the System was powerful, it had also just been born. Not only that but it was also created in my image according to the Main System.

It was an odd sort of struggle. In my initial interactions with the System, I'd believed it to be some sort of hive mind-like existence, retaining control over a large number of powerful beings. However, my melding with the new System was more akin to meeting a parasite. And the more I adopted the new System, the more I realized it wasn't exactly an intelligent existence—no, it was more similar to a type of universal energy. Like heart energy. Or the feeling I got from forming my Core.

But, somehow, not quite the same. It was more alive than a Core or pure energy.

I couldn't quite place the feeling. It was almost like energy had an intent of its own.

The electricity faded as I forced dominance over the newborn System and it eventually submitted to my stranglehold, much as my heart energy had done during the Core formation. It squirmed in resistance for a final second before I felt something settle in my mind.

[System announcement: You have subdued the new System.]
[New System renamed to the Desire System.]
[System type is currently being decided based on past achievements.]
[Deal type Dominance System applied.]

There were different types of Systems? I frowned, leaning into the armrest with my elbow and rubbing the side of my head in a useless attempt to soothe the splitting headache. Even with my high level of Will, if I didn't get some rest soon, I knew I would collapse from sheer mental depletion.

"System, explain what 'Deal type Dominance' means," I commanded and willed the System to answer. It took a moment, but it answered.

[System message: The Desire System is a skill obtained by Host Lilith Reiter that allows the Host to bestow System benefits to another being, titling them as a "Paragon." Each agreement individually restricts the Host's ability to command the Paragon. The Host will not be able to interfere with the Paragon's Path of Desire. The effects of this System exist within the Host AND Paragons; it is therefore not restricted to any specific location. Unlike the Main System, the jurisdiction of this System MAY NOT be restricted by the Host or Administrators, should any Paragon be raised to such status.]
[System benefits: Increased energy gain, obtaining skill sets, and other bonuses in exchange for acknowledging the Host as their queen.]

"What is a Path of Desire? What are other System benefits?" I asked. When no answer came, I turned toward my mind and pressed down on the System with some Will, but nothing happened. I repeated my question and finally, it answered. Sort of.

[System message: The answer to the Host's question is unknown. Details will be understood once a Paragon is created.]

I sighed and pushed to my feet. The world instantly tilted and nausea clawed up my throat in a rush of bile I barely kept down. I needed to sleep. Badly. All my heart energy reserves were utterly depleted. Perhaps if my Core had reached Silver level, I'd be able to rely on Core energy, what heart energy becomes after long-term marination inside a Core, but that wasn't currently available to me. Only the heart energy circulating in my Core would be useful. The energy inside my Core that I'd built was too low in quality and quantity to matter much.

"Are you able to purge me of the Main System?"

[System message: There are no traces of the Main System within the Host.]

My eyes widened with surprise. "It's been removed? Even Orpheus's blood?" A moment passed with no response and then—

[System message: The blood of the Main System's guardian was purged during the merging of the Host Queen and the Desire System.]

I remembered something the Main System had said about my Core. "What about the Core System? Will that be purged from me?"

[System message: The Host's Core System is not a True System. It is a mechanism to harness the energy of our Universe. Systems cannot interfere with natural energy mechanisms, though the way a System interacts with mechanisms such as the "Core System" can differ. In the Host's situation, the Main System attempted a direct interference with the Core System causing an error, though the interference was still accepted to a degree.]

I wasn't entirely sure what that meant, but when I pressed the System for more information regarding what it meant by "to a degree," it stubbornly kept silent. Since time was of the essence, I changed the direction of my questions.

"Do you have the ability to purge others the same way?" Though I couldn't see the System and it didn't have any physical attributes, I felt like I could sense it nodding as it narrated the red text.

[System message: Any being who agrees to become a Paragon will be purged of all other System influences. Only a direct invasion from a separate System can combat the purging.]

That last line was ominous, but there wasn't time to worry about the possibilities of other Systems and the morbid reality of what that implied for humanity's future of freedom as a whole.

Armed with the knowledge I could purge the System from others, albeit only when agreed, I knew it was time to follow up with Dralos. I reached out to the System for the last pieces of pressing information I needed to go forth with my plans.

"Do I retain the heart energy and skills the Main System provided?" I pressed, wondering whether I'd be able to still use the resurrection abilities. That, and if the abilities carried over, it would likely be a lot easier to convert the slaves.

[System message: A System convert will retain certain abilities if that is within the authority of the new System. All levels and energy provided by the previous System will be revoked as it is outside the new System's authority. Energy obtained by a System user while under a System Influence but not bestowed by the System will be retained.]

I wasn't sure what that meant, and the System refused to answer any more of my questions no matter how much pressure I put on it. Perhaps it didn't know. I'd try again when my Will had been rested. Still, at least I knew these Paragons of mine would keep their abilities and energy to some extent. This would make convincing them slightly easier. Hopefully.

My feet felt like they were lead as I left the laboratory and headed back down the hallway of slime toward the slaves' quarters. I tried to ignore the exhaustion and weight of my body and mind by turning my thoughts to the slaves. With the power already granted to them by the Main System and the addiction levels of Orpheus's blood, I didn't know who would take my offer. It was more than likely most would simply choose to stay with the

Main System. I didn't know whether the addictive quality was the dead Progenitor's blood or the System itself, and I didn't really want to find out, but at the same time, I didn't want to rely on fighters in withdrawal.

I paused, an idea occurring to me. "System, is my blood addictive like Orpheus'?"

This time the System's response was immediate and, unlike all the other messages I'd ever received from a System, it was said in an almost conversational manner, colloquial even.

[System message: Waaaaaay more.]

Shit. I wasn't sure if that was a good or bad thing, though replacing one addiction with another was somewhat of a solution. Only time would tell if addictive blood would result in a long-term benefit or not. I imagined a whole army of blood-addicted beasts clawing away at me for blood and I shuddered. It was a risk for sure, especially at my power level. While my System was different from Orpheus's, they had apparently been able to free themselves from his control with bindings. I didn't know if my System would also allow that type of switch in authority.

I really needed to get stronger.

It was an eerie walk back to the slave dungeons. I hadn't before noticed the way the hallway itself and the slime pervading it seemed to shift as if alive. Unlike when I'd been accompanied by another, the solemn silence of the trek began to stir a feeling of unease inside of me. The longer I was in the hallway, the more I began to see signs that this wasn't a hallway. It felt increasingly like I was walking inside the throat of some creature and that the slime was not actually slime, but saliva and phlegm.

I would have sprinted from the disturbing passage on any other day. Today though, I didn't have the energy. Physically, I was probably in good enough condition to run. But my energy reserves couldn't support the attempt.

So instead, I just trudged through and hoped if it was a throat, that the beast wouldn't swallow me whole right then and there. Fortunately, I never found out if the mysterious passage was alive or not and managed to exit it back into the dungeon cavern.

While I had hoped that the slaves would line up obediently upon Dralos's command, I wasn't surprised to find that many of them stood around the Draconian, red-faced and yelling slurs in his and Chella's direction. The ones at the forefront of the mob were Gronch and Romeo, catching me off guard.

In all my years, I had never once seen a half orc and an obviously noble-born human so in sync.

"I told you," Dralos said through gritted teeth, looking more annoyed at the inconvenience than frustrated by it, "Lady Lilliana will be here soon." In response to his words, a loud female voice struggled to be understood, her words coming out strangled.

I noticed then that Chella, who stood beside Dralos, was actually bound by the cuffs that the old Dralos had tossed at me, and her mouth was tightly covered by a leather gag.

"What is going on?" Romeo shouted for what was probably, based on the vein throbbing on his forehead, the hundredth time. "And why is she," he pointed to Chella, "tied up? Where is Lilliana?"

Dralos grunted when Chella squirmed in resistance before he kicked her legs out from underneath her. "I told you. I cannot tell you. We must await the Qu—Lady Lilliana's return."

"And how do we know she will return?" Gronch growled. His large orc eyes were narrowed into slits, and his hand gripped his axe so hard his dark green skin had turned nearly white. "She's been gone for hours."

"If the goal was to have her killed, they wouldn't have needed hours," Dralos responded dismissively. "She'll be here soon and wants everyone to be armed."

"Why are you all taking this so seriously?" Asked a woman from the back. I recognized her as the woman whom a man had attempted to prey on the first night. "She's just a girl."

"She's basically one of them," a man I had never noticed before shouted along with the woman. "A fucking noble! I bet she helped put us here. Probably got tired of being with us slaves and got herself an out."

Gronch turned on the man so fast that he was on the man before I had the chance to even open my mouth and punched him in the face. I saw murder in the war orc's eyes. I let loose a sigh loud enough to illustrate my exhaustion but also with enough force to cause Gronch's head to swivel in my direction. The moment he saw me, the tension in his shoulders deflated. A little.

That was still a particularly weird reaction. I hadn't thought the half orc to care about my survival beyond it increasing the chances of his own. Considering the Church's clear desire to see me killed and his empowerment by the System, I would have thought him first in line to wish me dead.

Ever surprised by the intentions and thoughts of others, I raised my hand in greeting but didn't return his smile. Nor did my tension vanish upon seeing the ragtag group of slaves I'd fought with. If anything, the pressure and time sensitivity of the situation descended on me, increasing the tension in my muscles.

"We're getting out of here," I said without pausing to give any verbal greetings. "Right now."

CHAPTER THIRTY-FOUR

Deal with the Devil

Getting out?" The first woman snorted, flipping her blond hair over her shoulders and glaring at me. "You may be able to walk out Lady Lilliana, O Great Saintess, but we'll get killed. Guaranteed."

I shrugged dismissively. "I just killed the scientist guy. If you stay, you're likely dead anyway."

Her eyes bugged and her mouth fell open as my words pitched the silent dungeon into furtive whispers and the occasional muttered curse. I ignored it all and focused on my compatriots who I'd fought side by side with. Starting with them was my best chance for success.

"I also killed the Sire," I said, intentionally using the local Sire title instead of Progenitor.

More shock from the battle slaves.

"Lies," the woman hissed. "I still have access to the System." Mutters of agreement and echoes of her accusation spread throughout the dungeon as even the slaves that had stood to the side at first were coming to see what the fuss was.

At that moment, my patience was already teetering on the edge as I remained overwhelmed from the wear on my mind. I didn't have time to deal with this.

"Silence!" I snapped, the corner of my lips curling into a snarl with the promise of wrath clinging to my words. I may have lacked the heart energy to pressure the woman, but I let the sheer commanding force of my personality carry the authority of my words. "The next time you interrupt me, you will not live to see whether my words are true."

The woman seemed more shocked than frightened but went silent none-theless. I turned away from her and continued, looking at all the slaves around me. There were more than earlier, many of the bystanders having approached at some point during the commotion.

I could explain to them everything that had happened. Explain to them that without switching to my System, they would die miserable, pathetic deaths as slaves. A logical man may be convinced. The issue was these people were not in a logical state of mind. One who has tasted power and who has grown addicted to it does not simply surrender those new abilities for a promise of some potential new power. It would be akin to asking a sword master to lose their sword skills for the potential of being a stronger energy user.

Finally, I pushed through the throng of slaves toward an older man. He couldn't have been younger than sixty years of age, white hair having encom-passed the entirety of his head other than his eyebrows. Despite the age and the layers of wrinkles pulling at his skin, the man's brown eyes burned with a desperate rage I would always recognize. There was also shame in his gaze. An endless, soul-sucking shame.

"What is your name?" I asked. To my relief my voice came out strong and clear, the high-pitched nature Lilliana's voice had initially carried was no longer so obvious. Either the body was maturing or my body Reformation was approaching. Perhaps both.

The man looked down at me and our gazes met in equal measures of curiosity and challenge, though the latter perhaps came more from my end. There was no fear in his gaze, though he did have some semblance of hesita-tion when he looked around to see everyone staring at us. I ignored them, focusing entirely on the man before me.

Seemingly confused as to why I'd picked him out of the crowd, the man gave me a little shrug. "Ethan," he said. "Ethan Brooks."

"Why are you here, Ethan Brooks? Are you a criminal?"

Ethan winced but shook his head viciously. "No. No! I am no criminal."

"Then why are you here?"

His hands curled into fists and his eyes dropped to stare holes into his feet. "Because I couldn't stop them," he whispered.

"Couldn't stop who, Ethan?" My voice was a whisper as I asked, still unmoving and unwavering as I silently urged the man to raise his eyes by not looking away from his shame.

There was a long moment after I asked where I wasn't sure Ethan would answer. Then he did, and I knew I would soon have an army. "I couldn't stop the slavers from taking my wife and my daughter."

"Did you kill them?"

He shook his head, crying now. Other than the soft beat of tears falling to the ground there was not a sound. No one whispered. No one moved. No one so much as dared to breathe lest they break the quiet tension. "I . . . I tried. B-but I couldn't. They killed my son like a pig and I-," the man cut off, taking a second to resist the sobs that had begun to claw at his throat. When he managed to bite down the sorrow, he gritted his teeth and pushed on. He looked up from his shoes to meet my eyes. "I did nothing. I watched, tied, and thrown in the corner." Ethan swallowed hard, and I could see the absolute fury building in him. Every time he swallowed back that sorrow, his rage grew. "At least my son was dealt an easy death. At least he was able to resist. What they did to my wife and daughter and my . . . my grandchildren . . ." He didn't finish. Likely couldn't. His jaw was clenched so hard I could hear his teeth grinding.

I showed him no pity. It was not pity that he wanted. Pity would get him nothing, but I knew exactly what it was he wanted. "Do you want to kill them?" I asked, still staring up into Ethan's dark eyes, matching the fury in his gaze with my own, one filled with rage.

"No," he growled. "Death would be too kind. I want them to suffer slowly. I want them to wish for death."

"Do you think you can get that justice with Orpheus's System?"

The man shook his head. "The power subsides whenever I leave the Arena. Even if I were freed . . ." He looked down at his shoes again.

"I can give you a chance at your justice, Ethan." The man's gaze snapped up. There was a sound of sudden muttering from somewhere, but I kept my focus. It didn't matter if some outliers began to whisper doubt at this point. Those who would desire my deal would take it once they saw its effect on Ethan. "But there is a cost to pay for that power. Nothing in this world is free."

Ethan nodded and I saw in his eyes that the decision was already made. There was still doubt in them, and a worry that I was giving him hope as some sort of trick. But that was a leap of faith he would have to take to be the first. The first of many.

"If your word is true, I will pay whatever the cost," he said with a set look of determination.

"The cost is simple. All I ask for is allegiance. I will give you the power you need, and I will not interfere in your path. But when I call, you will heed the summons. When I tell you to bow, you will kneel."

Ethan laughed with tears in his eyes. "Is that all? If you are true and the power you bestow upon me opens a door to my justice, my life is yours, Lady Lilliana." As he spoke the doubt in his eyes was quickly subsumed by hope. It was an odd feeling, to be someone giving others hope.

I didn't dislike it.

"Dralos," I commanded, motioning the resurrected one to my side. "Give me your dagger." Dralos obeyed without a word.

I reached out for Ethan's hand and, just like Dralos, he gave it to me without a word.

"Are we being serious?" The woman from earlier asked, incredulous. "This is a child. A noble child. Do you truly believe she has such power? This is a mockery of our pains."

Ethan didn't look at the woman and instead stared straight at me. "Perhaps Lady Lilliana is a fraud. Perhaps she is blessed by a God. Perhaps she is a devil or demon in disguise. I do not know. But I do not see what reason there is for her to lie and we have all seen what she can do with her heart energy. I choose to have faith that this is not all there is for me. Perhaps I am an old fool. In a moment, we shall see." I gripped his hand tightly and drew the tip of Dralos's blade across his palm. Red blood seeped through the cut to mix with his forgotten tears in the dirt under our feet.

This time, he didn't wince.

I repeated the same action with my left palm, the pain a small, dull ebb shadowed by the pounding exhaustion cracking my mind. Unlike Ethan's blood, mine came out red and black.

I didn't take the time to think about what that meant and slapped my cut to his.

The air around us crackled with palpable tension as the deal was struck, binding us together in an irreversible exchange. The atmosphere in the dungeon darkened, light given by torch fire and the vibrant hues of the world drained to a muted, twilight gloom. The shadows in the gloom grew and lengthened, twisting and curling in an eerily unnatural way.

A bone-deep chill radiated out from our clasped hands. It was a cold not of our worlds, biting through the skin and muscles of our bodies, and eating its way to the center of our bones. The temperature plummeted, our breaths coming out in frosty puffs of condensation. For a moment, just a moment, the memory of warmth ceased to exist within my mind, a figment of a distant reality.

I could feel part of the System splitting away from me in that chill, reaching out into Ethan and burrowing itself in the deepest part of his existence. At first, only a single streak of blue dripped like a tear from one of his eyes. Then more began to trickle out the corner of his mouth. Then, in a sudden burst of dark blue ooze from his orifices, the Desire System purged Ethan of the Main System's influences.

As the deal was sealed, a surge of unknown energy erupted, a shockwave of power that caused the dungeon walls to tremble in cowardice. The pact was sealed, I knew, etched into the fabric of our reality. As the chill faded and the trembling aftereffects ceased, an intangible force began to burn a mark along the cut of Ethan's hand. The man stared in shock at his palm as his flesh burned slowly into the shape of a crescent moon. Then, the instant the shape was finished, his flesh let off a soft hum and then it was as if all light in the world blinked off. When the light returned just a fraction of a second later, the crescent moon on his palm remained without light. Instead, it was filled with a deep, endless pitch-black.

And then there it was, a red glint in the corner of Ethan's eye. The Desire System.

[System announcement: You have gained your first Paragon. Congratulations!]
[Reward: You have gained the ability to reap a percentage of a Paragon's heart energy whenever the System rewards them with bonus energy. Do you accept this reward?]
[Yes/No]

I immediately slapped my hand against the red "No" button. There was no way I would voluntarily bind my growth to the rewards of a System. I would bind others to it. But I would remain free.

CHAPTER THIRTY-FIVE

Metamorphosis

I wasn't sure what class Ethan had been given as the older man reached out in front of him and gingerly touched some invisible option. He suddenly sucked in air like he'd been punched in the gut by a club, his face scrunching in pain.

Ethan collapsed to the floor, kneeling at my feet with his eyes affixed to the ground. For a moment, I saw something like hesitation in his eyes, but it quickly shifted into resolve. Still keeping his eyes on my feet, Ethan spoke. His voice was now deep and rough, a constant growl in his throat causing his words to come out in a powerful rumble. "Thank you for this gift, my queen. I will use it well."

I grinned, not entirely sure what was happening if I was being honest, but wanting to appear as though I did. "Rise, Paragon. A great battle awaits us against those who have wronged you." I motioned him toward the others, who had taken many steps away from us, leaving a large empty chasm between us. Even Dralos had retreated, admiration and awe shining bright in his black-tainted orange eyes. "Tell us of your experience."

Ethan nodded and then straightened. I struggled to keep the surprise off my face as Ethan stood at least an entire foot taller than he had earlier. Every second that passed, he seemed to grow younger. His wrinkles smoothed around his eyes and forehead, muscles expanding like wild vines along his limbs even as he continued to grow. At first, I thought Ethan had simply regressed, but there was no way the System had so easily granted him enough heart energy for a Reformation . . . was there?

When his body finally ceased growing, he towered over even Dralos, somewhere over seven feet tall. Ethan, as if knowing the exact reaction I desired, turned his gaze up toward the cavern ceiling and released a guttural war cry. The weaker battle slaves cowered away, hiding behind their friends, as the stronger ones gawked at Ethan's display of primal power. As the energy radiated from him, there was a bright flash as the tattoo mark on his right forearm shattered, freeing him.

What in Ashwash's name had the System turned the old man into? I wondered, reaching out with the remains of my sputtering heart energy to approximate Ethan's new level of heart energy.

My attempt was quickly made void as a black box with red text appeared in front of me as if reading my intentions. And just like with Ethan, I suspected it had maybe read my desires somehow.

[System announcement: Congratulations! Paragon 001 has achieved successful metamorphosis and a class upgrade.]
[Name: Ethan Brooks]
[Class: Primal Berserker]
[Race: Human?]
[System note: Paragon's initial level has been lowered by ten to match the amount of non-bonus heart energy obtained through the Main System before metamorphosis.]
[Level: 25]
[Open subwindow for additional statistics on Paragon 001.]

I briefly wondered whether the "levels" had some measure of comparison with Cores and heart energy and asked, "What is a metamorphosis?" I whispered the question so quietly under my breath I wasn't sure even Dralos, standing at my side, had heard me.

[System message: All Paragons will change and undergo a metamorphosis based on the Host's overall potential.]

"Explain more," I hissed, but the System refused to respond. "Ashwash curse this stubborn thing." I let out a breath and tried to refocus.

The System hadn't actually explained what a metamorphosis was. And were all Paragons going to match me in raw potential then? That didn't seem likely. The System had said "based on" rather than "equal to." I grit my teeth at the ridiculously ambiguous nonexplanation.

I waved my hand through the intangible subwindow button, and a much larger black window opened. I scanned it for a moment. The Desire System was providing me with numbers for various characteristics like strength, intelligence, and others for Ethan. I closed the window without taking too close a look. Without others to compare the numbers with, they were just floating numbers that held no meaning.

"My level is lower," Ethan said, "but all my attributes are higher now. And I can feel my potential, my ability to grow. It's like a fire in my gut, begging me to start on my path." He dug his fingers into his torn shirt that dangled limply from his neck, just barely hanging on. "I will not waste this opportunity granted to me." Ethan grinned wildly, all indication of his aged features gone. Even his personality seemed to have shifted, sparked with life and fire. "I . . . I feel like I can make the entire world tremble."

It looked like he was going to say more, and the woman from earlier had opened her mouth again to interrupt, but a scrawny woman burst through the crowd. The two men she struggled to squeeze between parted, and she tumbled forward, stopping hard when her back smacked into Ethan's leg, now more like a tree than the leg of a man.

"Can . . . can you turn me into that?" the woman begged, scrambling to her feet sheepishly. Her face had turned a deep shade of red, but her expression remained set. "I want what he has. I'll give you whatever you want."

I took the woman in for a moment. Not a woman. A girl. She looked only a few years older than me. No older than Romeo, so likely in her late teens. Even standing this close to her, I couldn't tell exactly what color her hair was. With the strands so matted and dirty, I could only guess it was a lighter brown color. Maybe orange. She was excessively pale and slim, underfed, and bruises littered her entire body, except for her face. Yellow eyes in the shape of diamonds glared from under her matted hair, contrasting with the tentative, soft sound of her voice.

"It doesn't work that way," I responded flatly, without emotion. Like Ethan, she didn't need my pity. If what she wanted was pity, she would not have come forward, much less so quickly. "You will be granted an ability that suits you."

Probably, anyway. It could be that all Paragons would upgrade to the same Primal Berserker. How would I know? I didn't say any of that out loud though.

The girl bared her teeth in an unnaturally animalistic way, the ends of her lips coming up in a wolfish snarl. Sharp, long canines punctuated the expression with clear lust for revenge. "I don't give a shit. Give me that power too." Her sudden outburst of aggression took me aback, and I raised an eyebrow. After a moment, the girl cooled, her sheepish smile returning. "Sorry. I really need it." Her eyes lit up for a moment and she kneeled. "Please."

I looked down at the girl, reopening the cut on my palm that had already started stitching itself together with Dralos's dagger. "Keep in mind, girl. I am not salvation. I cannot bring you hope. I will not get your revenge or fulfill your desires. I simply give you a chance."

The girl lifted her chin and stared straight at me. Not defiantly, but simply resolutely. "One chance is all I need."

Before I made the exchange, the wolf-like girl spoke once more. "My lady. If I did this, I request your aid in my revenge. Whatever you can do to help, I need it. My people are naturally much tougher and stronger than humans. If you help with our freedom and revenge, I can guarantee you the loyalty of hundreds of them."

I looked at her for a moment, chewing absently on my bottom lip in thought. I knew nothing about this girl. In fact, I wasn't particularly interested in whatever shit she was in. But if what she said was true, perhaps interfering with her homeland could prove to be rather beneficial . . . I supposed only time would tell.

Without answering her, I instead extended the dagger for her to cut her palm, and we repeated the binding ritual. This time, the room didn't turn cold. It turned hot. A boiling heat filled the dungeon, turning all the buckets of water into condensation, and wisps of flame enveloped us, lashing out randomly to set afire beds or someone's clothes. Where Ethan's binding had been one of death and hate, this binding instead emanated desires of life and love. Though both were desperate, I could tell her desires were much different from Ethan's. From my own as well.

The heat and flames eventually subsided, and I noticed the others had once again retreated away from us. A few of the stragglers had been caught in the flames, wailing in agony at their burned flesh. The girl and I remained in the center of a scorched circle, untouched by the flames. Just as with Ethan, a dark crescent moon was burned into the center of her palm. She closed her eyes, letting the feeling pass through her before she stood.

When she finally got to her feet, she too had begun to change. The first difference was her hair; the brown and red tint seemed to flake off, leaving only a bright, untarnished white with small black strands striking horizontally along the center. She grew only a few inches in height, but all her previous scrawniness vanished like Ethan's age. Her muscles expanded and tightened into bundles of power. Her nails elongated and then retracted before elongating again like a tiger flexing its claws. She smiled at me as the metamorphosis came to an end, two sharp canines protruding over her bottom teeth. Just like Ethan, blue fluid began streaming out of her as the Desire System purified her of the Main System's influences.

[System announcement: Congratulations! Paragon 002 has achieved successful metamorphosis and a class upgrade.]
[Name: Nida Keys]
[Class: Primal Tigerkin]
[Race: Therianthrope?]
[System note: Paragon's initial level has been lowered by twenty-five to match the amount of non-bonus heart energy obtained through the Main System before metamorphosis.]
[Level: 15]
[Open subwindow for additional statistics on Paragon 002.]

What in the nine hells was a Tigerkin? I figured it was something similar to a beastman, perhaps one from the Tiger tribe. I wanted to ask Nida what that meant and what she was, but the tension in the crowd had turned into outright excitement as people began to push forward, each wanting their turn to obtain power.

Some of the battle slaves refused to participate. I didn't give them much mind and continued to grant the System to those who came forward.

Around fifteen battle slaves in total stepped forward, not including Ethan and Nida. The fifteen were a combination of species and classes I'd never heard of before, with abilities I could barely understand. I glanced over their Paragon files as they popped up but didn't immediately pay the information much information, considering I barely understood any of it.

Seventeen was a substantially lower number than I'd expected, though, looking around at the scared expressions of most of the others, I supposed I would have been hard-pressed to say it was surprising. Those who had chosen to serve as Paragons stood behind me, opposing those who hid or scowled across from me.

After the last volunteer stood and underwent his metamorphosis, I pocketed my hand, hiding the slowly recovering scars. The many cuts on my palm screamed and throbbed with irritation. I'd been slowly draining what little energy my Core had gathered in a constant attempt to heal it between each deal in case I needed to act quickly. Luckily, passing on the System and creating Paragons didn't cost me any effort. It was as painless as it was effortless, a simple exchange of words and blood. Unluckily, healing was not without great effort.

The woman who had argued with Ethan earlier stepped in front of the crowd, stalking angrily toward me until we were nearly nose to nose. A strand of her blond hair slipped from behind her ear, falling to sway gently between us. "This is absurd. You are all being fooled by this little . . . by this insane child," she shouted, poking my chest with an ugly, crooked finger that had clearly been broken at some time and never set properly.

"Are you blind, Narissa?" Ethan grumbled, taking a step in her direction as though she had personally insulted him. "You think this"—he motioned to his new body—"is a trick?"

"I don't know what it is," she hissed in my face, "but there is something wrong about all of this. How are you breaking the slave bindings? Are you going to take responsibility for everything when the slavers find we've tried to escape? Will you be killed on all our behalf?" Narissa turned her back on me to face the others. "She's going to get us all killed when the slavers find out. For all we know, she is possessed by a demon. Do we really know what this System is? And haven't you guys noticed who's with her?" She glanced at Dralos and the tied-up Chella. "Who's to say she isn't with the slavers?" Narissa turned back toward me with her usual scowl. "You should know your place, Lady Lilliana. Didn't your mother ever teach you to not cause trouble for others? Gods, just when I'd managed to get a little leeway with some of the guardsmen, you're going to ruin everything and get us killed! I can't say I'm surprised, though; the guards did tell me your mother was your father's pathetic little bitch—"

Dangling feet. Blood. Empty blue eyes. My father's look of disgust as my mother's life left her. As it left her because of me.

I plunged Dralos's dagger through her heart in a single, swift motion. I gazed at her with a casual expression that disguised the pure rage her words had stirred. "You talk too much." As Narissa slumped to the floor, blue eyes wide and mouth open in shock, I withdrew the dagger. "Luckily, you have your use." I reached deep inside my Core, looking for a specific type of heart energy.

There it was. At the center of my Core, I found a bundle of hibernating heart energy. Energy with the attribute of a Soul Weaver.

With that, I reached into the puncture wound the dagger had opened and yanked out Narissa's heart, surrounding it with the force of soul attribute heart energy. Before Narissa's heart energy could resist the magnetic attraction of my soul attribute, I opened my Core to the homeless energy and pulled.

The raw heart energy didn't need much encouragement. It flooded into my Core like a hurricane.

CHAPTER THIRTY-SIX

The Beginning of An Army

Absorbing Narissa's heart energy left a rotting taste on my tongue. It was absolutely disgusting. Yet, the emptiness of my Core and the dire need to act now left me with no choice but to absorb the energy, repulsive as it was.

Some stared at me with awe. Most just looked shocked. A few were terrified. That terror was familiar; it was a basic lesson among queen and king candidates that fear was a necessary tool for leading a country to an age of prosperity. Those who could not tolerate hate and fear would lead to nothing but a weak rule.

"I know many of you don't understand what is happening. You don't understand how a little girl like me is wielding such terrifying power. You fear, as Narissa accused, that I am a demon or possessed by one." I gave them all a noncommittal shrug. "Does it matter what I am? I am here to give you an opportunity. What matters is what you choose to do with it. You may have refused the choice of power, but I can still offer you freedom. Still, your freedom is something you must fight for. Your life will never change until you pick up a weapon and change it yourself." I tossed Dralos his bloodied dagger, which I had dropped to extract Narissa's heart. He easily plucked it from the air, and I turned back to the scared slaves, many of whom had fought only a battle or two since arriving. Some had fought none. "Those who wish to fight for their freedom, step forth so I may remove that which marks you as a slave," I said, lifting my sleeve to reveal the section of burned flesh on my arm where I'd previously been marked.

This time, many more came forward. Nearly all the slaves came to have their marks removed. Even some who had cowered, trembling at the death of Narissa, stepped forward. Most of them screamed while my heart energy burned the marks away, though some only winced. The few who didn't step forward for their freedom were sickly or elderly. I noticed that the group Narissa had been a part of also didn't step forward. That was for the better.

The energy used for breaking the tattoo markings was significant. Even with the energy I'd regained from Narissa's Core, it didn't take long before I started to feel the drain. When I finally finished with the last volunteer, I let out a breath I hadn't realized I was holding.

"Let's go," I commanded, immediately heading toward the dungeon exit. I was honestly surprised no one had discovered what I was doing despite all the time that had passed. However, considering this was the slave area and both our slavers were with us, voluntarily or not, perhaps it was unsurprising. I didn't imagine many slave uprisings occurred in the city.

They nodded at my words, but their expressions turned puzzled when I moved not toward the exit into the city but toward the one we knew opened into the coliseum.

The seventeen Paragons moved instantly to obey. My comrades, who had all chosen not to become Paragons, were slightly more uncertain and cast doubtful glances my way.

"Shouldn't we use the passage to the city?" Romeo asked, his eyebrows furrowed in thought. His hands clenched tightly around his sword with such strength they turned white. Whether in excitement or fear, I didn't know. It didn't really matter. He looked at Narissa's corpse and bit his lip with palpable anxiety.

"Why would we do that?" I shot him a wicked grin, bending midstride to pick up a steel sword from the weapons bucket as I headed toward the passage. "We're already inside the home of our prey. Where would we go?"

"Wait a moment," Marisar said, his big fish feet slapping with their usual wetness on the floor. "I do not believe you have thought this through, Lady Lilliana. The fifty or so of us will not be able to defeat an entire squadron of guards. We are weak and underfed. And with the King and the Church here, there are only elites everywhere, ya know? We would be killed for treason and crimes against the Crown."

I nodded slowly, letting the Selenian finish before giving him the same grin I'd given Romeo. "Then we better not lose. Let's go." I knew an all-out battle in a city hosting royals was effectively suicide. But who said I'd be going to war against the city?

Dralos took the lead as we entered the passageway toward the coliseum and left behind the dungeon cavern. He continuously shoved Chella forward, who now only occasionally struggled against her restrictions. She was still taller than Dralos—taller than everyone except Ethan. But the cuffs and restrictions kept her somewhat compliant despite her towering monstrosity. Fortunately, the passage ceiling was vaulted enough that Chella and Ethan could walk through it, though Ethan was forced to hunch a little or risk scraping his head whenever the ceiling dipped from age.

Nida sauntered up beside me, still flexing her claws in awe. Mixed with her black-striped white hair, I noticed a set of ears that turned and twisted, as if tracking the sound around her. A similarly colored tail lopped around her waist, still but for its occasional twitch. I was, again, about to ask her about the title Tigerkin, but Romeo interjected from a step behind us.

"What did you do to that woman?" he asked a hint of accusation in his voice. "And how did you know you could?"

"I wasn't entirely sure I could," I answered honestly. "Do you remember Damien?" Romeo nodded, seeming to catch on to my implication. "It was something like that, but this time I initiated it."

"Was it necromancy?" His face looked like he'd sucked on something sour, though it appeared to be more from thought than disgust.

I laughed. "No, that was not necromancy." I debated whether I should explain further considering the risk of exposing my affinity to necromantic energy manipulation. In the end, I figured it wouldn't make a difference one way or the other and decided to explain. "Necromantic energy manipulation is the practice of inverting heart energy by stripping the purity using a Core. Its main purpose is to act against the inherent nature of heart energy, or life energy, which results in the decomposition of life or a manipulation of death. If someone tried to use inverted heart energy in the practice of necromantic manipulation to absorb pure heart energy, the forces would repulse and recoil quite painfully in both hearts."

Romeo was silent for a moment, apparently contemplating. Nida just stared at me with a blank expression, clearly having no idea what we were talking about.

"What about necromantic magic?" he asked, shifting his gaze back toward me. "Could that be used to absorb someone's energy?"

I shrugged. "I don't know anything about magic." With that, we all slunk back into a silent trudge through the stone hallway. The air was cooler than usual, no doubt due to the fact it was long past sun hours. As we walked, I let my hands run freely across the thick, rough-hewn stones lining the passage, each stone a story of centuries gone by in the dark.

Other than the red flicker of the occasional torch lighting the way, we were in total and colorless darkness. After a while, some of the newly freed fighters started to whisper among each other, some in anticipation, some likely in trepidation. I heard a few startled gasps as someone tripped over the uneven stone floor, and I resisted the annoyed sigh that threatened to escape my lips. I had to remind myself that these were not true warriors, but average individuals who had been forced into death fights.

When we came to a part in the passage where we could turn left, right, or straight ahead, we all instinctively continued straight toward the Arena. I hadn't even noticed I'd done it as well.

"Not that way," Dralos grunted, shoving Chella, who'd tried to match us in heading straight.

"What is over there?" Nida asked, looking at me. She didn't follow Dralos until I nodded and started heading to the right part of the forked path.

"Another slave group," he said, motioning us forward.

"We're freeing the others as well?" one of the freed slaves asked. I thought he might have introduced himself to me at some point.

"That would be good," a Paragon to my left agreed. "My brother is in one of the other slave groups. He will join us."

I pulled up his basic Paragon file with a thought.

[Name: Nasq Delacoire]
[Class: Primal Sorcerer]
[Race: Elf?]
[Level: 19]

Like Nida, Nasq was not human. His blond hair and green eyes were characteristics I wouldn't have found odd in a human, nor would I have his perhaps six feet of height. It was his nearly ephemeral beauty that had initially indicated his oddity, as had the pointed ears jutting out from his shoulder-length hair. Based on his Paragon file, I knew he was called an "elf," but that was not a species I was familiar with.

Elves. Tigerkin. Selenians. How many more species did this world have that Ordite did not?

"We won't have time to free all of them," I corrected as we turned down a third passage with Dralos still at the lead. "At some point, the coliseum officials will be alerted if we stay in the slave section for too long. In any case, our goal is not to free all the slaves, though that may be a result."

"Then what is our goal?" Romeo pressed. I turned to glance at him and nearly missed the young boy, whose clothes and skin naturally melted him into the shadows.

"Our goal is to find Radford Coldrun."

"Who's that?" Nida asked with a little bounce in her step and ran one of her fingers along a patch of fur on the back of her hand.

"The Slave Master," I said. There was no doubt in my mind they would have tried to ask more questions, but Dralos came to a halt at a large Silver steel door. The slab was smooth and plain, as if its edges and cracks had long since been washed away by the motion of a nonexistent sea. "Open it."

Dralos grunted and shoved Chella in my direction, then jammed his foot into the back of her legs so she knelt. "She must open it, my liege. My access is limited to your section."

I sighed and removed her gag. "Open it, Chella." She coughed as the brown leather restriction was removed from her mouth and stared up at me, her eyes small slits.

"You will not escape," she said matter-of-factly as if it was predestined.

"Just open the door. If you're right, then it won't matter if we get in or not." When Chella didn't move from where she knelt, I clicked my tongue. "Okay. If you wish to do this the difficult way, I don't mind." I lifted the sword in my right hand and collapsed it with my left as well, raising it above my head in a slow, dramatic fashion that caused Chella to bite down on her lip hard enough to draw blood. "I don't need you alive, slaver. I can simply bring you back."

"W-wait," she stammered, her cuffed hands struggling to come between her and the sword for all the good that would do her. "I—I am not a slaver. I'm only here on contract. With my help . . . with my help, you can escape! You can all get out of here."

"I don't want your help escaping. Open the door." I leaned in close, letting my sword rest against my shoulder. "I will not ask again."

She raised her cuffed arms. "I can't if my energy is sealed. The doors operate based on our specific energy signatures." I looked at Dralos, and he nodded in confirmation. Inwardly, I groaned. Then an idea came to me.

I glanced behind me toward the freed slaves. "Which one of you was the shapeshifter?"

A little rat-like man was gently nudged to the front of the group. He kept his elbows by his sides, and his fingers kept circling each other as if out of habit. His gaze seemed to be permanently attached to his feet, just as his posture was allergic to being straight.

"I am a shape-shifter . . . Lady Lilliana," the sniveling man said with an exaggerated bow. I instantly found myself disliking him. His energy was thick like sludge; it had some of the most contaminated heart energy I'd ever had the displeasure of dealing with.

"Does your energy also morph to match your targets?" I asked.

He nodded. "If . . . if I am given some of their blood, then yes . . . Lady . . . Lilliana. I can . . . please you that way?"

I resisted the urge to wrinkle my nose in disgust. "Yes. Do it."

Dralos took out his dagger again, slicing part of Chella's shoulder for the rat-man. The rat-man cautiously approached Chella until he was certain she was not threatening him. Then he leaned down and licked the blood trickling down her shoulder. His eyes rolled back as he swallowed, and a perverse expression spread across his face.

His flesh began to bubble, and something writhed under the surface. Unlike the metamorphosis of the Paragons, his change was slow. Slow and sickeningly unnatural. The air around him shifted to match the sludge of his heart energy. The air became thick with pollutants, and the space between bodies became heavy as if trapped underwater.

With a final disturbing snap of his neck, a second Chella stood in front of me. The new Chella, like the rat-man, was hunched over, sniveling with her fingers twirling incessantly around each other.

"Open it," I repeated, my ire rising at having to repeat myself for such a simple task continually.

This time, the "Chella" I spoke to nodded with a perverse smile. She reached over, and I felt her—his?—energy flood into the steel door blocking our way. It creaked open with a small *thunk* as whatever locking system released its hold.

CHAPTER THIRTY-SEVEN

Slaves No More

Just like the section of the dungeon that held me during my tenure as a slave, this second section was similarly dilapidated and smelled of shit and blood. White balls of energy illuminated the old and rotting furniture placed haphazardly around the admittedly much larger room. When the steel door first creaked open under the Chella clone's touch, I was surprised by the sheer number of slaves in this section of the slave dungeon. The space itself was also larger. Much wider and at least double the length of ours. In comparison, our living space had been ridiculously small. The white lights weren't stationary here like they were in our quarters, floating around the section as I looked on, and I saw why it was so much larger—there were many, many more slaves here. At least a few hundred were simply milling about.

"Hey, Chella, what are you doing?" The question came from a man with Chella's height and build, even sharing some of her appearance characteristics.

I didn't give him a second to process. I didn't even let him scream.

I encased my sword with heart energy and threw the steel weapon point first. It blasted over the distance separating me from the guard like a bolt of lightning, embedding itself in his throat before ripping out the other end. The guard's head, mouth still open in shock, tumbled off his neck and hit the floor with a splat.

"Explain the situation to them." I waved Dralos and the others forward toward the shocked slaves still bound to a master. While Dralos followed my order, I approached the guard's collapsed body. I knelt beside him and ran a hand over his eyes to close them. It was a show of mercy I had seen many do in war, though I had never done so before. Now, however, it seemed almost appropriate though I couldn't place why I felt that way. Still, I shoved my right hand into his chest. I didn't pull the heart from the body; there was no need for such dramatics anymore. I simply trapped the escaping heart energy and opened my Core to all the homeless energy.

I would likely need even more going forward if I continued shattering slave marks. My mouth filled with the repulsive taste as I absorbed the slaver's energy until his heart was left shriveled and desiccated.

I wondered briefly if I truly needed to be in direct contact with the heart. When Damien had offered his energy to me, I hadn't been in contact with any part of him, but then again, I had resurrected him.

Some fifty slaves led by my Paragons came forward, the rest standing in an enormous group some ways back.

"They would like to accept your deal, my queen," Dralos said, beckoning forward the first of the new section's enslaved fighters. I let out a breath and stood, stretching as the new enslaved watched me with doubtful curiosity.

"Let's get to work then," I said, reaching over to grab my sword.

An hour or so later, I'd finished with the dungeon's second section of slaves and Dralos had led us to a third section that had fewer slaves than the previous area, but more than where we'd been kept. I was in the middle of breaking the slave markings in the third dungeon section after adding another fifteen or so Paragons to my retinue when a shrill, ear-splitting alarm pierced the air like a wailing banshee. Hundreds of hands clamped over their ears in a desperate attempt to block even a fraction of the sound drilling into their heads.

The sound blared in every direction, seeming to originate from the white balls of energy still hovering over us. When the alarm had been set off, the energy balls began to emit a slight pulse, matching the constantly cascading pitch of the alarm. I wasn't sure how we'd been found, but considering the method of the alarm, I figured it likely had to do with the energy balls. Considering how long it had taken the alarm to go off, the security method was less than proficient.

I gathered heart energy into both my palms and launched rays of lunar light at the energy balls. The energy disrupted the flow and canceled out their center source, causing both hovering energy balls to wink out of existence with small pops. This sent all one-hundred-something newly freed slaves into utter darkness.

"Nasq," I said, "give us some light." An instant later red flames lit the room, bathing the slaves and barren stone walls in a flickering red and orange radiance. I turned to look at the remaining slaves who had not been freed yet. They carried a multitude of expressions, some promising use and others promising burden. "Those of you who have not had your mark removed will have to wait. We're out of time."

I half expected an outburst of protest, but none made to move or speak against me, as if united in resignation to their circumstances. It was pitiful to see but certainly made it easier for me.

"My queen," Nasq said, moving to stand by my side. When I turned to face him, he presented me with a nauseous-looking Chella. Not the clone, but the true giantess. "She wishes to speak with you."

"We don't have time," I said, wiping some loose blood from my palm onto my worn brown trousers and sheathing my sword.

"The slaves can free themselves with a Remover," Chella blurted, moving as if to take a step toward me but paused as Nasq raised a palm and thick orange flames erupted from it in threat. I reached up to place my free hand on his bicep and firmly directed him to lower it.

"Explain."

"Every three sections have a control room. This is Section F3." She pointed to a large bulge coming from the far side of the section's cavern area. It was difficult to see in the thinning light of Nasq's flames, but the bulge itself was quite obvious. "In there, you'll find a green prism. The prism holds a blessing from the Church of Light. It can dispel slave marks." After a pause, she added, "Or create them."

"Why are you telling me this?" I asked, finally turning to give the giantess my full attention but still wary that we were burning precious time.

"I am trying to prove that I am not your enemy," she insisted and again moved to take a step toward me, but stopped herself before Nasq raised the arm I wasn't keeping down. While I appreciated the man's loyalty to my safety, the cuffs strangling Chella's wrists sealed her energy and magic. His caution was overdone considering her current powerlessness.

"In honesty, Giantess," I started, giving her a single raised eyebrow, "I am not entirely sure what or who you are. Unfortunately, I do not have time to debate this with you right now."

"Aren't you curious why I didn't force you to the brothels?" Chella pressed, her words flying out in rapid succession now as if she had a time limit. Which, I supposed, she did.

"Not really. I appreciate the information." More alarms from outside the section had begun to emit the same shrieking noise and I was beginning to feel like this was the start of a conversation that would waste my time. "Nasq, relay the details of the Remover to those freed." I motioned the future Archmage toward a group of freed slaves who, when they saw my gaze, took on perturbed and uncertain looks. "I want them to focus on freeing the others with the Remover." Part of me wanted to punish Chella for not explaining the existence of Removers to me earlier. If she truly intended to help, then she should have been forthright from the start.

"I work for Duke Alistar," she shouted as Ethan stepped up to grab her by the shoulders. "There have been reports of many young nobles going missing and it was my job to report any sightings of them in this Colosseum. The Duke has suspected the Cael Kingdom of kidnapping Lysorian nobles and children en masse during this year's spring flooding of monsters."

Duke Alistar. Where had I heard that name before? I took a precious moment to go over what I'd learned about Lysorian and Cael aristocracy nearly three weeks ago in an attempt to remember the name. Alistar. Duke. The memory didn't surface immediately until I realized that he had to be a noble on the boundary between nations and then it clicked.

Duke Alistar was one of the lesser dukes in terms of authority in Lysoria. While he did have great wealth and a personal militia to boot, the Duke had, according to *The History of Lysoria*, focused all his attention on agriculture and the cold war against Cael that was waged on Lysoria's eastern border, forgoing the political fights within Lysoria as a neutral party. If Chella truly did work for Duke Alistar, then my plans would have to change.

I looked at Chella with a new perspective. If she was telling the truth, this could be extremely beneficial. "You're a ghost, then," I stated.

Her face took on a puzzled expression. "I apologize; I am not familiar with that term."

"A spy."

Nasq wrinkled his nose at my words, but Chella nodded. "I am."

"Aren't you kind of . . . large to be a spy?" Nida asked, who seemed chipper as always despite the blaring of the alarm around us. Her ears occasionally twitched, though that was the only indication that she found the sound annoyingly loud.

Chella gave a nervous chuckle. "That's the point. Who would suspect a half giant like me to be working for the Duke of a Lysorian major house?"

"Fair point," Nida admitted. Then she froze, as if a gust of wind had turned her entire body to ice. She looked at me, her smile dropping. "They're here."

"Shit," I swore, cursing myself for allowing the conversation to continue. I shouldn't have gotten distracted. Was I getting complacent in this world? "How far?"

Nida closed her eyes, her face twisting into a look of concentration. "A couple of minutes, maybe. Coming from above."

"How many?"

The tigress shrugged. "Hard to tell, Queen. At least the same as us."

I cursed again, turning to Chella and motioning for Dralos to join us. "Where is Coldrun?"

"The Slave Master?" Chella asked.

At the same time, Dralos answered, "It is likely he is in the banquet hall."

That caught my attention. "Banquet hall?"

"Yes," Chella said, nodding frantically. She talked so fast that I assumed she was trying to get the information to me before Dralos had a chance to. It was a misguided attempt at showing her value since it didn't change the fact that Dralos knew it. That being said, part of his memory was missing so her presence wasn't completely pointless. "Every night during the Sun-Setting Festival is a celebration. As the Slave Master in charge of the Colosseum, Coldrun is expected to host a nightly banquet for the festival's duration." She looked at Dralos with a slight frown. "Though he isn't expected to always attend himself. There's no guarantee he is there."

"He is," Dralos said, turning to me with a firm expression.

My patience finally ran out; I didn't bother questioning how he knew that. "Listen up," I shouted over the drone of the alarms, and all the mutterings in the room were sucked up into a silence lit up only by the on-and-off tempo of the alarm. "Those of you Nasq has spoken to about the Remover are tasked with freeing the others from different sections tonight. She and a Paragon will go with you to make sure it's done right." I pointed to Chella and a random Paragon with a slim build, but ferocious white eyes and long red hair that seemed to wrap around his neck like a mane. The Paragon moved to protest but backed down when I glared at him into compliance. "When you have freed the others, you may join us in battle or you may escape. The choice is yours. In the meantime, the rest of us will engage the guards."

There was no point in forcing unwilling men and women to fight in this battle. If our number grew too large, it might force us into a clash with the city guards rather than Colosseum guards and mercenaries. That was a situation I'd prefer to avoid until I had a more stable and trained force at my back.

No, what I needed was to turn Coldrun into a resurrected being like Dralos. That would give me control over the Colosseum and, by default, the ability to sweep everything under the rug. I needed out of the Colosseum's grip, but that didn't necessarily mean I wanted to tear down the entire thing. Although slavery, especially gladiator and sex slaves, was a dirty business that tarnished any hand dealing in it with the blood of the innocent and guilty alike, it was also extremely profitable, and my current finances were nonexistent. If I could turn Coldrun and take over the Colosseum, I could completely flip my financial situation. I would have to see how the "discussion" with Coldrun went at the banquet.

I turned back to Chella. "Are you able to contact Duke Alistar?"

"Now?" she asked, unsure.

"Yes. Now."

After a while, she nodded.

"Good. I have a message for him." I relayed the message to Chella and sent her and the others toward the control center to fetch the prism. As my group of Paragons and ex-slaves exited the third section, I sent Dralos to collect some stragglers from the second section. He nodded and ran ahead, turning sharply to the left in the distance to cross in front of the stairway leading to the Colosseum's Arena and wrap around to the other side where the second section would be located.

CHAPTER THIRTY-EIGHT

Path to a Breakthrough

By the time we were within earshot of the stairway, Dralos was already out of sight, and I could hear the heavy steps of armored guards clamoring down the steps. Judging by the number of discordant footsteps approaching us and the many different sources of heart energy, I figured Nida had perhaps underestimated their numbers.

There were around 150 ex-slaves and a little under ninety Paragons in total, yet I felt at least two hundred energy sources barreling down the stairs. Although I did not sense a Core among the guards, many had powerful auras resembling a Magic Core. It was much weaker than a Heart Core, but it explained why individuals like the Knight Captain and the Cael King's son-in-law could wield such power without their hearts exploding.

The stairway was no wider than that of eight armored soldiers, maybe ten if they eschewed the heavier sort. I chewed on my bottom lip, debating the best approach to clash with the soldiers. Strategically, enclosed spaces were best fought with traps rather than outright warfare.

The ceiling was unstable, so a collapse was a realistic plan. I shook my head, dispelling the thought. Unless I could trick the guards and mercenaries into fully entering the underground passageways while we took the stairs, a ceiling collapse would only crush the ex-slaves and Paragons.

"Nasq," I whispered, "can you shroud us in shadows?"

The "elf" took on a look of extreme concentration for a moment, then shook his head. "The passage is too small, and we are too many."

He was right. Even if the stairway could fit eight armored men, the dungeon passages could only accommodate five unarmored men side by side. I clicked my tongue in disappointment.

I looked again at the staircase. The guards would disembark the stairway toward the first section where I had been kept. We were coming from the third section, which was behind the walls of the stairs. If we clashed directly with the guards, we would at least have the element of surprise since they would have to turn the corner toward the third section to see us.

The dungeon layout was similar to a trident, with the stairs coming down the middle prong. The length of the base was the first dungeon section, while the left and right prongs were the second and third sections. So, technically, we did have the element of surprise even if they already knew we were down here.

When Dralos returned with the stragglers, I motioned him back the way he came. "Dralos, take half and wrap back around to the second section. Stay behind the wall and out of sight until I say so. Nasq, stay here with the others. Same as Dralos. Don't reveal yourself yet." I waved for Nida and some of the other Paragons to follow me. "We're going to start in the middle section so their attention is focused on us."

I felt some resistance from the Paragons I left with Dralos and Nasq. Even if they did not feel much loyalty toward me, they would inherently understand that their survival depended on my own. So I wasn't surprised that many were disgruntled by having me on the frontline. Still, they kept it to themselves. I brooked no argument and expected obedience in this situation—even the freed slaves who had no connection to me could feel my aura of command.

My group positioned itself directly in front of the descending stairs, leaving enough distance for the incoming guards to be well into the dungeon lobby heading toward the first section before reaching us. Hopefully, at that point, Nasq's and Dralos's teams could collapse in a pincer attack. There would be a few seconds for the guards to react before the other two could reach the foyer of the dungeon floor, but it should be a small enough window of time that the surprise would still send their ranks into chaos.

"There! The slaves are over there!" The armored guards and mercenaries swarmed down the staircase like hungry ants rushing toward food. For a moment, it seemed that fortune was finally in my favor as the guards would spill out into the foyer in a chaotic mess, allowing the pincer move to work without a hitch.

However, mere seconds before the first row of guards crossed the threshold, a powerful, deep voice echoed from the back of the armed mob with alarming command. "HALT."

The word wasn't shouted or screamed. It was spoken calmly, almost a whisper amid the clamor of soldiers and clanking armor. The order didn't need to be loud. Every soldier stopped, some taking a few steps back. Even the mercenaries in less armor and more ragged clothing stopped, turning their eyes toward a large, heavyset man in the middle of the pack. The foremost rows of armored soldiers did not turn toward the commander, though they did halt. I narrowed my eyes at them, sensing something off about their energy, but my attention was stolen when I spotted the man who had spoken.

I did a double-take. Not a man. Male, yes, but not a man. Even from my distance in the dim lighting of Nasq's flames and the moon shining down the stairway, I could see that the commander was blue. Though most of his body was clad in heavy Silver armor, a distinct belly protruded forward, and his face was bare, covered in black swirls of tattooed markings I didn't recognize. The design began at the base of his neck, snaking its way up his chin before spiraling up his cheeks to form new symbols on his bald head.

Despite the limitations of the stairs, the commander stood at least ten feet tall, nearly twice my height. The ceiling seemed to just barely miss scraping against his head. The foyer between myself and the blue warrior had a vaulted ceiling—the only part of the dungeon that did. If I could lead him into a pathway, perhaps the squeezed space would give me an advantage.

What in Ashwash's name was he? My confusion didn't last long.

"Holy Gods," Nida muttered from my left, gripping her spear more firmly with one hand as she used the other to push a loose strand of hair behind her ear. "It's a High Pandorian."

"Pandorian?" I whispered back. The name sounded familiar. Where had I heard that before?

"From the Pandorian Empire," Nida responded, voice trembling slightly. "I don't understand why he's here. High Pandorians directly serve the Pandorian imperial family and the . . ."

She stopped, eyes wide, and I pressed her with a hiss. "And the what?"

"The Church of Light."

I should have known the Church would have its own forces with it. I had no idea what a High Pandorian was, but when he stepped forward and some of the armed crowd parted to make way, I instantly sensed just how powerful the Pandorian warrior was.

Not only did the High Pandorian have that bundle of magic near his stomach that I'd been thinking of as a Magic Core, but he also had a Heart Core. An Ashwash-cursed Heart Core. And the Core was at the Silver level, even if its foundation did not strike me as particularly stable. Holy Ashwash.

My heart began to thump so loudly that it echoed in my ears. Those around me shuddered in fear and terror at the mere presence the Pandorian exuded. I didn't. I couldn't. My body was so filled with excitement and anticipation that there wasn't any room for fear.

Finally. Finally! I was about to get a real Core battle. That was exactly what my Bronze Heart Core needed to evolve into a Silver Heart Core. It was already on the verge of becoming Silver, and all it needed was one last giant push. This was it. This was my chance.

I shot Nida a giant grin and laughed. The sound cracked the silent pressure of the Pandorian like it was mere glass, and the aura around my own fighters lightened, their shoulders slumping slightly in relief.

"Listen, slaves," the Pandorian said, spitting the word "slaves" like it burned his tongue. "This is your only chance to live. Go back to your quarters like the good little rodents you are and stay there until the Slave Master decides what to do with you all. I promise you, if you fight, you will die." As he approached our smaller center group, I saw there was no white in his eyes. They were completely black.

I sneered at his words, unsheathing my sword only to let it drop complacently to my shoulder, and stepped in front of our group so the armored Pandorian could see me. "What is a follower of the Light doing here?"

The Pandorian's next words seemed to catch in his chest for a split instant at the sight of me. He recovered quickly, clearing his throat and withdrawing a two-handed battle-axe from where it had been sheathed against his back.

"I see our saintess candidate isn't one to sit still," the Pandorian said with a sneer of his own.

"Does the Church know you are here?" I asked, standing up to my full height and throwing the pressure of my heart energy forward. "I don't imagine it would take kindly to know an elite of its ranks is fighting slaves." It was a complete assumption on my part based on what Nida had said, but my assumption was proven accurate with the Pandorian's response.

He didn't flinch. "Her Eminence does not concern herself with such"—he peered down his nose at all of us—"with such trash. The Colosseum mercenaries and guards are enough to deal with the likes of you all."

"Then why are you here?" I mocked. "To ask for the Saintess's forgiveness for the actions of your subordinates?"

The Pandorian smirked and looked at me as one might look at a sick puppy. "My master does not believe you to be a true saintess. You should not have killed his niece. He will be quite pleased to hear of your death."

"Good," I responded, hefting my sword in front of me. "I guess I don't have to worry about killing you then."

The Pandorian chuckled, but the mirth did not reach his eyes, which remained cold as ice. "This is your last chance, Saintness Candidate. Go back. I do this out of kindness against my master's desires."

"That is funny, Pandorian." I pointed the tip of my sword at him. "Because you do not have any choice in your death here today."

He snarled, his previous casual chuckle nothing but a regretful memory in the face of my insults. With a wave of his hand and a shout, his men charged at us. Perhaps twenty rows of eight men shot down the stairway roaring with promises of death, clanking in their heavy armor and carrying their swords. They tried to make their way around me to the others in my group. Not a moment after the first row hit the floor, I leaped toward them, covering nearly fifteen meters in seconds, and thrust my sword forward between the first soldier's eyes. Gore and blood exploded out the back of his head. The mercenary dropped, his body falling back against the others like a domino, slowing the others' advance both physically and in apparent mental trepidation.

Behind the armored soldiers was a group of men and women in red-blue robes who had remained at the higher elevation the staircase provided. There were maybe a half dozen of them, give or take a person or two. I could sense a combination of magic and heart energy forming from them. I didn't have the opportunity to worry about what spells or techniques the mages and energy users would use.

The soldiers behind the initial row of mercenaries and guards made short work of the remaining distance, not even pausing from my show of dominance, following their other comrades who were engaging with us. Only as the second row of combatants approached did I finally realize that many of those I'd believed to be human were not. Some were, of course, like the one I'd dispatched. But a large number of them were not.

They weren't even alive.

It explained how the Colosseum leadership had managed to gather such a large force in so little time despite most of its guards likely being asleep in barracks or some off-Colosseum residence. And, even then, what were the chances the Colosseum even kept hundreds of guards at any one time?

No, a large portion of our foes were enormous humanoid golems. That was the Pandorian's true power, the power I'd sensed condensing near his gut. *Magic.*

"Pandorian Golems!" someone shouted from my right. When I turned my gaze toward the voice for a split second, I saw Romeo and Julius fighting with one of the large stone golems that towered over them with an empty, lifeless expression. I hadn't even noticed that they'd followed me to the center group. I hoped they would be able to hold their own.

I let my lunar attribute heart energy cascade over my body and sword like a veil as I charged the first golem that had attacked me. My sword shot like lightning through the air toward the humanoid golem directly in front of me. It deflected my initial strike with a fist of steel, and I understood that the golems were not clad in armor. They were armor.

I swore under my breath again, spinning on my heels to drive the empowered point of my blade through the golem's stomach to where I sensed its heart. I felt the thrum of power as my blade penetrated the creature's Heart Core and shattered it. An instant later the golem crumbled to dust, and I darted forward toward the next one.

CHAPTER THIRTY-NINE

Blood Will Run: Part 1

I didn't call Nasq or Dralos immediately after the skirmish started. For the plan to succeed, all of the Colosseum's forces, or at least most of them, needed to be in the foyer connecting the stairway and all three sections. Unlike the pathways, the foyer itself was a large circular space, able to fit what I estimated to be no more than forty people at a time. Over half of the armed guards had yet to finish descending. A good, technical strategy here would have been to retreat, allowing for increased space in the foyer for the rest of the soldiers to descend into.

Technically. And I might have chosen that path at any other moment.

Not today.

My adrenaline spiked to capacity as I barreled through golem after golem, crushing the creatures with a tornado of sword strikes fueled by the strength of a high-tier Bronze Core. In the wake of my ferocity, golems disintegrated, and humans bled as golem Cores shattered and human appendages were sliced clean off. Within moments, it was an absolute clusterfuck of gore and dirt-like ash, polluted with the screams of the dying and the piercing screech of steel clashing against steel. Magic and heart energy flew across the foyer in a wild mess, striking ally and enemy almost indiscriminately in the enclosed space. Some stray bolts of power struck the rocky foundation of the slave dungeon, causing large and small boulders to cascade into the battle, crushing unsuspecting men and women.

Freed slaves and Paragons climbed over their dead foes and friends alike to engage, as the bodies littering the space continued to fill and there was nowhere else to go. No matter where I went, my feet squished disgustingly into pools of deep red that trailed from guards and freed slaves alike. I stepped over a body, swinging my sword in elation at another soldier, my lunar energy-empowered sword slicing through his blade like melted butter and disemboweling him with a sickening squelch of flesh and organs.

Over the shouts and screams of battle, I yelled at the High Pandorian, who had yet to move from his spot high on the stairway, "I don't think you brought enough men."

His gaze scanned over me for a brief moment but otherwise stayed focused on the battlefield, causing a deep frown to etch itself on my face. Had I not shown enough battle prowess to attract his attention? Sure, I was still in the body of a twelve-year-old girl, but with the amount of blood staining me and gore covering me, I doubted my appearance still maintained the inherent innocence of a child.

Or perhaps he was simply fearful of engaging me. The thought made me growl at the disrespect and cowardice. My blade swung once more, cleaving the arm of a golem before I spun and embedded the steel deep into the creature's upper leg where I'd sensed its Core vibrating. In the distance behind me, I could still hear Romeo and Julius shouting at each other and the subsequent clashing of their blades against whatever foes they faced. I didn't turn to look, nor did I intend to help. If they survived or died, that would be their own fate.

Though I did not want them to perish, I was not their protector or guardian. A queen did not look back. A queen pushed forward, conquering and destroying any obstacles in her path.

And that is exactly what I would do—what I always did.

"Now!" I shouted when most of the Pandorian's forces had finally descended into the foyer. The majority of the freed slaves I'd taken with me were dead, as were a handful of Paragons. But still, we held, refusing to be pushed back into the thin pathway leading to the first slave area I had stayed in for the past weeks.

Dralos's and Nasq's groups surged forward from either side, crashing into the mercenaries like a wave of metal and flesh. From the corner of my vision I spotted Nasq slinging bolts of magic at the red-blue roped men and women, sparking absolute chaos among their ranks with the surprise attack. Other Paragons joined in Nasq's onslaught, piling on their own attacks as the group broke the defending soldiers from a distance.

I momentarily lost sight of the Pandorian when he leaped into the fray just as the three forces clashed, but I could still sense his Heart Core as it pulsed rhythmically, a beacon of dark energy amid the chaotic storm of combat.

From there everything descended into utter chaos. The dungeon filled with sounds to match that chaos and the cries of death and pain increased in multitude—it was nearly deafening to me as I was in the throes of it all. I heard the primal roar of Ethan as he surged into the throng of mercenaries with seemingly no fear of death and the crackling of Nasq's shadow magic as parts of the foyer blinked into darkness before being stained red with the blood of Ethan's prey.

I moved through the fray with lethal precision, decades of military and war experience dictating my every move with expertise. I was a blur of death despite being half the size of the mercenaries and guards, and a third the size of the golems I brought down one after the other. Each life I snuffed out filled the reserves of my heart energy and I could feel my Core growing stronger with each kill. I wasn't gaining power in the same way I had while being boosted by the Main System. Not exactly. It was as if I had somehow opened a passage inside my Core by absorbing the woman and the guard, a pathway that was now allowing me to absorb homeless heart energy from the recently deceased while I fought, and the more I did it, the easier it became until it was second nature.

I was reminded that there was no training, no practice, no form of cultivation or meditation that could force someone to learn like when their life was on the line.

All at once, a giant battle-axe cleaved a path toward me through the center of a golem, splitting it in two. For a moment I thought it might have been Gronch, but I knew it wasn't when I saw the dark blue skin and completely black eyes that glared at me with a bone-chilling coldness. To him, this was at most a job from his master. Maybe it was just a hobby of his, even. I didn't know. The Pandorian took off his helmet and tossed it to the ground with a look somewhere between boredom and expectation.

I met his glare with a grin fueled by the chaos of the battlefield and we engaged, steel sword to battle-axe. Instead of meeting his battle-axe head-on, I parried it to the side and used the momentum of the recoil to twist my blade into an upward arc, aiming to free the Pandorian of his arm. The move didn't take as the Pandorian launched a front kick at my gut with a speed I barely registered before my sword strike had neared him enough to be any real threat.

I stumbled backward but stayed on my feet and kept my guard up, dodging a wild sword strike from some peasant mercenary who I didn't have the time to kill. The Pandorian was, by far, the strongest fighter I'd faced since arriving in Graedon. Likely, he was well beyond the level of even the Silverwater's Knight Captain considering the low-tier Silver-level Core he possessed.

We engaged again, both of us drawing on our heart energy and turning it into pure Authority, an invisible, spherical force around its user that applied pressure to all living beings around the user into submission. An ultimate demonstration of dominance. My Authority had been weak previously. But now, at peak Bronze Core, it had some use. Even if it was minuscule compared to the force of my old Authority.

The surprise on the Pandorian's face was clear as our Authorities flexed into each other, struggling for dominance over the other force. My grin widened at the male's expression and I pressed even harder.

His face twisted into a look of utter shock at the force of my Authority and he switched tactics. Heart energy wrapped around his armor, hardening into the brown color of a golem, and he returned to a physical engagement as he aimed to crack into the side of my skull. I dodged to the side, weaving around the strike to launch a lunar-empowered punch of my own.

Unlike his, mine struck home but the innate rigidity of the golem armor covering his underlying armor sent a shockwave of pain up my arm and I could feel my fingers fracture from the impact. The Pandorian laughed when I winced, but it was quickly cut off when I jammed the hilt of my blade, still held in my other arm, into the side of his head. A helmet would have stopped the blow, but he'd already taken his off, the arrogant ass.

The Pandorian recoiled slightly and staggered backward, swinging his large battle-axe with a one-handed cleave. I redirected the axe with a physical manifestation of my heart energy forming a shield to sweep the Pandorian's weapon away at an odd angle just enough that I could dash into his guard once again and thrust up at his chest with my sword.

He growled and raised a knee to deter my advance lest I take the blow to the face. I twirled out of the way at the last second, dropping my sword so it spun around his ankle as I dodged. The sound my blade made upon contact was akin to sharpening a steel edge upon whetstone. When I looked, no blood had been drawn. The only indication I'd nearly cut his Achilles was a thin black line trailing around his heel.

The odd energy of "magic" swirled around the warrior for a split second before the bundle of that energy in his stomach spiked with power. The Pandorian muttered something under his breath and a twister of fire sprang into existence, blasting from the Pandorian's palms toward me.

I raised an invisible shield of heart energy which took the brunt of the magic's force. But I was still caught off guard by the use of magic and the resulting blow sent me tumbling backward. With some effort, I ceased the tumble and landed smoothly back on my feet, sword still in hand. My shoulder was scorched, flesh bubbling with the heat of what I realized was actual fire. Not heart energy with a fire attribute, but actual fire. Just like Gideon's had been actual ice.

I was beginning to get a better picture of what exactly magic was. It seemed that, unlike heart energy which could have many different types of attributes, raw magic wasn't used to cause damage. It was used as a catalyst to create or summon other forces to inflict harm. Perhaps magic could also be used outside of combat if it truly created something from nothing. Considering the time it took to prepare the magic, perhaps it was best suited for non-combat situations.

However, the ability to create something from nothing was the realm of Gods. I didn't—couldn't—believe such power could be as common as magic seemed to be.

I shook my head to clear my thoughts. Now wasn't the time.

Heart energy isn't the only thing that exists here, I chastised myself. I needed to keep "magic" in mind going forward.

"What in the world are you?" The Pandorian growled, hefting his axe into both hands, all mirth gone from his expression. His large chest heaved with the struggle to keep his breath stable, much as I was.

Sweat drenched me, plastering my hair to my dirt-covered face. As I squared off with the Pandorian, the hair was proving to be quite the annoying distraction since I couldn't just brush it aside in my current situation.

I wanted to return his cold stare with an equally cold glare of my own, but I couldn't wipe the wicked grin that seemed to be permanently etched on my features. I was just enjoying the fight so Ashwash damned much.

"How do you have such a solid Core?" he hissed. The Pandorian took a heavy step forward and narrowed his eyes as if attempting to see through to my very soul. "That is not something a lowly Pularean like you should be able to accomplish." The blue warrior scowled, "Is someone teaching you? Who dares to share the Pandorian cultivation with an outsider?"

"Aren't you Pularean as well?" I asked, genuinely confused by the Pandorian's taunt. Pandora was the largest nation and only empire in the Pulorean continent. What was the point of an insult that dishonored his own home continent?

The Pandorian smirked, looking down his long nose at me in superiority. "You don't even know where Pandorians are from, do you, child?" It was my turn to scowl, and I had to remind myself for the millionth time that by all appearances, I was, in fact, a child.

CHAPTER FORTY

Blood Will Run: Part 2

Whatever conversation was beginning between us was swiftly shut down by the wild roar of a blood-crazy Berserker. Out of the corner of my eye, without taking my concentration off the Pandorian, I saw Ethan rampaging against the building army of golems encircling him. His roar was so tremendous it shook the walls of the dungeon, causing even more loose rubble to tumble to the floor.

The Pandorian glanced toward Ethan for less than a second, but for that split moment, he was distracted, and I surged forward like a bolt of lightning. My heart's energy crackled around me in small explosions of power, wrapping around me like a physical aura as I leaped into the air to meet him at eye level and swung my sword at his neck. He raised his axe in panic, my attack catching him momentarily off guard. The edge of my blade struck powerfully against the flat of his axe, sparks of fire igniting off the clashing steel.

He tried to push me back, summoning his own heart energy and an aura of magic around him, but the crackling power I'd summoned kept me temporarily suspended in the air, my sword stretching for his neck. There was no stopping the adrenaline of battle that flooded my System and hyped the hurricane of rage deep inside me. Not him. Not his minions. Not his golems that had begun to turn toward us, sensing their master's struggle.

Before the constructs of rock and the mercenaries could turn to aid their commander, Ethan, and Nida cut them off. Ethan bellowed a challenge at the golems while Nida spun her spear in the direction of the approaching soldiers with a beast-like snarl.

Once again, the two of us shifted our heart energy into Authority, battling for dominance. The forces collided and our bodies were blown away from the point of collision, both of us sent spiraling backward. I felt myself slam into a wall of the dungeon, collapsing face first into a sticky mass of dirt, gore, and thick red blood. The taste of iron and dirt filled my mouth. I didn't have time to ponder how disgusting it was. I simply spat the blood out and snarled toward the Pandorian who was similarly uninjured other than a few cuts on his bare face. And a growing black eye. Served him right. I glanced down at the sword in my hand and its shattered blade scattered to bits around me. Then I noticed the Pandorian's battle-axe was also broken, though only into three pieces.

Without a word of warning, both of us dropped our shattered weapons and exploded into a flurry of movements ignited by our Cores and adrenaline. To say we clashed would have been an understatement. We went to fucking war.

Each strike was brought with the force of a falling tree. Each block with the stubbornness of a stone wall. Both of us circulated our heart energy to block and strike with lightning-quick reflexes, not pausing for even a moment's respite. The first to stop would be the first to die.

Despite my decades of training and the effort I'd expended to raise Lilliana's physical attributes, enhancing her physical body so far beyond its limits would only work for so long before her bones began to break and her muscles tore. The amount of heart energy I was forced to circulate in my body and the speed at which I did it were already causing internal damage. I could feel it in the roiling of my gut.

Just as the warrior landed a mighty uppercut to my stomach, breaking through my weakening defenses and shattering at least a couple of ribs in a single strike, a black spear shot through the chaos. It wasn't nearly as fast as we had been moving, but it was damn near invisible as it soared toward us.

Toward the Pandorian.

His focus was so intent on me that he didn't notice it. Ashwash, I barely noticed it and I was staring directly at it. The tip of the spear slammed into the Pandorian's back with a deafening *BOOM* that reverberated throughout the dungeon like an avalanche.

Although I couldn't see where the spear struck, I knew it had penetrated his armor by the look of utter shock and disbelief that twisted the Pandorian's features. It hadn't killed the warrior, but I could tell it had done some damage. In his moment of shock, I pulled all my energy into my fist and jammed it into the center of his chest. He didn't have time to circulate his heart energy to the area to strengthen himself, even if the spear in his back wasn't disrupting his ability to properly distribute the heart energy within his Core.

My fist crunched through his armor, a hole forming around my empowered strike. Unfortunately, the armor itself had still been quite tough. Tough enough that with my decreasing amounts of heart energy, it was able to put up a strong enough defense to shatter my middle and index fingers on impact.

Neither of us winced, both were used to pain. Both of us were already in significant pain anyway. My entire body was beaten sore despite the protective shield of heart energy I'd been circulating through it. The Pandorian was no better. With the spear, he was much worse.

"I thought," he hissed, "this was a duel."

"What in the worlds gave you that idea?" Nida said, her silver hair dyed red with the blood and gore of mercenaries and guards. Blood dripped from her mouth, her fangs flashing in the orange flickering light of Nasq's flames overhead. She didn't have her spear anymore.

The Pandorian's face flushed purple with anger, but there was nothing he could do about the spear without leaving himself open to my attack. "Bastards. The Goddess will curse you for all eternity."

I laughed at that. "I have been cursed since the day I was born. The Gods have failed to keep me down and they have had decades."

He looked at me with confusion at first. Slowly, it looked like a sort of understanding was dawning on him. "You . . . You are not Lilliana Silverwater, are you?"

All at once, I felt the excitement of battle give way inside of me to something darker. Something sinister that had been waiting patiently, all the while boiling with anticipation of release.

"No," I said. "No, I am not."

He stood to his full height with a struggle, a renewed look of determination on his face. Gone was the look of fear that came with certain death. Gone was the uncertainty. The Pandorian glared at me with a look of righteous indignation and zealous obsession. "Then, in the name of the Goddess and the Church of Light, you must be killed." The Pandorian dropped into a martial stance. "Today will be your last day in our realm, Demon."

I paused and just stared at the male, remembering that he was not just a High Pandorian. He was an elite of the Church of Light. One of the most powerful religious organizations in both Lysoria and Cael. His words and actions showed a religious determination, a belief that his death would be a worthy one.

For the first time since I'd come to Graedon, I realized I had finally found the perfect outlet for all my anger. For all my rage.

I had been betrayed and hanged. Then I was revived in another body only to be nearly killed. Again. And again. And again. It was all like some cruel, sick joke.

But this being before me, this elite warrior, this High Pandorian, thought I was the demon? A devil to be slain?

I was so fucking sick and tired of it. *So. Fucking. Sick. Of. It. All.*

My energy exploded unbidden from me in a tsunami of rage enhanced by the raw adrenaline that always drove me forward. The Pandorian must have noticed the change in my expression to one of pure, unbridled rage.

If he thought I was a monster, then so be it. A monster he would get.

I launched a flurry of attacks at the Pandorian that caused my previous strikes to seem slow and weak in comparison. Whatever emotions the warrior had previously been contemplating quickly fled his mind as they were replaced with an expression of heightened focus and determination.

I didn't care that he could wield magic. That he had a Heart Core. He was a Silver Core. A lowly fucking Silver Core and he dared to stand before me with such arrogance? A mere bug who hadn't even discovered his attributes?

He would kneel before me. He would grovel.

And then he would die. He would die pathetically and worthlessly, without a shred of meaning or honor to it.

Just like how they would all die. Every single one of them that put me in this situation would face my wrath, be it in Ordite or Graedon.

And I knew how I would do it—how I would defeat this warrior with double Cores. I would take everything he had. I would steal everything that mattered to him like he was trying to do to me. Heart energy poured into my eyes and the world lit up with the rainbows of colors that detailed for me where the Pandorian would move to next—just as Gronch had taught me.

A scream of rage tore itself from my throat as even more power erupted from my Core like lava from a vengeful volcano. I could see all haughtiness vanish from the Pandorian's face as he experienced true terror in the face of a superior being.

He tried to disengage.

"You aren't going anywhere!" I roared, refusing to allow his attempt at disengaging. I tore into him with every last shred of my heart energy.

I reached deep inside of me for my Soul Weaver attribute energy. It came rushing out, mixing with my lunar attribute as both attributes fed from the pure heart energy released from my Core.

The Pandorian threw himself to the side with reckless abandon, taking a massive hit from my combined attribute energy that slammed into him with a fury. I saw him twist with the hit, grabbing a nearby sword of a fallen mercenary and thrusting it toward me with desperation.

Heart energy rushed to protect my vitals, but I knew it wouldn't be enough to completely stop the sword and that was okay. I only needed to stop the blow from killing me outright. I didn't resist as my protective shield failed to stop the Pandorian's attack.

I did not so much as wince as the sharp steel, empowered by magic and energy, stabbed deep into my side. I simply shot him a smile.

His eyes widened in belated understanding, but it was too late.

I had let his attack reach me. I wanted it to. With only the momentum of his force and no pushback, he was off-balance and had no way to retreat. He was mine.

I stepped forward, pushed the sword deeper, and slammed both my palms into his chest. My Soul Weaver attributed energy flowed from me and into the Pandorian in a torrent of unbridled power until it found his Core. And his soul.

His Core may have been on a higher level than my own, but mine was better developed. My energy broke into his weakened Core, cracking it as if it were no more than an egg. All protection it had provided to his soul vanished within a blink and I commanded my soul aspect energy to extract the Pandorian's very soul from the confines of his withering Core.

Without even a whimper, the Pandorian's soul fled his body and presented before me in an intangible reddish-orange mass of energy.

CHAPTER FORTY-ONE

Reformation and Core Advancement

The Pandorian's lifeless body crumpled to the ground, his face a frozen mask of confusion and terror. I stood over him, panting heavily, the previously dull ache in my side now intensifying. It felt almost anticlimactic despite being near death myself, blood escaping my wound in heavy streams.

I stared in wonderment at the soul as it hovered almost playfully over the male's corpse.

Looking back, I wasn't sure how I knew how to do what I had done. In Ordite, it was well known that the Core formed within the heart, protecting it. That much was obvious. One could not reach the heart of an Awakened without first overwhelming their Core.

But the soul—the soul was not something even the scholars on Ordite had known about, at least not to my knowledge. This Soul Weaver energy of mine was unique. Gideon, or the man playing him anyway, had not had a Core. Stealing his soul, though I was not entirely sure what a soul was, had not been all that difficult. It was, more or less, unprotected.

The Pandorian, by contrast, had a Core protecting his soul making it much more difficult. And though I hadn't known for certain, I'd somehow felt the shielding over his soul had originated from his Core.

I physically shook my head, attempting to clear myself of distracting thoughts and to focus my vision, which had begun to blur. Questions concerning the details of souls and Cores were well beyond my scholarly prowess. Even in Ordite, I'd relied on countless advisers trained in Core research for answers. Even as a child, I had never been the best student.

Seeing the Pandorian's unmoving body at my feet, I was filled with both elation at my success and an overwhelming sense of exhaustion. The bone-weariness consumed me, and I was instantly met with an adrenaline dump that caused my feet to shakily give way as the pain from my stomach radiated through me like fire.

My instincts screamed to remove the sword. My training fought against that urge. Despite my self-healing abilities, the heart energy in and around my Core was in a statis much like the rest of me. Even if I did pull out the sword, I didn't know if I could heal it before I bled out. So long as my heart energy was frozen like it was, that was unlikely.

I had to find a healer. Where was Marisar? I tried to look around from the Selenian but my body refused to respond as the floor rose to meet my face.

Before I hit the ground, Ethan's large hands cut my fall short, his arms lifting me into the air. "Are you all right, my queen?" The Berserker's concern clashed with the anger in his voice.

I nodded weakly, my vision swimming and my blood running cold. A searing pain burst from my midsection. I stifled the scream that begged to rip itself from me and forced myself to look down at what pained me.

Nida stood there, her face concentrated as she grasped the handle of the sword still impaling my stomach nearly to its hilt. I wanted to shout at her not to take it out without a healer, lest I bleed out. I didn't have the chance before Nida yanked it out of me with a sickening squelch, followed by my grunts of pain as a flush of wet hot fluid flowed from the wound. Great.

Maybe I'd been too reckless.

"Marisar is a healer," I groaned, attempting to channel some of my reserves to the affected area and heal it myself, but the energy refused to move. All my energy was still in statis, though my Core continued to absorb the homeless heart energy escaping from the Pandorian's Silver Core.

I knew what that meant, and a small smile tugged at my lips despite the blood that seeped profusely from the wound. Even if the healing wasn't perfect, I simply needed it to keep me alive for the moment.

My Core was ready to progress.

And, with it, my wounds would heal through the body Reformation.

"There's no time," Nida said urgently. "I have some healing skills I'm going to use. Hold still, my queen."

That will hopefully be enough, I thought with a wince as she reached to gingerly touch the bleeding wound.

I nodded to the Tigerkin woman. "Do what you need to do." Then I looked toward Ethan. With gritted teeth and dried blood clamping one of my eyelids shut, I said, "Set me down, Berserker, and bring me the Pandorian's heart."

To his credit, Ethan didn't argue. He quickly found a fallen boulder to set me against and turned to face the battlefield, which had come to a standstill. I didn't need to be a telepath to understand the look of complete shock on the faces of the Colosseum's guards and mercenaries. With someone as powerful as the High Pandorian on their side, they had undoubtedly believed their victory was all but guaranteed.

It was no longer so assured.

Their faces transformed into fear and one by one they began to flee.

I tried to infuse my words with some heart energy, but my Core screamed in retaliation at the effort and instead of an empowered command I just grunted. Instead, I released a low growl and muttered, "Do not let them escape."

What was once a battlefield quickly devolved into a one-sided slaughter. Now bereft of their creator, the fearsome golems slowly collapsed into dust without the Pandorian's energy or magic, I wasn't sure, to fuel their existences. The remaining mercenaries and guards were left at the mercy of the overwhelming number of freed slaves and Paragons.

There was no mercy in war.

"A queen must make the wise decision," my father had warned, "not the emotional one. Not the decision you think is the fairest, but the wisest decision that will bring everything to an end. That will allow your people to thrive. You must never leave enemies alive to fight another day, to birth future enemies. There is no surrender in war. No mercy."

No mercy, I thought as Ethan returned and a brilliant green light enveloped me from Nida's hands as she began to heal my wounds. The pain lessened slightly as the power sank into me.

The Berserker brought me the Pandorian's heart, and I took it with trembling hands. I chose to believe they shook because of my excitement at progression rather than the weakness of blood loss. I tried not to dwell on it too much.

I pulled my arm back and squeezed against the Silver Core with all my strength. The flesh of the Pandorian's purple heart exploded between my fingers, swiftly followed by a shattering of Silver; the glass-like substance that was the Core of heart energy.

The energy surged into me, and I threw my head back in pure agony as the torrent of lifeforce rushed into my Core. I struggled to control the chaotic energy, while sweat poured down Nida's face as she focused on healing my wound. I vaguely felt her switch to using magic rather than heart energy, but I wasn't in the right state to wonder about the difference.

Nida looked up, her usual jovial expression now distraught as the scream that had been struggling to escape finally tore from me and echoed through the dungeon.

Unlike previous times I'd absorbed heart energy, the Pandorian's had been refined by a Silver Core. It was multiple times more potent than anything I'd been able to experience in this life, threatening to overwhelm and consume my own heart energy in the process. Perhaps it would have, had I not experienced this many times in Ordite. I knew what to expect from absorbing a higher-tiered Core, especially on the verge of the Reformation stage.

As the heart energy coursed through me, I fought to circulate it through my meridians as I'd been taught in Ordite. Previously, my heart energy had not been strong enough to clear the meridian pathways. Once they were opened, however, I would finally be able to initiate my first Reformation.

Ignoring the persistent pain in my stomach, I concentrated on circulating the quality energy. It surged through my meridians, seeking out the deep-seated impurities accumulated over years from exposure to mortal-world pollutants compounded by this body's prior abuse and neglect. Expelling these impurities was excruciating, as always.

This time, however, the agony surprised me. As I looked inward at my soul, visible for the first time since the Transference, I saw it as a massive diamond light twisted with a dark, wild purple of my necromantic attribute. Next to it was a much smaller flame, entirely enveloped in a dark, oozing black mass of impurities.

Lilliana.

With that thought, my body convulsed violently. My blood boiled, veins burned with intensity, combined with the pain from my stomach wound pushing me toward unconsciousness. My skin turned clammy and pale, beads of sweat sliding down my face. Each droplet fell, splashing into the dirt, blackened like the present state of Lilliana's soul, carrying away some of the toxins along with it. Soon, the black sweat turned into a heavy ooze that slunk to the floor, evidence that the Pandorian's Silver-Core energy was being properly absorbed by my evolving Core.

Inside our souls, my heart energy attacked the built-up grime of negative energy relentlessly, breaking it down before pushing it out through my pores much as the System had done to Orpheus's blood. The bitterness of bile rose in my throat, and my stomach churned. I was quickly overwhelmed by the acrid scent of expelled toxins, a testament to my Reformation.

With each purification wave, my body underwent a profound transformation. Unimpeded by Bronze-level impurities, the heart energy flowed more freely, penetrating deeper. It began to reconstruct my physiology at the most fundamental level. I consciously reached out, attempting to restrain the reconstruction from pulling too heavily on my "true self." Since Lilliana's body was that of a child, a full Reformation would tear it apart, and I wasn't sure I could survive that.

My bones, once burdened by physical and metaphysical impurities, lightened and strengthened. Each bone seemed reforged, denser, and more resilient, capable of withstanding great pressure without relying fully on flexibility or rigidity. The marrow would produce richer, more potent blood, increasing my vigor and physical capacity.

My muscles, too, underwent metamorphosis. Fibers were stripped down and reformed to be stronger and more efficient. Each sinew embedded with heart energy refined by my now Silver Core, enhancing my physical capabilities beyond those of an ordinary mortal. The power was both familiar and exhilarating.

My skin, once dulled by battles and abuse, shed dirt and blood, glowing with Silver radiance. It became supple yet tougher, able to withstand bruising and cuts that would have incapacitated Lilliana's meek body. Though I couldn't see my eyes, I could feel them regain their old brilliant red, replacing Lilliana's soft brown. A sharp pain lanced from my eyes as an old scar etched itself down my right eye.

When the mark of a fallen Lunari threatened to tattoo itself on my forehead, I pushed back on the Reformation. Accepting the mark would force my body to adopt the increased musculature of chosen Lunaris, a blessing prohibited for children, historically resulting in slow, painful deaths.

Although the Reformation would age my new body somewhat, likely throwing it into the midst of puberty, I needed to keep my true self mixed with Lilliana's until her body finished undergoing that natural process. That way my body wouldn't just increase in size but also grow and age into a better, stronger physicality than my previous body. There was also the risk that forcing a child's body to morph into the body of an adult through Reformation could cause lasting damages to the body's growth potential. I wanted to avoid that risk.

As the Reformation neared completion, I felt a clear shift in my Core. The ruddy coloring slowly faded, replaced by a Silver sheen that consumed the dull Bronze with fervor. When the Core completely glowed Silver, it pulsed with power. Compared to a Bronze-tiered Core, it had become a wellspring of heart energy. The once-foreign power now an extension of my own Will, ready to be harnessed as I desired.

I was one step closer to my former strength. My former glory. It felt damned good.

As physical pain subsided, I opened my eyes to see rows of kneeling Paragons. Many freed slaves knelt too, awe clear in their expressions. They knelt in blood and gore, among felled friends and foes without any regard. I belatedly realized I wasn't sitting anymore; Nida wasn't healing me. She was with the others, kneeling, eyes cast downward in respect.

Then, I noticed I wasn't standing either. I was upright, sure, but floating off the ground. The radiance of my new Core shone through my skin. I couldn't help but grin. To those who had never seen an Awakener with a Silver-tiered Core, I must have looked like a God.

I turned toward the closest Paragons: Ethan, Nida, and Nasq. For some reason, I was not surprised that those three were the nearest to me. Nor did I find myself particularly displeased with it either.

"Have the stragglers been dealt with?" I asked, my voice now too elegant for a child but still retaining a delicate quality.

Without rising, Ethan spoke with his usual grumble. "Aye, my queen. None remain."

"The magic wielders?"

"Them too."

"Good." At my words, Ethan's aura seemed to swell with delight, though his features remained stoic. "Then I suppose it's time for us to interrupt a banquet."

CHAPTER FORTY-TWO

Glory of Freedom and the Enticement of Cowardice

According to Dralos, the banquet would take place in a large manse adjacent to the Colosseum, where all VIPs and nobles could attend each night. Arriving there from the main battle area, where the path we had just liberated let out, wouldn't be difficult or time-consuming.

When I finally exited the dungeons, I was met with cool, fresh night air for the first time in weeks. It was a stark, incredibly pleasant contrast to the stifling heat of the latest accommodations I had grown accustomed to these past few weeks. The sensation was almost startling—a sharp, invigorating, and intensely refreshing change. Despite the scent of blood and gore wafting from both our clothes and the caverns below where many had been slain, the cold night air was crisp, filling my lungs with a purity I had almost forgotten. Not even the continuous blaring of the remaining alarms could disturb our temporary peace.

The coolness kissed my skin, causing a small, nearly imperceptible shiver to run down my spine. It was not from discomfort, but from the incredible novelty of the sensation, as if I were someone dying of thirst just granted rain. For a moment, I closed my eyes and tilted my head toward the sky, letting the night breeze whisper a gentle caress through my matted hair. It tugged gently at the ruined tatters of my clothing, reminding me that a change would soon be necessary lest the garment fall off in pieces.

When I opened my eyes, the stars seemed brighter, and the world seemed oh so quiet. I stayed there for a few more seconds, basking in the glory of the night and of freedom, before finally turning back toward my resurrected servant. True to his word, we had exited without a problem. If the truthfulness of his words continued, the banquet hall would be just through the north passage.

Though Dralos was still taller than me by at least a head, I was able to look at him without craning my neck. I must have grown around eight inches or so from the Reformation. It was difficult to judge without a mirror, but I guessed I was a few inches over five and a half feet.

"You will not be coming with us, Draconian."

He didn't even flinch in surprise, his face remaining stoic as always. "What is it you wish from me, my queen?"

"Do you know where the monsters are kept?" Considering the creatures that had been unleashed on us during the so-called saintess trials, there was a high chance that the Colosseum had many other beasts kept chained somewhere.

"I do," Dralos responded, confirming my suspicions.

"Set them loose," I instructed. "By the time I leave the banquet of pompous nobles, I want the entire city in a panic. Understood?" The Draconian nodded and bowed, disappearing without a word of discontent back into the dungeon so many of us had just managed to exit.

"You're going to release monsters into the city?" Romeo said, his face scrunched into a grimace of horror. Others joined him in quiet protest, echoes of whispers giving sound to the otherwise silent night. I realized once again that these were not soldiers, and that Romeo, as well as he fought, did not appear to even be twenty.

"It makes sense," Gronch responded, approaching us. The pale green half orc had been pretty badly injured compared to Romeo and Julius. One of his oral tusks had been shattered halfway down its base, while large, ugly gashes crisscrossed his now naked torso. At least none of his appendages were missing. Marisar was chasing after the stumbling half orc, a dim white light emanating from the clearly exhausted Selenian.

"How does setting such vile creatures on innocent civilians make sense?" Romeo spat, his voice loud enough to turn a few heads.

Gronch shot him a look of annoyance. "Shut the hells up, brat." Romeo's mouth dropped open in surprise, but Gronch kept his sour demeanor. "Why speak as if you know war? We can all tell you're some pampered noble's brat. Even enslaved, you have a fucking guard."

"Lilliana, if this is the path you are taking, I cannot abide by it," Romeo said, gritting his teeth as he cast an angry stare in my direction, outright ignoring Gronch. "There is no reason to kill innocents in the city when we can just leave."

"More innocents will die tonight no matter what I choose to do," I replied calmly, placing a hand on his shoulder and looking around at the freed slaves who cast us worried looks. "The reality of the situation is if we don't release the monsters as a distraction, we will all die. Even as we speak, I have no doubt the city guard is rushing to provide backup to their fallen brethren."

"We can do both if I go save them," Romeo retorted in protest, his eyes alight with determination as he attempted to shrug off my hand. I didn't let him and squeezed my grip until I saw him give a slight wince.

"Do you think they will care that a mere, dirty escaped slave saved them?" I shook my head. "No, they will simply throw you back into those cages like an animal." I looked at all in my sight. "You will all be thrown back into those cages. You may not yet understand, but this is war. And in war, you fight. You kill. You never look back, or else the person in front of you unburdens you of your head. When faced with a monster, sometimes you must become the monster."

Romeo's hand gripped the handle of his sword as if to give him strength. Eventually, however, he withered under my stare and took a step back. "How can you all be okay with the death of so many? The monsters won't just kill soldiers; you all understand that? They will kill children. Women. Everyone."

I clicked my tongue, urging our group to begin moving toward the banquet hall without any further delay. "Sometimes sacrifices must be made and people must die," I said to the young man, "but I do not waste life needlessly." I released my grip on his shoulder. "Put your faith in me, young one. By the time the sun rises, we will not only be free, but we will be victorious."

With that, I left Romeo and Julius behind to do as they willed. If they fled, blind to what I was doing, then that was their destined path. I did not have the luxury of debating morality with the boy, nor did I desire to. Though I had grown rather fond of the two, my words had not been spoken simply to soothe the restless mind of Romeo. I had been speaking to all the freed slaves. Until I was rid of this city, the larger my force remained, the better. And, even though the freed slaves were currently beneficial, I would need to deal with them later. It was too early in my conquest for them to begin spreading the fact that some thought of me as a queen. I doubted that would bode well with the royal family of Lysoria.

Following the direction Dralos relayed to me before leaving, the group of us flooded out the Arena gates like a swarm of ants. I was like the queen ant as they flooded around me, wild whoops of joy from Paragons and freed slaves alike as they crossed outside the Colosseum's borders and into the freedom of the city. Some of the freed slaves immediately fled into the distance, and I instructed the others to not interfere. While I was displeased and having the fact some referred to me as "Queen" spread into the outside world was not preferred, I didn't want to bother with some insects. No one would believe them anyway.

As the hundred and fifty or so of us remaining survivors milled about the Colosseum entrance, I raised my voice to be heard above the increasing sound. "Silence!" Once eyes had returned to me and words were whispered or silenced, I continued. "This is your final opportunity to flee. For those of you who continue with me here, we have a long and bloody road ahead of us. But if you put your faith in me, we will rise above the little kingdoms of this world. For those of you who wish to live your lives free of burden and pass away in a small forgotten corner of the world, you may leave now."

Words though they may be, I could see the profound impact they had on many of the freed slaves. Even though they had chosen to not become Paragons, I was promising them glory in their freedom. A few of the freed slaves trickled away into the distance, but most remained. Once the dead-weights of cowardice finished running away from the destiny of greatness, I grinned at those left. At least a hundred stayed, with a little under half being surviving Paragons.

For the first time since arriving at the Colosseum, I was able to take in what it looked like from the outside. Just like the inside, the Colosseum was massive, but from the outside, it looked more like towering walls than a stadium. Hundreds of windows for the audience peppered its thick layers, wrapping around it like hundreds of little eyes in a distinctly menacing manner.

The group of us stood on a wide gravel walkway that split into three directions. The first path was the most trodden and led back to the city proper. The second led back into the Colosseum—the same path we had just taken to leave. And finally, a path to the VIP manse that, according to Dralos, was used to house important guests for Colosseum events. That was the path we headed on. Looking ahead, it was an uphill trek to the mansion. I found the fact it was an uphill climb to be somewhat poetic.

I didn't bother telling those who followed to hush their steps or not to talk. I wanted them to hear us coming. To hear me coming. To know that despite all their precautions, plans, and schemes, they had not been able to keep me down.

At first, the mansion was too small to make out anything distinct about it. Then I spotted some ten or twenty soldiers with red embroidered uniforms standing guard and circling the territory. Some held weapons of steel, and others had what appeared to be sticks that curled at the top into fat nubs. Almost like a club, but not quite. I wasn't entirely sure what to make of them.

From the outside, the mansion stood less like a house and more like a stronghold, a testament to both opulence and strength. It was perched snugly atop a hill overlooking the sprawling city and Colosseum below. As we approached, some of the motivation of the freed slaves began to wane in the face of the commanding and protective presence of the structure. Massive gargoyle-like structures loomed ominously behind the posted soldiers, their eyes seeming to move as I moved.

The roof was covered in dark, slate tiles that glistened faintly under the moon's luminescent glare. A grand, wrought-iron gate marked the entrance to the estate, guarded by both soldiers and gargoyles. The gate was flanked by enormous stone pillars topped with three lanterns each that emitted a flickering glow into the night that was no less ominous than the life-like sentinels watching our every movement.

"W-we're supposed to get into there?" one of the freed slaves whimpered, losing his courage. "H-how?"

Before anyone else could answer, I simply said, "Just watch." The man's head snapped in my direction so fast I thought he might have broken his neck. His eyes opened wide and his mouth dropped agape as if he hadn't expected me to hear him. Then his face turned beet red, and I saw him grip his sword with a mixture of shame and determination. I gave him a light chuckle. "Your honor is not lost, warrior. There will be much glory to be had. Stay brave."

The aura around the stronghold instantly shifted into trepidation the moment the first soldier spotted us and shouted something I couldn't hear. Though the soldiers had been continuously on guard, there had been a layer of boredom to it. No real threat to stir their fighting spirits.

No threat to put fear into their hearts.

I led us into plain view without pausing or slowing, ignoring the shouts of the soldiers who drew their blades and readied their . . . sticks.

"Halt!" one of the soldiers shouted, a mass of burning blue flames shifting into a length of lava that twisted around him. "You are trespassin—"

The soldier didn't have time to complete his warning. Ethan's fist smashed into his red chest armor, crumpling both steel and the man inside. The silent peace of the night was abhorrently shattered by the primal roar of battle and blood that erupted from Ethan as his body grew beyond his already enormous size, reaching at least fifteen feet tall.

His roar stirred fervor and the will to fight even in my heart, whipping my heart energy into a frenzy. If that's what his roar had done to me, I couldn't imagine what it had done to the others. Luckily, I didn't need to.

The Paragons around me followed Ethan, surging against the soldiers with the destructive force of a tsunami. The freed slaves charged after, a half-step slower with the power of the Desire System aiding them. Just like it had been after the Pandorian died in the dungeon, what proceeded was a massacre. It wasn't quite as one-sided due to the exhaustion of the Paragons and freed slaves, but was nonetheless a complete stomp.

As if sensing the intrusion and losing the tide of their forces, the sentinel gargoyles began to move from their stony prisons, rock exploding off their surfaces as the creatures shrieked into the air. The gargoyles wore faces of both man and beast, with large, round eyes that seemed to suck in all light. They snarled as they broke free, revealing rows of sharp, menacing teeth and elongated tongues that flicked the air as if trying to drink it. A pair of horns curved back from each of their foreheads, giving them a devilish look aided by the bat-like leather wings that spread to their full lengths as the beasts took off into the air overhead.

I didn't pay them any heed, letting the others engage the creatures. I simply walked forward, an untouchable point in the battle. The Silver light from my Core radiated once more as I approached the gate separating me from my most recent torturers.

My heart energy flooded around me into a bubble of power and Authority. As I walked to the gates, the steel structures screamed as the sheer force of my energy commanded the gate to make way. With a single ear-deafening pull, the gate was yanked apart and flung away to hang loosely by the edge of their hinges.

I took a few more steps into the mansion's territory before letting a world of heart energy pour into my throat, enhancing the volume of my voice to a level those inside would have to use heart energy to protect themselves, lest my words rupture their eardrums.

"Good evening, ladies and gentlemen of Cael. Let's start with Radford Coldrun, the Red Cardinal, and Baron Silverwater. If the three of them come out of their own free will within the next fifteen seconds, I will let the rest of you live." After fifteen seconds, no one came out. I shrugged. "All right. Here I come."

The sphere of energy cloaking me blew apart the entrance door like it was made of sand and I stepped into the banquet hall, followed closely by Nasq, Nida, Romeo, Julius, and Marisar.

CHAPTER FORTY-THREE

Banquet: Part 1

Upon entering, my boots tapped audaciously against the floor of polished obsidian. The opulent crystal chandeliers hanging from the ceiling swayed slightly to the tempo of the raging powers outside, their flickering flames mirrored in a horrifically twisted manner in the shining obsidian. It was as if the flames were erupting from the floor in corrupt, black tendrils that curled and flicked with a sort of hungry randomness.

The chandeliers reminded me of my castle back in Aedronir, masterpiece artworks of crystals cut to perfection. The crystals magnified and illuminated the fires within, filling the lavish banquet hall with a dazzling array of light and color.

The walls were draped in heavy, luxurious tapestries woven with an intricate mix of silver and gold, depicting battles unknown to me. Where there were no tapestries, floor-to-ceiling glass windows allowed an incredible amount of moonlight to enter the room. My Core thrummed with pleasure under the rising moon, its power washing over me much as the night's cool air had refreshed my lungs.

At the far end of the hall, a raised dais housed the head table carved out of heavy black wood that, to me, smelled of death. The table was polished and smoothed, glistening under the light of the crystal chandeliers. Plush, velvet chairs with high backs and Silver embroidery snaked along their entirety, forming what looked like an insignia of some sort.

Before the dais, long tables of similarly polished black wood stretched out, laden with hundreds of different foods and drinks, many of which I had never seen before, much less tasted. After spending so much time in the dungeons, the smell was utterly intoxicating. I ignored the confused stares and shouts of outrage from the nobles as I came into their view, heading over to the table of delicacies.

Two guards in red uniforms jumped out from the corners where they'd stood guard, one with a sword and shield, the other with the weirdly curved stick I'd seen outside. I barely paid them any heed as Nida and Nasq surged past me to intercept. The first guard barely had time to gasp before Nida's Silver spear, I wasn't sure where she'd picked it up from, slammed into his chest, and emerged from his back. Nasq's victim died much worse, as a circle of shadows opened up below the soldier's feet and sucked him into whatever the abyss was. I didn't know what Nasq had done, but I suspected it was some type of magic. That seemed accurate considering his class was a High Sorcerer, though I would need to have a discussion with him about what that class meant.

I continued to the pastry table and snatched up a petal-shaped pastry about the size of my thumb. It shimmered with an otherworldly luminescence that reminded me of a full moon's beauty and power. I examined it for a moment, in awe at its translucent shade of pale blue and iridescent edges. It was thin and delicate between my fingers, and when I ate it, it had a velvety texture that all but melted on my tongue. A symphony of flavors released all at once, like an orchestra on my palate.

I memorized the look of the treat and promised myself that I would find out what they were later.

With a sigh of great satisfaction and a final lick of my fingers, I turned to face the tittering crowd of fancy, pompous nobles. The outrage on their faces was only equal to the pure disdain on mine. Considering my understanding of noble society, it was incredibly surprising they had not given up at least the Slave Master. The Cardinal I understood since she was a religious figure, and no one wanted to be the pariah of their religious community. And the Baron . . . Well, that was a little harder to understand since he was just a lowly noble, but perhaps that was more prestigious in this city than it was in my mind.

The Slave Master, however, should have been less important than even a merely wealthy merchant. Why would they risk their lives by not kicking him out of the banquet hall?

Possible answers ran through my mind as I glared at each of the present nobility. Fortunately, they were all here, so I didn't really have to think about it. I could just ask. Part of me was tempted to simply eviscerate the lot of them until the three I sought were all that was left. And I probably would have if I believed violence was the best choice to achieve my desired result.

It wasn't. Not yet. Nobles were individuals of pride and honor, or they pretended to be in any case. A few well-placed insults would do a lot more to uncover where my prey hid than random violence would, especially since the group of aristocrats had already refused to present the three to me.

"Where is the Slave Master, Coldrun?" I asked pointedly, morphing my expression from one of satisfaction at the pastry to one of bored disdain.

"He is not here," a tall man snarled, tugging at the lapel of his fine jacket as if to straighten his already upright posture. His hair, clearly once a fairly rich ebony, now bore streaks of silver that did more to benefit and frame his sharp aristocratic features than distract from them. The most notable thing about the man, however, was his viridian green eyes which said much more about his intellect than his crude tone.

"I did not ask if he was here," I corrected, switching my expression to one of casual annoyance. Despite my words, I continued to scan the crowd for a man that fit my image. I silently cursed myself for not asking Chella or Dralos to scout out more information about the man.

The green-eyed noble blinked a few times, taken aback as he was likely not used to being spoken to without any sense of formality.

"You cannot speak to him that way, disgusting slave," a woman hissed, waving at me as if I were a bug that would fly away if she mimed swatting at it. "He is an earl. Even if you are a slave, show some respect to the man of highest rank here."

"My word," I said with mock indignation, enunciating my words in an elongated fashion like the woman and man had. "Romeo, it appears that the lady is inappropriately intoxicated."

"I am no such thing," the woman hissed, her blond curls that drooped to her shoulders bouncing with each syllable as she punctuated her words with emphasis.

I nodded. "An imbecile, then. One who is unable to hold her tongue in matters greater than her limited intelligence."

The woman's eyes widened in anger, shock, and no small amount of embarrassment. But the man placed a comforting hand on her shoulder, and though she appeared as if she wanted to charge me, her shoulders dropped. If only slightly.

"We do not know where he is," the Earl responded, still holding the woman's shoulder.

"That is quite a lie," I said, not really sure if it was. "Since I can sense him in the vicinity." That was also a lie. I didn't even know what the man's heart energy signature would feel like. With a feigned sigh, I turned back to the pastry table and took another one of the delicious petals. Before I took a bite, I looked at the man almost dismissively. "I will allow you to avoid shaming your house if that is your fear. In fact, I will give you the opportunity to place many others here in your debt." The last was said to the room, my eyes wandering to meet the gaze of a handful of nobles. "I will not move from this spot, as I am quite famished. When one of you decides to share with me the location of Baron Silverwater, the Red Cardinal, or the Slave Master, I will reward you and four others with the freedom to live. You can go away, and I will not stop you."

"No one will step forward," a younger voice of noble intonation spoke from somewhere in the hall. I didn't bother looking.

"Perhaps," I said with a shrug, taking another bite of the petal. "However, for every thirty seconds that no one comes forward, I will kill someone at random." A second of silence before shouts of obscenity erupted and I laughed. Despite the rampaging of battle outside their little sanctuary, it was obvious they had never believed their own lives to be at stake. Such was the benefit of nobility, even in Ordite. The value of ransoming nobles generally outweighed the usefulness of their deaths.

"Enough," the Earl said, stepping forward ahead of the crowd. "I have entertained your threats long enough, young woman. Do you truly think we do not fear the combat outside the banquet halls because we are naive?" When I didn't answer he continued, his upright posture suddenly seeming less afraid and more military. "Those of us in these walls are not defenseless. Guards, for most of us, are simply formalities."

"Fifteen seconds left," I said, finishing off a third petal. Nasq and Nida moved ahead to stand between me and the approaching Earl. Unlike me, both of my Paragons stood over six feet, matching the Earl in both height and intensity.

That unfamiliar stirring of magic began to swirl in many of the nobles at my threat, and a few began to circulate some coreless heart energy. Even with whatever strength they would gain from magic mixed in, I remained appalled at the level of strength of the nobles.

"Five seconds."

A handful of personal guards wearing the standard red uniform tore into the room, likely running from wherever their standby station had been after being alerted to our presence. I doubted they were here specifically because of me—rather, I was fairly certain what the nobles here feared the most was the roars of the Berserker outside, not the ominous words of a girl who appeared no older than her mid-teens.

That would soon change.

"Zero." As the number left my lips, a bright white spear of condensed lunar attribute heart energy condensed around my fingers and surged at the woman who the Earl had calmed. Her face paled as she shielded herself with magic. The Earl shouted something, reaching over to cover her with his magic and coreless heart energy.

Their defensive measures did nothing against the raw power of heart energy refined in a Silver-level Core. My lunar energy tore through their shields like they were nothing, puncturing the woman through her throat and tearing out the back. In her death, the woman made not a sound, nor shriek.

She fell to the ground, eyes wide and full of fear.

I picked up another petal, this one with a bit of yellow coloring in it. "Thirty seconds."

The Earl shouted, his face contorting with a look of utter disbelief and pure hatred. "Dia!" He crouched to her side, tears streaming down his face as he turned his glare to me. "Do you have any idea who you just killed?"

"You see," I said with another sigh, flicking some crumbs off my torn shirt. "This is why those of the aristocracy are deemed by so many to be useless." I motioned toward myself and the five others who had joined me. "There are six of us, and none of you even bothered to fight us. Why? Fear?" With a nod, I indicated toward Romeo. "Two of us are children. What is there to fear against children? Or is it not fear?" Within a few steps, I was within arm's reach of the Earl and I bent down to look at the dead woman. "Perhaps it is the excitement you are filled with. Eagerness for bloodshed? If not, why wait?" The Earl attempted to move, likely to reach for the scabbard sheathing his sword, but I shifted my heart energy into Authority and bore it down on him like a mountain. "No? Well, then it must be arrogance." I stood, ignoring the coreless Earl and his pathetic magic, turning toward the rest of the nobles and releasing the full force of my Authority on all of them. Even the uniformed guards halted, their muscles unmoving. So weak.

"Ten seconds."

I kicked the Earl over, his muscles locked into place by the fear of my Authority. He fell to his side with a thud, his defenseless head bouncing off the floor with a thud.

"Two."

I lifted my foot and gently placed it over his head.

"One."

"Zero."

The Earl's head splattered under my foot with less resistance than a tomato but with all the red and fluid. When I lowered my foot, it squished against the gore and continued to make squeaking sounds as I made my way back to the pastry table.

"What is it about the three of them that holds your loyalties so tight?" I wondered out loud, wiggling my fingers over the tray of petals as I debated which flavor to try. No one else stepped forward, either stunned that a young girl had killed a powerful earl or feared having my attention directed toward them. After deciding on the orange one, I redirected my gaze to an overweight man in ridiculously lavish gold and silver-imbued clothing. "How about you? Where does your loyalty come from?"

Under the sheer pressure of my heart energy, the man's knees trembled weakly but he managed to mutter an indecipherable answer. I just stared at him until he repeated in a louder voice, "I—I—I am not loyal to a Slave Master, but I would shame my house as a traitor."

Instead of pressing him, I simply shifted my gaze to the small boy who'd collapsed to the ground at his side and said, "Five seconds."

With a shout the man fell over the young boy, covering him with his body and I couldn't help the frown that was starting to etch itself into me. What in the world did the Slave Master have over them?

I, again, raised a finger in the man's direction, allowing a minuscule amount of lunar energy to condense into a small sphere at the tip of it.

"Zero."

"Stop!" A woman screamed from the top of a spiral staircase leading to a second floor. The voice was ethereal, equally smooth as it was desperate. I allowed my hand to drop, releasing the condensed energy, and waved my hand for her to approach. That was a voice I would recognize anywhere.

"Ah. Welcome to the party, Madam Red Cardinal," I said, flourishing a slight bow in her direction and lifting my Authority from the room. "I see even in Sealrite the guests prefer to arrive fashionably late."

"You must cease your senseless killing," the woman seemed to plead, but I sensed the invasion of some sort of magic. My Core all but snickered at the attempt, batting it away with ease.

"Senseless? Oh, I don't believe it to be senseless. I just want some answers. Am I not entitled to some?" I moved away from the man and the boy toward the descending woman. "But I cannot say the saintess trials you put me through were very well thought out. A seer? Truly? As if that would ever end well."

At that, the woman paused, her eyes narrowing at me before her eyebrows shot up in surprise. "Lady . . . Lilliana?"

"Do I look that different?"

"How?" the Cardinal began her eyes expanding with confusion, no doubt trying to match my current appearance with how I'd looked prior to the Reformation. Her mouth gaped and I was confident a stream of unrequited questions would follow so I quieted her with a wave before she could so much as open her mouth to ask whatever annoying question she was contemplating.

"That is not for you to be concerned about Cardinal. You are only one of my three desired participants. Two are still missing. Fetch them."

She said nothing, her eyes cast down but then she lifted them, or, well, still down since she was at least six inches taller than me, but her chin still raised. "If I tell you, do you swear that you will bring no harm to befall the rest of those in this hall?"

"Yes. I swear that if I am presented with both the Silverwater Baron and the Slave Master Coldrun, I will not harm these nobles," I said.

The Cardinal nodded. "Bring them."

Naivety and hopefulness truly had a very thick, very invisible line.

CHAPTER FORTY-FOUR

Banquet: Part 2

After a few minutes, a large, heavyset man with a black swirling mustache was pushed down the flight of stairs, his irate voice barking threats at the two women dragging him. Both were clothed heavily in black uniforms, covering everything but their eyes. Less surprised than with the Pandorian, I was nonetheless still shocked when my Core thrummed with recognition at the Bronze realm Cores in each of the two Pandorians' hearts. Behind the Baron was a much slimmer man with a full head of silver hair and a very gaunt face. His cheekbones were so high I wondered if they weren't part of his forehead.

Both men were unharmed, but their wrists were locked with the same gold chains that had been around Orpheus.

"Ah," I said, "Baron Silverwater. I'm so happy we can meet once again."

The man blanched as he looked at me, no doubt taking in the ragged clothing, matted hair covered in blood, and the general aura of death that no doubt radiated off me like a stench this night. Then, as if something struck him, his face contorted into a look of outraged recognition.

"Lilliana? Is that you? What in the Gods' names happened to you? Why do you look so much older?" He looked around. "Get me out of these blasted cuffs. How are you even here? I thought you were enslaved. What is going on?"

"Why is he chained?" I asked the Cardinal who shrugged, both of us opting to ignore the Baron's incessant whining.

One of the Pandorian women responded. "He attempted to flee."

Fair enough, I supposed. The Baron was their main chance of survival. Made sense to try and keep him from running. Either way, this was fairly convenient for me. The irony of the Baron in chains while I stood over him would not be lost on me.

I turned to look at the five who had followed me. "I'm fairly surprised he managed to recognize me."

"He *is* your father, after all," Nasq suggested.

"Baron," I responded, ignoring his question since Nasq had all but answered it and went to stand a foot in front of him. "Tell me—who was it that sent me to my death in the Misty Veils?" He shook his head as if to say he didn't know, but I lashed out, striking the man with the back of my hand. "Do not tell me you do not know. Even I am aware that it was partly Morgana's handiwork. What I do not know is who aided her. I assume it was not you?" I asked, quirking an eyebrow.

"How the hells should I know?" The Baron's eyes were darting around the room now, widening at the dead bodies and the guards still frozen in place. I could tell he was shocked at the slap but didn't seem all that surprised. "What the hells is going on? We heard some conflict in the yard and then this bitch locked me in some room." He glared hatefully at the Cardinal. "Which you will still pay for. My family are direct blood relatives of the Lysorian King. Even if you are a Cardinal of the Church, do you really believe simply staying in Cael lands will protect you from our wrath?"

I sighed, losing patience. With a movement so fast no one else in the room would have been able to see it, I cloaked my hand in lunar energies and lopped off the Baron's right ear. He howled in pain, writhing against the golden chains that bound him, unable to escape from the grasp.

My knees bent silently as I squatted down above the bleeding Baron and picked up his fallen ear. Then I tossed it at his face where it hit with a sick plop.

"I will only say this once, so I hope you listen to me carefully. I do not consider myself to be a warmonger or particularly sadistic. War is a tool. Sometimes it is necessary. Just like torture. Or death." The words hung in the air for a moment until I chose to continue. "Tell me, Baron. Is torture a necessary tool for the answers I seek today?" I released my heart energy once again using the Authority skill to let the Baron know I was not the girl he remembered or knew.

Lilliana's father, the one who she so feared, glared up at me with contempt as trails of blood trickled across his face in varying directions. My expression remained calm and neutral, though the part of me closest to Lilliana raged with the desire to kill him. I kept it back, soothing it for the moment.

Then he shook his head and opened his mouth, the words coming out so fast it was as if they chased each other. "It was Morgana's idea, but the Goldenhearts orchestrated it. They'd been eyeing the Misty Veil Sire for years, but hadn't found anyone with royal blood they could use to lure it out."

I raised an eyebrow at that. "I have royal blood?"

The Baron grimaced. "Sort of. *My* family is distantly related to the royal family. The Goldenhearts more so." When he didn't look at me, that clued me into his words. He had specifically said "his" family. Not "our."

"What about me?"

He swallowed. "You . . . are also related."

"More than you?"

He swallowed again but nodded tersely.

"More than the Goldenhearts?" This time he didn't answer right away, his eyes darting around like a cornered rat.

Then he nodded and I shot him a wide smile. So *that* was why Lilliana was treated so poorly despite the potential I saw in her during the Mindscape event. Lilliana had some sort of direct relation to the Lysorian royal family.

"Explain."

"I—I . . . I don't know. I swear I don't," he blurted, finally seeming to break. "I didn't know she was a royal! I thought she was a maid. They told me she was a maid! Then they took her away and I never saw her again."

"They who?"

"I don't know, I don't know. They never said. I swear to the Gods, they never said, and I never asked. But they had the mark of the royal family," he blubbered, and I figured it was time to change subjects to my more pressing issue.

"By her, you mean my mother?" I asked, to which the Baron nodded in desperate jerks. "I thought, hmm. Did my mother not pass away in illness?"

The Baron snorted and seemed to want to say something more, but he remained silent despite the twitching of his left eye signaling he was in pain. When I reached out with my senses to examine the cruel man, I hit a powerful wall of energy curled around the Baron so deeply I doubted even a mind mage from Aedronir could have untangled the mess.

"Good. Good. Very good," I said, imitating the way the Baron had dismissed me the first time I'd met him. I'd sort of figured that Lilliana had some small amount of royal blood in her veins, but I hadn't expected it to be through her mother. The level of energy corrupting the baron confirmed the presence of someone powerful, likely originating from the Lysoria royal family. Interesting. Switching issues, I asked, "I see. So the Goldenhearts wanted to capture a sire?"

He nodded, his Adam's apple bopping slightly as he swallowed and he seemed to regain some of his earlier composure, his face turning slightly red. "And they did. The Demon Sire. With a potion from them." He sent an equally hateful look at the Cardinal who didn't react.

I barked a curt laugh, shaking my head. "You think you've captured a sire? With a little potion and the measly forces of a barony and a dukedom? I certainly do hope to one day return to your barony and see what has become of it in your absence."

Chances were the Demon Progenitor had burned most of it to the ground by now.

While the Baron considered my words with a growing look of apprehension and regret, I refocused my attention on Coldrun who was shivering with fear and smelled like piss. At first, I'd wanted to have the man turn over the rights to the slavery Arena to me. That had seemed like a solid plan, and in a way, it still was. Though I no longer needed any papers to do so.

Instead, I buried my fingers into his eyes with the full force of my Core, curled them to hook around his eye socket, and yanked his head off his shoulders with a sickening, disgusting snap as his skull dislodged from his spine.

I still fucking hated the guy. Not because he was a Slave Master. But because he'd pissed me the fuck off.

The Baron gawked while most of the room, including the Cardinal, turned away in horror or disgust. None moved to stop me. Whether from an understanding that I was much more powerful than they were, or because I had promised not to kill them, I didn't know, and it truly did not matter.

Finally, I faced the Cardinal. I could taste iron trickling into my mouth from the gore of Coldrun's face.

[System announcement: Congratulations! You have killed a Main System Administrator.]
[System notification: The Desire System has absorbed the remnants of the Main System left within the Administrator and purged the body of any traces.]

That was interesting, but I'd consider it later.

"You never really believed I was a possible saintess, did you?"

"No," the Cardinal said flatly, clearly unsurprised by my question.

"Then why bother?"

She shrugged. "Just because I did not believe it did not make it not so. The will of the Goddess is not for me to question or attempt to foresee."

I debated for a moment how to go about my plan. When I finally decided, I slapped my hands together. "It truly was an unfortunate series of events, wasn't it Romeo?"

The ebony boy cast me a confused expression, his face looking somewhat green and I noticed he'd distanced himself from the head I'd stomped.

"The daughter of a Lysorian Baron was betrayed by corrupt Lysorian nobles. Knowing that Cael slavers were at an all-time high in the borders, they conspired with the Slave Master Coldrun to capture her. After finding out about his missing daughter's whereabouts, the Baron of Silverwater rushed to her rescue! But when he got there, he discovered that even the Cael King was in on the plan. Oh, how the King laughed in Baron Silverwater's face. Baron Silverwater, however, couldn't let his daughter rot as a slave. After all," I said giving the Baron a rueful smile, "she has royal blood in her veins. So, he helped her escape, only to be stabbed in the back by a Cardinal, a member of a neutral religious organization. His daughter, the young Lady Silverwater, fought hard to save her father. Unfortunately, he died in the process of protecting her from the Cardinal's two Pandorian warriors. In fact, everyone died in the crossfire. The Cardinal of a church couldn't risk any bystanders or witnesses to her traitorous deeds with a Slave Master. When the Cardinal revealed herself to be a user of undead energies, she knew even more so that her great secret couldn't be revealed. When Lilliana finally arrived at the scene of her father's last stand, there was no one left. Then, just as all seemed lost, a powerful Lysorian force broke through the gates of Sealrite, rescued the citizens from rampaging monsters in the city, and saved the recently freed Lilliana from death at the hands of a Colosseum beast released by the Slave Master in a desperate attempt to flee."

Nasq clapped playfully and Nida laughed. Both Marisar and Romeo had paled noticeably, clearly catching on to what I was indicating.

"You're inciting war," the Cardinal said, her red eyes aghast. I could see her mind processing everything I'd said at a rapid pace. She didn't need to know all that; it wouldn't do her any good in the moments to come. But I wanted her to know. I wanted them all to know of my vengeance. I wouldn't just kill them; I would sully their names. Their houses. Their family and honor.

"No," I said, turning toward her and allowing my darkest attribute of heart energy to turn the air in the room to a heavy muck. I let it crawl over me, drenching my Core of mostly lunar energy black with necromancy. "You already incited it. I was simply a witness to the Church's betrayal."

"You promised you would not harm them!" she screamed, her ethereal voice cracking.

"And I won't." I smiled, raising my hands. "I won't even touch them."

Suddenly a scream resounded from a few of the nobles in the back and magic followed, tearing at something moving and cracking.

The nobles' magics and coreless heart energy were too weak to completely obliterate the undead corpses, so even when one managed to knock an arm off the Earl, the arm simply crawled back to the body at a frightening speed.

"Holy Goddess," the Cardinal whispered, grabbing a golden circle hanging from her neck by a string; the same symbol I'd seen embedded into the chairs. "That is not resurrection."

"No," I said, grinning wide as a noblewoman died with a scream on her lips and my dark necrotic energy infested her from the Earl as the walking corpse sunk its teeth into the noblewoman's neck. "No, it's not. But thank you for your help."

The two Pandorian warriors clad in black armor dashed toward me, opening their Cores and shifting their heart energy into spheres of Authority to repulse my own.

An hour ago, perhaps they would have defeated me in tandem. When I was a Bronze Core. My Silver-realm Core exploded with light from within me, showering the area around me with a brilliance that those nearest to me couldn't help but turn away from. I enveloped the approaching Pandorians with my Authority, completely crushing their pathetic defenses against it.

I didn't just crush their bodies under the pressure of my heart energy.

I dominated their minds and their Will. Even the Cardinal was forced to her knees as her Pandorian guards cracked and broke against the obsidian floor that was more red than black now.

The Baron still spluttered at my feet. I looked down at him, disgusted by the blithering fool of a man. I leaned over him, the unmatted portion of my hair spilling over the side of my face to cast a shadow across it as I whispered to him low enough that only he would hear. "Lilliana sends her regards. Good bye, Cedric."

His face was shock, confusion, outrage, anger, panic, desperation, and other emotions I didn't bother to recognize as I picked up a sword one of the Pandorian women had dropped and drove it slowly, painfully through the Baron's heart. "Maybe in your next life, you will choose your victims more wisely. Lilliana was not a girl deserving of your disdain. Without you, she could have grown to be great."

The Baron squirmed and twitched, the golden chains still binding his abilities with a dull, golden flare. When eventually the flare stopped, so did his twitching. I knew he was dead.

With a bit of necromantic-attuned energy, however, he began to twitch again, and his eyes shot open. Lifeless and unseeing as a moan of the undead escaped him in a wail.

"You . . . are a necromancer . . ." the Cardinal wheezed, her eyes filled with disgust and shock. "But then . . . how . . . resurrection . . . ?" A great amount of energy surged from her stomach where I believed mages to harness their magic, but I waived a finger of energy and cut her flow off as easily as one might take candy from a child. She opened her mouth, shocked, but seemed to understand her death was coming. Based on the feel of her power, I'd known from the beginning she was more of a utility user, not one of strength or power, so I hadn't been worried. Especially once she'd attempted and utterly failed in her manipulation. The gall of her to attempt the manipulation of a Core user while she was coreless, regardless of whatever level her magic was.

More and more I was beginning to view this "magic" as being rather useless and particularly weak.

Adopting Gronch's way of speaking, I said, "None of your fucking business, lady," and then kicked her in the face. My foot crunched into her skull, and I felt her head shatter from the impact. "Nasq, Nida, get the Cores from the Pandorians." Turning to the rest I said, "Let's go. He should be here soon, and we need to get out into the city before he arrives at the gates."

Even as I said that, new heart energy continued to flow into me from my undead creatures who, whenever they consumed heart energy, directed it toward me.

Romeo looked up, having bent over to vomit at the sight of undead corpses mauling at the living. "Who?"

"Duke Alistar, of course."

The mention of Alistar's name cast a palpable excitement over the others. Nasq and Nida moved swiftly to extract the Cores from the fallen Pandorians, their expressions reflecting a mix of urgency and grim satisfaction. The air crackled with tension as the rest of my group rallied, preparing to leave the scene of the massacring undead atrocities.

As we made our way toward the exit, the sounds of battle and chaos outside grew louder. The city would be in chaos already from the released monsters, and our actions tonight would only stoke the flames higher. I could vaguely sense the Duke's presence drawing nearer to the city, his formidable power a bright beacon in the night. Somehow, I wasn't too surprised to tell the Duke had a Core. According to Chella, despite how Duke Alistar's proclivity to focus solely on protecting the border had caused his political influence to be the weakest among the dukes, in terms of power, he was, by far, the most powerful. He just preferred not to broadcast it.

Still, I couldn't help but wonder where he'd learned about the Core. Or, perhaps more likely, if I'd been wrong to judge the power of an entire world based on small examples. But even the Cael King did not have a Core, so how was it possible that a duke did? Was Cael just weak?

Questions I would ask the Duke later if my plan worked.

We emerged into the courtyard and were greeted by the great roar of Ethan who had, somehow, grown even larger. I roared back at him, letting loose from my throat a sense of rage and pride at my Paragons. I was still full of necromantic-attuned energy when I released my roar, and the sound did more than spread rage and pride, it echoed to the city with a rumble reminiscent of the Mist Veil Beast King.

I grinned at Ethan. "I'm going to have to teach you some energy tricks to bring you back to a normal size," I joked and slapped his thigh, which was about level with my shoulders. "Otherwise you'll never sleep in a bed again."

**[System announcement: Congratulations! You have killed a Main
System Administrator.]**
**[System notification: The Desire System has absorbed the rem-
nants of the Main System left within the Administrator and
purged the body of any traces.]**

Another administrator had died? I glanced back at the banquet hall, now
burning down with a black and orange fire that worked tirelessly to consume the screaming and shrieking creatures within. I rubbed my hands
together again and cleared my throat. All the surviving Paragons and freed
slaves looked at me, waiting.

"From here on out, we're splitting up," I instructed. "Paragons, you can
go start your own paths. Those of you who did not choose the path of
Paragon must also go forge your own lives now. But heed my words now. A
new force will soon be entering the city's borders. Do not attempt to stop
them. You will not be able to, and I do not want you to. Let them come, for
they will bring all of us a truer freedom than simply the deaths of Cael
nobility."

One of the freed slaves stepped forward, kneeling at my feet. "Though I
do not wish to become a Paragon, Queen Lilliana, I still wish to serve you."
I could hear his heartbeat pounding in his chest with desperation, so I
remained silent. "I wish to serve but . . . I cannot . . . I cannot be tied to
such a System again."

I laid a hand on his shoulder and nodded. "For those of you who wish
to continue serving, you may follow me into the city proper. We will be
protecting civilians from the monsters we released until Duke Alistar's
forces arrive."

CHAPTER FORTY-FIVE

The Duke's Forces

Dralos had done his job well. The city was a chaotic mess of fire and screams where violence reigned supreme.

Though we had only just crossed the Colosseum area into the city proper, I could already hear and smell the beckoning of death. Monstrous shrieks rang out from all directions, spread throughout Sealrite. Even the protective walls embedded in the city stone gates flickered weakly, their enchantments strained to the breaking point. It was a scene of utter devastation, at least in the sections closest to the Colosseum.

Buildings with thatched roofs were collapsing in showers of sparks as enormous monsters of all shapes rampaged through them, chasing the screaming residents from their homes and to death. The streets I imagined were once filled with the sounds of everyday life were now choked with smoke and the acrid stench of burning wood and flesh. Despite my distance, I spotted a large bell tower looming over the broken city. Where the clock had been hung was an enormous brown creature with eight legs and a large bulbous body. Two pincers clicked at the side of its head, centered by hundreds of tiny little eyes that darted in every direction.

The bell itself was twisted from the heat, drooping at an ugly angle that was a beacon of the city's peril.

I stopped, gazing at the city now engulfed in a hellish inferno. Dralos had done his job a little *too* well. I had wanted chaos, but if the city was destroyed, there wouldn't be much financial gain from having a business there. How could I run a Colosseum in a city filled with nothing but ash, blood, and corpses?

"Is this what you had in mind?" Romeo asked in a whisper. Although his skin had returned to its normal shade, I could see a renewed sense of horror in his expression.

I didn't answer as we tread the path into a residential district. A grand fountain sat in our path at the plaza's center. But where I would have expected crystal-colored water to spray from it now only ran red with blood from the corpses that lay haphazardly strewn about.

Everywhere we went, the flickering light of the fires cast a ghastly glare on the destruction, turning the denizens' previously peaceful night into a scene cast right from a nightmare. All around, shadows danced malevolently along the walls as if chasing us, distorting our shadows into an illusion of moving ghosts of the city's dead banished to darkness and silence as their homes and families burned to nothing or were devoured by the creatures they'd cheered for during Colosseum fights.

Despite the overwhelming destruction under the bright moon, there was clear resistance. Soldiers and civilian defenders alike streaked past us shouting warnings and directions to safe havens. Their faces were all the same, smeared with soot and blood, yet the look in their eyes was one I recognized to be a resolute determination to save and protect.

Heart energy and magics radiated and crackled all around us as city soldiers fought against the innumerable monsters Dralos had released, unwilling to yield to their despair.

At first, I simply continued to walk in silence, taking in the excessive carnage and heading toward the western gate where I could sense the enormous power of Duke Alistar and his men approaching the city.

"Okay," I said finally, turning toward those who had remained with me. About half had left, leaving me with a little over fifty, only fifteen of which were Paragons. The others, eager to begin their paths of vengeance, had left with my blessings. "We will fight off creatures and head toward the West Gate over there." I pointed ahead of us down a winding stone path and residential homes. "Do your best not to interact with any of the guards—no reason to inform them of our . . . situation. Once we meet up with the Duke, it should be a straight shot from there."

"How will he get in?" Gronch asked, his face red and covered with beads of sweat while his fingers gripped the hilt of his twin axes with a desperate focus. "Something must have been keeping him from attacking this city."

I nodded. "I had the same thought at first, but according to Chella, it was simply a political restraint. Cael and Lysoria have avoided a full-scale war for decades, though I'm not entirely sure why. I can imagine it being some political maneuvering." Gronch coughed as my thoughts trailed off into possible reasons. I nodded in acknowledgment and resumed. I needed to sleep soon. My focus was slipping. "In any case, the Duke's hands were tied. There was nothing to justify Lysoria declaring war on Cael. At least, no reason with enough pull of morality and justice to force the Lysorian King's hand."

Gronch shot me a quick grin, wiping away some sweat with his forearm. "And now there is."

I nodded. "Now there is. And the city guards are all busy fending off the monster infestation. Whatever guards are still posted on the city walls won't last long, if at all."

"Is that why he had Chella in the Colosseum?" Julius thought out loud abruptly, his face similarly wet with sweat under the heat of the flames around us. "To come up with a reason."

"That is what I suspect," I responded. "I imagine Chella agreed to place me in the Colosseum to give the Duke a reason to invade."

"To save you?" Romeo followed up with a confused expression. "But he didn't even try."

"No," Julius replied even as I opened my mouth to answer. "No. He was waiting for Lady Lilliana to die."

I nodded again. "My thoughts exactly."

Before Romeo could put words to the puzzled expression twisting his normally handsome features into one of confusion, a handful of nightmarish cries reverberated around us. The flames of a nearby residence warred like the waves of an ocean for only a moment.

Then they split, parting with the force of a massive beast who strode our way with a vicious hunger clear in its eyes, twin beads that glowed with an eerie light and pierced the smog with a sickly yellow gleam.

It lumbered slowly into view, its sheer size and presence a terrifying spectacle. Standing nearly twenty feet tall at the shoulder, the beast was a horrific blend of primal ferocity and supernatural menace. Its fur, dark as the sky above us, was matted by blood and singed slightly by the flames around us, and clung tightly to the creature's hulking frame with muscles that even Ethan would envy.

"Holy Gods," Romeo muttered, taking a step back. "Is that a fucking body in its mouth?"

Rather than a single body, multiple torsos and appendages remained skewered on the beast's great fangs; two colossal canines that jutted from its lower jaw, each one as long as a sword and looked to be just as fatal. Probably more so. Saliva dripped predatorily from the maw as it snarled, showing off its lined rows of serrated teeth, easily capable of snapping even bones empowered by heart energy and magic.

Compared to the bear-like monster rampaging toward us, the beasts we'd fought in the Arena had been appetizers. When it leaned forward to swoop a massive paw the size of a human at our group and four more of its kind followed from the parted flames, I shouted, "Spread out!"

Paragons and freed slaves dashed away from where the monster had gouged deep furrows into the cobblestone, forming a half-circle crescent with me and the bear beast in the center. The edges of my lips arced into a frown as the handful of bear monsters turned their muzzles toward the sky and released a deafening roar that echoed through the burning city, sending a visible shiver down the spine of many freed slaves and even some Paragons. The monstrous bellow was not simply a battle cry. I felt in my bones that this was a creature of territory. That it was declaring to all under its roar that this was its dominion.

The challenge stoked my rage, and I relished it for a moment, then I pushed it down. It wasn't the time to enjoy the frenzy of a chaotic battlefield. When the Duke arrived, he needed to be impressed beyond belief if he was ever going to take a twelve-year-old girl seriously. Even if I now looked more sixteen than twelve, it wouldn't matter much if he simply disregarded me as the pawn noble girl for his plan.

On Nasq's command, a small section of the Paragons launched projectile heart energy and magic toward the bear beasts, scorching and even melting the arm of one of them with some type of acid attribute I had never seen before. I momentarily wondered when Nasq had managed to claim a hierarchical position among the Paragons, but I was quickly shaken from those wonderings when the lead bear monster slashed at me with his giant paws.

I released a burst of Silver-Core heart energy in a ray of power, my energy reserves immediately refilling as my Core was bathed in pure moonlight and began to purify energy at an astonishing rate. Under the moonlight, I was renewed and empowered, all the lunar energy in my body thrummed with delight and cackled with increased vitality. My blast of lunar energy tore through the lead bear beast with ease, spraying sinew and gore out the back of the beast, but leaving nothing except burnt flesh in the front.

The one with the melted arm roared in protest but Nida's spear surged forward like the bolt of lightning it was, sparkling with an iridescent green flash. It buried itself into the beast's shoulder right before Nida herself followed the weapon, bulldozing her mass into the bear-like thunder to her spear's lightning. Her body morphed without warning into a long, lithe-looking creature with the same black and white stripes that her hair usually adorned. Her canines sank into the beast's flesh and it roared in pain, its neighboring beast reaching over to swat her from its neck.

Before it could, Ethan was upon both of them. He could not physically tower over the beasts, being around the same height, but his sheer aura overwhelmed them as he grabbed their skulls and slammed them together with a roar of his own.

The four creatures scampered away as Ethan bellowed, Nasq's long-range users following the retreating beasts with a rainbow of energy and magic that even I had trouble distinguishing. I waved Nasq and the rest off from further pursuing the creatures. Our focus needed to be on the western gate where Duke Alistar approached so I could head him off before any narrative other than mine reached him. The last thing I wanted was for someone to paint the freed slaves as aggressors toward civilians. I knew how righteous nobles such as he prided themselves on concepts like justice and protecting the weak.

Instantly I started to bark orders, rearranging my force to spread out further into the city proper and begin breaking a path toward the western gates. We would break up into five groups, each led by me, Ethan, Nasq, Nida, or Gronch. My team would clear a direct line to the western gate while the rest cleaned up the nearby areas. I knew that Romeo and Julius would want to help the civilians, so I had them join Gronch's group, which would head into the residential area. I made sure that there were more Paragons in Gronch's group than the others since I at least knew Nida, Ethan, and Nasq could hold their own against more powerful enemies.

We split, and my group of mostly freed slaves with a few Paragons charged toward the western gate. Considering I was the strongest, I figured the other teams would need the extra strength more than I would.

As we ran toward the gate, we cut down a variety of different beasts, ranging from four-legged horses with bird beaks to smaller versions of the arachnid I'd spotted on the bell tower. The path to the western gate was fairly straightforward and we followed the cobblestone path toward it. There were often turns or switchbacks that cost us more time, but no one complained. In fact, the red glint in the eyes of my Paragons, whenever we defeated another monster, suggested they were rather enjoying the extra points.

No. What had Gronch called them? Experience points?

Occasionally, I'd make a point to stray off the path to rescue or save someone in an attempt to spread word of my "heroics." The first few times I tried flashing them a smile, but Marisar ended up warning me against it. There was too much gore and blood on me to make a smile anything less than horrific. One woman even screamed, the exact reaction opposite of what I desired. So I stopped smiling and simply saved them, then moved on.

By the time the gate came into view, looming large ahead of us, we'd lost quite a few of the freed slaves and the rest of us were completely drenched in gore. Some of it red, some of it other colors, but all of it smelled like shit.

There was a sudden resounding *bang* as two things dropped behind us and I spun around to face it, leaping forward to place myself between the newcomers and my group. One was heavy and dense, a massive bell. The other was surprisingly light given its bulbous mass.

The arachnid.

The bell was the giant metallic ball that had been hanging from the tower after something had melted it. Webs cascaded around the bell in a blanket-like wave, edges frayed as if it had been yanked apart by something fierce.

From the distance, I heard the roaring of at least two of the bear creatures from earlier. They were getting closer. Had the beasts been tracking us?

I audibly groaned. Why could nothing ever be easy?

I reached out my senses to get an idea of where the Duke's forces were, but before my senses expanded enough and before I could engage the arachnid creature, a massive tidal wave of heart energy enveloped the entire city. I felt my jaw nearly drop open at the familiar power of a high-tier Gold Core, all three heart rings around the Golden Core already formed. I could see the power radiating from the Core flickering between gold and platinum, as if the Duke should have already progressed and wasn't able to.

"I . . . I can't move," one of the freed slaves behind me whimpered, his words echoed by others similarly frozen in place.

"It's all right," I answered, letting the Silver glow from my Core aura fade. I wasn't sure what exactly Duke Alistar's capabilities were, or whether he could differentiate between my foundation and his own.

It hardly made any sense for anyone in this world to be that strong. I'd met the Cael royal family. None of them even had a Core, yet this man had a high-tier Gold Core? It couldn't have been an issue with Cael since the Silverwater Baron had also been coreless, strong only compared to powerless mortals. And it couldn't have been a religious issue either, considering the Red Cardinal had also been coreless. Since all three Pandorians had Cores, perhaps it was due to ties with the Pandorian Empire? I was missing something.

"Citizens of Sealrite," came a throaty, booming voice from somewhere above us. "By the decree of King Aizen, Ruler of the Lysorian Kingdom and Master of the Four Seas, war is hereby declared against the Kingdom of Cael. Put down your weapons and allow the Knights of the Alistar Dukedom to free you of your nation's negligence."

Without warning, nearly five hundred knights in shining gold and silver armor began to pour from the sky like an Iron Rain. It wasn't until then that I noticed other creatures were flying above us, winged creatures. I couldn't tell their length or power at my distance, but there were many of them.

Thud. Thud. Thud. Thud.

Knight after knight landed in the city. They slammed into the ground causing hundreds of craters to birth in their wake, instantly engaging and slaying the freed monsters with great training and even greater ease. Each knight I spotted radiated an aura of heart energy that bordered on forming a Bronze Core. It was both awe-inspiring and boggling.

I resolved to research more about this world. I shouldn't rashly jump to conclusions, especially regarding power structures. I had very clearly missed something about the way the nations here dealt with power. The way of creating a Core was not lost or unknown; it seemed to simply be held in great confidence.

Or kept secret.

"Ah," said the same booming voice, no longer with the voice amplification but still somewhere above me. "There you are, Lady Lilliana."

A bolt of yellow-blue lightning raged downward from one of the winged creatures above, colliding into the arachnid. A bloom of dirt rose from the ground at the decimation, and I couldn't help the surprised intake of air I did when I could no longer sense the arachnid's existence.

Yes, the Duke was, indeed, a threat. I had expected him to be strong, sure. A high-tier Gold-level Core? That, I had not expected.

"Duke Alistar," I answered, giving a slight bow toward the now dispersing cloud of dirt and smoke. Even as we spoke more knights surged around us, cutting down monsters that had begun to push back the freed slaves. "It's a pleasure to meet you."

"Where is Chella?" the Duke grumbled his lack of formality fairly surprising and quite irritating, his rumbling voice a perfect partner to the whirlwind of power around him that caused the smog around him to dissipate in a rush.

His very presence was rather commanding of respect. Though he radiated a calming aura, there was also something close to dogmatism in his eyes that reminded me of a bloodhound. His age, however, was etched as deep lines in his weathered face adorned with a myriad of scars that traced across his face from his collar bone to the top of his left ear. His hair had thin strips of ebony still but was mostly a silvered mane. It reached down to his shoulders in a loose mess, pushed back by his broad forehead. Underneath were ferocious golden-brown eyes that promised both kindness and justice.

"She is freeing other slaves from the Colosseum," I responded. She was also fetching me the prism to create more slave tattoos. Leaving that out was likely for the best. "There were many more enslaved in the dungeons." Dralos was also down there, fetching the Progenitor's Core before returning to my side.

Duke Alistar nodded and swore, his eyes narrowing. "Cursed Caels and their slavery. Barbaric." He looked down at my much smaller form as he finally reached where I waited for him, standing to my maximum height. Our postures were oddly similar, a testament to both our lifetimes of disciplined military experience and training. Just like his knights and soldiers, the Duke bore a thick silver-golden armor with the symbol of a great golden-maned beast painted brightly on the front of his chest plate. "Is it true that your father, the Baron, has passed away?" he asked, those golden eyes of his glancing down at me with a weight and authority I hadn't yet experienced in Graedon.

"Yes, Your Grace," I said, forcing my eyes to tear, a small quiver in my voice. "While attempting to protect me, he was slain by the Red Cardinal's High Pandorian guards."

The Duke's eyes widened in what I guessed to be either shock or disbelief, but he quickly hid the emotions and went stoic again. Though when he spoke again, his voice was greatly softened. "I see. At the very least, your father died an honorable death in the protection of his daughter. Do not be dispirited at his sacrifice, daughter of the Silverwater."

I did my best to look pained. By the look on Marisar's face, I wasn't doing a very good job of it. Still, the Duke seemed to accept my words.

"An honorable death," I repeated, lowering my head in feigned sadness.

The Duke gave me a pat on the shoulder. "We must make haste, young Lady Silverwater. You were lucky in your escape, as was your father. Had the Sealrite city lord not been called away, an undertaking as we have done here today would not have been with such ease. We must fortify the city walls and send word to King Aizen that we were successful." The large man turned toward his soldiers, stroking a beard of white and black with a look of concentration sketched along his wrinkles. He called out to a short woman who had floated down to the ground in his wake, though she had done so with a silent and gentle grace. "Anastasia, contact the Pandorian Empire and the Church of Light. If Lady Silverwater speaks true and there were High Pandorians in Sealrite causing harm to Lysorian nobles, this war will not be between only two nations."

Duke Alistar rose into the air, a giant sphere of golden light erupting from the darkness behind him and bathing us all in a brilliant light. He roared his next words with a shout that I knew everyone could hear over the fire, over the screams, over everything.

I hoped it would reverberate even through time as my first step toward true vengeance.

"It is time we push back against the bastard Caels!" His soldiers and knights cheered back under his banner of command and golden light, thrusting their weapons into the air as their brethren thrust them into monsters. "For Lysoria," he shouted, his words echoed in screams of pride by his men. "For Honor!" It was repeated again. *"FOR JUSTICE!"* The roar of his golden-silver knights quaked the ground, and I could see monsters attempting to flee the area swathed by Duke Alistar's banner of justice.

I let loose a grin once his back was turned, the blood of beasts still trickling down my face.

It was time for war.

About the Author

Fudge Esquire is the author of the Queen of Conquest series, originally released on Royal Road. An attorney by day and writer by night, he trades in both legal briefs and sword fights, cross-examinations and spells and monsters. When he isn't tangled up in courtroom battles or penning epic fantasy plots, he can be found at home in Seattle with his beautiful wife, dashing husky, and mischievous Bengal cat, who runs the house.

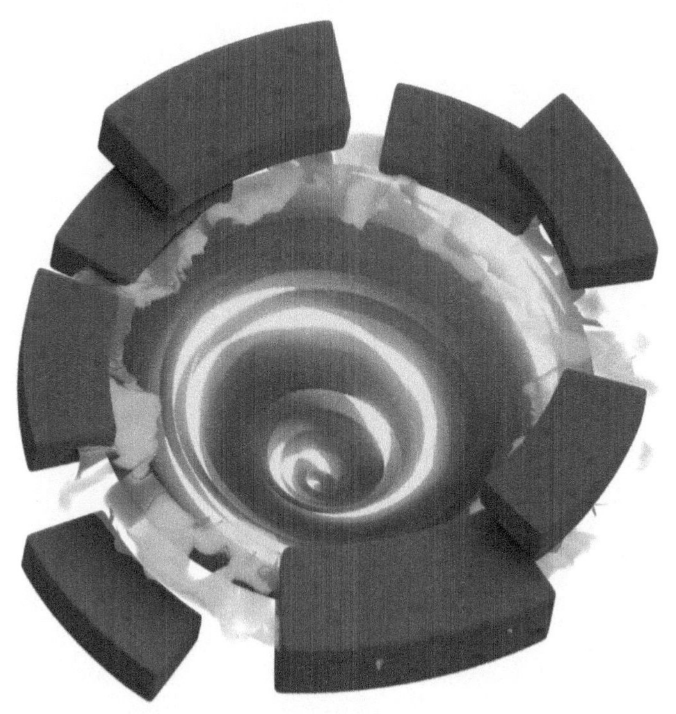

RESPAWN YOUR CURIOSITY

follow us on our socials

podiumentertainment.com

@podiumentertainment

/podiumentertainment

@podium_ent

@podiumentertainment